Property of the Green Bastards

The Badlands Orc MCs

Flora Quincy

Copyright © 2022 Flora Quincy
All rights reserved. No part of this book my be used or reproduced in any manner whatsoever without the written permission of the author, except for in the case of brief quotations for use in critical articles or reviews.

The characters and events depicted in this book are fictitious. Any similarity to real persons, living or dead, is coincidental and not intended by the author

Contents

Property of the Green Bastards	v
From the desk	ix
Content and Trigger Warnings	xi
Prologue	1
Chapter 1	3
Chapter 2	22
Chapter 3	43
Chapter 4	65
Chapter 5	82
Chapter 6	94
Chapter 7	112
Chapter 8	126
Chapter 9	145
Chapter 10	164
Chapter 11	179
Chapter 12	197
Chapter 13	211
Chapter 14	227
Chapter 15	239
Chapter 16	251
Chapter 17	264
Chapter 18	278
Chapter 19	296
Chapter 20	308
Chapter 21	320
Chapter 22	339
Chapter 23	354
Chapter 24	368
Epilogue	383
Bonus Epilogue	390

The End	399
The Green Bastards MC Hierarchy	401
Glossary	403
Also by Flora Quincy	405
About the Author	407
Acknowledgments	409
Full Content and Trigger Warnings	411

Property of the Green Bastards

~He is the monster who rules the Badlands.~
When Axe discovers a traitor is determined to destroy the Green Bastards, he must eliminate every threat to his territory, no matter the personal cost.
Then a chance encounter with a human woman brings out primal instincts impossible to ignore.
When Dinah's secret is revealed, he must decide between loyalty to his club and protecting the only person he can't live without.

~Her humanity makes her fragile, her past tells another story.~
Dinah survives in the human world by altering her appearance and lying about her past.
A dream job in the orc controlled Badlands is the perfect opportunity to start fresh. But until the proof her family betrayed the Green Bastards is destroyed, she is a dead woman walking.
After an explosive confrontation with Axe, she is forced to face all her darkest desires and fears.

~The drums of war will sound, and blood will flow.~

*This book is for E"W"H for her love of orcs and maps.
And a special shout out to Frank. You came into the process late but
without you...I'd have lost some of the fun.*

From the desk

What to say?

After realising orcs and motorcycles were a match made in heaven, I stumbled head first into this world.

I hope both lovers of monster, fantasy, and motorcycle club romance will enjoy this.

As with all my work, this is meant to be fun. Enjoy the ride.

And always remember:
Save a motorcycle, ride an orc.

Content and Trigger Warnings

This book is meant for mature audiences.
There are graphic depictions of sex and violence.
Consent rules.

Full list of content warnings can be found at the end of the book.

GHIN 'HREN

THE BADLANDS

Prologue

A millennia ago, the humans and the creatures possessing magic took to the battlefield to see who was the greater.

Neither could gain against the other because their rival advantages, technology and magic, lost their power in a land called the Badlands.

Sick of war, a powerful necromancer called Frey travelled the battlefield every night for a full turn of the moon. She collected blood and bone from all the fallen, human and magical alike. And with those parts, she created a new species that she charged with the job of creating a buffer between these ancient enemies.

These people called themselves orc'i, blood people. They divided themselves into or'des, blood clans,called hordes by humans.

At the heart of their society were the twin concepts of or and sol, blood and bone. Or was the inherited, collective bloodline. Sol, the bones of an individual and the centre of the orc'i ancestor worship. To the orc'i, desecration of solteng, an ancestor's bones, is the greatest crime.

Flora Quincy

In a time of famine, the orc'i turned to humans and magical creatures for help. Both sides agreed on the condition that the hordes disbanded. Desperate, they agreed. Unable to let their ways die, they formed outlaw motorcycle clubs and instead of riding wargs, they adopted motorcycles, chrome wargs.

But even with the assistance, the smallest and poorest horde continued to suffer. In desperation, they stole solteng from the holy mountain and sold them to humans because orc bones were believed to have magical powers. When the other hordes learnt of this betrayal, they sentenced every orc who participated in this barbaric act to death. And to ensure that their evil blood, their var'or, would not pass down to future generations, the heartsongs and children of these criminals were also condemned. Their horde name, the Driftas'orde, was made taboo and henceforth they were known as Disavowed.

According to ancient laws, any descendent of the Disavowed was to be executed for the crimes of their or'teng.

Chapter One

DINAH

The fortune cookie I opened on New Year's Eve read: *You are destined for great things.*

When I read the words, they felt more like an omen than the restaurant trinket it was.

For the first time this year, I do a great thing. I successfully park without assistance. Not bad for someone who got their licence three weeks ago.

Better than that, I parallel parked the dinky former-rental car I bought forty-eight hours ago in a tiny spot between two concrete flower-filled planters right outside the little red-doored antiques shop where I will work for the next six months. Elmeer's Antiques and Oddities might be small, it might be in the heart of the Badlands in a town called Dwen'mar, but it's Mecca if you want to get anywhere in pre-Union orcish antiques. And south of the border, I am the only expert in orcish antiques. Even if I wasn't, I'd still be the best.

I take a deep breath, almost shaking at the prospect of working with the great Elmeer himself. My last interview was by landline, so I haven't had the chance to meet him in person. This far into the Badlands or any of the Northern Territories, internet is spotty, and most people only have dial-up internet if they have it at all. All because the further you get from the border, the more magic works and the less human technology works. Something I know a little more about than most humans who prefer their magic nice and tidy. But that is not important now. What is important is ensuring I make a good impression. My position depends on this final interview—and if I don't pass, the twenty-eight hours and fifty-six-minute drive from the Capital will be for nothing.

"You got this, Princess," I tell myself, using my gramps' nickname for me. It is his faith I need right now. He passed into the Night seven years ago, but I know he watches over me. A quick glance in the rear-view mirror confirms I look normal and human, which is vital since my government paperwork says:

Dinah Smith
Human
Born: 7 February
Parents: John Smith and Grace Smith

If they find out my entire identity is forged, my family and not-quite-human me will end up in jail. Failure to disclose non-human genetics is arguably the biggest offence in the eyes of countries ruled by humans. So, until I can make things permanent here, everyone must believe that I am undoubtedly human.

For the next hour or so, nothing else in life matters. This is for me without the weight of responsibility or any other bullshit that usually haunts my life.

I'm early for my first day on the job, I get the perfect parking spot, and I parallel park my car. If that isn't confirming my destiny for great things, I don't know what is.

Hopefully, destiny will continue to smile, and I'll be made permanent at Elmeer's. I'll make myself a home in the Badlands. *Home*. Home means belonging. Safety. Security. *Fuck it*. I deserve those things after everything I've been through. I can't help the self-deprecating laugh. I won't have a home if I get caught. I'll be lucky if I have a grave.

With a final calming breath, I grab my bag which fell off the passenger seat when I slammed the breaks to gawp like a tourist at the Allteng, the orc'i's sacred mountain. It was just like the postcards I've been collecting since a little girl, except more magical and transformative. I swing open the door and put both feet on the ground at the same time. I am going to take my first step towards my destiny with one emphatic step.

Destiny. The word rings in my ears, clear as a bell–it sounds so romantic and I feel its grip deep in my bones.

Dwen'mar is everything a Badlands town ought to be. The lack of tall buildings gives you a large, open view of the sky with the Allteng in the background. The weather is hot during the three summer months, and bitterly cold the rest of the year. Today, 15 August, is just perfect. The heat is no longer oppressive, but the land isn't frozen over yet. And the air carries the fresh scent of freedom. No stench of pollution or the oppressive stink of prejudice I grew up with.

I grin at the sun, adjusting my cat-eye sunglasses a bit because of the glare. I've got this. From the conservative hem of my black and white houndstooth to my sweetheart-neck, mid-century vintage dress right up to my shiny black-pin curls. The five piercings including cuffs hiding my pointed ears–the only hint that I might not be one hundred percent human–are hidden behind my curls. My makeup is on point, my eyebrows are the perfect shape, and my cat-eye looks like it was photoshopped. I look the part: city-educated and certified orcish art and antiques expert. That is who I am meant to be, according to the resume I sent via snail-mail in June. Maybe not who I am, but on this perfect day, it is exactly who I am.

At least, it makes sense in my head.

Then, my perfect day gets even better. The rumble of pipes heralds the arrival of a pack of motorcycles, those chrome dogs you hear about. I turn and see it isn't your everyday bikers. The leather-wearing bikers are the Green Bastards. The 1% of 1%ers. The orcish motorcycle club known for being an outlaw's outlaw.

They have a reputation for dealing out swift and sometimes bloody justice to anyone who threatens Dwen'mar or their territory. They deal in guns and protection. If you go through their territory, you pay. I already handed over a bribe to the Green Bastard's Collector at the border. And that was after I'd paid the official government tax for crossing into the Badlands. Their income might be illegal, but everyone turns a blind eye because the Green Bastards, like all the other orc MCs, act as a buffer between the humans to the south and the truly magical creatures to the north.

As I watch them drive by, my heart hammers in my

chest, wondering if they will notice me. When they pull up, bracketing me against my car, I wonder if Destiny really has me marked out for great things.

This could be it, I think. *This really could be it.*

All those stories my gramps told are coming to life. What if...what if one of them sees me and declares I am his fated mate? That I, Dinah Smith, am his heartsong? It was about as likely as a star falling from the sky and landing in my lap, but like a lot of orc-related things, I know a bit more about heartsongs than a lot of humans. And like all orcs, I dream of the day my heartsong, my soulmate identifies me, throws me over his big broad shoulder, and breeds me in a cave on the Allteng.

"Don't get ahead of yourself," I quietly warn myself. I only carry the blood of orc'i on my father's side. He was half; I am only one quarter. Perhaps even less seeing as my dad lied about so many things before he died. Still, I have three genetic markers that only orc'i have. But that means jack shit if I don't have a heartsong. Only orc'i of the blood have heartsongs. Nope, not happening for me. My life is built on lies, deception, and human greed. Which is why I really applied for the job with Elmeer. I need to find out who I truly am, who my orcish family is. My life and the lives of my human family literally depend on it.

"Who the fuck do you think you are, human, parking in our spot?" The growl comes from a large orc with a thick white handlebar moustache and mutton chops. I jump a little at the curse he mutters in orcish under his breath. No one wants to be referred to as "having the brains of a teenager humping a rock."

"I–" I look around, confused by the obvious hostility. The orc'i aren't naturally aggressive. Distrustful, yes, but straight-up in-your-face unwelcoming isn't exactly the policy of dwenweh.

"And how the fuck did you park your car in that tiny ass spot? No cars ever manage that," another orc asks. "You a hag?"

"I–"

"She's human… smell 'em," the first one says. His eyes narrow, and his satisfied smile makes him more sinister than his words ever could.

"That's enough, Eel," an elderly voice cracks behind me. I spin around to see Elmeer himself watching us. He is old. Ancient, almost, but it is hard to know the true age of Pilgrims. Despite the obvious lines on his face, his neat dreadlocks show no signs of grey. "The girl just got into town."

I throw back my shoulders and face these Green Bastards again. But all that courage melts when the one called Eel gnashes his teeth at me.

"It isn't a motorcycle spot," I finally blurt out. "In fact, according to the...you won't care which section of the road code, but this is definitely a car parking spot. The motorcycle spots are over there."

I point to the swathe of open spaces just across the road.

"Besides," I continue because when I fixate on a topic, I can't stop talking. "You could fit maybe one bike here. And your bike is at far more risk between..."

No one says a word, allowing me to trail off like an idiot. I see it in their faces because I've learnt to recognise that point when I miss some subtext, and they don't know how to respond.

"Never said we were going to park our bikes there, Princess," the orc in the middle says. Until he spoke, I purposefully avoided looking at him because he looks mean. Not kick-a-puppy mean, but the kind of mean if he

Property of the Green Bastards

caught you kicking a puppy, you'd wished you'd never been born.

I swallow and finally give myself permission to study him. He isn't the biggest, but even straddling his motorcycle, I know he is tall. Those jean-covered thighs are thick, his shoulders wide, and because he is wearing nothing but his leather motorcycle cut, I can see that the muscles on his torso are like carved marble.

My first impression, beyond his size and meanness, is that he looks exactly like the statue of Frodrick Ash'or'ash, the Horde King, and the most important orc in modern history for his role in brokering the Peace between humans and orc'i one hundred and twenty years ago. Hell, I'll bet my red-soled stilettos, Frodrick is this orc's great-grandfather. He has those hard planes on his face, the dark-green skin with flecks of lighter green in the orc version of freckles over his nose and honey-coloured eyes. His tusks, nestled just at the corner of his mouth, are capped with gold indicating he is the Horde King.

Shit and cookies, the actual Horde King spoke to me.

But more than a king, the patch on his cut tells me his name is Axe and he is the MC's prez. I know these things already. I did my research, but it is something else coming face to face with the most powerful orc in the Badlands.

Nevertheless, my insides melt a bit. He is handsome. Cruelly handsome because he clearly is not overjoyed that I am here, taking up his parking spot. But I suspect he isn't happy that a human is here at all. Not good if I want to get out of here alive or, better yet, guarantee I can make a home here. I need to stay on the good side of the Green Bastards. And I've just pissed off their prez.

And he called me, "Princess," in that growly way that makes me want to rub my thighs together, be naughty, and call him, "Daddy."

Flora Quincy

Oh, yes, I am in T. R. O. U. B. L. E.

AXE

A WEIRD KICK in my chest tells me something is off with the tiny human in front of me. And not being able to put specifics to that something irritates me more than her ignorance about the parking spot—we really need to put up a sign. But mostly, I want to castrate Elmeer for defending her and challenging my authority. He'll answer for that. Not to Eel, though. That fat shit would kill him, and I do not want a pillar of the community and owner of a lucrative business for the club murdered because Eel has no filter. Fucking Elmeer, the wizened man might be orc-kin and an honoured Pilgrim but he has no say in how I run this town. Why he wants to offer the tiniest amount of assistance to this...itch. She makes my chest itchy. To use one of Swot's fancy words, she irks me. And I don't need irks in my life.

I get off my bike and stalk over to the woman who if I stripped that dress off her would look right at home on a pin-up poster. I cage her against the car, really getting in her face so she knows how fucking serious I am.

"You seem like a good girl." I don't hide how pissed off I am. She pouts her lips, clearly trying to keep some smartass, sassy comment inside. "Now listen up."

I lean in until I catch her scent. I hate it. Not that she stinks, but she doesn't smell right and the only way to fix that would be to cover her with my cum. I growl, furious at myself for even thinking that. Thankfully, she takes it wrong and flinches, a spark of fear in her eyes.

"I don't like humans inserting themselves into my busi-

Property of the Green Bastards

ness. They call me a monster for a reason."

Her eyes blow wide like a rabbit caught by a warg. "I don't mind," she says. Her voice is huskier than when she was spouting all that bullshit before. "I don't care that they call you a monster."

I don't blink at her bravery, if anything her backtalk makes me want to put her in her place more. "You want to know something, Princess? Monsters don't bring good girls flowers. They bring good girls to their knees."

"Oh." Her rose-red lips part and she licks them. Fuck if my eyes don't go straight to that pink tongue. Then some speculative look crosses her face. "I've never been called a good girl before."

My dick perks right up because it is a traitor to my good sense. I slam my hands on the car, making her jump. "I want you out of my town before I remember you're here."

I get back on my bike and focus on the shit I actually have to deal with. But who has time to fuck about with a woman when some var coward rode through the mar last night banging war drums–fucking war drums? Scared the living shit out of my mom and sister who were out in orc'helm. We didn't even catch the shithead because most of us were in church and the prospects were slow little shits. Now I have a new sheriff to break in, one who probably only cares about crap-for-balls human politics.

The MC–back when it was the King's Horde–might be older than the town, older than motorcycles for that matter, but these days there are only forty patched brothers and a handful of prospects. Not exactly an army to deal with trolls to the north, varor fuckers in the shadow of the Allteng, and stankass humans to the south.

Yeah, I don't need a motormouth woman who makes every fibre of my being itch. That would be throwing another variable into the mix. Even if she has curves that make my dick feel strangled in my pants.

"Park somewhere else," I order her. Then rev my bike and back away, driving off before she starts arguing. Hawk will take care of it, and hopefully, make it clear to the old Pilgrim that the girl is to be out of here before dawn tomorrow. She can go back to whatever fancy place she came from, and I can focus on the fuckery I'd been on my way to face. Now I have to make nice with the cock-sock sheriff. At least I got to look at a nice pair of tits before noon.

Deliver me, Frey, from fucking humans.

I laugh at my phrasing. Fucking humans. Yeah, I'd fuck her. But no way would a little thing like that be able to take orc cock.

Princess, you wouldn't be able to handle the fucking I'd give you.

Too bad she can't hear my thoughts. It would be nice to see how scandalised that prissy little bitch could get.

―――

DINAH

I watch the MC's president ride off and feel like I've been rejected by the love of my life, which is stupid. If we were heartsongs, we would know. Our heartbeats would pound erratically until they were perfectly aligned. Rejection is one thing. The fiery hatred he obviously has for me? It scares me.

"You heard the prez. Move the fucking car. If it is still there when I come back in…" The one who asked if I was a hag frowns at the sky. "I'll give you one loop of the town to get that rusted tin can pointed out of town and back to wherever you came from."

Property of the Green Bastards

They tear off after their leader, leaving me coughing at the dust their bikes kick up.

"Do they really mean it?" I ask Elmeer, who stands next to me.

"Yes," he says, his voice grave. "But they'll let you stay after I've talked to Bonnie and explained. You can park around the back. There is a small garage I never use. The entrance to the alley is just around the corner. I'll wait to show you where to park."

There aren't any other options so I get back into the car. The second my back hits the seat, all the fight goes now that I've been rejected by the MC. Why does that hurt so much? Why does it feel like my heart is going to break through my ribs with how hard it's beating? The only time I've felt like this before was in middle school when Steve Francis pulled my shorts down in gym. I blink before tears can form like they always do when I think of that time. "You got this, Princess. Gramps always said I belonged to the Badlands. I will belong here. I have to."

Getting out of the spot is harder than getting into it, but I just about manage before a motorcycle comes down the street. As he passes, he spits at my car, hitting my window with a thunk. Yeah, that hurts. What if they know? What if they've already guessed who I am and why I am here? My life was forfeit the second I crossed the border, but the reason I'm here is to destroy any proof of who my orc ancestors are, therefore, preventing my head from being separated from my shoulders.

The alley is narrow when I turn into it and smells of garbage in the summer sun, which is oddly comforting amidst the otherwise terrifying newness. Before heading out to the Badlands, I had only known what it was like to live in the Capital, which in the summer smells of too hot, week-old garbage in our neighbourhood. Three generations of my family live in one of the century-old, tall, narrow apartment buildings in the Stews. We take up the top two floors for twenty people across eight bedrooms. It is cramped but it is where I've lived for the last fifteen years.

Yeah, Dwen'mar's alley might stink but that ripe garbage smell reminds me of love and laughter–not that there is much of that these days. But with the money I'll earn this summer and send back, I'll finally be able to pay them back. I have to drive slowly up the alley because of how cramped it is with the garbage cans sitting at odd angles against the cinderblock and concrete garages.

Elmeer waves me towards a narrow spot under the protection of a corrugated metal awning. I back in, turn off the engine, and give myself another pep talk. "You still got this, Princess. You made it here on your own."

Elmeer knocks on the window.

I can see his mouth moving but can't make out the words through the glass until I use the hand crank to roll the window down. "I'm sorry about that. I should have mentioned the parking." He kindly repeats himself and even though he doesn't sound apologetic, he smiles like he wants me to relax, have a little faith in him. "They rule this place. Keep us safe."

"Why the parking spot?" I ask. "The one out front."

"That way, I can keep an eye on their bikes. Everyone needs to have line of sight." He looks sheepish. What can a man as old as him do to prevent a thief from stealing their bikes? It isn't like cell phones work out here. "Not that anyone would touch them, but orc'i are serious about collective–"

"Collective responsibility. I know. Or'dwea'ki" I bite my tongue the moment the words are out of my mouth. "I'm sorry. I didn't mean to speak over you. I obviously

Property of the Green Bastards

studied orcish culture and the language but I rarely get to use it down south. Or'dwea'ki. Responsibility of the people. I am rambling."

"Your pronunciation is very good," Elmeer says. This time he sounds genuinely surprised. "Come in. I am hoping that your knowledge of old orcish will help me with my current conundrum. It is what made your application stand out."

"Oh? I would have...well, of course. I want this job. It is my dream job." I feign a giggle because people laugh to make conversations a bit more lighthearted. "Sorry. I'm nervous. They make me nervous."

Which is the truth.

"They have that effect on some people." He chuckles. "You get a lot of groupies coming up here to find a way into the club. They probably thought you were one of them based on the way you are all dressed up. A pin-up girl like those old posters? You know the ones. Once they know you are here to work, they'll just expect you to follow the rules."

I nervously brush my fingers over the cuffs disguising my pointed ears. This is good. They all think I am human, a groupie even. That is much better than the alternative. Isn't it?

Other than an ease with lying when necessary, my worst trait is a tendency to overthink other people's words and actions. The question is: do I want them to discover who I am, even a tiny part of it? Or at least, who I've been told I am. Will they help me if they know or will they destroy me? I smile brightly. "Rules I can follow. I love rules."

"We better get started then," Elmeer says after clearing his throat. Oh shit, did I space out while he was talking? "This way."

Flora Quincy

I follow him into the shop and gasp at what I see. Physically, it is just as narrow as it appears from the street but it's deep. An entire block deep–possibly deeper if there are any dwarfish beams in the ceiling. And every surface is thick with objects. This isn't like the upmarket, posh gallery I worked at. Nope. This is the real deal. Even the smell is right. The deep scent of dried spices, the sharper field grass tea which all orc homes have a constant supply of. Then waxed All'pine because so many of the objects are made with that hardwood tree that can only grow at the base of the Allteng. It is a scent I smelled in a large white cube gallery but that whiff pales in comparison to the drugged-out way I feel huffing in all-pine like some addict.

This store is what the elders call a kol'tap, a place of goods. The literal translation hardly does justice to the meaning, which comes as the Hordes began to give up their nomadic lifestyle and built more permanent dwellings and other buildings. All their most precious goods were stored, hoarded in one place to be used or sold as needed. Always for the benefit of the Horde.

"That is correct," Elmeer smiles, his eyes hidden by the wrinkles on his face.

"Oh! I didn't realise I was speaking out loud. I'm just. This place feels wonderful."

"I'm glad you like it. Come over here and let's look at the map."

I flatten my skirt around my legs and walk over to the large table that is comparatively bare to the rest of the shop. On it, lies a beautiful vellum map of the entirety of the Badlands. Each detail is more beautiful than the next including markings for the best warg whelping sites along the northern border, about three hundred miles northwest from Dwen'mar. My fingers tremble, hovering just above the surface.

Property of the Green Bastards

Sil'kot of the Badlands

"Now. What do you think of its condition?"

I reach into my bag and pull out my specialist glasses with their high-power LED light and magnifying lenses. Once on, I bend close, squinting a little because the ambient light is uneven. In the gallery, I have access to a range of scientific testing materials. I have a mini version in the car, but this is about instinct and raw skill. There isn't a lab north of the border that can run tests. I need to be good enough to look at the objects coming into the shop and know beyond a shadow of a doubt if they are genuine or not. And this? This is like finding out you can shit out a gold nugget. Kind of hard to imagine, impossible to believe, and the most thrilling experience I've ever had.

"It is perfect." I sigh. "Too perfect. Obviously a second empire forgery but even then…"

I straighten to get a better look at the rest of the map. It is about eight-by-five feet with carefully preserved, uncut hides which is significant because an old superstition said the scraps could knit themselves together to make a haunting of the same animal. Made from exactly seven hides–though you wouldn't know that from looking alone. Horde maps like this always have one hide from each Horde to demonstrate the unification of knowledge. Or'd-wea'kot, or blood responsible knowledge. The knowledge of the orc'i. But what makes it so perfect is this one has a hidden eighth panel. One pressed between the layers…one I am going to steal and destroy because, on my father's deathbed, he confessed it is the only record of my grandfather's true name, my father's true name…my true name. An Or'sol'kot, a family tree, hidden away in case he could return to claim his birthright.

. . .

Property of the Green Bastards

All I need is a couple of nights to unpick the seams and remove the damning evidence. Then I am safe to stay here.

"Too…" I shake my head, overwhelmed by the success that is within my reach. "I didn't even. I've seen the pictures but to see it…"

"You are convinced it is of that time period?"

"Convinced? Mr Elmeer…the ink couldn't be more genuine for a forgery of this time period. The forgers of that time were artists. These…" I tap the tech perched on my head. "These are so powerful; I can see the areas the ink has degraded slightly because of chromoclorphlorence damage."

"If you say so." He chuckles. He looks back at the map and what might be regret darkens his face for a minute. "Job's yours. On one condition."

"Yes! Whatever you want."

"Hear it out first."

"Deh, zaza." The words are out faster than I could think. "I…"

"I know a bit about who you are, little one."

"No…"

"You must have some orcish blood. Otherwise, why would you, with your work history, take a job like this? I can't pay you what the Halo gallery does. Not with your skills."

"I…" I am about to argue my work history is a forgery as well but catch myself in time. I don't do authentication or curation for Halo. I'm a cleaner because while I might have graduated with honours and top of my year, I'm poor trash from the Stews. Connections, who your parents are, are everything in the Art World. Meritocracy? More like aristocracy.

"My condition is simple. You forge this map. You forge it so well that not even you would know."

"I can't. That would be illegal." Shit. Shit, shit, shit, shit, shit. I cannot have him look at me like that–with that twinkle in his eye.

"I know your Uncle Frank." Elmeer raises an eyebrow. My human uncle Frank owns a pawnshop and "antiques" business. I learnt to forge at his knee. I learned everything there that art school didn't teach me at his side.

"I didn't know that," I admit. My body relaxes a little. Okay, being Frank's niece isn't a bad thing when your boss wants you to forge an artefact worth about one hundred million in common dollars.

"On paper, your job is to ensure everything we sell south of the border is authenticated. And on top of that, you are going to make forgeries. No orc-kin would ever allow an authentic piece to leave the Badlands. But there is a demand, and I need the money. Badly. Things aren't what they used to be."

"So I forge documents, the map…anything else?"

He grins. "Frank says you are the best. A natural. When he called and mentioned his niece had applied." Elmeer shakes his head. "Promise me, Dinah Smith. Promise on your ancestor who called you to this place. Promise you will take this job and protect the hoard, no matter the cost."

I know he means the goods in this store. But instead of stuff, my mind goes to the Horde instead. The people of this mar, of this territory, of the Badlands. The weight of the promise–as I hear it–causes my shoulders to drop. In the split second I have to think about it, I can't decide if this makes it easier to achieve my real aim.

"Sure." I decide. I'll be working with the original. I convince myself it is a lucky turn of events. Fuck, I should have thought of this before. I vow to send Frank a message

Property of the Green Bastards

for not warning me…but also a thank you. "I'll forge the map for you."

"And," he continues. "You do anything to make sure this place continues to exist. No matter what. Get on your knees and pledge on the spirit of your orcish ancestor that you will keep this place safe from harm, even if it comes from one of the hordes or the Green Bastards."

I don't fall to my knees or make any promises on the ancestors. My ancestors are Varor, they are Varki, they are Disavowed. And the whole reason I'm here is to destroy every piece of evidence that I am one of them. Descended from their last MC president.

"Why don't I sign the contract instead?" I laugh. "I can't exactly drop to my knees in this dress and heels. I mean, I could, but the fabric–"

Laughing, he holds up his hands to forestall whatever I was going to say. "Stop! You are definitely related to Frank. Let's get that contract signed and then I'll show you around."

Chapter Two

AXE

I'm meeting the new sheriff at the Compound. I've seen his official picture in the post office. He looks a couple of years younger than me, but humans age funny and rarely live past one hundred.

I can see him parked outside the Compound's gates. His car's nicer than the beat-up bit of metal the girl was driving but still shit for the Badlands, especially in winter which will be here soon. He leans against the hood, smoking a cigarette, clearly thinking his dark green sheriff

Property of the Green Bastards

uniform gives him some sort of status. He looks like an Allpine and is probably as smart as one too.

Fuck, I hope not. Dammit, I do not want a smart lawman.

Old Digby did his job, which was to ignore us and our work. All he needed to do was sign off on the reports and drink a flagon of ale at the bar in the Orc-helm…on the club's tab, of course.

I drive by him into the Compound, where I park my bike and swing a leg over, hearing my hip pop. I did a long ride hunting for traces of the cockshit from last night. I need to stretch my legs but that will have to wait. Dumbo, one of the prospects, runs up and lets me know that the human pulled up thirty minutes ago. "But Ryder got here about an hour before that."

"Ryder?" The growl is deep in my chest. "What is that rockfucker doing here?"

"He says it is about last night."

I grit my teeth. Too many people know about last night. The sound of war drums carries over one hundred miles. I didn't expect anyone to come here in person, though.

"Hawk?" I look at my enforcer who is getting off his bike. The fucker is huge and creepily unflappable–Swot is rubbing off on me with these fancy words. "Keep Ryder occupied while I get rid of the human."

"You sent her packing?" Raine, Hawk's heartsong, asks. He was originally Old Horde, where Ryder is prez, but for some reason, he wanted to prospect with us and then BAM, he sees Hawk, Hawk sees him, and they realised they were heartsongs.

"Don't play stupid, shithead. Of course, I did," Hawk snaps. "And don't let a pretty human with big tits turn your head."

"Get out of here, both of you," I snap. Something about the two of them thinking the woman is attractive bothers me. If anyone gets to think about her, and the problems I know she will cause, it is going to be me. "By next month, there'll be enough human pussy and ass up these parts to open a brothel. All wanting to ride orc cock."

"Fucking Equinox Breakers." Raine howls at his own joke.

I leave them bickering about her and walk to the gate. A better look at the sheriff tells me this asshole is full of his own gold-plated shit.

"Axe Ash?" he asks as he straightens and holds out his hand. I know he is getting my name wrong on purpose because of the way he watches me, hoping for some kind of reaction. But I know men like him and this isn't my first time dealing with humans.

I consider how I want to react then think of my little human and how she ran her mouth when she started talking about road codes. As if the president of a motorcycle club doesn't know the laws of the road–legal and illegal–better than the piggy cops set to enforce them.

"If you want to know a bit of history," I start slowly like I'm talking to an idiot who doesn't speak the common tongue. "Orcish names and an orc's human name are never combined. My orcish name is Ash'or'Ash." I smile because he knows this. I can see it in his eyes when I don't give him my personal name either. I hate the name Den, but my dad got off on the idea of his heir being called King of Fire. Asshole, but I grin. "My government name is Axe. No family name–just Axe. So, you call me Axe and only that. More important is the fact I am the president of the Green Bastards."

"All right," he says slowly. "I guess you can call me Logan."

Property of the Green Bastards

"Sure thing, Sheriff Logan Clarkson." I smile. Did the idiot really think I wouldn't know who he was? "Welcome to Dwen'mar, Sheriff."

"Logan," he says like he has all the time in the world. Well, look at that. This fool thinks he can play my game.

"I like formalities," I tell him. "Sheriff. Sheriff Logan if we get to know each other."

I watch as he grits his teeth. This isn't how he thought it was going to go. What? Did he think he would walk into Digby's role? That he would be given the right to personal names? Yeah, not going to happen.

"I wanted to talk–"

"I got family visiting. I have to perform the K'tav. Maybe we can meet at your office. Tomorrow? At noon?"

"Fine. But what happened last night? I heard about it first thing when I arrived. We need–"

"Tomorrow at noon."

"If the President of the Old Horde is still here, bring him along." He tips his cowboy hat and opens his car door. Leaning through the open window, he waves. "Bye, Axe. Good meeting you."

I smile despite the irritation. That prospect is going to be scrubbing shit with a mascara brush for a week if he doesn't have a good explanation for how he missed seeing the sheriff spying on us.

I kick at a rock so it flies up, catch it in one hand, and throw it at the prospect who is sure as hell fucking attentive now. He ducks just in time for it to smash into the wall behind him. When he finally meets my eye, I can tell he doesn't know if he should have let it hit him or not. He licks his tusks nervously and plays with the piercing at the centre of his lower lip. Looks like a proper orc, but his ears are so big we had to call him Dumbo. It'd be rude not to.

When I'm in earshot and don't have to shout my business for everyone in the mar to hear. I ask him some life-changing questions. "You wanna suck your food through a straw for the rest of your life? Because I'm confused, how'd the lawman know Ryder was here before me?"

"Don't know, Prez," he says. "I was watching at the gate."

"Walkie Talkies," Swot pipes in from the doorway he's standing in. He is our... technical expert? He's more than a mechanic, at least, even if that is his main job. "I know the cells don't work because I cut the lines myself a couple of days ago. And we pick up the radios. Walkie-talkies. Simplest answer because I don't have any other. It is what I would do."

"Next it will be paper cups and string." I spit in the dirt. Humans can be as crafty as the Fae. "Right, where is Ryder?"

"Your office." Swot flexes his jaw. "Took a swing at me, Prez. I was a good boy and didn't reciprocate but can you kiss my boo-boo better?"

"Keep an eye out. And find out who has been ordering walkie-fucking-talkies. And give the prospect something interesting to do."

Swot grins. "Sure thing, Axe."

He puts up his fist, and I pound it. We prospected together, and, between us, we come up with the best jobs for the wankers who want to become a Green Bastard.

The main room of the Compound stretches the whole front of the building with concrete columns spaced about three metres apart and metal trestle tables slotted in between. The bar is at the back, and a patched, heavily-tattooed brother, Rift, is wiping down glasses. He raises a hand but keeps on with his work. Otherwise, the place is empty, which is good. I need my people out there looking for whoever–

Property of the Green Bastards

The thought cuts off when I push open the door to my office.

Ryder. The orc is older than me, and we have an understanding he isn't supposed to step into my territory for another five years. The fucker.

"Give me one reason not to shoot you in that ugly mug not even your momma can love?"

"Axe." He grins and leans back against the back of the sofa, arms spread like an eagle. "How is your sister?"

My other brothers straighten up.

Raine is the one whose lips curl up to reveal his teeth and the ruby embedded in his tusk catches the light. "Ryder," he warns.

"Simmer down, cuz." Ryder can't keep that shit-eating grin off his face. "What would I want with a spoiled brat?"

He refuses to meet my eyes. Yeah, keep lying to yourself, fucker. "Why are you here, Ryder?"

"I heard the drums too." He is the only one sitting. A human might believe he is posturing by having his ass on my fine leather couch. That he doesn't care there are three fully grown orc'i in the room who could tear him apart. What outsiders don't understand is that by sitting, he is telling us he wants a Meet. By standing, we are telling him to get out or we will drag him out. "Axe..." He looks away and mutters something I can't make out. "Ash'orde..."

I try to turn my laugh into a cough. This pathetic little shit thinks he can make up sweet calling me by that title? No one calls me Ash'orde, Horde King. My title is merely a symbolic, inherited title that means nothing in the Badlands now that the hordes no longer exist. It still carries weight for me but no one needs to know it is a burden to be the last Horde King.

"What the fuck dude?" Raine laughs. "Ash'orde? What century are you living in?"

"Axe, I came in good faith," he says through gritted teeth. "You know I wouldn't break our bargain if it wasn't serious."

Shit. Shit. Shit.

"Out," I tell my enforcers.

Raine complains but Hawk drags him out with a few whispered comments.

I walk behind my desk and sit, staring at the other MC president who came into my territory without a word of warning, against a bargain we made five years ago, and alone.

"This is about Kendle, isn't it?" I ask after a minute. I really fucking hope it is just about my sister. I can handle that.

"Yes." He looks away. "And no. We heard drums last night. My people are dealing with it but...I had to know."

I close my eyes and ask Frey for patience. "Five years," I remind him. "Five more fucking years. Next time, pick up the phone or send a prospect you don't like very much."

"Now."

"No."

"She is twenty-three. Legal age."

"You are fifteen years older than her," I try to say without boiling over in anger at the fact the orc across from me is my sister's heartsong. "She doesn't even know."

He sits forward, elbows on his knees and rubs both hands over his face. "Which was my decision. Shit. She was eighteen. I was older than you when I found out you were about to become my Sol'sin. It would be like taking a kid. I'm not into kids, Axe."

I respect him for not sweeping in and dragging Kendle off kicking and screaming. Or worse, watching her go happily because that would kill Mom. Doesn't mean I want my little sister mated to this rockfucker, though.

"The drums," I prompt him.

"From what Raine said, it was coordinated." He leans back again, now looking more like an MC prez than a lovesick Gok. "Witching hour. Our people were in bed. The orc'kin curfew meant none of them were out–"

"Shit...you are old school." I shake my head.

"Yeah, but it meant none of them were killed." This catches my attention. Other than the drums, there was no violence. "They shot up a couple of orc'kin businesses and the schoolhouse even though our Goki study there. No one was hurt..."

"Your lawman?"

"He is writing it up as a drunk and disorderly since he doesn't want any friction. But, of course, some of the orc'kin will say something."

"What do you want to do about it?"

"You aren't going to tell me what happened here?"

"Kendle was out with friends." I grin, knowing how much it will piss him off. I'm not disappointed. He bares his tusks at me. The rubies in them pick up the light. "She was fine. My mom was with her."

He nods. Mom has a rep. Sweet as sugar but when it comes to my sister? She's fiercer than a warg with day old pups. The way she stands guard over Kendle is the only thing that makes me worry Ken would happily ride off on the back of the first horny asshole to suggest it.

"I think we need to call a formal Meet," he says. "We can't be the only ones."

"From what my guys saw of the car–yeah, car–it could be Disavowed supporters." I throw the lure out just to see the way his green skin goes white.

"No," Ryder says in flat denial. "Impossible."

"You think their families have a short memory?" I ask. I almost like reminding the other MCs that no matter what we pretend, three generations later, a few people are still angry that the Disavowed were legally executed. The Green Bastards might have carried out justice but they voted for it as well and I won't let them forget. We are all responsible. "Starting a war means nothing—"

"The Disavowed are dead," he says, his voice clipped. "Your grandfather cut their heads off and offered those k'vari poison if they were too cowardly to take justice. They took sol from the Allteng. They dishonoured the teng. My solteng's bones were taken and were sold to humans to be crushed for human vanity." He grips the back of the sofa like he'll lose it if he lets go. Even though he knows my bloodline, my sol'weh carries the responsibility for killing two hundred and ninety people. Another sixty escaped to human camps where they died. Their bones didn't even have the chance to be dishonoured by being discarded on the sides of the Allteng, because the humans took them. "Axe, I don't forgive the Disavowed… If you think they are back I will put my blade through their necks."

"Hey." My instinct has me snapping my fingers in his face to break his focus. "Sol'sin, me or'teng, me sol'teng, ki'weh jak. Or'dwea'ki. You did the right thing coming to your Ash'orde."

He blinks at me like I'm some kind of ghost. I don't give him anything with my expression. Hells, I'm surprised I just told him he did the right thing bringing his concerns to his king. I reminded him that orc'i have a collective responsibility to look out for each other. Fuck, I do not need to pile more shit on my plate.

"Meh Ash' Orde—"

"Yes?" I smirk this time. Got him. He just acknowledged I am his king.

"Bastard. I'll have one of my people keep you

Property of the Green Bastards

informed about what happens in the North Shadow of the Allteng."

"You do that. Now get out."

"Tell my little cousin to come visit his mother."

"Do you really think Hawk will let his pretty little heartsong out of his sight?"

He flushes. It must rankle him that we are taking one of his blood family who chose to leave the Old Horde and prospect with the Bastards. But then he gets our Horde Princess. Fair swap, even if we hate it.

"And Kendle?" His voice is cautious. A youth asking for his first blow job.

"No."

"Soon. Or I'll take her."

I shrug. Kendle might want out from the hard heel of the club's protection, but she is strong, and the image of anyone trying to manhandle her makes me smile.

"Fuck. I hate you, you smug little shit." He means it.

"You can go now." I stand to open the door for him, and he stands with me. He is a little shorter than me but so broad he'll have to turn to get through the door. Damn, that is funny.

"She'll have rubies in her tusks before the new year," he snarls, daring me to contradict him. I can't. I know he means it. Five months instead of five years. But I won't let him know that.

"You'll be sucking my dick before she even sees you."

"I could almost like you–almost…" he says. No shit. We are cut from the same cloth, we are the heirs to our fathers and ancestors. Countless generations of ruling just turns into instinct after a while. It is proof that the Or, our blood, runs pure. It is why all the Disavowed are on a death list. No one wants Var'or to taint future generations. And no matter what, Ryder carries dw'or, good blood.

Flora Quincy

I let Raine show him out, then shut the door and go back to my office. Hawk follows me and he sits where Ryder was less than a minute ago. Then the rockfucker farts.

"Frey. Warn me." I open the window a crack. We are up on the first floor, so I'm not worried about people eavesdropping.

"Don't want his stink in here. My farts are fucking roses in comparison. So, what did he want...other than to kiss your ass until you hand over Kendle?"

"Fuck d'you know about that?"

"Enough," the smug fucker says. "Pretty obvious when you think about it. Explains why you let Raine prospect. Swot doesn't hold a monopoly on grey matter."

There is a comfortable pause while he waits for me to speak.

"I'm going to call a Meet at the next full moon." I tug on the metal bar running through my eyebrow that marks me as the former gok-ash, crown prince, but resist the urge to run my tongue along the gold caps on my tusks. It isn't like I need a reminder that I'm the last horde king.

"Sounds about right. You think we will hear the others had war drums too?"

No need to answer that. Of course, they have. A knock at the door has us both starting to talk about warg racing until we see it is Raine. He patched in with the MC two months ago–same night that Hawk claimed him. Their bond is new but it is Hawk rather than Raine who seems uncertain about what to do.

"We need to have a party tonight. Show solidarity with the or'kin." The younger orc sits on the sofa and swings his booted feet onto his heartsong's lap. "Big ass party. Invite the new humans and a few others."

Property of the Green Bastards

"See if they talk to anyone," I agree. "It is a good idea, brother. Get Boonie on it."

"I'm not your bitch, Prez. You can tell her yourself. She saw Ryder." He laughs like it is a great joke.

I don't even have time to say something when my mom storms in. She had me at nineteen, so her hair is still as black as night and there isn't a hint of age around her eyes, but she dresses like a ninety-year-old or'ma–a shapeless black linen dress over black leggings and sturdy flat shoes. Like most widowed heartsongs, her head is shaved, exposing her piercings and neck tattoos. My tough enforcers mutter, "Hey, Boonie," before retreating to the safety of the bar.

The door hasn't even closed properly before she is hissing at me. "He isn't taking–"

"We have bigger issues. Also, how many people know?"

"The officers." She bats my questions aside. "Tell me."

"Ryder. Someone sounded the drums in All'mar. He was checking on Ken."

"You are calling a Meet? At the next full moon?"

"What makes you think that is your business?" She isn't part of the MC and as backwards as it is, she doesn't get a say in club business, which she knows.

"Don't give me lip like that in private, son. I'm just curious because you might meet your heartsong."

"We both know I'm heartless." I cross my arms and frown. She hasn't brought this up in years.

"I dreamt I delivered your daughter." My mother and her fucking dreams. They actually mean something. "I want to hold my grandbaby. Watch little Ash'goki running around the Compound."

Maybe I should frown because I want that too, but since I hit puberty, I've walked by almost every unattached orc and not one irregularity in my heartbeat. "Not happen-

33

ing. I don't want to get some bitch pregnant for the sake of your dreams. I'm not that desperate."

"Find a nice girl then." She reaches into her pocket and pulls out prayer beads which she flicks through rhythmically. "Find someone at the party tonight. Elmeer's girl, maybe. Just met her. Pretty and smart, which is more than the honeys hanging around you."

I sit up. "You know about her?"

"He hired her to forge a map and authentication documents for us. I vetted her."

"Do I need to remind you, Boonie? You are a heart-song, not part of the MC."

"I like to screw over humans as much as you do." Yeah, that is my mother. "She's a good fit. The Pilgrim thinks so too."

"Fine, organise a party tonight. I'll tell people there will be a Meet. But I'm not fucking the human to give you grandkids."

———

DINAH

I'm absorbed in reviewing the archive when Elmeer knocks on the office door.

"Five o'clock, time to go home," he says. "Do you need help moving into the Barracks? I assume that is where you are staying?"

"Yes. I was thinking of driving over—"

"Good idea but leave your car back here. Don't worry, I don't use the space."

Gratitude makes my heart swell. "Thank you. I mean it."

There isn't parking near the Barracks but according to

my instructions, I'm to leave it running out front until I'm moved in and then find parking.

The Barracks was never a literal barracks, but because only humans live there, someone thought it would be funny to make a connection to the imperialist past. It looks more like a nineteen fifties motel from the outside if you tacked on a deep wooden porch. I knock on the door and jump back when the door abruptly swings open to reveal a tiny brownie wearing a violet-coloured muumuu with her hair in an elegant crown braid.

"Dinah Smith. I see you standing there. Come on in. I'm Miss Krystal," she says.

"Hi, sorry. I should have come by right away..."

"Elmeer called. And no worries. You come and go as you please."

I swallow down more questions because I have a strange feeling I've been incredibly rude. "I offer apologies for putting your day upside down."

"That sounds more like a question. And when I say, 'no worries,' I mean it. Elmeer did call so it's no problem. Now, it is just you and the new lawman staying. I won't be cooking your meals unless you want but that is an extra–"

"I'm used to cooking for myself."

"That is excellent. I hate cooking. Come on in, girl."

The interior is another style entirely. Hells, it is another century as well. More seventies nursing home than motel but with a strong Victorian gothic vibe.

"There are a lot of styles here during the quiet times," the brownie says, as she points out the dining room and then a lounge crammed full of sofas and chairs. "The house is very magical and sensitive to the people staying. It will settle into a style soon. Don't be worried if it changes its mind though. Happens sometimes with these old guest houses."

She points at the staircase which is definitely nineteenth century. "The first iteration and my personal favourite. Now, take your pick of the rooms. I suggest one not facing the street. Kin'helm can get rowdy on weekends."

By the time I've carried my things up and returned the car to the spot behind Elmeer's, it's late and I'm starting to wonder what I'm going to do for food. I'm on the landing when I first notice the difference.

Truly, utterly magical, I crow internally.

All my dreams come true. The motel-retirement home vibe is gone. In its place, the ground floor is exactly what I pictured: dark-stained wood, gas lamps, lace doilies over the backs of sofas covered in rich burgundy velvet. Absolutely too much, an antiquities maximalist's dream space.

"That you? We've been invited to a party at the Compound," the brownie tells me. "There are some rumours about the drums."

"Drums?"

"Yes. Some idiots drove through town banging war drums last night."

"Oh."

I don't know what to make of it. The last time war drums were sounded would have been about the time this guest house was built. That the map at Elmeer's was forged.

What the fuck is going on in the Badlands?

―――

AXE

The sounds of the party filter into my office around nine o'clock, but I'm stuck sitting in front of a busted-up

Property of the Green Bastards

computer attached to dial-up that keeps dropping the line. Reconnecting sounds like a normal phone call until the high-frequency bings and white noise kick in. Worst thing is, once you've heard it you can never unhear it. Like an earworm, it buries into my brain, driving me crazy when I need to focus. I'm trying to do some research on the new sheriff, and except for being top of his academy and looking like a total de'garad in the picture, there isn't anything I can use against the pretty boy. His whole demeanour this afternoon when we met has my instincts screaming that he is more than he seems, and his timely arrival the day after the drums sounded makes me jumpy.

"Come to the party, Ash'ee," my half-sister, Kendle, says. "Mom's pissed."

Mom means Boonie who raised both of us but we only share a dad. And at first glance, you'd never know her biological mother is a fiend because her skin is the same dark emerald green as our dad's and she tucks her tail behind her. But it whips like a cat's when she gets angry. Since yesterday she's shaved the sides of her head to reveal her pointed ears and rows of piercings. She dresses like the protégé mechanic she is and the idea of seeing her in a dress or anything feminine is about as believable as someone thinking they could get away with sounding war drums in mars protected by MCs.

"Axe..."

"Yeah?" I roll my shoulders, not used to hunching over a computer. Fuck I wish I could have been doing something instead of stuck in here all day.

"Come to the party. Have a drink. Say hi to people before the families go home."

She'd make an amazing MC prez. She knows what to do and how and when. Instead, she'll be a heartsong. Still fucking unbelievable at that job but not enough for someone as skilled as her... Just a shame it has to be the Old Horde she ends up with.

"Yeah, fine." I pull open the large filing drawer in my desk, pull out a bottle of whiskey, and pour out a dram which I throw back. "Fuck, my back aches. How do people sit at a desk all day?"

"How am I supposed to know?" She laughs. "I heard the Old Horde prez came to see you. Hope you threw him out on his ass."

"Did you see him?"

"No. Raine came by the garage and told me. Come on."

Fucking Raine, I don't want Kendle knowing anything about that prez 'til she has to. I follow her into the main room. The party is in full swing, noise coming from the back where I know more are in the courtyard enjoying the clear weather while it lasts. About two hundred of my people and townies are living their best lives, drinking and dancing. There are a few adolescents hanging out, shooting pool, and learning what club life is like but when the clock strikes ten, they are out of here. We might not be traditionalists, but if you haven't done your Run, you've no place with the orc'i when they really let loose.

I make my way through the crowd, greeting the orc'i who live in Dwen'mar. All of them want to know what is going to happen, who sounded war drums in the very heart of their community, and what the repercussions will be. I grow more and more frustrated because there is nothing new to tell them.

I finally make it to the bar, my eyes passing over the bottles of liquor to see if we need to restock on anything. Dumbo puts a beer in front of me and lifts his chin towards Elmeer who struggles to hoist himself onto the barstool next to me.

Property of the Green Bastards

"Axe..."

"Boonie told me." I take a sip of my beer.

"Her uncle is a great way—"

"Elmeer. I don't give a fuck about some human girl. But don't think you can disrespect me, old man."

"Axe, I know. But..." He looks like he is about to shake right out of his skin with how nervous he is. I need a full apology. A formal fucking apology for acting like he is orc rather than kin. "She has—"

"That doesn't sound like a fucking apology," Eel growls. He is from my grandfather's generation and has never been made an officer. One of the last things my father said to me was that Eel was as slippery as his namesake and had varor on his mother's side. A pretty big accusation, but it means he will never get promoted. All the same, he is loyal to the club and a brother. I trust him with my life.

"Ash'or'ash, by meh'teng and meh'solor, I apologise."

I grunt. "Just remember or'dwea'ki is the law."

"Deh, Axe."

"Get out of here." I wave him away, then think better of it, and pull him back to say in his ear, "You are kin, a most respected Pilgrim."

"Thank you, Axe." The old man awkwardly slides off the stool and melts into the crowd.

I swivel around to survey my people. At first, the party looks like a normal gathering, but now that the kids have started to leave, you can see people settling around the edges, heads bent close as they talk about last night. I signal to my mother to get the rest of the kids out. The moment the last young one leaves, the whole place gets quiet and all eyes are on me. I see the human girl and lawman in the crowd. They aren't standing next to each other, though. She is standing next to Goth, the brownie who runs the Barracks where humans visiting Dwen'mar stay. She hasn't changed out of that ridiculous dress and stands out, looking expensive and untouchable. I wonder how many of my brothers and sisters have offered to buy her a drink since she walked in with all those curves on display. Fucking pisses me off because that itch is back. When I turn to the lawman, he is looking over at her. Now that is not what I want. If I have to get rid of her, I don't want any limp dick rockfucker looking at her. Especially not the new sheriff.

She is my itch. Mine. No one else's.

There is a gentle cough that shakes me out of the spell she's cast on me. I am standing with over a hundred people looking at me while I look at the human. I shake it off and raise my right arm above my head, my hand spread wide before clasping it into a tight fist to beat against my heart. One beat for each of the disbanded hordes. A formal gesture to the unity of Frey's children who were born from the same blood and bone that covered the battlefields of old. All orc'i know. They will listen to me tonight and repeat my words to those who weren't here.

"As most of you know, someone dared to ride through the town and sound drums last night. Tonight, we show no one breaks the strength of the ki'Dwen'mar. We are not afraid of cowards who ride at night on a new moon. Their weh is var!" My men stamp their feet and a few women ululate. "If any orc'i or kin hides this coward, they are k'var and not welcome in the helms of Dwen'mar. Some of you might also have heard that the other MCs have received similar cowardly rides. As Ash'or'Ash'Den, your Ash'orde, your horde king, as the president of the Green Bastards, I am going to call for a Meet on the next full moon. All of you are meh'sin, meh'see, meh'ze. Meh'ki.

Property of the Green Bastards

Meh'weh toa ki on Dwen'mar. Weh'teng and weh your Ash'orde, for I honour you!"

There is another cheer from the orc'i but the only person I see is the human with her left hand spread out over her heart. This human bitch dares to give the old sign of loyalty? Fuck that. Is she trying to win my affection by showing she knows the old ways? A smile flickers on her face when she sees me watching. Our eyes meet and that itch is back. The minute the party starts again, I'm reminding her that I'm a monster who'll put her on her knees. I'll wipe that smile off her face when I give her exactly what she clearly needs.

Big. Thick. Orc. Cock.

"Party on, my friends," I shout and smash my beer bottle on the floor. "We are the ki'on'Dwen'mar. We are the ones to hold the line."

The spell breaks and the conversation picks up again. Only this time, the air is full of excitement and urgency. People swarm the bar to get drinks, and others come up to me, touching their hands to their hearts. It only reminds me of the woman I need to deal with, so I push through, acknowledging them but not waiting to speak. Their questions can't be answered tonight anyway.

The closer I get to her, the angrier I become. I want to do so many things. Fuck those plump lips until the red lipstick is smeared all over my cock. I want to turn her ass the same colour as her lips. Then I'll make sure she gets out of this place. Fuck what my mother and Elmeer want because I do not need the distraction she represents.

When I'm finally in her space, I keep going until her back is against the wall. Up close, I can't escape how rich she looks. The kind of money tourists who breeze into our territory to look at us like animals in a zoo seem to have. The black and white dress hooks up the front and pushes

Flora Quincy

her tits up. Their soft roundness would be more than a handful. Her skirt flares, hinting at hips, and yeah, I want to push that skirt up and get my hands on her ass right now–in front of everyone if I have to.

I'm aware now more than ever that I lied about wanting her gone. I need her under me and then out of my town and back to her human world. I take in a deep breath, ready to speak, instead, I get the scent of honeysuckle. I don't want to wonder if her cunt smells so sweet, but I do.

"I thought I made myself clear," I growl deep and low. "I want you out of my town. Outsiders, especially human ones, should be smart and leave at a time like this."

"I can't. I promised Elmeer I'd work on the map." She is only tall enough to sniff my pits, but the way she looks down her nose makes me want to put her in her place. No one in this mar, in the Badlands, looks down at me.

But I like that she doesn't back down, even though I can hear the tremor in her voice.

"Don't care." I grin, showing off my teeth.

"I'm not going." She crosses her arms, pressing her tits up even more.

"You want to be fucked by an orc, Princess?" For the first time, she looks away. "Well?"

"Why would you want to fuck me?" she asks in a soft voice that I have to strain to hear.

"Oh, Didi..." I lean in close. She might be tall for a human woman but I still have to bend down to whisper in her ear. "I'll fuck you so hard, you'll run away crying for your mommy."

Chapter Three

DINAH

Sweetheart?

I don't think he knows my name or he wouldn't call me that. He just thinks he is mocking me, but I like how it sounds coming from him.

I know he is trying to intimidate me but it isn't working. Okay, it is working but not how he wants. Mostly, I'm turned on. Really turned on. In a way I didn't know was possible. It is as if my body is preparing for him to stuff me with his big, thick orc cock and then fill me with his seed until it runs down my legs like a waterfall. The only thing stopping him from smelling my arousal is the smell of stale beer and sweaty bodies that fills the common room.

I am about to lick my lips when I remember I'm wearing lipstick and I don't want to smear it. If anyone is going to make me messy, it is the orc in front of me.

Instead, I swallow. "We never actually met. My name is—"

"Don't care what your name is, Princess." His breath lingers on my cheek, then pulls away enough for me to see his eyes flash and nostrils flare like he can smell my arousal. But that smirk just reminds me this is his game and I don't know the rules...yet. The danger only makes my heart beat harder, faster, so irregular that I worry I'm going into cardiac arrest. Then those same thick fingers tuck a strand of hair behind my ear, trailing along the sensitive skin along my jaw until it rests under my chin, tilting it up. He leans close until our lips are barely touching, and my heart thunders in my chest. We are in public, anyone, everyone can see us. "Don't need to call you anything while I fuck you. You'll be screaming my name, not the other way around."

"I know," I breathe. My heartbeat is an arrhythmic gallop taking me closer and closer to the orc who would kill me if he knew my secret. But for a few brief moments with him, I'll risk it. "Oh, Goddess. I—"

"This is your last chance," he growls. "If you say no, you won't ever fuck an orc in the Badlands. And if you fuck me, I'm the only orc you ever fuck. Understand me?"

"No...I mean, okay. I want this..."

"Would you like to play a game, Didi?" I nod, anticipation and a delicious thrill of fear course through my blood. "Either run out that door or run down the hall next to the bar. Show me how brave you are, little human." He steps back, letting me duck around him. The first thing I do is

Property of the Green Bastards

scan the crowd. No one is watching us which seems strange. Does he do this all the time with all the women who come to parties here? It makes my stomach churn at the thought of them with him. Not jealousy but envy, because if I listen to my head, I will walk out that door and avoid Axe for the rest of my life.

So...do I stay safe and keep up the masquerade that I'm human, or do I risk being discovered when he spreads me open and sees my second clit? Then I feel Axe's heat at my back. The fear of being caught melts away. Instinct tells me if he is at my back anything is possible. "Are you afraid, little rabbit?"

Does he sense the turmoil boiling inside of me?

I take my first step forward. Then my next until I'm winding my way through the crowd to hide my trail. I'm not going to make this easy on him by taking the most direct route. Let him wonder what I'll do.

Slipping through one conversation after another, I make my way towards the door that leads into the cool night air. I reach it in time to duck behind a large orc with Hawk on his patch just as someone leaves. I hope Axe thinks I've left because even if I am the prey, I'm not stupid. I need to see...something. Instinct drives me, and I'm blind to whatever the end game is. From there, I snake along the back wall, shimmying between a table and an orc I don't know. She gives me a steady look but doesn't try to stop me. I smile, embarrassed by my behaviour which seems childish, which makes me glance around to see if there are any more witnesses. Axe is talking to Hawk. Is he asking if I left? I don't have time to worry and make it to the bar as quickly as I can. I pause for a moment, victory thrumming through my veins. He hasn't caught me yet. And other than the two orc'i whose eyes I met, it seems like no one is paying attention, which only heightens the thrill.

Flora Quincy

My hand is on the handle when a strong, solid body presses me into the cool wood of the door.

"That was a very clever move back at the front door, Princess. I'm impressed. You almost fooled me."

"You cheated if that guy told you," I hiss, wriggling against the wall of muscle.

"Oh, he wouldn't do that." I can hear the smirk in his voice, which is twisted and predatory. I am no match for him. Yet, my brain whispers, you could be. Your heart is beating fast and irregular as if it is trying to match the beat of his heart. I push the thought aside. I won't let myself think that he is my heartsong. No, I'm just not used to playing games of cat and mouse. "All right, Didi, you need to make another decision. Do you open that door and get—"

I don't wait. I turn the handle and open it barely enough for me to slip through then tug it closed, twisting the simple lock. He could rip it open, more likely use a key but every second is precious. He might think I'm at a disadvantage because I am wearing heels, but I've been wearing them for eight years. If he thinks I can't run in four-inch stilettos, he is going to be sorely disappointed. I sprint down the hall.

I hear the door open behind me and veer to the left, running up the stairs as fast as possible. There is a closed door at the top of the stairs, and I jiggle the handle. It sticks a little, making me think it is an unused room—exactly what I want. Finally, it opens. I shut it and lock it. The room—not a closet—is dark except for a bit of light coming in through the window that silhouettes a large chair and desk with an old-fashioned computer directly in front of me. I collapse against the door, which is cool against my heated skin. My heart races inside my chest, which has nothing to do with heartsongs, or so I tell myself.

Property of the Green Bastards

The combination of adrenaline and the fact I'm out of shape must be the culprit. Then the door gives way, swinging into the hall–the opposite of how I opened it.

"Shit!" I cry out and stumble forward until I hit the desk and am bent over it. He'll have a perfect view of my ass. Instead of getting up, keeping an eye on him, I stay exactly where I am.

"You did very well..." he purrs behind me. I hear the door close and the snick of the lock. "I like how you thought to lock the door. That is exactly what you should be doing when you are stalked by a monster. But...silly rabbit. That only works if you know that person doesn't have the key."

I curse again.

His boots don't make a sound as he crosses the wooden floor. I giggle. How can someone so big be so silent?

"You should have hidden."

"You'd have found me," I pant.

"True. And I like you like this. Bent over my desk, presenting yourself like a–" He cuts himself off. Was he going to call me a slut or a bitch? I should be offended but it is kind of thrilling when he talks like this. Sick and twisted as I am. This is how I want to lose my virginity. "I'm going to fuck you...just like you want. Are you going to deny me?"

I whine, arching my back where I stand. When I feel his hand land on my ass, he squeezes each side, then runs his hand between my thighs and grinds the heel of his hand against my clit. There might be layers of fabric and lace between us but I swear by all that is holy, he can feel how wet I am. I'm so lost in the sensation of his large hand...oh, Goddess, it is so large, I have to spread my legs apart to fit its width. I almost miss when he pulls me back a little. He pushes my skirt up, each layer of fabric resting around my waist, and then pulls my panties down my thighs, leaving me completely bare.

"Stay just like that...poor, Didi. You're soaked," he says, mocking me. I feel humiliated and turned on, desperate for more of his touch and his words. I hear the sound of a zipper dragging open a pair of jeans. I want to risk turning around to look at him. "Face forward. If you want to take me, you need to spread wider."

"I–" I want to tell him I'm a virgin before this goes any further but he doesn't let me. When he kicks my feet apart and rocks his giant cock between my thighs, I realise I don't want to see the weapon he calls a cock. It will be a battering ram, a club. So long and thick, I'm afraid I'll break. "You need to know–"

"No excuses, Princess. You need to know that if you come into my Compound dressed like this, you are begging to be fucked. And I like it when my women beg...and you've begged so pretty."

"Actions speak louder than words," I gasp as he rocks his ridged cock along my slick sex.

"They do." He rams home, straight to the hilt, tearing through my hymen and causing me to scream out a string of profanities. He lands a sharp spank on my ass before withdrawing and unknowingly rubbing against my too sensitive second clit. My heartbeat begins to beat in that same strange irregular rhythm I'm starting to associate with him. He fills me again, grinding his hips into my ass, adding to the addictive pleasure of his cock inside of me. His thrusts are shallow, never letting up. Even then I'm gasping with each movement. He pushes me to the edge of pleasure. I feel like I'm flying, higher and higher until I'm shaking from the most powerful orgasm of my life. My body collapses against the table, boneless and weak.

Property of the Green Bastards

"Fuck, yeah. Come all over my cock like a good girl, Didi. Just like that."

Even dazed from my release, I rock my hips back on him putting delicious pressure on my second clit that sits right at the opening of my sex. If he discovers it, then he'll know I have orcish blood, but right now, I'm not thinking about that. I'm focused on the way his cock stretches me, fills me in a way that makes my breasts feel tight in my corset. There is a tug on my hair as he pulls me against his chest, arching my back, and forcing me to stand on the balls of my feet. One breast pops out, my nipple tightening in the cold air. But Axe isn't paying attention, instead, he is pulling back, the ridges on his cock making the pleasure almost too much for me.

There is an unearthly silence followed by him cursing. "Shit, shit, shit. Are you—"

"I was a virgin before you fucked me," I gasp.

"Good," he growls and slams back into me. "This virgin cunt is mine. Say it, Princess."

"My virgin cunt is yours, Da—" I swallow the word "Daddy." He wouldn't understand, or he might misunderstand.

"That's right. And when we are done." He grunts as he thrusts into me, fills me. Impossibly full. "I'll have your virgin blood on my dick and my cum will flood your womb. Gik'or, Frey Gik'or sol."

"Fuck," I cry out as my body is forced over the edge again by the possessiveness in his voice and his merciless ramming. My sex squeezes around his cock, desperate to make his words true. Even as my body seeks to milk him dry, I know I'm risking everything. I'm not on the pill; I need to tell him. Tell him to pull out. "I'm n-not on the p-pill," I manage to gasp out.

All he does is thrust harder, taking his pleasure, not

Flora Quincy

thinking about mine, and if that doesn't trigger my next two orgasms, I don't know what does. The knowledge I am his to do with as he wants makes every grinding, grunting thrust sweeter than honey.

Without warning, he falls over me. His hand so close to mine, they're almost touching. I flex my hand, and my pinky brushes against his wrist. Lightning fast, he pulls out, flipping me over on my back, and plunging back in. His eyes are focused on my face, there is no escaping how inhuman he is now. His size, the way his tusks stand out, the gold caps reminding me he is the king. An orc fucking away my virginity, my fear, my need for control wrenched away from me–oh, Frey. I never imagined I would love sex so much.

Something changes in his expression and when he glides back in, he smears my lipstick with a thick thumb before pushing it between my lips. "Suck."

I do as he commands.

"Good girl. Now, unhook that torture device and show me those pretty titties."

He keeps his thumb in my mouth so I can't respond. I want to drive Axe out of his mind with actions the way he drives me wild with his words. Only, I've zero experience with the opposite sex. I've never seen a hard cock, even the one I'm impaled on. But I want to seduce him like I think other women would: by teasing him with my body. Smoothing my hands along my sides I untie the bow that holds the halter neck up. I lower my left hand, drawing the fabric down, across my nipple which has pebbled. Then the right side, all the while he keeps a steady, even rhythm while he fucks me.

"What a good girl." He pulls out and pulls my dress off, letting it fall on the floor. I'm sprawled naked on his desk as

Property of the Green Bastards

he jerks his cock until with a fierce growl he comes all over my breasts.

There is so much cum that I know there is no way I will be able to get it off and leave this place without everyone knowing what he has done to me. Then when you can hardly see my skin, he begins scooping it up and fucking it into my cunt. He takes his thumb out of my mouth and feeds me his cum. It is salty and a little sharp. I suck on his fingers without being told. "This is what you wanted, isn't it? My cum covering your body. The taste on your mouth, the way it feels in your cunt..."

He smirks and twists one of my nipples until I protest, and he soothes the ache by rubbing a little on my clit. He hasn't noticed my secondary clit. I open my mouth unsure if I should say something.

"Such a needy little piece of ass. Well, Princess. You're not a bad fuck for a virgin." He slaps my clit hard with four thick fingers causing me to gasp–part pain, part pleasure. All indignation.

"What?" I barely get the question out. He's left me speechless and not in a good way. "I'm what?"

"This is what you wanted, isn't it? To be fucked by an orc? Some twisted fantasy you read about? Now that you got what you want, you do what I want, and get the fuck out of my town." It is mocking and dismissive like I'm one of those girls who hang around and don't care whose cock they are riding. He tucks himself into his jeans and walks to the door which he unlocks before closing it and locking it behind him. Shit. Why did he lock the door? Was it to give me privacy while I clean up or to make sure I couldn't escape? For some reason, this is all I can think about instead of the fact I'm literally covered in cum, which is beginning to soak into my skin. If I don't wash it off soon, I'll absorb his scent. Orc'i who scent me will think he has claimed me, and after that shitty goodbye, that is the last thing I want.

"Well, that's one way to lose your virginity." I look down at the unholy mess he made of me. I don't have anything to clean myself with except my own clothes. Then I spy the pillow on the sofa. "Oh, Goddess, what do I do?"

I don't even want to know what my face looks like. His taste is still on my tongue. I lick my lips, no longer afraid of smearing my lipstick.

I grab the thankfully clean cotton cover off the cushion and wipe my thighs and stomach. Mostly, I smear the cum but it does the trick. At least it isn't running down my legs, anymore.

It sucks but I only have my halter dress, which is ruined because his cum seeps into the material. Then I toss the cushion cover back on the sofa. He can deal with his own mess.

I laugh.

"What the actual fuck?" I go from drugged and dazed by too many orgasms to bewildered and finally pissed at myself for giving my virginity to someone who didn't even check if I'd come. Who didn't touch my clit until the very end. He made a mess of me and left me to clean up on my own. "You asshole! Just because I came doesn't mean that you can get away with being a selfish dick... Even if that was hot. Fuck. What am I meant to do?"

I look around and decide I'll leave him a note. See how he likes that. There is pen and paper on his desk and I take my time composing a suitably scathing diatribe against his ability to make a woman come. Who am I kidding? I loved every second of it and he knows it.

<u>Thanks for taking my virginity. I can now fuck</u>

Property of the Green Bastards

<u>someone and not be one of those awkward virgins who don't know what they are doing.</u>

But this effort is just as weak.

I look at my words and realise that he won't care. I tuck his pen into my pocket and crumple up the paper to bury at the bottom of the waste paper basket. I do not want him to find it, but feel stranger taking it with me.

Now I'm stuck because how the fuck do I get out of here without everyone smelling me. Knowing how their MC prez wham, bammed, and slammed the door. No "thank you". Just a threat that I need to leave.

Bullshit, am I going. He might not be my heartsong, but he sure as fuck doesn't scare me anymore. I know exactly what kind of orc he is. A high-handed asshole who thinks he can get whatever he wants. He is the easy lay. He was the one who pursued me. Now that fucking him is out of my system, I can focus on why I am here in the first place.

I straighten my shoulders. "You've got this, Dinah. You have…okay, you haven't dealt with this but…the President of the Green Bastards, the last Horde King, just fucked you. And marked you. That is not something to be ashamed of. Imagine how many of those groupies he mentioned would kill for even a tenth of what just happened to you. Head high. Let them think what they want. You aren't going anywhere; might as well show him he can't intimidate you."

Except, of course, I'm shaking in my four-inch heels and scrambling to gather my courage.

A knock on the door makes me jump. I collect myself and open the door as proud as a queen. Like the President of the Green Bastards coming all over me happens all the time, that it is no big deal.

Flora Quincy

THERE IS an orc standing in the dimly lit hall. He looks about my age. A sharp frown on his handsome face, and a ruby glints in his tusk, telling me he is from the Old Horde.

"Here." He holds out a wet towel. Without a word, I take it from him and wipe my mouth, trying to remove the smeared lipstick. I dab at my chest in a purely symbolic attempt to get rid of the rest of Axe's cum. Finally, I throw the towel over my shoulder into the office.

"Thank you..." I leave the sentiment hanging, hoping he'll give his name since I can't make it out on his patch.

"Raine."

"Thank you, Raine." I turn right to head back downstairs and to the bar. "We are consenting adults. I did nothing wrong."

"You don't want to do that," he warns. "Everyone—"

"I won't let him scare me away," I say with a lot more confidence than I feel.

Raine grabs my upper arm and twists me towards him. "You don't get it. You, a human, can't just walk back in there smelling like you bathed in his cum."

"He left me like this," I snap. I suck in a deep breath, hold it for a count of eight, slowly let it out. "If he didn't want me to smell of him, he should take responsibility. Two people were fucking in there."

He lets out a string of curses in orc'ish dedicated to his prez's stupidity. "You aren't stupid which is why I have no clue what you thought you'd get from fucking him—"

"He propositioned me," I tell him. "I don't want anything from him. Fucking Axe has nothing to do with why I'm here." I wave my hand around. "It was a mistake," I say more clearly. "Trust me, I do not plan on repeating what just happened. It was a huge mistake."

Property of the Green Bastards

"Look—"

"If you don't want me going out that way, then how do I get home? I am assuming you want me to go back to the Barracks?"

"Fuck. Fine. I'll take you," he grumbles. "This way."

I follow him down the hallway until we get to a fire exit with an illuminated sign. He pushes the bar and opens the door for me like a gentleman. I step out into the cold night air. We are on a fire escape stairway, and when Raine sees my shoes, he helps me climb down the metal stairs.

I want to laugh. This is so fucked up. I should be more attracted to this Raine guy than Axe who treated me like trash. But even though I don't plan on sleeping with Axe again, it doesn't mean I will lie. If given the choice, I'd pick Axe every day of the week. I'd repeat everything we did in his office.

No, Princess. You do not do repeats with the President of the Green Bastards. Zero good ideas there.

"Hey...you okay?"

"What?" I look at the biker. He has his hair tied in an elaborate top knot that the more northern orc'i have. Further south—

"Yeah, I know about hairstyles."

I frown. That is twice in one day that I spoke without realising it. "I'm sorry, I'm very tired. I was driving for twenty hours straight. I should probably get a few hours of sleep."

"You haven't slept for twenty hours?"

"More like twenty-five...I had to stop for food and breaks. So that ate into driving time."

"That isn't healthy."

"I don't need a lot of sleep." I inhale but only smell Axe's scent, which makes me grin like an idiot because the smell of his cum feels like armour. Clearly, I'm still cum drunk, but anyway, no one in their right mind would touch me when I smell like him. I turn and smile at Raine. "Thanks, I can go from here."

"Yeah? You think Axe would let me watch you walk home on your own?"

"I don't think Axe cares." I roll my eyes. "Deh, sinsin. Or'dwae'ki on fro di k'in."

"You speak...wait." He jogs to catch up with me. "You speak old orcish?"

"Obviously. Elmeer hired me to forge authentication documents."

"Shit." He rubs his hands over the shaved sides of his head. "Yeah. Let's get you back to the Barracks. You really shouldn't be out here."

I watch him walk past me. He mutters under his breath about arrogant Green Bastards. I speed up so that we are shoulder to shoulder.

"So, you are from the Old Horde?"

"Look..." He stops, and I skid to a stop. "Do you have a name?"

"Dinah."

"Dinah? You know you aren't his heartsong, right? You aren't an orc even if you speak the language and probably have a bit of magical blood. You can't be his heartsong. He is heartless. So don't start getting attached. You aren't part of the club or the horde. Stay out of Bastard's business. Okay? For your own good."

More than Axe walking away, Raine's soft words are like a knife in the heart. So I force that rich-person smile I've been practising since my first day at the art history and appreciation society. "That isn't what I want. I only want to do my job."

"That's great."

We start walking together but instead of talking, Raine

Property of the Green Bastards

is looking around. His eyes dart around for any potential danger, like another possible drive-by where war drums are sounded. I want to ask the only member of the MC I've actually had a conversation with, but the words don't come. From what I understand, the Green Bastards aren't like a human motorcycle club. Orc MCs don't keep club business from women. But it is a club versus everyone else. And they still think I'm human.

It is maybe a twenty-minute walk from the Compound to where I am living. But the feet disappear in seconds and we are standing in front of the Barracks.

"Okay. Thanks," I say and hold out my hand like I'm so used to doing. He looks at it strangely then takes it in his. My gramps would say he had a weak handshake, but orc'i don't shake hands or care about human customs. "Sorry. I forgot. No handshakes."

"Yeah. Why–" His question cuts off and he pulls me behind him. "Shit, shit, shit."

I look around and see what the shadows had hidden. Someone has spray-painted Human Pigs over the door. The kind of thing one person could do without being noticed.

I roll my eyes and push past him to inspect the paint. It is still wet and I recognise the make from the rich chalky scent behind the tacky aerosol stink. It is the same that my cousin uses when he tags the neighbourhood for his gang. The stuff will come off easily. Especially off the glass and the high gloss paint on the door.

"Kids," I tell Raine who paces back and forth, speaking into a walkie talkie. I nearly laugh at the sight of the big orc and the blue and red kiddy toy in his hand. But his posture tells me something is up. "Raine?"

He looks at me. "Gotta go, Hawk. Deh, pahpah."

I blush, realising that Hawk is Raine's heartsong.

"You can't stay here," he says.

"Why not? Some kids getting cheeky because there is a new human lawman in town? Or do you think this is more serious? The glass isn't broken. It is only on the door. It's harmless. Look, I grew up in the city. My cousin runs for a gang and does this kind of thing all the time...with the same spray paint. Shit, Raine. Do you think you are the only people who—"

"You don't know what you are talking about," he snaps and takes a menacing step towards me. I see the exact moment he gets close enough to smell Axe on me because his nose wrinkles. "Fuck. Get inside. Lock your door. Only open for me or Axe." He hesitates for a moment. "Or Boonie."

"All right but I still think it is bullshit." Then it hits me. "My bag! My jacket. Shit. All my stuff is at the Compound."

I turn around to head back the way we came. Raine stops me with a hand on my arm, but what pulls me up sharp is the sight of the sheriff standing watching us. He is handsome for a human, short cropped blond hair that probably curls if it grows out. Tall and muscled but compared to the orc'i, he looks malnourished.

"Ma'am." He tips his head like we are in a movie, and I hear Raine snort behind me. "I see you need rescuing."

"I'm fine. I just need to get my—"

"Keys. I have mine." He dangles them from his fingers. "And I think everyone would be happier if you waited inside while Raine here returns to the Compound for your stuff."

"She isn't your business, lawman."

"And she is yours?"

I look up and see the way the street lamps catch the white of Raine's tusks. "Everyone in Dwen'mar, even you,

Property of the Green Bastards

is my business. Or'dwea'ki, weh meh teng. Or did you come up here as stupid as you look in that city slicker get up? Wrong month for Halloween."

"Sheriff." I grab both their attention. "If you let me in, I'll sit in the dining room."

"No," they say at the same time, though for very different reasons.

I dash forward and snatch the key from the startled man as he stares at Raine. "Thanks."

Their eyes are hot on my back as I unlock the door, leave the key in the lock, and walk in. The boarding house is quiet and dark. As far as I know, only me, the sheriff, and my new landlady live here and we were all at the Compound. I turn right into the large dining area with its heavy communal dining table in the centre. Everything about today is catching up with me as the adrenaline from losing my virginity dissipates. I pull out the nearest chair and sink onto the unforgiving wooden seat.

"You want to take a shower? You can use mine." The sheriff is standing in the archway looking at me. "I... I know it isn't my business—"

I narrow my eyes at him and channel all the energy from the bitches who looked down on my background when I was a student. "What gives you the right to stick your nose into my affairs?"

"Shit. Why? Why is everyone pissed off at me? I came up here to keep the peace. And we need to stick together. I need an ally here and so do you."

I raise an eyebrow. "Wow. You think I want to associate with you? Maybe I should let those kids in and they can spray-paint your door."

I see how he straightens and takes a step forward. "That isn't what I meant and you know it. I meant we are both new here. They want to get rid of us."

Flora Quincy

"Look, lawman," I sneer the word. "I am here because I want to be. Because working with orc antiques and objects is my dream job. I'm not going to fuck that up. You're a pathetic cumdribbling little dickshit if you think I want to be your friend."

Is this too harsh? Probably. But my instinct tells me to keep him as far away as possible.

"Cumdribbling?" He blinks, shakes his head like he can't make sense of what I said. When he speaks next his voice is slightly deeper. "Wait...are you from the Stews?"

I don't answer, I just close my eyes and try to rest.

"Seriously, I–"

"Go to bed," I tell him. Surprisingly, he does. As he stalks off into the darkness, I think about how I genuinely don't know what to think of him. Part of me wants to believe he is racist so he's easier to hate, but why take the job here? Our landlady was very clear that he'd asked to be transferred to an orcish town. It isn't my business, so I put it out of my mind for now. I look around for a clock and the only one is an ancient grandfather clock that must be two hundred years old, but the hands are stuck at three-forty. At least I know it will be the correct time twice a day.

Now I'm alone, I begin to sort through everything in my head.

Starting with my job. The forgery will take all winter, and I expect I'll have other jobs along the way. But I do have an entire backroom to myself to do the work. There is a lot I'll need to order in but Elmeer said whatever the cost. It goes against his claim he needs money but we both know the hammer price will more than make it back. The thing is that I know he'll get at least five times what he thinks he'll be able to sell it for. The map is exactly the kind of thing collectors are desperate for. They are buying up everything they can because import duties on magical

Property of the Green Bastards

antiques will be going up next year after the elections. The current liberal-left party won't be re-elected. The opposition is trying to sell itself as pro-magic. While you might think that would make antiques cheaper, they are going the other way so that "preservation of historic, local culture is prioritised over human greed." Bull-fucking-shit. The higher duties will just go to "pro-business" interests. Buying human will be cheaper and all the magical imports and exports will be cut out. So, this map? It will sell for more money than anyone can imagine around here. And looking at the state of the main streets and the worn furnishings of the Compound, they could really use the cash. I'll do more than forge the map, I'll use all my connections to help them. Every good deed will hopefully keep me in the MC's good books enough that I'll be permitted to stay.

"Dinah? Whatcha doing in this dark?" Miss Krystal is switching on the electric lights which flicker pathetically before she curses and turns them off again before lighting a gas lamp and walking over. "I passed Raine. But I already had your bag and told him to get to bed. Now...oh."

Now I'm blushing. It was one thing for the sheriff to insinuate I smell of orc cum, but the way Miss Krystal refuses to meet my eye makes me realise just how the long-term residents might interpret what happened. "Why don't I..."

"Please...what will people think?" I ask, suddenly shy. "I need to know."

"Well...most won't know. Axe didn't come back, and I just assumed you'd gone home but forgot your things. How did you get in?"

"The new sheriff."

"Well, that was nice of him...tell me, sweetie. Are you going to be okay? There are a lot of girls, humans, you understand. Who come up here looking to get in a family way with an orc. I just don't want you to get your heart broken. Orc'i don't settle with humans unless they are invited to join a heartsong pair."

"I know," I rush to say. "I don't want that. To be a slut. I don't want people to think I'm a groupie, I mean."

"Oh, dear. First, no slut-shaming. Sex, enjoying sex, isn't a crime. The honeys here aren't sluts because they choose to sleep with the club members. It isn't a crime to enjoy sex. And no one would think jack about you wanting to try orc cock."

"Still..." I am unprepared to deal with the aftermath. When you fantasise about your first time, you never think about what will happen afterwards.

"All the same, I hope no one else saw because they will think you belong to Axe if they catch you smelling like you do. Axe doesn't do long term, never has. Everyone knows he is heartless. For your own good, forget tonight happened."

I nod and grab my things from her, muttering a hasty embarrassed goodnight under my breath. My room faces north, and I can see the Allteng out my window. I flick the curtains closed and make my way in the dark to the little bathroom. "Shit."

I go back and dig out my solar-powered lamp out of the box marked stuff and turn it on so that I can see what I'm doing in the bathroom.

It looks exactly like something from a historical movie. The tiles are small, white, and laid out like the ones on the subway. The bath–the first one I've ever gotten to use–sits on four claw feet. The toilet cistern is attached to the wall way above my head and I will need to pull the chain to make it flush. The basin is huge with two taps instead of a mixer. There is a faint scent of lemon, probably from a

Property of the Green Bastards

cleaning product, but otherwise, it is bare. I play around with the bath taps until I figure out how to get the shower working. The water splutters out at first and is freezing, but eventually, I feel it beginning to warm up. I strip out of my dress and toss it in the sink. I'll have to soak it in the tub if I want to get rid of his scent.

The clean-up post primal virginity loss is not nearly as sexy as the act itself.

The smell of Axe's seed on my skin is even stronger now. The part of me that wants to be a strong independent woman is ready to strangle the side that positively swoons at the idea of being marked like this.

Strong and independent me wasn't so excited about the prospect of acting like the single most significant experience of my life was about as exciting as a week of leftover bean casserole. Nothing to bruise a powerful man's ego like acting as if the orgasms he gave you didn't positively wreck you for any other dick. He did, but no way will he ever know that.

I step under the almost too hot spray and all thoughts of Axe vanish. I've never taken a shower where I didn't have to worry about someone walking in or using up all the hot water. This moment is luxurious compared to what I grew up with. I begin by just letting my body get used to the water's temperature and how soft it is compared to the hard, chemicalised water from down south. When my hair is wet all the way through, I reach for the shampoo and lather the heavy weight of black hair, removing all the hairspray and product I use to keep it looking like I've walked out of a fashion magazine. Axe's, uh, efforts earlier mean there are tangles in it that I slowly work out with my fingers. Only after applying a deep conditioner and pinning it on my head do I begin the long task of washing my body.

Flora Quincy

It begins with an industrial-strength soap that strips away the layer of makeup I put on most of my body to hide the orc green freckles that cover my skin. I'm also washing away the rest of the drying cum which takes away from the primal passion of just an hour ago. *Shit*. Why don't I feel more different? Or maybe, why do I feel lighter? More in charge and safer than I did before he came up to me in the bar and dared me to play his game.

Some people prefer losing their virginity on a bed covered with red roses. I dreamt of being dragged to a cave and ravished by a fearsome monster. A dark office and an orc aren't exactly the same as my fantasy but it was so much better than any fantasy that I just do not care. My hand drifts down to between my legs and where I find a smear of blood along with my own slick. Whatever cum he pushed inside with his fingers has long disappeared, but the stretch is still there, the ache that will stay with me hopefully until I see him again. I feel a smirk tug at my lips.

What are you thinking, Axe? I wonder...

Chapter Four

AXE

I watch her silhouette against the curtains, and my dick twitches in my jeans.

A virgin. And I was an asshole because when I saw her lying there spread out on my desk, I didn't know what to say. She looked too perfect covered in my cum. She had me fucking speechless. She left my brain scrambling and that never happens, so I said some kind of crass scripted bullshit to piss her off.

What else could I do?

When I first saw the blood on my dick, I thought I'd

ripped her open. Most humans aren't meant for orc cock, and I hadn't exactly prepared her to take me. Only to find out she was a virgin? I'm a total caveman to get off on the fact her first cock was mine. I'm acting like virginity means something. Some virgin snow white bullshit. Fuck if I care, but she can't pretend she didn't want it. She played my game and begged for it.

Fuck, maybe I played her game.

I don't give two shits whose game it was. What happened in my office was the best sex I've ever had. Stalking her through the crowd had my instincts flaring. When I caught her, there had been no fear in her eyes. Only anticipation. And who knew a woman could sprint in fucking feet breakers? She took off, ass taunting me, and I followed.

I popped her cherry and I don't even know her name. How she picked my office, I don't know. And I sure as shit don't remember leaving it unlocked. I'll talk to Boonie or Swot about it tomorrow. Fuck, I hop it just messed up and forgot to lock it.

For now, I watch my little human as she gets ready for bed.

"Axe?" Raine asks. He's found me skulking about and...well, fuck him and his opinions.

I grunt. "She got in just fine."

"Yeah? So why did you follow?"

"I was curious."

"Curious enough that you fucking stalked her while I walked her back. Then stayed in the shadows? Why couldn't you do all this gentleman stuff? Isn't exactly how I wanted to spend my night, Prez."

"Yeah, but you did it," I point out. Then it occurs to me. He might have thought because she was with me that she'd be with him too. I don't know his deal with Hawk. If

Property of the Green Bastards

they have an open relationship or not. "Did you think you were going to fuck her? Because I already told her the only orc cock she's coming on is mine."

"Damn, Prez. I never thought you'd get jealous over some girl. You gonna hand her your balls after one fuck?"

He's baiting me. And I'm getting mad too easily. "You think I'm in love with her?"

"In love with her pussy...you marked her up good. You are lucky, Prez. If anyone had scented her, they'd have seen it as a formal intent to claim her."

I grab his wrist, spinning him around and twisting it up his back, which will aggravate an old wound from a warg run a couple of years ago before he prospected. "You do not tell me the consequences of my actions. She was a fuck. She wanted it...but it wasn't a fucking claiming. You think I'm going to put my cum in her cunt? Risk getting some random human pregnant?"

Except I risked it. Coming on her instead of in her, doesn't exactly work when I was pushing my cum into her quim.

"Frey! Ash'or'ash, she is orc'kin. You got to know that...Prez, let me go." He tries to shake me off. "This is serious shit."

I release him and push him just hard enough that he stumbles.

"Don't go calling me king," I warn him. "I'm your prez. If I put on that king bullshit, that is for them. I'm not a king."

"Sure thing, Axe." He glares at me. "She's orc'kin. I'm telling you. There is something—"

"Who she is doesn't matter." It does, if he is right and she is orc'kin, I need to be more careful than if she was human. "Fuck it, she was just a fuck. I need a drink. You coming or are you gonna keep PMSing?"

"Nah, prez. You need a shower. You smell almost as bad as her." He waves his hand in front of his nose like he doesn't spend most of his nights smelling of Hawk. "So if you aren't claiming her, does that mean I can persuade Hawk to fuck her with me? If she is willing to play hide and seek with you, bet she'll be into our kinkier play."

He flashes a smirk at me, those little rubies flashing in the light, reminding me they have a thing for knives. It is like drawing blood is their love language. The thought of a single mark on her unblemished skin, though, makes my stomach churn.

"Fat fucking chance. She got her taste of orc and tomorrow she leaves. Fuck, I'm going to bed. All of you are taking her too seriously. Just some human, you got me?" I point a finger at him. He snorts like he doesn't believe me. "Asshole. You're lucky Hawk likes you intact or I'd carve your balls out."

Now the rockfucker actually full out laughs like this is the funniest shit he's ever heard. I shake my head and head off to the Compound with Raine catching up.

"You're taking what happened too seriously. She is just some human," I repeat.

"Maybe if you say it enough, you'll believe it." Raine's words follow me all the way back to my apartment that covers the top floor.

It is the same as when my dad was alive and lived here with Sandra and Boonie.

I'd always planned to let my heartsong decorate it, but that isn't happening. Thirty-three and still no heartsong. Pretty sure it's never happening. Fuck, everyone knows I'm heartless. Maybe that is why they pay attention to who I fuck.

I smirk thinking about the uptown, rich girl I just screwed in my office. Bet this place with its furs and leather

Property of the Green Bastards

would make her gag in disgust. Even the priceless weapons on the walls will look barbaric to her fancy eyes. Yeah, someone like her wouldn't fit in my life, no matter how perfect she feels around my cock.

I hunt down a bottle of moonshine Sandra made and drink straight from the bottle. No matter how much I drink it, it burns going down. Not the beer I wanted, but if I go back to the party people will smell her on me. Boonie will want to know why and who. And the brothers will have a fucking field day like Raine did.

I scratch the skin above my heart.

My itch. Cor. That's the orcish word. Fuck my ancestors for getting their words all messed up. I'm not an idiot. I know cor is heart in one of those dead human languages. But she isn't my heartsong.

I fall asleep thinking about heartsongs. I never think about heartsongs. Not me. Not the monster of the Badlands.

I WAKE up with a cramp in my left hand. I make a fist and flex out my fingers until the tendons stand out, but that shit hurts. I glare at the battle axe that hangs on the wall above the door. Frodrick's war axe isn't that impressive until you know the handle is iron and the blade is as sharp as the day it was given to him. My father and grandfather didn't touch it. It wasn't the blade used to end all those lives. But it is mine and every once in a while, my hand likes to remind me.

I roll out of bed and grip the handle, feeling the cold metal against my palm. For a moment, I rest there with my forehead against the door and just let the sensation of or'gre take over. That battle rage had humans thinking orc'i and the creatures they met on the battlefield were two

Flora Quincy

different races. They said our battle blood made us cannibals, child killers, something terrifying to help their populace get behind the war that drained their resources and would never break the stalemate.

The history lesson passes over me as the weight, the meaning of this weapon, rushes at me. Last night, I told Raine I wasn't the king. But as of yesterday, I've played that role twice. First with Ryder and then in front of my people. Perhaps the high from calling on my blood right urged my more primal side to claim—no, not claim. I did not claim the little human. I fucked her to scare her off. To make it clear she is not ready for orc cock. For orc life. For MC life. This isn't the same as her sunshine and roses life down south. I need to find the itch, which has only gotten more distracting, and make one thing clear. She needs to leave or else because I can't lie to myself anymore this morning. My wrist hurts, too. Because I woke up in the middle of the night and jerked off to the memory of her. Probably gave myself carpal tunnel syndrome.

I release the axe's handle and step back.

"You're fucked, Axe," I tell myself. All because a little human played my games, then spread her legs. Her fancy exterior hiding my perfect kinda sex freak. I grin. If she is orc'kin like Raine says, if she wants to stay, she can. I haven't had a good lay in a while, but she'll have to follow my rules. Instinct tells me she'll follow even if we never get naked together again.

I take my time showering, eating some breakfast, and reading the newspaper that gets delivered every day from the human world. Seems like the politics down south are as restful as they are up here, which is good for me. The more their media focuses on their political upheavals, the less it will care about whatever shitstorm is brewing in the Badlands. Hawk scrapes out a chair and sits across from

Property of the Green Bastards

me. I pour out another mug of coffee before filling his cartoon character mug.

"I want to do another sweep. My gut says he hasn't left," Hawk says after downing half the bean juice in one go. "I'll take wargs."

"Yeah, was going to ask that, brother. Thanks. You were busy securing the perimeter but Grass and Goose don't have your tracking skills." Our road captains are twins and have the fastest bikes so we had to send them. But Hawk got given that government name for a reason.

Our eyes meet. We really shouldn't be talking so out in the open, but with Hawk's instincts, I'm relaxed enough for us to go over this delicate subject.

"Take him to the foot of the Allteng and let the Sisters take care of it."

"That will take all day," he grumbles.

"What? Did you plan on trying to convince Raine to be submissive and breedable?" I joke.

"Nah, Prez. That's your kink. I like them when they fight back."

I grin but keep quiet about the way the woman ran from me. The chase meant something to her. She wants to be prey. My dick twitches like it doesn't realise she is a walking, talking distraction. All it cares about are her tits and cunt.

"You gonna do something about your little bird?" Hawk asks.

"Boonie wants her to stay..." I say despite the fact I've been telling myself all morning that she's got to go. I decide to ignore anything about me and the girl. Focus on the reason I'm going to give everyone else for letting her stay. "She is going to be doing the authentication bull they were talking about."

"That will be good money."

I grimace, knowing he is right. We aren't pressed for cash but modern times means diversification. Human tourism is picking up, and they all want something authentically orcish. Easy enough to sell crap to the tourists, much more lucrative to get those high-end collectors. Or, at least, that is how Mom explained it to me months ago. I'd given her my okay and now some itch drives into my town looking like she stepped out of a wet dream, loses her virginity on my dick, and I'm expected to let her hang around making money for me? It should be perfect but something tells me this is a trap.

"You are thinking too hard," my mom says as she comes into the kitchen. It is nine in the morning which means she has been up for hours with the wargs. "There is a burnt-out car by the gap...you gonna tell me what that is about?"

"If I knew, I'd tell you." I smirk at Hawk. Well, well, well, I'll send one of the prospects. We can check it out. Then I'm not actually lying to her. 'Sides, it gives us a place to start.

"Hawk?"

"Sorry, Boonie. And I have a message to deliver to the Sisters. Want me to pass anything on?"

My mom, who was born into the Silver Amazons, also known as the Sisters, has their superstitions and their viciousness in spades.

"Tell them the cat is out of the bag. Oh." She slams a hand on the table, making the mugs jump. "Tell my crazy cunt of a sister I was right about you know who. She'll get it."

"Yes, Boonie. I'll tell Mom." We all laugh. Hawk's mom Kat never left the Silver Amazons but since boys don't live on the sides of the Allteng, he came to the Green Bastards to be raised by his aunt.

Property of the Green Bastards

"You shoulda been born a girl, Hawk." My mom smiles. "You'da made one hell of an Amazon."

"Lucky for me, he wasn't. I wouldn't want to live separate from my heartsong. I like getting laid too much." Raine saunters in, a shit-eating grin on his face. "Got news about that graffiti on the Barracks. Some kids thought it would be funny to scare the pig. Seems like Dinah was right."

Her name. No. Gotta not think too much about the itch and what happened last night. I've got real problems. And knowing her name? That just makes it real. A real fucking big deal.

"Pigs are useful," Hawk points out. I sit back and enjoy the way my family banters. With meh'or around me, I can put aside being prez, being the king, and just return to those few stolen years of being Den.

"Ashee? Earth to Ashee?" My mom waves a hand in my face. "You gonna go easy on that girl? She disappeared last night before I got a chance to talk to her properly."

"Eh, why not? I'll go over to Elmeer's today." I shrug. My brothers stare at me like I've turned into a pig. "But she has to follow the rules of the mar. If she lives here, it is because I will it."

"Urgh. Why do you have to play king in the morning?" Now Kendle is wandering in looking worse for wear with a giant hickey on her neck. I catch Raine glaring at it, but it is for the best. She needs to live her life before being dragged off to live with the Old Horde.

"Well, now that the whole family is here, I have news. Meh'weh, keh'i." We all look at Hawk like he has grown a second head. What honour oath is he talking about? "The Seh'wed'or has ended. The old farm is reverting to the club at the end of the month."

That is good news, and we pound the table with our

Flora Quincy

fists. My great-grandfather had leased the most profitable farm in the district to a Fury three generations ago. Parasitic shits have slowly been running it into the ground because they rely on magic to tend the farmland. Seems like they forget this is the Badlands where the land is literally bad for growing things. Magic doesn't replenish the nutrients in the soil, so they've mortgaged it three times in the last two years, not even using the farm as collateral but using the granddaughter. The only woman born into the family since the first lease was signed. This generation's fury's power is ours, and I don't even know if the bitch knows it. Anyway, we will need her magic if this turns into war.

"Good. Take care of it." I finish my coffee and stand. Stretching my arms over my head and letting my shoulders pop. Kendle chucks an apple at me—she absolutely hates the sounds of bones cracking. Nothing like pissing off a sibling to start the day right. "I'll stop by Elmeer's and then head over to the garage, see what they have going there."

I know they are looking at me, or at least Raine is, with a lot of meaning. I flip them off, push out of the kitchen and into the main room. There are a few of my brothers still passed out on the sofas. The place smells of sex and stale beer, which is, in a sick sort of way, comforting. At least the rest of the club and the partiers think that the world is normal. Totally unaware of the shit about to land on our doorstep.

I consider walking to Elmeer's, it is only a ten-minute walk, but that won't look good. I veer towards the line of bikes and run a hand over the carefully tooled leather of the closest bike. It is one I don't recognise. "Prospect!"

The kid is skinny, his face covered with such pale freckles he looks jaundiced. "Axe?"

"Whose bike is this?"

Property of the Green Bastards

"Mine..."

"Pretty fancy bike for a prospect." I try and remember his people. There are ten thousand orc'i in my territory. He isn't a townie and stinks of the farm in a way that doesn't smell.

"Uh...if you mean the leather, I did that. My da' is a tanner."

"Oh? And why did you leave Gill'mar?"

"Because it is a fucking asswipe, and I'm the seventh son of a seventh son."

The weight of that, magically, carries everywhere. Doesn't matter what your race is, if you have magic or not, on this island, that means something. "What is your name? Do you even have a road name?"

"Don't have one yet," He flushes making him look like he has a fever as well as jaundice. "My government name is Jon."

"Tool," I tell him. "From now on, you are Tool. If you want to do more of this work, talk to Swot...actually, get on your bike and come with me."

"But—"

"Wake someone up inside. I want you with me." I go to my own bike and run an expert eye over it. When you grow up around bikes, you get an instinct. You know something is wrong, long before some idiot takes their dying chrome dog to the shop. But she looks good. I swing a leg over and settle while I wait for the kid, who comes back in record time. We leave the Compound and head into the centre of town. On one side are the orc shops, the other are those owned by kin. The spot outside Elmeer's is empty. And as I back my bike into a real bike space across the street I grin because I can't shake the memory of her spouting the road code at a bunch of bikers.

Tool parks next to me. "Should I wait..."

"Nah, kid. Ordweaki. If something happens to a chrome dog belonging to the MC..." I let the threat hang in the air. Gill'mar is too close to the Allteng for him to have much experience with humans and kin, but he'll learn.

I cross the street and push into the koltop, the bell tinkles, which is the most annoying sound in the world. Frey. I remember coming here as a kid and pretending I was some kind of ancient warrior or adventurer.

"Axe!" The old man waves from the back of the shop. I process what I'm going to say but Tool is too close to my back and I have to walk deeper into the shop or have him riding my ass. I wanna spit at the idea. Gives me the ick.

I'm bigger than a bull in a china shop but I move like a cat so it is no problem to snake through the junk to get to where the map is.

She stands over the map. Not tarted up in her fuck-me dress and heels today, she wears a fitted button-down that shows off enough cleavage to be indecent. Makes her tits look perfect and gives my dick reason to twitch in my pants. "Whatcha looking at, Princess?"

She looks up briefly, flashes a distracted smile and then gets back to looking at a fucking map. This woman? Does she really understand what happened between us? I fucked her brains out. Gave her more, and better, orgasms than she's ever received in her life and the bitch is ignoring me? I took her virginity last night. She should be–she should have some kind of pissy remark or reaction, at least.

"Dinah...maybe you should tell Axe, the President of the Green Bastards MC, what you are looking at."

Dinah. Her name is Dinah. I heard Raine say it at breakfast, but looking at her, it fits as good as those trousers

Property of the Green Bastards

and more of that red lipstick. Or it would if she was an orc. Sweet berry. Di'or'nah, sweet blood berry it means.

"Oh, sorry, Elmeer. Axe, I'm examining the quality of the hide. If I'm going to...oh, can I talk about that?" she asks like peroxide has destroyed every brain cell in her head. But her eyes flash at me like she is just daring me to remind her that I fucked her. A smirk tugs at my lips. She's just sealed her fate. I'm fucking her again, and enough times after that until I get bored.

"You can tell them," Elmeer says, smiling at her like she farts sunshine and rainbows. Hell, maybe she does.

"This is a forgery," she declares.

"Impossible," I say. It was the most prized possession of the Disavowed before my grandfather took it in compensation. It is a genuine ninth-century original. One of the first Horde maps.

"No! It's a good thing," she insists. Her eyes are bright green like someone used paint to give 'em colour instead of her genetics. Which works because she gotta be some kind of artist to be making this map for us. "The forgeries of the mid-nineteenth century are works of art in their own right. The challenge is forging a forgery. I'm trying to determine if they went with the Millener technique for scraping the hides or the Carter method. Two very different schools, each brilliant in their own way."

She glows when she talks, and I can't help but be drawn in.

"Don't know anything about art," I tell her and walk up to her and bend close. Part to get a whiff of the honeysuckle coming off her, but also to look at a map I'm just learning is a fake. "Did you know?"

"I suspected, but Dinah confirmed it. You don't need to crowd the girl, Axe," Elmeer tuts. "She knows to be respectful."

Fuck, respectful, I want to say. I've been a whole lot closer to her than this. "Well, Didi," I say, relishing the fact I kinda got her name right last night. "Tell me. How you gonna convince your people that–"

"Wow." We all turn to look at Tool who is bent so close his nose is almost touching the hide. "They double scraped in a v shape."

"You..." She slips around me to get close to the prospect who is suddenly a little too close to my itch for my liking. "I haven't looked at this quadrant yet because there was too much detail work."

"The hide probably has less wear because there is so much intricate work on it..."

They start nattering about tanning techniques, and I want to scream that this is not why I brought Tool along. He was meant to be the skinny-not-Axe so that she knew exactly who she fucked last night and who makes the rules. They have to stop long enough to breathe, and, in that Frey-blessed silence, I drop the bomb and watch all the pretty colour drain out of her face.

"I never said you could stay, Princess. If I remember the right of it–"

"But!" She sounds pissed off. "I need to do this–"

"Elmeer, why don't you show Tool some of that leather you have in the back while Dinah and I talk?"

"Sure, Axe..." They sneak out like kids told they can't have candy for dinner. I can't promise that Elmeer won't eavesdrop, but Tool absolutely knows that I don't want to be interrupted, so he'll keep the gossipy Pilgrim away.

"That was rude. We could have moved," she says the minute we face each other like magnets drawn towards true north. My heart stumbles into double time when our eyes meet, which switches a thing in my dick that grows hard so fast, a lesser man would faint.

Property of the Green Bastards

The itch is back. I consider fucking her over the map to prove a point, but her frown has some other part of me tapping the breaks. The need to explain all of it to her taking precedent. Then we can get to me putting my dick inside of her again.

"See, the thing is, Didi, I own this town. This territory. The whole fucking Badlands belongs to me...and everyone follows my rules. I gave you the courtesy of asking you to leave twice..." I let the reminder hang in the air. I won't, I can't push her away even if I say I want her out of my mar. "Now, I'm going to be nice and let you stay to finish the map because it will make my mom happy, and I like money."

"You are such an asshole," she almost spits. I can see the fire in her. Last night, she was a little rabbit who wanted to be caught by the warg. Today, she is all in-my-face energy. I don't know which one my dick likes more. I take a step closer, then another. Her chin tilts back, exposing her swan-like throat, and revealing her racing pulse. I struggle to hold back from grabbing her by the throat so that I can feel how fast it beats. Maybe I'll run my tusks along the exposed skin, letting them promise the mating hold we inherited from some ancestor.

"You got me there, Princess. I'm an asshole. But a fair asshole. You do the job you were hired to do and I will let you stay. So long as you follow my rules."

"Of course, you have rules." She rolls her eyes, which is going to stop right this fucking second. Disrespecting me like that might be okay from a child, but she is a grown-ass adult and needs to know better.

"First rule. No sass. None of your back talking, especially in front of patched members. No swearing–I don't like it when ladies swear."

That gets her just like I hoped it would.

"You fucking arrogant jerk. You cannot tell me what I can and cannot say."

"Three," I continue like she didn't have a little tantrum because I'll pay full price for those flushed cheeks and flashing eyes. "You don't do anything that puts yourself or the mar in harm's way. Dwen'mar is a safe hearth for all orc'i and kin. I don't want it burning down because you need to blow dry your hair and start an electrical fire at the Barracks. These are old buildings and we don't have the–"

"I would never put the mar or its people at risk. I'm not some doh'gru."

I bite my tongue to stop me from laughing. There is something cute about hearing her swear in orcish. Like me drinking a fancy, girly cocktail with those little umbrellas. It takes a real man to pull off drinking a tequila sunrise. "Aw, Didi, I said no swearing. That means any language."

"Stop laughing at me." But her eyes sparkle. Yeah. Okay, this itch is getting too comfortable. I need to tell her what's what and then get out of here.

"Just don't get in my way. Remember you are just here to work." I put as much aggression in as possible, just waiting for her to snap. The fucking woman just smiles and asks if that is all. "If you don't follow my rules, I'll tan your hide."

Now that gets a reaction, perhaps not the one I expected, though. Instead of looking afraid or worried, she gets that same rabbit look in her eyes, which dart around as if trying to find all possible exits. No fear, though. This rabbit thinks it can stand up to the big, bad warg.

"Yeah, Princess…you wanna run from me again? Cause if you do, I'll catch you and own you just like I did last night." I reach down and make a big ass deal of rearranging my dick in my jeans. Her eyes are glued to where I've got my hand around the hard ridge in my jeans. She

Property of the Green Bastards

licks those red lips. All I want right now is for her to run so I can throw her over my shoulder...no. I want to fist that blacker than night sky hair and feed her my cock until she is gagging like a good girl who has never tasted cock. "You ever choked on cock, Princess?" I ask.

"No," she breathes the word. It is so quiet.

"Maybe if you are a good girl and follow the rules, I'll let you taste the tip," I taunt her. Fuck if it isn't getting me going the way her pupils dilate and her tits fill out that shirt with the way she is practically panting. Yeah, okay, this was not a good idea getting involved with a little human. But fuck if she isn't perfect. In fact, except for being human, everything about her is perfect. She has everything I want in a woman except a second clit. "You weren't so shy last night..."

"Axe, you need to believe me..."

I'm close enough to see her eyes are kinda glazed, alerting me that something isn't right. This girl is going to faint on me.

Chapter Five

DINAH

I don't think I've ever felt so lightheaded before.

I nearly fall to my knees right then and there and confess everything.

That I'm in Dwen'mar to destroy evidence that I am descended from the Disavowed. That my paperwork is a lie, but once all the proof is gone, I just want to live amongst my people. Fuck. Fuck. Fuck. I want to beg him to help make my dreams come true. His eyes are shrewd and he clearly knows enough that his mocking smile turns into a cruel smirk. He lets go of his cock and I think I'm

Property of the Green Bastards

free. Free-ish. I must be seeing things because he goes to unbutton his fly and pulls his half-hard cock out.

"Are you a good girl, Dinah?" He all but purrs my name as he fists himself from root to tip. And with each pass, it gets thicker and harder. A weapon of cervical destruction. I can still remember the ridges along his cock. Frey, the maker of orc'i, must have been a genius devoted to the pleasure of those who love dick because an orc cock is the sort of thing you could only come up with if you cared about g-spots and prostates. Or sex in general, for that matter. The head is flared like a human's but the length is covered in ridges and a pattern of nodules unique to each orc. Human biologists say it was because they are warlike people and the cartilage is there to protect their giant green dicks as they run into battle. Knowing what it feels like to be fucked with that monster cock and now seeing it in daylight convinces me that Frey was just a horny bitch.

"Tell me what is..." His words fade out as my eyes go kind of fuzzy at the un-fucking-believable size of that monster cock.

I don't know if I want to prove something to him when I drop to my knees or if I really am just that weak for him. But here I am, the hard tile floor underneath me, hands resting on my lap as if it isn't my first full day at work. As if my boss and a prospect aren't on the other side of the door into the back room. I do it anyway because my heart races, a thundering gallop that only evens out now that I am on my knees. I have to lift my chin to meet his eyes. And while I'm submitting to his unspoken commands–giving up all control–I still feel oddly safe as he swaggers towards me. He stops close enough that all it would take is for me to lean forward a little or for him to thrust his hips forward and just the tip would be in my mouth. Like this, I can smell that same heady, addictive scent that makes my insides melt and the place between my legs throb against the lace of my panties. Goddess, why didn't I just wear cotton today? Why did I have to hope that something like this would happen and, therefore, wanted to wear pretty panties for the monster in front of me?

"Be a good girl..."

I take a shuddering breath, determined to tell him no, but my lips part just enough that before I get the chance to say anything, the hot flared head is resting between my lips, butting against my teeth with each not quite a thrust movement of his hips–like he can't help the restless motion because he wants to be in my mouth as much as I want to taste him against my tongue.

I'm staring up at him now, my eyes open as wide as they can go because I don't want to miss a single damn expression on his face.

"You okay? Uh...Dinah?"

I'm blinking. I'm kneeling. That is real. But Axe is fully clothed and looking down at me.

"Fuck." I was caught up in a fantasy where I was about to give him a blow job? What is happening to me around this orc? I struggle to get back up on my feet, but when I do, I take an unsteady step back, grateful I'm wearing flats rather than heels.

"Oh, hell the fuck no," I say, backing away from Axe as he watches me with genuine concern on his face. "Not you. Or your rules. Sorry. I accept your rules. I'll make sure to follow them. Thank you for stopping by." I wave my arms, hoping he'll take the hint and leave me to my turbulent thoughts. "My head. I feel a little—"

"You look..."

"No need to worry about me! Thanks. I need to get back to my work." I look around, wishing Elmeer and the

Property of the Green Bastards

prospect who arrived with Axe would come in and save me from myself. I meet Axe's frowning eyes.

"When did you last eat?" he asks out of nowhere. "What did you do this morning?"

"This morning? I had some really shit coffee because there is—"

"You've just had coffee?" He cracks his neck like he is about to do some heavy lifting. "You realise that people get altitude sickness coming up to the Badlands?"

I blink. "I didn't think it would affect me."

Because I have orc blood, I don't add. I know humans can get it. The tourist guides all discuss it but they never mention how people with orc blood respond. And they never call it altitude sickness.

"Frey, save me from arrogant humans," he grumbles. "Come on. I'm taking you for breakfast."

"You don't have to," I say as I edge around the table to avoid the steady progress he makes as he stalks towards me.

"I don't, but I am going to because you are my responsibility. Meh'Dwea, Didi," he growls. "Stop running away from me."

That has me stopping, my back going ramrod straight and words coming out of my mouth before I can stop them. "You liked me running away last night."

"Oh? So we are going to talk about that now? Well, I don't want to hear you discuss how I blew your mind while waiting for you to faint on me."

I miss it. Or maybe he just moves that quickly but the world is spinning and I'm looking at firm, jean-covered orc ass because he has me in a fireman's carry. He walks out the door with my disorientated perspective on this morning all out of whack. I wiggle trying to get some leverage on the situation. "You can put me down."

"Nope." The word pops at the same time he slaps my

85

ass. "Stop that. You'll eat breakfast, and then I don't want to hear a peep from you or about you until the map is finished."

I open my mouth to argue when I see Elmeer and the prospect walk into the room. I cry out for help, but they make no move to rescue me. The prospect even gives a thumbs-up.

Axe doesn't put me down when we get out on the street, he just keeps walking past people who I only see afterwards because I'm looking at their bemused faces, or worse, their outright gawping. It feels like the whole town is witnessing my humiliation. Orcs, orc'kin, and others stop and stare at the spectacle we are making.

"This is weird," I finally say.

"No shit, Princess," he snorts and hitches me higher on his shoulder.

"Can't I walk?"

"No."

"Axe—"

"Be quiet. We are almost there."

Then I'm slithering down his front. When my feet hit the ground, his hands find my waist and squeeze, pulling me hard against his front until I feel the bulge against my stomach.

"Before we go in. Remember you promised to follow my rules. Don't care where we are if you don't follow them, I'll take it out on your ass. Now, say 'Yes Axe, I understand.'"

For a split second, I consider disobeying him. Quick on its heels is the feeling of…protection. And if I say the words, I'll be more enmeshed in this community. After today, I might never see him again. But this moment still happened. The memory is mine forever. "Yes, Axe. I understand."

Property of the Green Bastards

The best I get from him is a grunt, so I turn around to face what turns out to be a diner called, surprisingly enough, The Diner. I've seen images on the town's website and like the rest of Dwen'mar, it could have come straight out of a postcard. The exterior is slatted wood that is an aged brown-grey you can't fake no matter what chemicals or tech you use. And the neon red sign declares that they are open for business in common tongue. On the outside, at least, there is no orcish, which isn't a huge surprise since we are on the kin side of Main Street.

"Booth," Axe says as he pulls me by the wrist into the cool interior. With the way my blood has been rushing around my body, I'm a little unsteady and more than a little annoyed at the way he instinctively cups my waist so I don't wobble. He makes me go ahead of him as we walk through the half-full dining area to a corner booth in the back. A second later, I hear the bell chime again and then as I'm sitting, the prospect, whose name I need to learn, slides in across from us.

"The Pilgrim stayed at the shop," he tells Axe, but his eyes are on me. "I'm bringing her back after we eat."

The waitress arrives. In a flash, I realise why Axe was the way he was last night. She appears human with tits like melons and done up to look exactly like a pin-up girl. I love her look. This is the kind of woman I want to be friends with. She is giving me vibes with her cherry-red hair and matching lipstick. "What can I get you today?"

"Morning, Cherry. She'll have the kids' breakfast," Axe orders for me. This feels more like a fantasy than when I imagined he put the tip of his dick in my mouth. I squirm, wanting to argue and order for myself, and wanting to be taken care of. I know it has nothing to do with me. He doesn't care about me, Dinah Smith. But even knowing that, I can't help but wonder why he is doing this because last night, he couldn't get away from me fast enough and now I'm sitting in a diner with him while he orders me breakfast. "And water."

"That what you want, honey?" the waitress asks. "If you want something else..."

"No...that is good. It seems I have altitude sickness." And now that I think about it, the light-headedness, the slightly queasy feeling in my stomach, and the shortness of breath. It isn't because of nerves or the proximity to Axe but altitude sickness. I don't know if I should be relieved or disappointed. I slump back and stare at my hands, twisting the rings on my fingers.

"Ah. Kids' breakfast it is." She smiles. "Gentlemen?"

"Coffee for the rest of us," Axe finishes up the order. He turns away from her and angles his big body, watching me with a scowl on his face. Cherry nods and scoops up the menus we never looked at. As she walks away, I catch sight of a forked tail the same colour as her hair sweeping behind her. Not human then. I wait, expecting him to say something, maybe ask how I'm feeling. He scowls at me once more and then turns to the prospect. "You stay on her. Offer any help with the map leather stuff. Make sure she gets to and from work okay. She is an asset."

"Do you have a name?" I ask the prospect, who is maybe nineteen.

"Tool." He gives me a lopsided grin which I can't help return.

"You aren't here to flirt with her," Axe growls and pulls me back by my ponytail when I reach across the table to shake Tool's hand. "No flirting with the prospect, Princess."

I check to see how Tool is reacting to Axe's cave man behaviour. After Raine's comments last night, I didn't expect any special attention from Axe today. Today. Today

Property of the Green Bastards

Axe has me caged in after carrying me through one of the most populated parts of town. Tool looks relaxed, sitting back and looking around like he has never been here before. Like the diner is more interesting than his Prez getting territorial over a human.

"Drink," Axe grunts when Cherry returns with our drinks. He pushes one of those classic large plastic cups you get at some diners with the pimpled, texture up until the rim which is smooth in front of me. The glass is clear but the fingers holding it are green and strong. The nails are neatly trimmed, and I hesitate to reach out and see what my 'human' hand looks like next to his orc hand.

"Dinah, you need to drink some water...slowly," he warns me. "Elmeer's playing fast and loose these days. His employee nearly fainted while we were having our little conversation. He—"

"It is probably the lack of sleep," I interrupt not wanting to get my boss in trouble. "I was too tired to sleep last night."

We are all saved from talking because my food arrives. The plate has half a dozen silver dollar pancakes, sausage patty, extra-crispy bacon, scrambled eggs–runny, just like they should be–and toast. Next to the plate, there's whipped butter and a large container of maple syrup that smells so divine, I nearly start drooling. I pick up the knife and fork, ready to begin eating when Axe steals my plate and begins cutting up my food like I'm a kid.

"You need to eat small bites. Let him take care of it," Tool reassures me. I blink at the men around the table who seem completely unfazed that the most important orc in the Badlands is cutting my breakfast sausage into uneven wedges.

"This is not normal," I say, hoping one of them will

snap out of it. "Outlaw bikers don't cut up food for strangers. I don't know–"

Axe gives me a look, daring me to say more. I narrow my eyes at his too attractive face. He wouldn't tell these people we fucked. Would he? I'd been so confident last night about not caring what the people of Dwen'mar thought about me sleeping with Axe. But the cold light of day makes me nervous because he smells of leather and an aftershave I don't recognise. This is my catnip, I realise. These smells. This orc with his dark green skin and tusks. My heart flutters and I lick my lips, knowing I need to put a stop to this but not wanting to break the spell where he is taking care of me.

"Axe, neh go. Meh se'd daw. R'ak sin–" I make a grab for the plate, but he slaps my hand away…gently. "Fuck. Hi'dfi, Ahni–"

The table gets quiet. Hell, the whole diner is quiet, which doesn't mean I'm talking loud. They are just that focused on our weird little table.

I dare to meet his fierce scowl.

"Fuck it, fine. Give yourself indigestion," Axe snaps, throws the cutlery down, and slides out of the booth. "Tool, come on."

"I thought–"

"Think whatever you want, Princess. Tool, come on. Let's leave the civilians to their breakfast."

I swallow, wanting to apologise but not knowing what I should be apologising for.

"Wait–"

The President of the Green Bastards smirks at me. "Wa'la, Didi. Car'ki meh'weh. Hala k'feen dwel. Get that map finished."

He raises an eyebrow daring me to talk back, but his words cut deep. Deeper than he could ever realise. He

Property of the Green Bastards

called me k'feen, a person without inner strength, which is one thing I've never been allowed to be. You don't grow up the family charity case, wearing hand me downs into your twenties, and relying on government support and come out weak. The shame wriggles into my voice when I finally find the words. "I didn't ask for your dwel, Axe."

"Nothing I didn't willingly give." He growls. "You're an asset. I only ever do what I want to do. I'm the Prez of the Green Bastards. If I–"

I block out the rest of his angry rant and turn back to my food which I eat in careful small bites, sipping water as I go. You don't get to where I am and cry over bullshit like this. At least, not in public. And why should it matter? Why should how he sees me matter? He doesn't matter to my plans, because he doesn't know who or what I am...and I vow he never will.

"You know what? Fuck this. Eat your food. Drink your water. And stay the fuck out of trouble." He slams his hands on the cracked laminate and pushes out of the booth. I watch Tool hesitate for a moment, clearly uncertain if he should stay or go. But when Axe doesn't say anything, Tool sits back and takes a sip of his coffee. I finish quickly after that because it suddenly becomes imperative to get back to work and prove my worth to Elmeer.

"Here. I'm paying for my meal," I say to Cherry as I hand over the cash at the cash till set up next to the door.

"Axe already paid," she says with a wicked, toothy grin. "Sorry, I can't take your money this time."

"What?" It sounds like a squawk of indignation... which it kind of is. I pull myself together and think fast. An idea pops into my head. *You're gonna get in serious trouble*, I warn myself. Myself doesn't care. "Fine. If he wants, he can pay for this meal. But the next time he comes in, bring him a kids' meal and say I've already paid for it."

This time, she takes the cash.

Cherry snorts. "Sss'wassi, girlie. You are a beast. Shit. People don't sass the President of the Green Bastards like that, but for you? Damn, I'll make sure everyone knows you paid for his next meal in case I'm not on shift."

"Thanks," I say, then laugh because the way she is smiling rubs away some of the shame.

No one here knows, I remind myself. No one here knows who you are, where you came from. These aren't people who can smell the food stamps and the fact you were on benefits. They are like you. Hardworking, honest, and not rich. This is your chance to make a fresh start. "Thanks…I'm Dinah. And new, obviously. I don't have any—"

"Friends. Yeah. You have one now. We don't have a lot going on but there is a rocking bar that the kin go to and orc'i that aren't really into MC life. You wanna go?" Her smile reveals pointed teeth and a closer look shows a Fiend's curling horns. I wonder if she dyed her hair to match the colour of her horns or if it is natural.

"Yeah. I'd like that."

"Cool. Uh, tomorrow night work for you? Like eight? Wait. Are you staying at the Barracks?"

I nod.

"Great. I'll pick you up."

"It's a date."

She winks at me and then shoos me out.

Tool waits on the street, his hands in his pockets, and a frown on his young face. "I'm sorry. I should have…it's just, you and Axe…it was like a force of nature. Fuck. Maybe I should have stepped in."

I consider telling him it is okay, but that would be a lie

Property of the Green Bastards

and then some. "Next time?" I offer it as an olive branch. "I know I'm not your responsibility. And he is…who he is. Just do what you think is right for you."

What I don't say is that is what I am going to do.

"I need to stay on the good side of the Bastards, Dinah," he says softly. "I haven't been in this town long. Getting patched in is important. You heard him call a Meet last night." He looks away, gathering his thoughts. "You're human. And I can't be your friend exactly, but I'll help you out." He gives me a boyish grin. "Outsiders sticking together, right?"

"Right." I smile right back.

"Look…I need to get back and see what he wants me to do." With a final wave, he jogs after Axe. I wonder if he'll catch him or what.

"Fuck." I slap my cheeks. I need to get my shit together and get back to Elmeer's. What the living shit is he going to say? Hopefully nothing.

Chapter Six

AXE

That fucking itch.

She makes me hard in a way that makes me want to do something stupid, like fuck someone I shouldn't...namely her. Without trying, I can still remember the feel of her slick, hot cunt milking my cock.

Frey, I should be grateful she started spouting nonsense about being able to take care of herself. I was making a fucking fool of myself cutting up her food like that. Jaysus, what if I'd made the mistake of feeding her? What if we'd shared a meal? What if I'd taken a bite of her food? There was grain, meat, and egg on the plate–the Dwra'er. The meal heartsongs share. Would she know? She knows about the orc'i and our customs. She could have misinterpreted and thought I was claiming her. I wasn't. The girl nearly fainted while we were talking. She needs a strong hand to make sure she doesn't inhale her food and end up sick. Vomiting over the table would have embarrassed her. And her pride calls to my own. I grit my teeth together and spit. I look up. Where the fuck is the prospect? Then I remember I told him to stay with her.

"That was harsh, Prez. She isn't k'feen."

"Go back to the Compound, beg Boonie for a tube of mascara and then clean the toilets with a mascara brush," I bark.

I shouldn't be taking this out on the prospect but there is nothing worse than someone saying out loud what you know is the truth.

She has my wires crossed and everything I shouldn't be doing I am and vice versa, which is why I need to put her as far out of my head as possible. Physically out of sight, hoping it will keep her out of mind.

"Sure thing, Prez…but earlier you wanted me watching her?" He makes it sound like a question. We both know it isn't.

A tick in my jaw that did not exist before this morning begins to twinge. "You can do the toilets after they close up. Go on." I wave to the shop just at the moment that I watch her walk in. The brat didn't even look in my direction. What the fuck? "Go. Now. Before I change my mind."

I ride straight to the garage. It is a bustling hive of activity and probably the largest, legal business the MC owns. We even have a halfway functional website for tourists to use. My sister is working on a bike in the first bay.

"That belong to Heph?" I ask.

"Yeah. Can you believe that an actual giant brought their bike from the Great Mounts just because he knew I fixed up bikes?"

She sounds a little in awe of the situation. Immediately, I get a flash of Dinah and how excited she was talking about the map.

"You are the best, go'see." I ruffle her Mohawk. She wrinkles her nose in disgust at being called kid sister. "I'm your sol'sin—"

"Deh, deh, deh, Ashee," she laughs. "You are such an old man. Oh, Hawk is in the office."

I give her shoulder a quick squeeze, thinking when she goes with Ryder, I'll need to make sure she gets her own garage. Even tell her clients where she has gone. He might take my sister from me but he isn't going to take the one thing that gets her up in the morning from her. "Thanks, go'see. Finish Heph's rig up and I bet he'll bring you more business."

"You think so?" She sounds so hopeful, completely unsure of her own talents. I nod at her to let her know I mean it.

The office is up a flight of metal stairs that lets you look out over the paddock where the warg pack is playing with the current litter. The pups are about as big as a wolf now but nowhere near full grown. Boonie stands at the fence watching them roughhouse, next to her is Sandra, one booted foot propped on the bottom rung. I wonder why Kendle didn't mention that her birth mother was here, but then Sandra might not have stuck her head into the garage yet.

"You look like you have too many other peoples'

Property of the Green Bastards

worries on your mind," Tara, our secretary, says. Her background is hard to pin down just by looking at her. Her dad is a mothman and her mom is one of the nymphs from off the island. Looking at her, she passes for a pixie mixed with a werewolf who has a moth antenna flicking about nervously. Doesn't help that she is painfully shy and doesn't leave the office unless forced to. She has a honey-sweet voice to go with her personality. I like the girl, I do. She grew up with Kendle, but she is so quiet and tiny. I'm pretty sure I'd step on her if she didn't wear the company issue t-shirt that says Green Bastards in the brightest neon blue anyone could find. And no, we didn't pick it because of Tara but...if she is the only one required to wear it, well…

"Yeah," I say and scratch my neck. "Too much going on. Anything I need to know?"

"Hawk's in the back."

I thank her and push into the back office, which is more a base of operations for my veep, Grim, who runs this place. He is working at his desk, going over some inventory or other. Hawk, meanwhile, stands at the window that faces the Allteng. Neither of them move or jump to or any of that bullshit. Which tells me it all. My men are on a knife's edge and that turns us into dangerous beasts. And the best way to keep the beast in check is to meditate. Now that the door is closed, the noise pollution from down below is cancelled out, and I can even hear Hawk mumble the Words of Silence under his breath.

"You found him?" I ask.

"Yeah. Eel is with him now." It is Raine who answers. He sits on the sofa, looking far more relaxed than the other two but the blood on his knuckles is telling of his activities this morning.

"You beat–"

"Neh, Prez. Just a good old-fashioned left hook. No permanent damage. I had to…" He gives a significant look to his heartsong's back and I know, somehow, that whoever they caught is gonna trigger some kind of shit that I really don't want to examine too closely.

"Who?"

"Not here," Grim looks up. "Tara is already afraid of Hawk after his reaction."

I whistle through my teeth. That is some strong words right there because I've known Tara her whole life and the only thing that makes her nervous are crowds, loud noises, and snow.

We make our way back through the office, Tara not looking afraid of Hawk at all, and veer into the paddock. Boonie waves me over, but I get away with flipping her off as I vault into the ring. My favourite mountain of a warg, Shadow, lopes over, tongue lolling out of his mouth. His giant canines remind me that this creature is a predator. Just because I've raised him since he was a pup, broke him to saddle, and raced him, doesn't mean I don't have a healthy respect for the fact he is a wild animal. The native predators of this land.

"You riding somewhere?" Boonie asks.

"Yeah…to see about that burnt-out car."

My mom nods. She wasn't my dad's heartsong and property for her whole adult life for nothing. She did her duty reporting the burnt-out car and until I say otherwise, that is all she gets. It is a shame because she'd have made an amazing sister in the club but she had to take on a different role, being dad's heartsong.

I look at Raine. If he hadn't prospected and been elected to the club before meeting Hawk, he'd be riding bitch too. Thank fuck we got him before the old laws did. There are responsibilities for being property–really fucking

Property of the Green Bastards

important ones. Doesn't mean the divide can't hurt a club. I help mom saddle Shadow. He stands still, but his ears and tail tell me he is on high alert.

"Hold up, toddler." A sultry voice pulls me to a halt. Sandra. I turn and open my arms wide for a hug, which she wrinkles her nose at, just like Kendle did. "You know I don't touch."

Her Fiend tail lashes behind her and her fingers do an agitated dance in the air, the well-maintained claws catching the light in a deadly way.

"Aw, Sandy, why don't you wanna hug?" I pout. As a kid, I never got her dislike of physical contact but since her aversion covers everyone but Boonie and, when he was alive, my dad, I now just enjoy teasing her.

"Orc'i, disgusting creatures, always wanting affection." She pretends to puke before straightening and tapping my chest with the tip of her tail. "There is movement up north. It is why I came down to find out if my Kendle was okay."

"Give her a hug this time?" I prompt.

"I always hug Kendle." Her tone is defensive. As long as I have known her, the only people she voluntarily touched were my parents. Still, it pisses me off that she doesn't hug her daughter. Boonie might have raised Kendle as her own but my sister carries Sandra's blood. "Now go deal with that vark scum, little Ashee."

I hear the guys snort behind me. For all her personality, Sandra is tiny and hearing her treat me like a go'k is gonna make anyone laugh.

"You be nice to Boonie, too." And then more softly. "She misses you, zaza."

"Ashee, always caring about other people. When are you going to let someone care about you? Give your mom some grandkids."

99

"Not happening."

Sandra waves me off with two fingers, and I turn back to my warg and the task at hand.

Boonie stands at the gate, holding it wide while Hawk, Raine, and Grim trot behind me on their wargs. She ululates and shakes her hands above her head. The bangles on her wrists clatter together, click-clacking blessings on us as we ride out. This is why property and heartsongs are so important to clubs. They are responsible for setting the wards and creating the charms to protect everyone else. And honestly, I don't know what we will do when she dies. Kendle can't take her place, and I'm heartless. It could mean the end of the club when there is no heartsong tied to the leadership in the club.

We skirt around the back of the Compound, taking the long way rather than riding through town which will be busy at this time of day. No matter how well trained, a Warg lunging at a car is never going to end well.

Once we are farther out, Hawk breaks to the left, his black beast's strides lengthening. Shadow looks at me and I nod. He knows to follow but it's been a week since we've been on a run, and I want him to stretch his legs and reacquaint his nose with the countryside before we join the others. But, instead of sniffing around on his own, he follows after the others at an easy lope. I ask him to go faster because the thought of what is going to happen in a few minutes is enough to wish that Grim felt he could have told us in the office. There is only one thing that might cause my brothers to get that angry.

A traitor.

Hawk takes us up a ridge which we ride along in full

Property of the Green Bastards

view of Dwen'mar and anyone who looks in the direction of the Allteng.

Human MCs like to hide when they have to get information out of someone. We do it out in the open, with honour. In the old days, anyone would be permitted to ride out and watch the questioning.

But people have lost their love of violence and the stomach for blood is less. Non-existent really.

I'm okay with that.

What I do, I do to protect my people. If that means protecting them from seeing this side of me? If that is what it takes to keep them safe, I'm happy to do that.

The part of my or that makes me the Ash'orde revels in the clear skies and the heat of our two suns. My work is not done in shadows. The other side of me that worries the orc'i are turning their backs on the old ways and embracing human customs, knows people will ask uncomfortable questions. I'll have to lie. Say it is MC business, so it's none of their fucking business. Keeping civilians out of the ugly side of life is something we learned from human MCs.

The ridge ends and we have to dismount to walk down the stairs that have been carved into the cliff face. I'm surprised to see Dumbo there looking white as a sheet.

"What's with him?" I ask Raine, who pushes his aviators back and glares up at the cloudless sky.

"Dumbo doesn't like heights."

"Yeah, fair." I'm not going to give him shit over that because needles scare the living crap out of me. Why I don't have a single tattoo on my body. One day, I might get my back piece, but fuck like I want anyone knowing I'm going to faint like a little girl when it happens.

"You aren't gonna take the piss outta him?" Raine snorts.

"You want to take the piss out of Swot when he faints giving blood?" I ask. "Nah, I'll buy him a beer."

"Frey. What crawled up your ass and made you mister sweet?" Hawk asks.

"Bet it wears dresses and drives a wreck." Raine provides.

All the joking is masking the nerves in the air.

"Fine…break it to me."

"Traitor is a prospect," Grim says with a growl. This fucker never shows emotion. He hasn't since his heartsong died ten years ago but the idea of one of our prospects threatened the mar? And with war drums?

"Which one?"

"Kid."

Proportional anger is in order because I'm seeing red. An unnatural haze fills my vision as the or'gre begins to rise.

I don't even take the time to climb down the stairs, jumping straight onto the ledge fifty metres below. I should land like a tonne of bricks but I'm light as a fucking breeze. My knees bend to take the impact, cushioning my landing.

They've got the prospect tied up to the rock face. His hands are cuffed above his head, and he shifts his weight back and forth like an impatient child. Something twigs and he looks in my direction. His eyes are blown so wide you can't see the whites, making him look like an animal. I kinda doubt he can actually see me. Something has messed him up good.

The anger leeches out of me at the sight of him; at how pathetic he looks now because it sure as fuck is gonna get worse for Kid.

We'd named him Kid because he was a pimply-faced seventeen-year-old and high school dropout who wanted to prove himself. It had been a close vote letting him prospect but his family had been part of the MC, fuck. I think of Eel. Kid is his nephew's kid. Not near sol, but still sol'kin. That is going to sting for an orc as old school as Eel.

"Why?" I ask.

Finally, his eyes focus, shattering the dazed expression to reveal one full of fierce hatred.

"Greesh'at Sin'vark Si'doo," he snarls. "Ash'or'Ash or-s orc'i on gre-ad Ha's Var'or I'll so Driftas dw'orsol."

I let him spit it all out. Then tell him like I'd tell someone their farts stink. "Bat'sta. Meh'weh is orsol ao or'gre til Disavowed varki. Rockfucker."

He starts thrashing when I don't say the name of the disavowed–Driftas, Wind Riders. But the thing worrying me most is his claim to be of blood and bone of the Disavowed.

"Shit…"

I look over my shoulder. The others stand on the stairs.

"You heard?" I ask. Hawk nods. "He say any of that bullshit before?"

"Neh, Axe," my cousin says with a deferential tilt of his head. "The warg followed his scent from the car. When we found him, he was wandering the plains, drugged out of his mind."

Now I'm getting the information I should have asked for before jumping off the cliff.

"Fuck, okay. Let's slow down. Where?"

"Towards the east border where the sun no longer touches the ground." He is talking about the gorge, a giant slit in the earth from where the Fiends come from.

"Why?"

"Suicide," Raine suggests. "What else would a var-weh ratshit do? Did you think the Fiends would rebirth him into the world?"

"The Green Bastards are as weak as the others! Let the

Prophet rule and give back unto the blood that was forgotten. The heir shall rise and take back the land from the blood-shedder!" Kid screams. This isn't the orc I remember. The more he talks, the crazier he sounds.

"Sounds like a religious zealot," Grim says with a frown.

"Whatever it is, we need to learn more. You got that shit ready?"

I get confirmation when Raine shrugs off a backpack and begins to unload some of the kit. A bottle of vodka, the cheapest shit you can buy, another equally shit whisky, and a blow torch.

I'm about to show them why they call me a monster.

I kneel and pull out an eight-inch blade that is wicked sharp–wicked because according to Sandra who gave it to me, there is a fiend's curse on it.

"You recognise this, Kid?" I ask him, flashing the blade in front of him. Letting the afternoon sun catch the light and bending it into his eyes so that it blinds him. "This is Cuddles. Now, I didn't name Cuddles. But you know what? I don't think Cuddles cares about that. Cuddles does care about the truth, though. So here is how it is going to go. I ask you a question, you tell me the truth, and Cuddles doesn't cut you. You lie? Well, supposedly, it burns like Hellfire."

I wait for him to say something but with three of my officers at my back, he seems to have lost all that fighting spirit. Maybe he knows it is done. Maybe he is just fucking crazy. Who knows.

"Tell me who put you up to this? Who told you to bang drums in my mar?"

"The Prophet," he hisses, eyes darting around like the rocks have ears.

Property of the Green Bastards

The blade does nothing. This is going to be twenty questions.

"Okay." I use the tip of Cuddles to scratch my nose for a minute. I rest the blade on his forearm, just above this tattoo with the club's colours which are only a few days old. He shouldn't have gotten it yet but argued he was as good as patched. I never should have let it stand. Now I have the chance to cut it off, or if he wants, burn it off. "How about we play it this way? You either talk to me and Cuddles, or I let Raine and Hawk have their little pyro playtime. Why did you betray your oaths?"

"The resurrection has come. The blood and bone of the Driftas has been made again! Frey, Bless the blood and bone heir of the Driftas."

I look down at the skin that should be broken and bleeding but nothing. Cuddles hears the truth and won't cut.

"Fuck," Kid whispers, his eyes are on his skin as well like he can't believe what he said is true. "She?"

The skin is uncut.

"He?"

Cuddles slices and digs into his flesh. Now that I have a literal edge, I bare down strong until the blade hits bone. It is a forearm so not exactly where I would like to start, but I have the spice of or'gre teasing at my senses. I grasp the threads of truly monstrous power and angle the knife away from me and drag it up his arm to his elbow, cutting through the muscles and tendons until an entire chunk is sliced off. Kid is screaming, crying, pissing himself. Hot blood spurts from the wound. It looks ugly, but he won't die on us soon which is kind of the point. He tugs at his bindings, trying to get away and when he can't, he kicks back like he wants to bury himself into the cliffside. There is blood everywhere. My clothes, hands, fuck, there might be some of this scum's blood on my face.

This is why we have the blowtorch. I step away and Raine is there pouring vodka on the wound and then cauterising it in a single fluid motion. The stench of burnt flesh has acid churning in my gut. The white of the bone– his sol, what makes him unique–chars, on display which should only happen in death.

"Is the pain that bad?" Raine asks, eyeing cuddles.

"Yeah. It burns like a motherfucker." I clean Cuddles and place her back into my boot. "Let's see if he wants to talk now."

I step back and let my enforcers do their job. But either he is actually fucking loyal to the kvari scum or he is just some pawn because he can't give us any information.

"Come on, Kid. You aren't doing this on your own," I snap when all he does is whine and beg.

"Maybe leave him here? Get someone else to watch for a bit? Because the only thing we've learnt in the last hour is that his piss stinks and that somehow there is a–"

"Yeah." I don't know what to call it either but the last thing I need is for any of us to call the she-orc out there, the heir to the Disavowed.

I hear a bellow from up above and then Eel is barrelling down the stairs. He stumbles down the last few steps because he sees what we've done to his sol'kin. Kid wasn't winning any beauty contests before. But now in addition to my handy work, there are some pretty ugly burns on his sides and a nasty looking cut near his ear.

Grim restrains Eel before he can get any closer. I curse under my breath. We haven't had time to discuss what happens with the rest of Kid's family. The rules are complicated and in place for a reason. When we get down to it, the laws of blood and bone are clear in

Property of the Green Bastards

times like this: Kid carries the dw'or of Eel and his whole line. But the MC bylaws? They condemn Kid and Kid only. He betrayed our brotherhood. For that, he loses everything–his cut, his place in our community, and his life.

I spit out a curse far too old for it to have any meaning in this world. But the gist is simple. My life fucking sucks because of some punk-ass kid.

"What'd he say?" Are the first words out of Eel's mouth.

"Some bullshit about a prophet and the Disavowed," Raine replies. The guy is a freak of nature. A moment ago, he was a psychopathic violence machine. Now he is back to his gives-no-fucks self.

Eel stiffens up. In the MC, he is the only one who remembers those times when Disavowed were brought here, their heads severed, and then with their bodies thrown off the side of the mountain. Their bones were left to be ravaged by Mother Nature rather than cared for in the caves under the Allteng.

"Var'weh's ji'sol," I hiss at the thought of what had to be done to protect the Or and the goki orsol.

My brothers follow my words with curses of their own. Except for Eel, whose eyes stare at Kid.

"Why?" he asks. "Why? The Prophet?" He roars the words in a way that echoes around us.

I wonder why Eel isn't trying to beg for this fucker's life. Likely he is just as pissed off as we are. Hells, if my sol'kin had done something so cowardly, I'd be the first one to burn colours off their skin.

"Leave him for carrion," I say to the others.

"Let me talk to him," Eel asks without asking. I sigh, not wanting to but also not having a good reason to say no. Eel is club. His history with the MC gives him standing and he wasn't happy when Kid wanted to prospect. Shit. How am I only remembering that now?

I glance at Grim who shrugs like he thinks it won't hurt. "Yeah. Fine. Just don't kill him."

"You don't kill something this stupid," Eel continues screaming at Kid, spittle flying from his mouth. His body even begins to shift with the Or'gre. Those ancient shoulders growing broader and more powerful, causing the seams on his cut to stretch. But my eyes are on his hands. His fingers are already talons sharp, black, and vicious. "You stupid fucker."

"Find out who he means by the prophet. More–"

"She lives!" Kid sing songs. The first thing he has said since Eel got here. "The queen lives! The prophet's words. The ones–"

Eel's fist flies out and smashes into the prospect's jaw. I see teeth literally fly out of his mouth and then the blood, followed by screams. They are different to when Cuddles had him. These screams are hysterical, almost happy. They turn my stomach in a way that the pain didn't earlier. It isn't a nice business. Kid howls like a lunatic, making the hairs on my arms stand on end. Creepiest thing I've ever heard.

Eel doesn't stop. Just keeps at it until it snaps into place that he'll make it impossible for us to get any information from Kid if this keeps going. Raine clearly has the same thought, and he and Hawk pull the other orc away, it taking both of them. Eel pants, his back pressed onto the ledge and his arms pinned to his sides.

I hold back the anger churning inside of me. Eel took this too far.

I turn back to the traitor. His face is bloody as he slumps against the rock, bloody and almost unrecognisable. I've seen a lot of violence. Done a lot of violence but

Property of the Green Bastards

seeing a pimply-faced, barely legal prospect tortured like this isn't for the weak. What pisses me off, the longer I look at him, is we aren't going to get any more information out of him. I don't know what makes me angrier, the fact someone got to his face before I did or that it was Eel. The old orc can wait, I grab Kid by the throat.

"So. You—"

"He can't speak, Prez," Eel grumbles.

"His ears broke, Eel?" I ask.

The muttonchop fucker shrugs. "I hit him hard."

"And what gave you the right?" I flex my hands around the scrawny kid's throat.

"Sol. He is my sol."

I throw a punch that lands right next to the traitor's head, causing the rock to crack. The bastard whimpers and I smell him piss himself again. I'm not even at a quarter of my or'gre and this prick is losing his mind. But it is Eel who makes me want to grind bones tonight.

Someone brought drums into my mar. Scared my sister and mother and the people who should not need to be afraid because I am there to protect them. And it was this runt?

I growl something in the primal orcish that has no words. Our mother tongue because when Frey raised us, blood and bone from the great battlefield, there was no one to teach us language. We are one of the youngest races and yet we remember a time when we had no language or culture. That most primal part of me sings out to do more than cave the head in of this cowardly kvar.

"Axe...don't, you'll kill him," Raine warns me from where he crouches next to Eel. "He doesn't deserve the honour."

"His jaw is broken."

"Not his mind. Fuck. Hawk, get him off…"

But Hawk isn't going to remove me from this. He does check to see if Kid is alive though. "He's awake but Eel's love tap means he can't talk," Hawk clarifies.

I nod. Love tap is about right. Eel broke the guy's jaw. "I'll mention discretion," I say. "Take him and dump in the waste. Nature can take care of him."

Eel doesn't say anything, just lies there, panting hard. "Thank you."

"Yeah. Well, you get to carry him up." I don't bother waiting for them and head back up the stairs to where Dumbo is waiting. Then it hits me. How did Eel know we were here? "Dumbo, how'd you think Eel found out?"

"You were riding on the ridge," he says. I shake my head for forgetting.

I hear the others coming up behind me. Eel has Kid thrown over his shoulder like a sack of potatoes. Raine brings up the rear, frowning at some deep and meaningful thoughts. I'll need to grill him later because he rarely leads us wrong.

"You need a run," Hawk says. My cousin knows me too well and probably still scents the or'gre—a whiff of ozone floating around me. "Take off. Grim and I'll take care of it."

"Nah. We need more information." I scrub my chin. "We'll need to speak to his family...shit. They live out Steel Prophets way—"

Fuck.

Steel Prophets...Kid said something about a prophet. Could they be messed up in this shit? Too obvious but there is what they say about the simple solutions being the best. Fuck. "We need to head out now. Get there before this news gets out."

I hate it a little, to be honest, because I don't mind doing a long trip with the wargs normally. And the

Property of the Green Bastards

symbolism will be important. I look at my brothers. I can't go on my own but I can't rob us of three officers either. Not at a time like this. "Grim and Hawk, you come with me. Dumbo and Raine, you are on the Compound. Throw the garbage out."

"How long will you be gone?" Raine asks.

"Couple of days. Keep this shit locked down. Say...fuck it. Say we are following a lead about who sounded the drums. Or some bullshit about mercs. And point them east, okay?"

Chapter Seven

DINAH

On my second day I'm cleaning out a low-ceilinged attic room above the shop where I can begin working on the map. I was surprised to see Tool waiting to escort me, riding his bike while I walked the fifteen minutes from the Barracks to Elmeer's.

Then he came upstairs and helped with the lifting and eventually the long process of dusting and mopping the floors.

"Didn't think you'd do hard work," he says when we take a break in the afternoon. We are sitting at the front, windows thrown open to entice a breeze. I look down at myself and the stained sweatpants and long-sleeved t-shirt.

"What? Didn't think a city girl could clean?" I joke.

He gives me a one-shoulder shrug. "I don't know anyone who lived in a city, like one of those big human ones, and never met anyone who went to university–except the club's lawyer but he isn't an orc. Why would you need that kind of learning? Seems like what you are doing for the club doesn't need book learning."

"Education is important," I say slowly because it's important he understands. "I was lucky. I had a scholarship. I grew up poor."

"You?" He snorts. "Whatever."

I grit my teeth. They believe my lies so easily but dismiss the truth. "Break. Is. Over."

"Hey. I'm not saying you are a rich bitch. You are cool. You work really hard," he says, at least noticing I'm not vibing with his attitude.

I don't have it in me to reply and just grab the bucket we've been using to mop the floor. I carry the dirty water downstairs and pour it down the drain in the ally. There are a couple of Kin dragging trash cans out, ready to be picked up by a crew of gnomes, who will take it to a Brown Spot. I hadn't given it any thought before but it seems like gnomes still do most of the dirty jobs north of the border. Equality is in the eyes of the beholder. I raise my hand in greeting and smile when they wave back. I find the spigot, refill the bucket, and carry it back up to the attic room.

Tool hasn't moved.

I get to work. The same work I wanted to get away from so bad. The last year, working as a "gallery intern" was really being an underpaid cleaner. They let the girls who came from wealthy families, whose families actually bought art, wear their little black dresses and stand around

Flora Quincy

looking bored even when they were chatting up potential clients. But me? When they saw my home address, because it was on my government identification, I got put in the back room, and then when the cleaner got sick. "Oh, Dinah, can you do it? And why don't you put the uniform on so that you don't get your...pretty...dress dirty." The cleaner never came back. They had to pay her minimum wage, they only had to pay my travel expenses and lunch. One day had turned into a week until my job was a cleaner in all but name.

Luckily, those late nights gave me access to the back room and the lab. I'm a grifter through and through on my mom's side, so I took advantage of every uninterrupted moment. I never stole from the gallery. I wasn't stupid. But I did improve the forging skills Frank started teaching me from the moment he saw I could draw anything from memory. "At least you have one skill the family can use." He would say.

Then, the job at Elmeer's came up. No one at the gallery was fluent in orcish. My bosses, of course, whined that they didn't have an applicant on staff, they said so in front of me.

It didn't break me, though. I applied. I got the interview. I quit and told them where they could put it, making sure to use the most vulgar combinations my petty soul could muster. And I never looked back.

"So...how did you get into this?" Tool asks when he finally gets up.

"Uh." I carefully squeeze out the excess water. "My uncle runs a pawn shop and forges documents. Fake IDs."

"Damn." He whistles. "We could use someone like that."

I roll my eyes. "Anyway, I worked for a gallery. One of their jobs was assessing if pieces of art were forgeries."

Property of the Green Bastards

"Cool."

"Yeah. I learnt to make things which could, um, circumvent the marks of forgeries." I can't help the smile and pleasure my talents evoke. "I never did anything illegal, but I gathered information and knowledge like a magpie."

"Then, you really are an artist. Did you go to art school?"

I shrug. "Never needed to. Are you going to help or am I doing all the work?"

"You aren't my swis's du," he grumbles but gets up and takes the mop from me. "Go make a list of the materials you need. I'll finish up here."

"Kom'sah Tool'sin."

The process is long. Not just getting everything organised but getting it up the stairs too. Tool calls in a couple of his brothers to help with the table I'll be using. Watching three topless orc'i grunting to carry a table up a narrow flight of stairs is hot. Not quite the melt-your-panties-hot of Axe but pretty damn fine as fuck. Their muscles bulge in a way that human muscles just cannot. And the way the light picks up the sheen of sweat on their dark green skin. Yeah, a girl could get used to watching them work. I wonder if they go to the gym. If they lift weights. What I do not think about is how much I wish it was Axe here. Growling and prowling Axe who would snarl as he follows me down dark corridors, ordering me to take it easy because I shouldn't be doing any heavy lifting. But, to rankle him, I'd keep hauling boxes because I am not weak but I'm strong like an ox. I laugh.

"Strong like an ox," I mutter in a guttural voice.

"You are so weird." Tool laughs. "Guys, she thinks she is strong like an ox."

"An oh'she, maybe," the one called Dumbo says.

"Leave me alone!" I wail in mock distress, laughing along with them. Dust and curses fill the air as we finish up the work.

I decline their invite to go back to the club because while I can be brave about Axe when he isn't in the room, walking into the common room and seeing a honey on his lap leaves a bad taste in my mouth. No. Better to stay away. Keep my head down, prove my worth, and forget that I lost my freaking virginity to the last Horde King…fuck, like that will ever happen.

When I get back to the Barracks, all the good feelings from working with Tool evaporates. It is only me and Logan here, so our rate has been cut because we aren't being served meals. Which means I'm cooking for myself for the first time; I may have exaggerated my ability to cook to Miss Krystal. I get to the kitchen which is large enough to make food for fifty, and see Logan standing at the stove heating up a can of soup. It has that too salty smell and I feel myself wanting to offer to cook for him. I'm no cordon bleu graduate, but being one of a large family that lives paycheck to paycheck, you learn how to cook the basics on next to nothing. And I have next to nothing after paying for Axe's meal at the diner and then drinks the night before.

I can normally stick to my budget with ease, but here, everything costs money. Not like I didn't know that before but for the first time, I'm paying rent and the fresh produce in the Badlands is expensive because almost everything is imported. Meat, I can't afford and root vegetables are all that there was at the store. Miss Krystal told me to go back on Thursday for when things get discounted but Thursday is three days away. Which is why I'm making an omelette.

Property of the Green Bastards

Back south, an omelette would have been a treat but eggs are cheap here. I got a whole flat of eggs, twenty-four in total, for two dollars. I whisk up a three-egg omelette. It ends up being more scrambled than omelette but the taste! These eggs actually taste of something. Richer than anything I'm used to.

Out of the corner of my eye, I watch Logan spoon soup straight from the pan. Every time I see him, the less threatening he appears, which has my instincts screaming. My dad gave very little advice that was worth taking to the bank except one piece. "Never trust someone who is as out of place as you." It was why I avoided all of the kids who had even a little bit of magic when I was at school. Why I changed my style so that I fit in with the humans from middle and upper-class backgrounds. Even a whiff of other would have put me at risk, so the spark of empathy I feel watching him reduced to canned soup is squashed by the concept that he poses the greatest threat to my family down south and my chance to stay here. If he learns, then–

"How was your day?" he asks out of nowhere.

"Busy."

He sighs heavily, obviously hearing my clipped tone. "What do I need to do to make you trust me?" he presses.

I carry my dishes to the large porcelain sink and wash them along with the pan I used and his pot. I don't say anything for a minute, letting him hang. Waiting for him to come in with a complaint or some other bullshit.

"Come on, Dinah. We've been here the same amount of time, but the best I've gotten from the MC is a fuck off and Axe missing a meeting with me. You have a prospect trailing you. You had breakfast with Axe..."

"How do you know about that?" I snap.

"It is all over the mar."

I wince internally. Of course, it is. I have to remember

that while people might not have cellphones here, this place is small and people talk in small towns. Especially if it involves the freaking president of the local MC taking a human out for breakfast.

"I work for one of the MC's companies. Goodnight, Logan." I wipe my hands on my sweats and scurry out of there before he can say anything else.

The minute I get to my room, it is like entering a sanctuary. There are familiar smells and sights that remind me of the family I have down south; the reason I am up here in the first place. I clean up, taking a long shower before filling the tub and soaking until my skin begins to raisin. My bed is a double, and I'm getting used to sleeping on my own, but still, only one side has an indent on the pillow. The first two nights, I was too exhausted to notice, but now I'm too wired not to notice. The silence becomes too loud. There's none of the city sounds I'm used to. The rumble of the subway that makes you feel like you're being rocked in a cradle. Even the murmur of voices as the people who were on the graveyard shift head out.

I curl up in bed, bringing my knees to my chest as I focus on my breathing. Deep, even draws of air which now feel thin, and long, slow exhales. But my heart pounds louder than everything. The tug going north and west. Axe. The one person who I've connected with...no, I just feel it because he took my virginity and I can still feel the delicious ache between my legs. That's the only reason.

I pat under the blankets for my e-reader, a going-away present from my boss which I'd almost sold because why would I need it? Now, I'm glad I didn't. My cousin filled it with books by linking my device to her account with the warning that I wasn't to tell anyone in the family about her reading tastes–who would have imagined that sweet, seamstress Elise reads dark mafia and tentacle erotica. I set up an account with an eBook library for access to art history journals and books, but I'm currently reading a dragon shifter romance written by a dragon shifter, which is pretty freaking cool. The hero has a hemipenis and I wish I had an internet connection so I could find some visual references. Instead, I'm imagining two giant orc cocks...I shift to a seating position, readjusting myself, and feeling only a little self-conscious when my hand drifts between my thighs.

My fingers are slim, but I work them furiously, playing over the memory of Axe between my thighs, the way his cock felt gliding through my slick folds...

AXE

I HAVE saddle sores from riding a warg for twelve hours.

I've never done it before—not for that long anyway. We stopped for a piss and a bite at a dinky roadside cafe with an attached gas station. The food was watery potato soup and good crusty bread. I'd murder for a burger if you dangled one in front of me.

We arrive at the Nro'mar at dawn and the Allteng dominates the skyline. Somewhere to the northwest is the invisible line between my territory and the Steel Prophets. Closer than I like though. The idea of those fuckers being responsible for any of this business has my hackles rising. Steel Prophets were the only MC to stand against my great grandfather. When the humans forced us to disband the hordes, the current generation's orsolteng demanded the right to carve the Badlands up into separate countries. When we needed to put up a united front, when our people were at their weakest, they cared more about themselves than the orc'i as a people. I don't care if we have our different traditions, if old rivalries still exist. After thousands of years stuck between the humans and the purely magical creatures to the north, I do fucking care about banding together in one unified country, no matter what that looks like.

I push my sunglasses up and squint at the stretch of scrubland between us and the post fence that demarcates Kid's family's ranch. Overhead, I can see a few huddles of Glassfinch swooping in the sky, which tells me they must grow tubers and possibly potatoes. Not a big operation, though. They likely sell to the Silver Amazons and the smaller mars in the area. Fuck. Local boy gone bad is never a good look for anyone.

"We gonna have any trouble?" Grim asks. He assumes I have a plan; I suppose it is part of being Prez and King. Fuck, why does that title seem to mean something these days?

I cross one leg over Shadow's whither, trying to stretch out my hamstrings a little before I have to jump down and act like the horde king or the MC prez. I don't even have a minute to think about it or answer Grim's question because an all-terrane is speeding towards us, kicking up dust. Someone has tipped them off. The only people who knew where we were going are here and Raine, who isn't going to say shit.

"Fuck," I mutter. "Yeah, we're gonna have trouble."

I reach into the holster and pull out a pistol which I just rest against my thigh. Safety is on. Shadow hasn't been trained around guns even if the kennel is close to the firing range. Firing a gun when I'm on top of a wild beast is likely to end up with me on my ass. But I'm not taking risks when there are only three of us.

"All hail the Ash'orde!" a woman screams out through

Property of the Green Bastards

a megaphone. "We were warned you would visit us. We are unarmed."

Yeah, that sounds bad, the fact they feel they need to let us know they are unarmed before we get off the wargs. And then I see why they might want to be extra cautious: the person driving is pregnant. She looks like she's in her early thirties and her hair is in a long braid over her shoulder. I can see how she kinda looks like Kid or Eel with the same square jaw and snub nose. And the passenger is some scrawny adolescent whose nose and cheekbones are covered with pimples, looking like he might shit himself. But his sister, as she introduces herself, is steady as a rock.

"We are to escort you to the hearth, Ash'or'Ash," she says when they are close enough. "Sorry about hollerin' at y'all like that. But good news never travels fast and this came down like lightning."

"Just want to learn the whys and wherefores of happenings a couple of nights ago," I say. "You got a place for the wargs?"

"Yup...but not really much to feed them."

"We'll pay for a pair of goats," Grim interjects. "Even if they only eat the one, you can keep the money for the second."

She tongues her tusks in thought before nodding. "This way."

Their house is a low bungalow built from local rock but with a new, solid a-frame roof. This close to the mountain, they likely get enough snow for it to make sense to spend the money to convert the roof. Grim catches my eye and indicates that he noticed the expensive extension as well. But other than that, they are clearly hard-working farmers. No other luxuries are visible. No bikes out here. Just the one all terrain and mated pair of wargs in the back. The bitch looks pregnant, which will be good if they can sell the pups.

"Who lives here?" I ask. "Just you?"

"Yes. Since my daddy died. My heartsong is away selling our last crop. We have some hired help from the local mar during picking times but, otherwise, it is just the three of us until the baby comes." She looks between us, taking in a deep breath that lets me know whatever is coming out of her mouth next won't be good. "He'Or'Fee...you called him Kid. He was my third cousin. His folks sold me and my heartsong the land a couple of years back when Kid prospected. I don't know where they are. Until I got the call from Eel, I only knew good about Kid. He wanted to be one of you real bad. I don't know why he would do anything to risk that." She talks fast, earnest. I've seen people scared enough they'll spill all their secrets to keep themselves safe. She's one of them.

"He do drugs?" I ask, remembering Kid's wild eyes.

"No...no more than anyone else. A bit of weed, maybe."

"So, you don't have kin with the Steel Prophets?" Grim continues with the questions while I listen. He has an avuncular vibe according to Swot, which makes him good around skittish warg pups and anyone who comes asking for help from the club. They like talking to him. Me? Supposedly, I am not so friendly. Hawk stands on my left, silent and watchful.

"We have kin in the Steel Prophets," the boy says. He looks angry like somehow we are the reason Kid went loco and sounded war drums.

"Those kin talk about Disavowed?" I ask him. The woman flinches and the boy's eyes dart to her. Shiiiit and salt the fucking threshold. "Do your kin talk about the Disavowed? Anyone talk about war drums?"

Property of the Green Bastards

"War drums?" both of them squeak the words out.

"Yeah. Fuckers like Kid decided to drive through the mars banging war drums. All the mars and you're telling me you know nothing about that?"

"No. Our kin don't talk about war drums," the boy says, sounding afraid. "Just talk about how there should be grants to the families who lost loved ones in the Purge."

Purge. The only ones who call it that are sympathisers. A growl begins to rumble in my chest. Paying the families whose kin stole solteng from the Allteng is a taboo topic in Dwen'mar. They might not live in my town but they sure as shit live in my territory.

"What Jessy is saying is there are some who think the sins of the father shouldn't be passed down to the child," she says. "That is all."

"Bullshit," a new voice shouts. Only this one is old and breaking with anger. "Bullshit, they talk about war drums. Those kvari scum killed our heartsongs. Killed our chances–"

A small frail orc appears wearing some kind of dressing gown over a t-shirt and grubby pyjama pants. This orc could be male or female, it is hard to tell because of their age. Or perhaps, it's illness because the smell of medication wafts into the room with them. "You! You have the deaths of those var'weh orc'i on your hands, boy? You kill 'em? No. You didn't."

"I hold that or and the weh of my forefathers," I say. My temper simmers, but I am more curious than angry. "You said there were only three–"

"She is visiting from the Allteng. I–"

"Yeah, and my heartsong...I watched your grandfather chop his head off. I watched that. And then he spat on the one corpse in all creation who could have given me happiness. He sold sol from the Allteng and deserved what he

123

got. I blame my heartsong. But if I hadn't been with child? My head would roll too. I'm no coward to take poison. What did I do? What did the babe in my belly do? Nothing...yet I would have been condemned. I know why Shelly ran south, fearing death at the hands of humans. Perhaps she would die but her child might live."

"Nana..." the young woman pleads.

"No..." the old one brushes off her relative. "I'll say my piece. The only reason I'm alive is because I did not know who my heartsong was until I went to watch the executions."

Ice in my veins. That is all I can think of. Ice in my veins. This orc should by law be dead. All the heartsongs of the Disavowed were executed. If they knew who their heartsong was...yet...why? A small voice in the back of my mind pokes at old logic. It says this orc had no reason to be murdered.

Grim, however, is more focused and asks a question to the ancient one. "Who is the prophet?"

"One of the Steel Prophets. Their false wise one. Very, very young." The wrinkled face contorts in anger. "Despicable lies to think some rebellion will fix their problems."

Fierce white eyes meet mine. "You think on this. People will band under that lunatic's banner because they are unhappy. You called a Meet, Ash'orde. You are willing to bring down all kinds of anger on yourself because you decided to act like a king, go'k. You aren't no king of mine or theirs. You best be remembering that when they want to crown someone else."

My heart skips a beat as the or'gre rises in me. "We never had kings. Not like the humans," I snarl, flexing my hands which are growing their long black talons. These talons, according to our legends, can cut straight through chain mail at the height of my power; I'm yet to experi-

Property of the Green Bastards

ence them full grown. "What you saw goes against the rules of the Teng."

"The rules of the Teng? And the honour of the or'weh?" the crone howls.

"This whole family is mad," Grim says and takes a step in front of me.

"Nene." The woman pulls the old orc back. Her eyes are wide with horror. "What is this?"

"I watched him die!" she screams. "Ignorant child. I came to you with a warning. My cousin cares for his kin more than you. He knows the truth when he sees it but is blind to what it means. If you wish to be king, ignore the pieces and look at the board."

Chapter Eight

DINAH

The next night Cherry is on time, with a shit-eating grin on her face as she pushes into my room and looks around. Then spins in place for a double-take of the bare room.

"Wait. I thought you were some city slicker girl. Rumour says you worked at a fancy gallery. Where are the rags? The…what is the word? Not dugs, that is tits…digs? Hmm, no, that is home…your rig? You know what I mean; the expensive clothes."

"I have no idea what you are talking about. And I never said I was a city slicker or wealthy."

"Wow. Wow. Wow. I've never met someone with so many surprises. You are like the solstice come early with sprinkles. Are you telling me–"

"Yeah, I am poor. My clothes might look expensive but they're hand-me-downs or donations that my cousin Dolores alters." I run fingers through the curls I unpinned when I got back. "I haven't bought new clothes in years."

"Damn girl." She grins big, her pointed white teeth flashing. "I like you.. Now, whatcha gonna wear tonight?"

I look her up and down. She has a Rosy the Riveter vibe if the coverall had been shrunk down ten sizes and been turned into cut-offs to show off an ass that looks like it was moulded from silicone. I look at her tits and then her ass and lips. It clicks. "Are you part succubus?"

"What?" She laughs. "No. Def no. I'm a boring old fiend…I just wanted to get some work done."

"Oh, sorry. You just have so much sex appeal."

"Precious, you have no idea how cute you look when you are embarrassed. Has Axe seen you like that? I've been trying–" She sits on my bed and crosses her legs like a pretzel, leaning forward so she can rest her chin on her upturned palm. "You and Axe…Tell me everything. You seem pretty bright with a lot of spark. But Axe doesn't go for kin let alone humans, so spill. What are you crossed with?"

I bite my lip uncertain how much I can get away with saying. Then again, the best lies are cloaked in truth. "My dad is a quarter hobgoblin. He can pass for human, which is how I ended up being born in the Capital."

I give her my best sorority smile and keep going along with the version of my life that I've told so many times over the years, I almost believe it myself.

"I've got pointed ears but that is it. Of course…" I wait watching her for any tells that she might be too interested in my background. "Being one eighth is a bit–"

"Pull the other one, sweetheart. Orc, maybe troll or elvish. Not hobgoblin. Maybe humans wouldn't see it but everyone north of the border will be able to tell. But, like, don't lie about being part orc. No one is going to turn you in for saying you are human. You are safe in Dwen'mar."

I relax. Thank fuck. She thinks I'm relieved that she isn't going to out me to the authorities. I'm relieved she thinks I'm just one-eighth orc and isn't going to ask more questions. Humans buy the hobgoblin stuff. Hobs are domestics, it makes sense that a poor orphan from the Stews might have some domestic-goblin blood in her. And because I don't sense extra interest, I feed her a bit more of my story.

"My dad has orc blood, yes. I don't know much about his family…" I weigh up my options. The practised nervous concentration on my hands. "He drinks a lot."

"Shit."

The weight of this tiny lie hangs between us. For the first time, I actually feel a little sick in my stomach about the lies. "Cherry, I'm sorry I lied. It isn't drinks. It is drank. Both my parents are dead. Poor orphan is never a good look. And humans are more accepting of hobgoblin blood than orc heritage. I'm so used to the lie that I sometimes believe it."

"No…I mean, I've never been south of the border, so what do I know about humans except sightseeing sugar daddies? But with everything I've heard? Yeah, lying to get by and not be treated like shit sounds good to me."

"It isn't that bad." I burst out laughing. "Fuck. I mean, it is. A lot of humans are horrible but that is where I grew up. On my way north, I stopped by a couple of the cities, sightseeing. It was cool. There were mixed households out on the streets. There are a few famous mixed couples in affluent neighbourhoods but not where I grew up."

"Damn, you say you are poor and then spout big words like affluent."

"Scholarship kid," I tell her with a grin.

"Whatever. You can talk books and shit with Swot. Though, maybe don't smile at him when Axe is around...or do. Not sure if you find spanking–"

I choke. I will deny it, but the mere thought of Axe putting me over his knee makes me tingle.

"Nothing is happening there," I hasten to assure her. "Axe–he was just looking out for me. He wants me gone."

"If you say so. And if you really aren't into him, then let's introduce you to some of the local hotties. Put something on that screams fun. Like that!"

She points excitedly at my dress which is air drying over the back of a chair. I splutter that it is still damp and instead dig out a pair of black jeans and a black peplum shirt. All very conservative but with a pair of killer heels and red lipstick? It will look sexy without asking for it. I have a black, backless dress that screams asking for it but the idea of wearing it when Axe won't be around to appreciate it means it stays on the rack.

"Shit, this place is rammed," I say as we walk into a bar called Mable's located deep in the kin'helm. Cherry chuckles behind me and prods me towards the bar, which is set up on a dais on the left. The place is a one-eighty from the Compound which has a worn-down feel. This is...it could almost be an upmarket speakeasy. When I tell Cherry, she laughs and says that the owner will give me free drinks for life if I tell her.

The quality of the booze, though, is just what I could get at the Compound. Even the cocktails are made of generic or off-brand liquors. Adding to the atmosphere, all the drinks are served in straight-up pint and half-pint glasses. Even the wine is poured into a half-pint glass.

In the Capital, it would be chic, but here, the economy is clearly king, I think until I see the prices. Maybe I am wrong and this is just an aesthetic.

However, when I taste the bizarrely named Nighthawk's Doom, flavour explodes in my mouth. Even my snooty, art world ex-colleagues wouldn't be able to complain about this witchery. So fucking delicious that I know I'll need to pace myself if I don't want to get smashed and show up hungover for work.

"I like it here," I tell Cherry when we grab a pair of bar stools along the wall where a thin ledge of wood serves as a table. "It has a great atmosphere."

"You are such a city girl," she cackles. "Oh! Friends!"

Suddenly we are surrounded by people she knows. Names are being thrown around and I'm meeting two other fiends, an orc who has nothing to do with the MC by her own admission. Finally a man who can't quite be all human called Dennis.

"I'm part wraith," he says when I work up the courage to ask. "So, you made friends with Cherry?"

"We met at the diner the other day."

"Nice. Cherry has excellent taste in people. So what do you do, Dinah?"

The conversation flows from there. They all do various things around town, and I start to piece together that what the tourists are sold and the reality are very different. A lack of internet and modern technology means I have zero points of popular culture knowledge to share with them. All the music on the jukebox, and then later by a band, are either a couple of decades old, lacking electric guitars, amps, or mics, or it is local from the Badlands or further

Property of the Green Bastards

north. Some of the orcish songs I've heard before but when I hear them live, they are louder, rawer, and less refined than the recordings I've listened to.

I feel out of my depth which surprises me because being able to adapt to every situation is how I made it here; by masking my true self behind layers of protective lies. Here, I thought I would fit in. Maybe some of the wistfulness enters my face because the orc pulls me to the bar with her to collect the next round of drinks. While we are waiting, she looks me dead in the eye and asks, "Why do you look so homesick?"

My instinct is denial: put a smile on and deny it. But I relent when she raises both eyebrows at me. Her expression is so...human. It hits me in my chest that I am Othering her. Expecting people here to look, talk, and act differently because they aren't human.

"I thought I would be better prepared," I admit.

"Your dad? One quarter? So like, you never had any of our traditions...or any of it? No Rite of Weh'ni'teng?"

"None," I confess and step closer to her so that I can say it more quietly as if will minimise my embarrassment. "I thought it would be a homecoming."

Her eyes get sad, and I realise just how much truth I've given her.

"I didn't think I'd find a heartsong," I reassure her in a rush. When she smiles, I know she can tell I'm lying. "I want to. I assumed I would find one...maybe not right away. Like, who meets their heartsong on the first go?"

"You'd be surprised. But don't sweat the heartsong stuff. It could still happen. There are only fifty thousand of us left. Compared to one of your cities, that is small. You and–" She cuts herself off and I wonder what she could possibly have to say. "Anyway. I'm sure your heartsong exists. That magic won't vanish. I feel sorry for your dad though and grandparents. Most of us meet our heartsong when we are in our late teens or twenties. If you haven't, then you go to a Meet and mingle. The magic always brings us together."

"You have to be my age…"

"Oh, I know who my heartsong is." She grins. "I'm just waiting to scare the fuck out of him."

"Why?"

"Because he used to pull my pigtails. I'm going to make him suffer before I pull his dick."

"Your drinks, ladies." The barman puts down a strange assortment of glasses in front of us.

"Let me—"

I freeze. The arm reaching across the bar and handing over a stack of notes is familiar. I see Raine and grimace.

"Hi, I'm Raine." He smiles at Erika.

"I know who you are." She doesn't smile. "We don't need your charity."

"Please…"

"Are you that dense? These ladies' drinks are on the house." The barman smiles but he is a troll so it is not friendly or welcoming. "I won't take your money."

Raine tenses. Same as when we'd talked about what had happened with Axe. "I'm not here on club business," he grits out.

Erika takes half our drinks and pushes past Raine without a word. I take a bit longer, looking him up and down.

I don't say it. I don't even let my face give anything away but I get it now. He is an outsider. Here he is part of the MC. At the Compound, he is Old Horde. My world shifts a little. Our commonality makes him more dangerous, not less. Empathy leads to confessions. Confessions lead to exposing your most vulnerable spots.

Property of the Green Bastards

"Did you hear our conversation, ss'thee?" I ask. Ss'thee, orcish for bastard.

"Yes," he says. Our eyes meet straight on since I'm perching on a barstool, then he smirks. "Your secret is safe with me. I won't tell Axe you think he is your heartsong."

"Never said that." I force a smirk. This asshole has no idea what he is talking about. "I don't think he—"

"Dinah?" Raine sounds exhausted. "Just fucking relax. I came here for a drink."

"To this place?"

"Yeah. What am I not allowed or something? Because I'm an orc or because I'm part of the club?" His words draw attention to his cut. The black leather blends into the tightly fitting black Henley. I can't lie, he looks good.

"Club." I don't know if it's the alcohol or Raine's vibe, but my confidence rises. "I've seen the other orc'i here. They look nothing like you."

"Then can we forget that bullshit? I'll join you for tonight and walk you home. And before you ask, I'm doing this for my peace of mind. Axe is away for a couple of days."

"Fine. Order your drink and pay the nice bartender for ours because he shouldn't give them to us on the house."

He tips an invisible hat and turns around to the Troll, who pulls him two pints of dark local stout and takes the cash he offers without a word. One nice thing about having Raine is he takes half the drinks with him and people get the fuck out of his way. We get back to the others and all conversation stops.

"Dwas-weh," he greets everyone, letting a touch of a northern accent slip through. Weirdly, the others relax even though I'm not sure they all speak orcish. Except for Erika who frowns at the other orc. "Walked Dinah home

Flora Quincy

the other night, so just following up with the gentlemanly duties," he says with a wink.

His grin could disarm nuclear subs, it is so charming. I wonder what Axe looks like when he is relaxed and happy. Pushing the memory of the MC prez aside, I make introductions. Not that he needs them. The club rules this town of twenty thousand; they all know who he is even without the patches and cut.

Conversations around us quiet down as they wait for the big orc to say anything but he doesn't. Just leans against the wall drinking his beer and ignoring everyone. After a while, I can't help but nudge him with my elbow. He grunts in acknowledgement.

"Why aren't you with Hawk?"

He makes an annoyed sound and finishes off his beer. "He and Grim went with Axe."

He turns silent but now I know why he is in such a sullen mood.

"So..." Cherry cuts a glance towards Raine. "I'm hearing that all the towns had people ride through and there is going to be a Meet."

"Yup," he says even though there is no question and he is under no obligation to confirm what she has said.

"Your prez going to get permission from the town first?" Erika asks. "Or are we–as always–bending over backwards for the MC's plans?"

"Well, your ma could come by and talk with him first...being mayor and all," Raine throws back. "Jaysus, Dinah. You certainly made some interesting friends."

No shit. Erika is the mayor's kid? You'd never guess with her heavy eyeliner, ripped jeans, and band t-shirt.

"Look city-power and all that nonsense is good." Raine leans in. "But the MC–"

"The MC does a lot of good, but this is the twenty-first

century," Erika hisses. "I didn't go to law school to come back to a society that still kisses the ground of a king only in name. The hordes are disbanded. We live in a democracy."

I throw back my drink and decide to call it a night–with every intention of bringing Raine with me. I think he can hold his temper...Erika, I'm not so sure. When I apologise for heading home so soon, it is strangely gratifying that they want me to stay and party a bit longer. It takes some persuading to get Cherry to stay and enjoy her night. I whisper to her that I want to separate Erika and Raine, and she practically pushes me into his arms. I file away the tension, determined to learn what it was all about and what it means for me. I don't want to lose the friends I made.

Raine downs his other drink and wipes the back of his hand across his mouth. "I'll walk you back."

It is only ten, but we are so far north that the sun hasn't set. I'm overwhelmed but the difference between the place I grew up and Dwen'mar, feels more like two separate galaxies rather than driving across the border into another country.

"I hate impressionists," I grouch, as I watch the light take on a warm lavender glow that reminds me of an impressionist painting.

"What's an impressionist?" Raine asks.

"Artists who painted what they felt."

"Isn't that what an artist is supposed to do?" He scans the empty street as if expecting a hidden threat.

"They don't think they have to paint the world as it is."

"And what is that?" he prods.

I'm drunk enough that I answer his question. "The world is ugly and messy and dangerous. And art is one of the places where there can be precision. Where a rose can be a rose. Not blobs of paint where people have to guess what it is. We already guess with people. People lie. People and art. They can tell the truth or they can lie."

"You don't like liars?"

"Everyone lies, Raine. I'm a liar. You too." I shake my head and change the topic. "Why did you come out tonight?"

"Axe is going to be away for a couple of days. And Hawk is too. I'm not really close to anyone in the club. I prospected for a year, but I'm still Old Horde. I'll not take out my rubies, and they know that. Fuck it, I just wanted a quiet drink."

"We ruined that?"

"I should have drunk in my room."

We walk the rest of the way in silence. It feels more like a gentle stroll, keeping shoulder to shoulder, allowing the rest of the mar to pass us by.

"You've had a pretty crazy intro to Dwen'mar," he says after a while as we turn onto my street.

"I like it." I can't help but grin even while my head is starting to spin. The alcohol probably wasn't the best shout considering I was diagnosed with altitude sickness yesterday. "I like being away from humans."

He side-eyes me, and my grin grows. "What? I never got to say that before. I'm twenty-three. And my whole life, I needed to be human. More human than human so I never–"

I'm talking too much and it has nothing to do with the drinks. These people–my people, I remind myself–make it easy to forget years of carefully woven lies and masking.

"You aren't in the human country anymore. You passed through GrandVerne to get to the Badlands. You don't have to lie about being human..." he says softly. "Fuck. Look, your timing is shit. But you should just, I

Property of the Green Bastards

don't know, re-register here. Or apply for citizenship. You are orc'kin. You'd get a new passport here, easy."

"I want to. There are just things I need to take care of first."

"What about your human family?" he asks. "You must have one."

"They are..." I stop, unsure of where I stand with any of them. Unable to trust them, but needing a friend. I look back towards the bar. People who are not part of the MC, people whose loyalties are not with Axe or the Green Bastards. People, even orc'i, who might not want to uphold the old laws. Who don't believe in the horde king and his laws. They want a civilised, democratic Badlands. Before I open up, I need more information. "Tell me about the difference between the town and the MC."

"Fuck..., whatever. Can we get a drink though?"

"Why do you need another drink?"

"Long fucking day," he answers and pulls me across the road to a narrow building with a few shallow stairs down into the basement entrance for a bar called The Nighthawks.

Unlike Mable's, this place is quiet, dead quiet. All the patrons sit drinking at tables and not talking to each other. But as I take the place in, I see every table is full except the bar, which is bathed in an earthly glow of mage light. The barman is a Fiend about seven-feet tall before you count his curved black horns. He is shirtless, and I can't help but stare at the startling complex spells tattooed on his skin. I'm not sure why I think they are spells but they pulse in the muted light.

"A drink." Raine puts a bill on the table. The fiend looks at me and I pull out my own money. It hurts to be so profligate with the few bills I have, but I need to keep up appearances. I'm always playing catch up. I grit my teeth.

Raine isn't like the people I went to university with. I won't compare those wealthy kids to an orc–even if he has real rubies in his tusks.

"Yeah, two drinks." The barman's voice is deep. "There is a table in the back, orc."

"Wait, I need to order." I step into the ambient light. The fiend shows no emotion, just picks up my money.

"People don't order here. I will bring you a drink. You drink it."

"Okay..."

"Take the girl to the table," he snaps at Raine, who does a poor job of suppressing his laughter.

Our table is tucked in the back, a couple of sturdy chairs that look like they belong in some kind of medieval fantasy fair they have down south. The table, though, is something else. Polished stone. "This must be worth...Meh teng no' grat'tani."

"What is with humans and money? And you and orcish?" Raine snorts. He rolls his shoulders, arms crossed against his broad chest. He looks worn out and instead of snapping back, I swallow my retort and shift in my chair, trying to get comfortable under his assessing stare and finding it challenging to keep my face passive. "Go on. I'll let you ask your questions."

"Is Axe and the club really devoted to the old ways and the old laws? Is the mayor and mar at odds with the MC?"

"The mayor convinced herself the MCs are just a workaround for the hordes and old ways."

"And the MCs? Do they hold with Var'or var'weh sh'rook?"

He re-crosses his arms and stares me down.

"I was just asking a question," I say at last. "Just trying to understand."

"Fuck. You make simple questions sound fucking

Property of the Green Bastards

meaningful. Look, I came to prospect for the Green Horde because Axe is my Ash'orde. My king. The last Horde King. I realise that might seem like a fairytale to you, but here? There is magic in the blood of the orc'i. Our people were raised from the blood and bones of fallen warriors. That means something. So, yes. Axe follows the old laws. He follows them because he has no choice. He follows them to honour the Or and the Sol of all orc'i. H'ish no weh ten. Do you understand that? You cannot be his heartsong, not because he is the last Horde King. He is heartless. There is no fated love for him. And he won't make you his property, because the club won't accept you."

That makes me jump. Property.

"I don't even know what that means," I admit. I've read my fair share of orc motorcycle romances, but I know there is a difference between fiction and reality. "But what I do know makes me think it is really misogynistic. And why do orc MCs even have them when heartsongs exist?"

"Holy fuck. You are exactly what you look like, aren't you?" Raine chuckles. "A rich bitch from the south."

I stuff my hands between my thighs, fingers tensing. I rarely taste the or'gre, battle blood, but tonight, I feel talons growing in place of my nails. I focus my breathing and force them away. Nonetheless, the anger slips into my voice. "Orsol she'w har. Go'ki to zaza per'a don dwea. I thought wealth wasn't a way to judge a person."

"You shouldn't Falk'jwo on things you don't understand," Raine warns me, his voice clipped. Fuck, his whole demeanour has changed. He looks dangerous now. "If you don't want people to call you out on your bullshit, keep those questions in your pretty head."

"I am not a rich bitch," I grit out. "I never have been. I never will be."

"Sounds like she believes she isn't a rich bitch," the

Flora Quincy

Fiend says out of nowhere. He puts a tumbler full of a liquid that has the consistency of water but is, like everything in this place, black and smokey. I lift the glass and watch as smoke swirls inside the liquid. Knowing there are two sets of eyes on me, I sip. Citrus and smoke but it doesn't taste alcoholic.

"What is this?"

"A tonic to fix your altitude sickness." the bartender says. "Here is your change. Raine, take this to Hawk. And respect my customers and keep your voices down."

He drops bills on the table and walks away without a word.

Raine's drink is clear but smells like beer. "Are the drinks here magic?"

"No. The bartender is magic...his drinks are whatever he senses you need." He drains his glass, wiping his mouth with the back of his hand before looking at the beer bottle– just some generic brand–that the bartender brought over. Raine's sigh is heavy but a reluctant smile tugs at his lips. It disappears when he looks at me. "You came here thinking orc'i ride wargs and sang war ballads. An MC isn't like a horde. No matter what citizens think. If I hadn't prospected, I'd be Hawk's property, at best. I'd be wearing bangles and making offerings to the ancestors. Sound very progressive to you? Fuck. At least we allow women to prospect."

"So a heartsong becomes property?"

"Frey, no. Property means something to the club. Means you are trusted, that you will take your role and place in the MC hierarchy. Not the same at all. But you'll always ride bitch."

I know the alcohol is affecting me. The buzz in my head makes my thoughts reckless, and my tongue loose. "That means I could–"

Property of the Green Bastards

"Not you. Sorry, Dinah. You aren't part of this world. Even if you stay here...you grew up with them. Everything about you screams human. No one here is going to care that you have orc blood in you. Unless you have a real reason to think..."

I'm drunk and pissed off with always needing to prove myself. Well there is one easy thing to prove. I raise my eyebrow and then use my nail to scrape away some of the makeup on my collarbone. He leans forward.

"Freckles." I giggle. The alcohol swirling in my head making it feel fuzzy. "I've got a lot of freckles... green freckles."

"No way. And you cover them up? Makes sense."

"There's more," I say full of confidence that this orc isn't going to freak out on me.

"What are you telling me? You have a second clit?" He sits back laughing. My cheeks heat. It is one thing to say it but to hear him sneer at me works on my anger.

"Do you want to see them?" I snap the question. The or'gre swirls inside of me.

"You're shitting me." He sits forward. "Sure."

"You really are nothing but a bunch of shits, aren't you?" I snarl. "All of you. Just a bunch of snobs. As bad as humans. Well, you can tell your prez," I sneer at the word. "You can take all of it and shove it up your loose assholes, you kibling fucker."

I push away from the table, my chair falling back with a loud clatter that forces all eyes in the bar on me. An ugly flashback hits me hard, and nearly turns my guts when I recall the memory of when I was eight years old and had just arrived at my grandparents. When a little too much anger had sent my cousin to the ground after she'd teased my stained clothes and freckles. My cousin Dozy's broken wrist had meant a week in my room, one meal a day, and a month without dessert.

Except, no one at the bar says a word. There are a few annoyed looks but it seems the people at the Nighthawks come here for their privacy.

"Thanks," I say to the bartender, who waves me out as I escape the bar.

In the time I've been having whatever conversation I was having with Raine, the sun has set. The fresh air sobers me up. A pair of gnomes are lighting gas street lamps. There are fewer people out, but I keep my head down the final few feet. My luck doesn't hold. Raine catches up with me.

Out of nowhere, he stops. "You want to know why they call him the monster that rules the Badlands?"

"I assume it is advertising?" I genuinely am not interested. Not anymore.

"Fucking ignorant and acting like you know everything."

In the dark, he can't see my cheeks go red with shame. Why do his words make me feel so small? "Then tell me."

"He doesn't play nice. That whole unity crap in the common room? Never in my life–that is before I came here–have I seen him want to bring us together. He doesn't take that king stuff seriously but he knows he is the king. He isn't the biggest but one on one, he can take anyone down. He does not forgive. When a patched brother from another club made fun of his sister, he broke the guy's leg in five places. When he caught the fucker who sounded drums, he cut out a chunk of flesh– the guy's whole forearm. I don't mind beating the crap out of traitors but I can't do that kind of thing. And you know what? No one would be surprised if he beheaded him. Not even the Kvar's family would have argued.

Property of the Green Bastards

Maybe he made love to you or some shit but if you betray him? He'll kill you and sleep with a clear conscience."

I keep quiet through the whole speech and any warm feelings evaporate. The fears I wake up with are still there. "Fuck you, Raine."

"Believe it or not, I like you and want to help. Not just because you are pretty and I like pretty things. Tool says you work hard. I believe that. Everyone will too. But you don't fit in because you are too good for a monster."

"Fuck you. I never said anything like that. I've never been too good for shit."

"Let me be your friend."

"You call this friendship?"

"Yeah."

"Then this friend is going to tell you this: fuck off. Leave me alone. I'm here to work, not deal with all your MC drama."

The asshole grins like I just told him we are BFFs.

"Night, Dinah. See you around."

I want to scream my frustration but swallow the impulse like always.

Any hope that I can go straight to bed shatters when I walk into the Barracks.

Cloaked by shadows, Logan sits on the stairs with a large glass of water next to him.

"Were you waiting up for me?" I ask. Too weary to be careful, I push past him.

"Yes...I was worried. The president of the MC and some of his officers were seen riding wargs along the ridge yesterday."

I stiffen. "Is that meant to mean something to me?"

"Why don't you tell me? Why don't you tell me who you really are? Ja? Tell me how a girl from the Stews speaks

143

orcish and is hired by Elmeer? I'm not here for you. Unless you are breaking the Drum'mar Treaty."

"The only reason your people–"

"Our people."

"The only reason humans have a lawman in the Badlands is because they–"

"We are a peacekeeping force."

"Whose peace?"

The silence becomes tense.

I continue up the stairs. When I get to the landing, he says, "I want to protect the peace. I am not picking sides. I don't want a war."

"And the people who live here don't want one either. They want to have their–"

"War drums were sounded in every major city in the Badlands the night before we arrived. War drums. You know what that means. War is coming and just be honest with yourself, you are a romantic idealist who is too caught up in being here to understand the bigger implications." He talks fast like he needs to get it out before I interrupt him. I'm finished with all this drama. Yet another person who only wants to get rid of me. And then there is Axe, who, if Raine can be trusted–and there is zero reason to doubt him–would kill me in a heartbeat. They've all made snap judgements. I'd be naive to continue believing things would be different here.

"Fuck you," I hiss, apparently, it's my phrase of the night. "You don't know anything about me."

But I'm starting to think people here see me all too clearly.

Chapter Nine

AXE

I'm back home, exhausted and pissed off. There is a big electrical storm in the air, and the sirens are already wailing like some heartbroken banshee.

It is early for a storm this powerful and the blaring alarm sends people running to prepare for the winds and rain. Shadow and the other Wargs have their tails between their legs. I'll have to send someone to tell the mayor to turn the horn off so they can settle down. They are wild animals and don't need this blaring.

After getting the sirens turned off, I consider riding

past Elmeer's on the off chance I can see the girl, but something unexpected sneaks up on me. I know where she is. I know where she is at all times. My heart tugs in her direction, and any reminder of her is a fucking distraction I can't afford when the club and my people are under threat. But I just know seeing her will ease that tightness. She walks out of the shop, locks up, and struts down the street with Tool at her heel like a puppy. Nah, that ends now. No more prospects trailing her. Besides, Tool is too young for her. She needs a stronger hand.

"Fuck."

I cut off that line of thought before it gets too much. I can't keep her with me the whole time, can't be with her always. I'll have to be content with a prospect.

Tool is too young, I remind myself. I can leave her with him and know nothing is going to happen.

The storm will blow in from the west, out across the endless sea where the sea serpents live and swim with the merfolk. An hour later, we are gathered in the common room with flagons of beer and grilled meat ready for the party we'll have when the storm comes. It's just what I need to keep me away from the human, make me forget it has been two days since I was between her thighs. Every night away from her, I've fucked my hand twice before I could fall asleep. And I wake up every morning hard and frustrated by dreams of her when I should be focused on learning more about Kid and if there are more traitors who need to play with Cuddles before being left out in the elements.

I'm halfway into my second beer when Raine returns from his ride, making sure everyone is indoors. We extend or'dwea'ki to the mar whether they like it or not. Asshole makes a beeline to me and says like he is telling me he

Property of the Green Bastards

prefers apples to oranges that he saw 'my human' walking down the street towards Elmeer's.

He isn't loud about it. Doesn't make a big deal or raise it. I should be putting my fist through his face but my anger finds a better target. A prettier target who knows what will happen when she breaks my rules.

Instead of a bike, I get into one of the trucks the club keeps for weather like this. It's a cage but I'm not risking my bike when the wind picks up. I park right outside the shop because only idiots go out in a storm. Yeah. I know what that makes me. But, let's be real. I'm doing my neighbourly duty. Checking in on the new girl in town. Kicking the truck's tire doesn't help me shake the feeling I'm turning into a complete simp for this girl who will bring me nothing but trouble.

I walk into Elmeer's shop and freeze. Dinah perches on a rickety stool placed on top of a glass cabinet. If that weren't enough, she balances on the soles of her bare feet, arms stretching above her head while she changes a lightbulb that flickers as it fights against the inconsistent electricity. She might start an electrical fire. Might get a small shock and fall, breaking bones and possibly damaging valuable, dusty junk. She's also completely fucking oblivious to the siren that should make a human cover their ears, not sing a ditty about an elf and a dildo. I'm not even going to ask how she knows the words to that.

There is no old orcish word for patience because we are a people of action, but that perfect peach of ass stretches her jeans, and only an asshole wouldn't stop for a moment to appreciate those curves. Fucking poetry. And I know it will be even better when I bend her over my knee and turn those cheeks red for putting herself at risk.

Thank Frey, she missed the word "patience" when creating the orc's genetic code. We got the blood of predators instead, ones capable of silently stalking prey. And, right now, I'm grateful since any sound might cause her to lose that precarious balance and seriously injure herself. An injured Dinah is no good to me. I'm in no mood to wait for her to heal before I remind her of the rules I carefully spelt out a couple of days ago. Rules she agreed to follow.

"There you go. How many people are needed to screw in a lightbulb? Just one Dinah." The little brat sounds proud of herself. Everyone knows the sin of pride comes before the fall.

I move fast, wrapping my hands around her waist and plucking her off her little perch. Pulled against my chest, I cage her there, enjoying how she struggles in my arms. Not screaming to be let go, just complaining I surprised her.

"That was very, very stupid, Princess," I growl in her ear. "I warned you there would be consequences if you broke my rules. There is a big storm coming. You could have caused an electrical fire. Could have shocked yourself, fallen and broken your neck–"

"Like you care," she hisses. "Let me go, oaf."

"I said–"

"You just want an excuse to get your hands on me," she dares me, sounding way too smug like she can read my mind, or maybe she can feel my hard-on pressing into her ass. Sue me, she's been wriggling against me, and I'm not dead.

"Maybe. But I don't need one when you'll beg so pretty for my cock. Bet you go to bed at night dreaming of it. But only good girls get orgasms. Bad girls like you get spanked so that you remember to be a good girl."

"You wouldn't dare spank me." She can sound offended all she wants, but her voice is all husky and dripping with sex. "And how dare you talk to me like that."

Property of the Green Bastards

Well, I'm not admitting dirty talk isn't my thing and I'm flying by the seat of my pants with her.

"Princess, this is a perfect example of fuck around and find out. Now, I'm going to put you down–"

She is off, just like I had hoped. Smart girl doesn't run out into the storm but deeper into the shop. She glances over her shoulder for half a moment, flashing an obscene gesture before ducking behind a shield made for a giant.

She couldn't be more perfect.

I put one foot in front of another, no need to rush. We have the whole storm to work on her little attitude problem.

Clever human sought the higher ground, but the stupid Didi has just cornered herself.

There is still no need to rush, but I take the stairs three at a time. When I cross the threshold into the low-ceilinged attic room, I talk to her like I'd do a nervous warg. "Dinah...be a good girl."

I spin, grabbing her wrist which holds an iron skillet. "Where'd this come from?"

"We." She tugs against my strength. "Are. Using. It. You are strong. We–"

"We? You mean Tool and you?" I grip a little tighter as furious possessiveness flashes through me. Forgetting I told Tool to help her fills me with anger at myself. This human girl means nothing to me except as a tasty morsel to be enjoyed but eventually discarded like all the other honeys who come looking for orc cock. "What are you doing with him?"

"Making the map," she grunts, still fighting against my grip. She dips, twisting her own arm in a way that must hurt as she tries to gain enough leverage to throw me. I'll need to teach her the proper way to defend herself against a creature that is so much bigger than her. I pluck the skillet out of her hand and toss it on the floor.

"Now. About that spanking."

"Barbarian…"

I catch her chin in my free hand and meet her eyes which spit fire.

"Say a word and this stops." The memory of some drunken conversation with Hawk about consent and this kind of stuff reminds me she needs to want this as much as I do.

"I can take whatever you dole out," she breathes, almost panting.

"A word, Dinah."

"Steve."

"Why a man's name?" I do not want to hear any name but mine when I'm with her.

"I hate that name…I would never willingly say it."

"Did he hurt you?" Because fuck no. If someone in the mar touched her while I was away, they are going to meet the wrong end of the axe hanging above my door.

"He was a bully." She doesn't want to talk about it. I'll deny how I know that, but I'm not pushing her even if I want to.

"Another word. I don't want you to think of that name ever again. Like swearing, it is banned from your vocabulary."

She rolls her eyes. "Butterfly."

"Good enough." I tug her to the large crate pushed against one wall. I'm sitting with her between my legs, my hand still wrapped around her wrist.

"Why do I need a safeword?" she asks suddenly.

"A what?"

"A safeword…something that means I want it to stop."

I frown. "I thought you were a virgin. What kind of

Property of the Green Bastards

virgin knows enough about kinky shit to know what a safeword is?"

"I read, asshole. You know books? Romances, erotica...I like the ones–"

"No," I interrupt her because I do not need to know what kind of books she reads to get off. Discipline first, because I'm not having her break my rules and this thing is going to be something kinky. Maybe if she is good, I'll make sure she gets off. She squeaks when I pull her over my lap.

"You going to spank me with my jeans on?" When she realises I'm not exposing that pert derrière. "It won't make an impression if you do it like this."

Frey knows, I want to pull those jeans down and relive what they are covering, but I'm not giving the brat what she wants. "Good girls get their asses spanked with jeans off."

"That isn't how it works," she says and tries to twist.

"It works how I say it works. Now take your punishment, Princess. We both know I want you to be a good girl." To make my point, I spank her without warning, making her shout a protest. "Just because you have your ass covered, doesn't mean you have any protection."

I've smacked an ass while fucking, who hasn't? But have I spanked someone because they broke the rules? Nah. It won't ever get said out loud, but I am a spanking virgin, and you know what they say about virgins? What they lack in technique, they make up for with enthusiasm.

"Ooff." That little sound goes straight to my cock as I land the first one on her right cheek. I like it enough that I catch the other side with the same swing and force. Bless her but she repeats that gasp of surprise.

"Think you can take it?" I ask her.

"You hit like a girl."

The brat is bratting. Cute. Real fucking cute, but she needs to know that I'm being nice. "You're being rude to females of all types. I won't have you talking yourself down like that. Another strike to add to the list."

I lay into her then. Not keeping any rhythm because I don't want her expecting the next one. I'm not easy on her either. Which I know because she squirms and tries to reach behind to shield herself against the onslaught. She doesn't use her safeword though, and when I pause to rub the tenderised buttocks, she arches into my hand. Trailing my hand between her thighs, I cup her sex and feel how hot she is. "Are you wet? If I took these jeans off, I bet you're soaked. Your cunt just begging for my cock."

"Axe," she breathes, rolling her hips against my thigh. I tuck to the right and am hard as diamonds, and the way she is draped over my thigh means her sex is rubbing into my cock. I give her a quick set of smacks because I need to distract myself, which leaves her panting.

"Yeah, Princess? Are you ready to say sorry?"

She sniffles and nods.

"I need words, Didi."

"I'm sorry," she moans the words like she is begging me to fuck her.

"Sorry?" It's hard to ignore how husky my voice is. I am going to fuck her because she is mine and the thought of anyone else touching her drives me insane. "Whose rules do you follow?" My question is out of nowhere, but her answer is far more important than if she is sorry. "Whose. Rules. Do. You. Follow?"

"Yours."

"That's right." She doesn't need to see my smile, but she does get to feel my palm landing on her ass a couple more times. "You're sorry you didn't follow my rules?"

Property of the Green Bastards

"I'm sorry I didn't follow your rules. I'll be good. I'll be good for you."

"Fuck, yeah." I don't care if she hears how pleased I sound. My heart sings at her confession. "Ten more. That's it. Count them out for me."

"One—"

She says it before my hand connects. "I'll let that slide. But you count after contact."

She obeys. I knew she would; knew she could obey if she wanted.

We are both breathing hard after the last one. The silence is broken by the first clap of thunder, which has her jerking in my lap. I help her into my lap and see the tears for the first time and the way mascara trails down her cheeks. If her nipples weren't poking through her thin shirt, I'd be worried. I want to be inside her, and because I'm a sick bastard, I reach between her legs and undo her jeans. I watch how her eyes are focused as I slip my hand in and rub her lace-covered pussy.

"So wet for me…"

She buries her moan in my shoulder. And then I feel the small bite of her blunt teeth on my pec.

"Stand up, Princess. I want to see if your lesson made an impression."

"Yes, Daddy."

"What?" Shit. Daddy? That shouldn't be hot but coming from her…I'm grateful she isn't able to feel the way my cock throbs. "Daddy?"

"I mean…it isn't what you think. I'm not calling you that."

She means papa which kinda sounds like pah'pah. Yeah, she isn't calling me heartsong. But if she wants to call me Daddy, my dick and I don't mind.

"Yeah. Don't do that. I'm not your heartsong. That isn't ever going to happen, you hear me."

I put her on her feet and pull her jeans around her thighs. The pink lace she wears doesn't even cover her ass. More like frames it, especially since I'm sitting and it is right in front of me. Then there is her ass. It almost matches the pink of the panties.

Her ass is even better now that I can see the curves. First, I palm one cheek then the other, soothing the flesh that is hot from her initial spanking over her jeans.

"This is beautiful…"

"I…please, Axe."

"Yes, Princess?" I prompt. "I want to hear your words. You were doing so well during your spanking."

"I need you to touch me…" I watch her shift and wait for whatever she wants to say. "Please, I was good—"

"Cheeky, Didi." I lean close and bite that sweet peach. "I am touching you."

"I want you to touch my pussy."

"What a dirty mouth." But she was good, so I reach around and cup her pussy, pressing my middle finger between her folds until I'm rubbing right along her clit and slit. I rest my other hand on her lower back, urging her closer. "Go on. Take what you want."

There is a kittenish growl from her. Seductive even when I'm the one aching and she is grinding against my finger taking whatever she wants.

"Give it to me," she whines.

"Words, Dinah," I remind her.

"All I want is your cock inside of me."

"Whose cock?"

"Daddy's?" The word is careful, testing the waters.

"That's right, Princess. Daddy's cock is going to split

Property of the Green Bastards

you open again." I slap her pussy hard because, fuck I need to be inside her right now.

"Frey. Again, Axe," she pants. I can't disappoint her, so I repeat the assault on her clit. Fuck, her slick coats my fingers. I lick my fingers, doing what I forgot to do that first night and taste her. My throat goes dry and that thirst can only be quenched by drinking from the source. I'm not careful when I pull her panties down and spin her around. There is a thatch of dark curls covering her sex. Dark pleasure fills me knowing I'm the first, and I'll be the only person to ever see her like this.

"You're beautiful. Fuck me, but you are beautiful." I arrange her on the trunk, lifting one perfect leg over my shoulder, getting my first look at her dripping sex. I use my thumbs to spread her open. At the top, her clit is swollen, its small hood can't cover that perfect little pearl. My eyes travel down, appreciating each needy part of her. That is when I see it. The bottom of her sex, just behind the opening of her cunt, is another clit.

"Two–" I stop. My mouth waters and my cock leaks pre-cum in anticipation. This woman has two clits. "Orc."

"Yes. Axe–"

I don't need to know what she is going to say because I'm sucking her second clit and using my thumb on her other. I was born for this. To bring her the pleasure she deserves because there is no way some human could give an orc woman the tongue-fucking she deserves. I tilt my head, letting my tusks glide along her clits. Tenderly getting her used to the feeling of the gold caps on my tusks. I can feel her pulse against my lips and her sweet nectar on my tongue, but I'm the one in heaven because I've discovered my itch has two clits. It is enough to make her an orc but not enough to make her my heartsong. That doesn't mean I won't worship her body.

She's bucking, blindly thrusting against my tongue as I fuck it into her quim while her clits rub against my tusks.

"That's it," she moans. Never one to disappoint a lady, I keep it up just like she asked until she comes undone. I lap her cum, working my tongue like a fiend. "Oh, Goddess…I need something inside of me."

I transfer my mouth to her top clit, sucking on it. Filling her with one, then two blunt fingers I push them up to the knuckle. She's so tight that I can't believe I actually managed to fuck her with my cock. Looking up her body I watch her breasts rise and fall as she tries to keep some kind of control. "Let go, Didi. Come for me. I want to see your pretty face when you lose control."

Damn. She does. Eyes blasting open to meet mine, mouth letting out a string of words that let me know just how good I make her come. Her cunt pulses around my fingers. I dip down so that I can get another taste of her cum.

"Next time, you're coming on my cock," I growl into the soft skin above her sex. After one last lick of her slick sex, I sit back to watch her pant but, like a gentleman, I keep pumping my fingers into her. "I need to get naked, so I want you to finger yourself while I do that."

She whimpers but almost too eagerly she pushed my hand out of the way, plunging her slim fingers inside of her. Another time I might watch her fuck herself like this with her eyes screwed shut, mouth open, and sexy little sounds telling me how good she feels. Not right now though. I pull my t-shirt off and shove my jeans off, letting my leaking cock bob free. I stroke myself enjoying the show she's putting on for me.

"Hey, Princess," I say, causing her eyes to snap open. "Hey, there."

It's fucking quiet, the storm settled down, as I kneel

Property of the Green Bastards

between her thighs and line my cock up with her opening. She presses her thighs wider and uses her fingers to spread her slick folds open. A perfect invitation to fuck her.

As I enter her, she hisses at how my cock stretches her to accommodate my cock. I can't take my eyes off where we are joined. Watching the ridged inches slowly disappear inside of her until I'm balls deep. Like this, I tell myself. Whenever I fuck her it will be like this. The vice-like grip on my dick, the blissed-out look on her face.

"Please, I need you to fuck me," she begs so prettily that I won't reprimand her for swearing. Poor thing is too orgasmed out to remember the rules.

"Like this?" I pull out until just the tip rests inside her, probably putting pressure on her second clit. I look down at how I'm covered with her slick. "You're so wet. I'm going to make this so good for you…screwed you like a monster that first time, didn't I? But now, I'm going to make you come so hard you pass out."

"Axe, are you going to ruin me for every other man?" I'm not sure how she can ask me a question like that.

"Fuck, Princess. I already have."

"Then fuck me."

I grip her thighs, spreading her legs even further apart, so I can pound into her. With her, I can't go gentle. I can't take it easy or let her get used to me. And I refuse to think too hard about the instinct to claim her. To brand her, make her my property. Ravishing her like this should be enough to let her know I'm not letting her walk out on what we have–animal magnetism.

She's with me. Agreeing with her eyes which don't leave mine. Some kind of magic makes it impossible to think of anything but the way she squeezes around me.

"Fuck me harder, Daddy."

Okay. Yeah, she gets a pass when she says that. Fuck

me harder Daddy might be the hottest thing anyone's ever said to me. Jaysus. That does it for me. Her trusting need that I'll give it to her like she wants it.

"Whatever you want, Princess." My words come out in a fierce growl. "You want Daddy to fuck you? Just ask, Didi. You've been such a good girl for me."

"Fuck," she shouts as she comes all over my cock. Not just coming but shaking with the strength of her orgasm.

"Yeah, that's right." I'm now losing that last bit of control. Thrusting hard and fast into her until I feel my balls draw up and I'm shooting cum deep inside of her. I'm not even thinking when I shout out my release. "Daddy's going to breed his good girl."

We stare at each other. I don't know if she is thinking about what I just said. If I can even lie and say it was all part of some fantasy. In reality, it is an uncomfortable truth that from the moment I said the words, it is all I want. Breed her. Fill her with cum until she's round with my kid.

Shit, I need to wipe that from my future plans. I've been trying to put her out of my head because I've got shit to sort out. That plan's right out the window now. My instincts are too pressing to ignore. I sit back, feeling my cock slip out of her and with it a whole lot of cum. I'm a saint because I don't push it back into her and order her to tilt her hips back so that it doesn't go to waste. At the same time seeing my seed leaking out of her is its own kind of reward.

"Stay," I order and leave her resting on the chest while I gather some old quilts and rugs to build a makeshift bed in the corner furthest from the window and door. The storm is at its height, but if it was me, I'd take advantage of the bad weather to commit crimes. That done, I stand over her and take a moment to enjoy the sight of my cum dripping out of her and the sheen of

Property of the Green Bastards

sweat covering her body. I worked her over pretty hard, and have to imagine fucking a rock to distract myself. I'm tired, my cock is not.

"Get up," I tell her.

"I'm legless." She pouts, which is cute. Yeah, I'll call it cute. I'll even lie and tell her I think she looks pathetic when she does it rather than show how I really feel. She is just an itch. One I need to stop scratching or I'll never be able to stop. "Please, Axe? You fucked me so hard, I don't think I can stand."

"Fuck me." But I pick her up and carry her to the nesty thing I made for us. She tucks herself in and I slide in next to her like a complete sap. If she says one word about how I'm pulling her close, I'll make sure she can't sit for a year. She twists in my arms and we lie there watching each other. Prey and predator, face to face, trying to figure out how we got here. Her makeup is smudged, and I run my thumb over the patch of skin not, I realise, covered by makeup.

"What's this? Do you always wear so much makeup?"

"I–" The word is a breath. Then her chin lifts and her face goes blank for her next words. "I have freckles. I normally wear makeup but–"

I swipe my tongue over her. "Fucking delicious. No more makeup."

She rolls out of reach and sits, legs crossed, glistening pussy on display with my cum dripping out of her. The look on her face is anything but seductive. "I can wear as much makeup as I want. Whenever–"

"That...fuck. Fuck. What is with women? Doesn't matter if they are human or orc. A man says he wants to see her without makeup. She always acts like–"

She dives at me, catching me by surprise so I fall on my back. Her hands are on my shoulders, her face in mine. I

159

focus on that rather than the way my cock gets rock hard at the heat of her body against mine.

"Men, human or orc, sometimes need to be quiet. I wear makeup to protect myself. My paperwork says I'm human. If I had…if anyone had ever seen my second clit, or my freckles. Or my ears." She pushes her hair behind her ears and tugs one of the intricate cuffs on her ear. Pointed. Her ears are pointed. "Three genetic markers, Axe. They would be arrested. My family who took me in when my father died–the one with orc blood–would be arrested. Fined. So yes, I wear makeup to cover my green freckles."

I look closer. They are green. Fuck. Three genetic markers. The number three rocks my world, and I say the first thing that pops into my head. "You don't have to worry about lying anymore. I'll make sure your family is protected. As my–"

"Shut up." She kisses me, sucking my bottom lip in between her teeth. "I'll wear makeup if I want. Don't you like the idea of mascara running down my cheeks while you fuck my mouth? Or what about smearing red lipstick all over my face?"

"Dirty girl, Didi." I cup her breast as a reward, making her hum in appreciation. I want more, I finally accept. All of her tonight. Because tomorrow, we'll have to move on from this. "How about we do that."

"I think I want to sleep. You wore me out. Any more and I might die." She blinks up at me, sleep slowly taking over but before it does, I pinch her arm, jolting her awake. "Ouch. Not necessary."

"I want to play with your clits while you sleep." The words are out before I think she might not want to wake up with my cock in her. "Everything, I want to breed while you are asleep."

Property of the Green Bastards

"You're serious?" she asks breathlessly.

I massage where I pinched her with my thumb and nod. "Yeah."

The brat rolls her eyes as if her eyes aren't blown wide with lust. Then a smile peaks out. "If it makes you happy."

"Nah, Princess. It is going to make you happy."

"Does that mean I can wake you up with my mouth on your dick?" She challenges, sounding a lot more alert than she did a few minutes ago. Her cheeks turn a perfect pink but she holds steady. She means it.

"Any time you want. Go to sleep. I'm gonna go clean up."

"Or you could play out your fantasy…"

"Thought you wanted to sleep?"

"I'm too tired. And the first time I get on my knees for you, I want to be wide awake. But if you wanted to…"

"You're gonna die of orgasms, Didi."

"Is that such a bad thing?" She lays back, moves a little so that she rests her cheek on her hands. A picture of innocence, except that she spreads her legs for me, her sex parting, exposing her clits to my hungry gaze. J'mera. I don't say it out loud. She doesn't need to know how glad I am that I got to her kinky, cheeky ass first. J'mera twa fir hwe. My two-clitted goddess.

I wait until her breaths even out and I know she is asleep before running my thumb back and forth across her slick sex, making sure with every pass that I tease both her clits. I'm not gonna make her come right now. Her body is worn out from all the fucking we've done. This woman, passed out from so many orgasms, is perfect. Fuck my life, this ends me.

Two clits. Green freckles. Pointed ears. An orc even though she passes for human. I want to pull down her lips and check her teeth, see if she has tiny tusks. If she does, then I need to get my cock in her mouth as soon as she is awake. The feel of those tusks around my cock? Fuck. I reach down and give my already hard cock a pull. I can't take my eyes off that second clit though. So perfect. How did I miss it when I fucked her that first night?

Probably blind to the details because all I saw was a human. And a virgin.

My heart itches. The sensation was hard to ignore when I thought she was human. Now I know she is–I won't acknowledge she is my heartsong. I could have got it all backwards. Her heartsong might be another orc. After all, I've been labelled heartless without a soul mate for the last fifteen years. I haven't even bothered asking what it feels like when you meet that special one. Not asking now, either because the club–hell, my mom–doesn't need to know how on edge this all makes me.

I almost forget I'm touching her when she lets out a little restless moan. I lightly spank her top clit which she liked so much earlier. Seems she likes it in sleep too because she arches under my touch.

She is just another variable I need to contain. Her only objective value is copying the map. But under my fingers, fuck it, I dip my fingers inside her hot channel and feel the combination of her slick and my cum. Yeah, under my fingers, around my cock, her eyes flashing at me, or when she smiles, I can forget that I have responsibilities.

I move down her body until my mouth is at her sex. Okay, so maybe I didn't tell her I would do this. But fair play, right? She gets to wake me up with a blow job, why can't I blow her mind with my tusks and tongue while she sleeps? She's been such a good girl, after all. Everything we've done must have left her sensitive because she comes quickly, blindly grinding her hips into my face. Even while her cunt pulses around my fingers, I move up her body until my cock slides into her. I want her to sleep, so I don't go hard. But with the way she is clutching at my cock, I can't last long. She's coming again and the plaintive, needy moan she gives me sends me over the edge. That and the fact she is an orc. Mine. The restless thought surrounds me as I withdraw, drawing her against me, and cup her sex so that my seed stays where it needs to be: in her womb.

Chapter Ten

DINAH

I didn't think it was possible to wake up from a fantasy only to discover that fantasy and reality are one. He bred me while I slept. I can feel the evidence between my thighs, and my heart catapults in summersaults of fucking amazing, out-of-this-world delight.

I'm sprawled over a dark green chest that's rising and falling with gentle snores. Gentle is not a word I would use to describe Axe in normal circumstances, this morning, though, it makes sense.

The morning sun filters through the windows, catching

Property of the Green Bastards

dust motes and casting a warm glow over our...cave. I flush and bury my face in his chest because all too easily, I am thinking things that aren't possible with Axe. Made even more obvious since I can hear his heart's steady rhythm under my ear. And mine? It races a thousand times faster. If we were heartsongs, they'd be the same.

Never mind. I had another amazing night with a hot as fuck orc who found out I was an orc and told me he would protect my human family. So far, he has every one of my firsts. Except, I haven't had him in my mouth…yet. I lick my lips and trace my fingers down his taut abs to where his morning wood taunts me. "Damn…"

I'm finally getting to see him in all his monstercock glory. Sitting up, I lean forward to see if I can capture the image of his cock in my mind. For the good of cock-loving kind, I must try to draw his erection with every possible detail. Years from now, I can show it off. The "that dick was inside me" kind of bragging you can do at the old folks' home.

It is as long as my forearm, thicker than my wrist, and darker than the rest of his skin, making the ridges and notches almost disappear. Except my cunt remembers them. Each delicious drag against my internal walls and second clit. My nipples tighten with arousal; I want him so bad the ache takes over my thoughts.

I promised to wake him up with my mouth. I won't tell him, but falling asleep with his tongue exploring my pussy, when I knew he was tasting his own cum, was the hottest experience of my life. Yeah, so what if all my experience is with this man. Each time we come together it is fireworks and a revelation.

I lick the pearl of precum off this tip. His taste bursts in my mouth. I suck the tip, teasing the slit with my tongue in hopes of teasing more of the precum from him.

Flora Quincy

"Fuck, you look good. What are you doing?" a grumbled voice has me twisting to look up at Axe who is blinking awake.

"I am waking you up with a blow job."

He grumbles something and looks out the window. The sun streams in the window, no evidence in the blue sky that there was a wild storm last night.

"Fuck. No. Not right now." The snarled words are softened by his husky voice, and the fact I know he wants me as much as I want him.

"Axe, come on…" I wrap my hand around the head of his shaft, watching each play of ecstasy on his face. I play with the head, feeling the way the foreskin slides over the head. I run my thumb along the slit, gathering the precum. I put that thumb into my mouth and suck. Salty and all him. Frey, I need a taste of him. I want to swallow a cock that I know will touch my heart if I manage to take all of him. My heart skips a beat making me sway a little. "You taste like–"

He surges up, hands gripping my shoulders pulling me close until our noses are touching. He doesn't look sexy now. Now he looks angry. "No. I did say yes. Now I am awake, and I am saying no. Get dressed. I have to go."

He sets me down and rolls to his knees, swiping up his t-shirt. Then it's his jeans, and he tucks his erection in–and thankfully, it looks uncomfortable because I am pissed off at this double standard.

"What the fuck? So I don't get to wake you up with a blowjob?"

"You–" He grits his teeth. "Any other time, yes. And last night was great, but this isn't a democracy. I said no and I need to go."

"Fuck that."

"Swearing. Why are you always swearing?"

Property of the Green Bastards

"Because I grew up with people who swore and drank and fought and fucked. I grew up around people not so different from you and your club."

"Yeah?" His eyebrow arches and the smirk is back. "You know much about any of that?"

"Yeah, actually." I'm nodding. "I do. Except the fucking. I'm pretty good at drinking. I can throw a punch even if it isn't much good, I know how. I'm not a snitch. I'm not some pussy little bitch—"

"No woman of mine has a mouth like yours."

"Yeah. And you don't know what this mouth can do. So thank fuck I'm not your woman!" We are at some kind of stalemate. Glaring at each other and our breaths coming out hard like our heart beats. "Get out."

"Are you telling me to go? I am going."

"You wanna be here when Elmeer unlocks at nine?"

"Fuck." He moves out fast. No goodbye, thank you, or see you soon. Nothing to say he isn't ashamed of being found with me.

"Coward!" I screech, feeling bruised and broken because last night was so perfect. Everything was so perfect until he told me no. And I know, I know I should respect that and I do. Still, it feels like the worst kind of rejection.

The sound of the boots on the stairs stops. Then he is stomping back up to the attic room. "Dinah, I have a fucking meeting with the sheriff at nine, which I missed the other day. I don't give a fuck if Elmeer walks in while my cock is shoved in any of your holes. He could walk in with you sitting on my face, my tongue buried in your cunt, and I'd not care. If you don't believe me, I'll prove it to you. Just not today."

I'm left speechless. He grins. The first real smile he has given me and all the anger, even at him telling me it is just sex, melts away. I give him my own tentative smile, a nod telling him I get it. "Promise?"

"Princess, you can smother me with your pussy, and I'll die happy."

I blink, and the bastard is gone and with him, my heart.

This can't be love, I tell myself as I pull on my own clothes. We've known each other for five days. Not even. He was away for some of that time too. But I'd do anything to see him grin, to hear him reassure me. I suck my lips between my teeth and try to bury the feelings threatening to overwhelm everything. My fingers comb my hair enough that I can braid it over my shoulder. My eyeliner is probably smudged, but I can smudge it out more and call it a smokey eye.

I sneak downstairs to the small bathroom in the back of the shop.

When I see my reflection, I decide to get rid of as much of my makeup as possible. And I smell of sex, which is heavenly to my nose, but less so to customers, Elmeer, and Tool who will no doubt be wondering why I'm not at the Barracks.

Fuck. My night with Axe might as well be public knowledge now.

I strip and have what my auntie would call a whore's bath. She said it with a lot of respect for the profession and the insistence that being able to clean yourself up just using a small sink was the height of sophistication. I smile because auntie would have been proud of me going after Axe. She was the one who told me to only lose my virginity to someone who wasn't going to freak out that I had two clits.

"Just stay a virgin. Most men don't know what to do

with one clit. You might end up in jail for manslaughter because they'd die from the confusion of two."

"Or because they turn me in." Her face had fallen. All the teasing disappeared.

Now, I'm staring at myself and liking what I see. My freckles are splattered across my face. On an orc, they are light green but on me, they are dark moss-coloured. There are even a few spots on my upper lip. I flick at those ones with my tongue.

"You are playing a dangerous game." Elmeer radiates fury when he sees me. "Do you know how dangerous… how much danger you could be in now he knows? They will close ranks. The Green Bastards protect their own, and you aren't one of them. I don't want to see you getting hurt. You know that—"

"I don't think he is my heartsong," I interrupt him before he says something to break my heart. "We are just having sex. It doesn't mean anything," I lie. But I am so good at lying that he just nods.

"Will you be fine when you walk into the common room and a human tourist is on her knees with his cock in her mouth?" His words are the opposite of what I expect to come from him. I suspect he is purposefully vulgar to get a response from me.

My anger is immediate, visceral, and ugly. Worse, it is impossible to hide.

"Hold on to that anger and know it means you have to stay away…unfortunately, I need you with me today and we are going to the Compound."

But when we walk into the courtyard in front of the Compound's main building, Boonie gives me one look and tells me to stay in the common room until Elmeer collects me.

"Darlin', you go to the common room. Elmeer and I need to talk." Axe's mom stares at me.

"I'll go back to the shop," I tell Elmeer.

"Tool can handle it for today," he replies.

"But–" I look at Elmeer who insisted I come and leave Tool to keep watch. "Please, let me go back to the shop."

"No, darlin'. Wait in the common room," Axe's mom commands, a sharp bite in her voice that has me jumping to obey.

My heart races as I turn towards the large, intimidating building. I consider returning to the store; I have work to do. I need to finish the list of items we need to create the forgery. There are export documents to alter. Tool can come back and tell them I told him to come back here.

"You aren't a coward, Princess. You aren't going to let him run you out of town. It is sex. Your hearts aren't aligned. He isn't your heartsong. You can wait for Elmeer and no one will judge you. If they do, fuck them." I decide I'm going to grab my new sexuality by the horns and embrace it. Hell, if I was them, I'd be jealous of me. Axe fucked me. He went out into the storm for me, and then stayed with me. We might not be fated to be together, but there is nothing to be ashamed of.

"Why are you here?" Raine asks when I enter the empty common area of the Compound. It is dark except for the bar where a few downlights bathe the bartop in warm light. I swallow as I start forward, aware that my freckles are obvious now. My ears too since I didn't put the cuffs on.

Property of the Green Bastards

"Elmeer has a meeting with Boonie and she told me to wait here." I shrug like I do this every day.

Fake it 'til you make it. Fake it 'til you make it. Repeats in my head.

His eyes nearly bug out of his head when I get close enough for the artificial light to touch my skin and reveal my makeup-free face.

"Fuck," the prospect, Dumbo, whispers. "Frey...jikl'a sred'dweary en'ia. Hot shit, you are..."

En'ia. Spicy. Hot. Dumbo thinks I'm hot.

"Get her a drink, Prospect," Raine growls. "And keep your eyes to yourself. She isn't your heartsong, is she? Yeah, then don't go calling her en'ia. Got me? You want your heartsong to enjoy your cock? Then keep your eyes employed with their own business. What'll you have, Dinah?"

It isn't even ten in the morning. But I'm starting to think I could use a drink.

"Beer. Thanks." I smile at the prospect who snaps the top off the bottle without looking at me.

"You fucked Axe again," Raine says without preamble. Dumbo chokes, telling me it wasn't common knowledge. I scowl at him as he eases himself onto the barstool next to me. "What? Everyone knows he doesn't fuck the same bitch twice."

"Bitch?" I ask.

At least he looks apologetic. "No offence meant, just a turn of phrase. He doesn't do repeats, Dinah. Does he know about the freckles and the ears?"

He is pushing me, wanting me to react. But I've had all this orc bullshit right up to my eyeballs. If he wants to pry into my private life he's in for a shock. I can punch back as hard as the next girl raised in the Stews. Hells, he won't

171

even know what hit him. "He knows. And about my two clits."

"Fuck," he hisses. "Doesn't change things. Axe can fuck you, we can all smell him on you. Boonie probably sent you away because she doesn't want–"

I flinch, and he curses under his breath.

"I'm sorry. We can be…rough. Dinah, everything I've seen tells me you aren't a bad person. You are tough. So, just let me say this." He waits for me to nod. "You're an orc. You'll find a heartsong, it just won't be one in this club." He rubs a hand over his mouth. "This isn't what you imagined club life to be like, is it?"

My shoulders drop all the fight going out of me.

"I never really thought that much about club life. But, not so much." I use a bright red thumbnail to scrape at the label on the beer bottle which is damp with condensation. "I thought…I don't know what I thought, Raine. I guess the hope for my heartsong clouded my judgement."

"You shouldn't want Axe as a heartsong. He needs to fuck you out of his system. Then I want to find a way to get you to where you belong. Far away from the club and this place," he says but in a way that is so full of fucking sympathy, it breaks my heart. Just another person telling me I don't belong. "He has a lot of responsibilities, and you are a distraction he can't afford."

"I already know it isn't him. Heartsongs are soulmates. They are meant to complement each other. Axe and I…we don't mesh like that."

He snorts and rolls his eyes like he can't believe I just said that. "Yeah, you don't mesh."

"We are just having fun, even if you don't believe me, that is all it is." I sigh. "I still want to find a heartsong even though I'm not orc enough."

"Not your fault, kiddo. Having hope isn't a bad thing."

Property of the Green Bastards

He smiles and wraps an arm around my shoulders. "Gods. Also, you are more than orc enough. But you're too tidy for a place like this. Just go back to the city, yeah? Back to that fancy job with that fancy hair. Fuck. Yeah, you can't go back with those freckles, though, and you shouldn't hide them. But there are other mars. Des'mar is big. You'll have the money to set up there, the club can help you apply for citizenship…"

This time it is my turn to laugh, but it is bitter and angry. "You think the Capital or any human city is tidy? Clean? Nice? I grew up with twenty people in eight bedrooms with cockroaches for pets. Until I came up here, I'd never had a bed to myself, never had a room to myself, never had a bath. Just showers. If you were lucky, it wasn't tepid. Always timed because there wasn't enough hot water for everyone. You're all such hypocrites for judging someone by the way they look."

"Shit, but you look…"

"I look the way I do because my cousin worked as a seamstress and would take clothes from the vintage place she worked at that were being donated because no one wanted them. Shit, my shoes aren't designer. Knockoffs." I'm on a roll now. "I worked all the way through university. I flipped burgers. I cleaned. I didn't grow up talking like this."

I look around the bar taking everything in but with fresh eyes. It is real leather on the booths. The handles for the kegs are brass, not something cheap. Even the aged, run-down look isn't grime or hard wear on cheap materials but patina. The shine and age that comes from centuries of wear. That priceless quality we looked for with every object that came into the gallery. I thought these guys were not wealthy exactly but not rich either. But they fake the rough side of their life.

Flora Quincy

From talking to Tool, I know there is always enough food and clothing because the orc'i look after their own. The teenagers all go to school. None of them dropped out the first chance they could to help make money for the family. I'd lived that. I'd been at the end of a lot of hate from my family as I made something different of my life. They'd called me so many names, but the only one that mattered was always a slur of hate, "youfuckingselfishlittlebitch." Those had been the words Auntie Tee shouted at me as I drove away. It didn't matter that I left for them. That I drove to the other end of this continent to destroy evidence that I was Disavowed. Then I was going to disappear and never be a burden to them.

"You know what? Fuck this place. I don't belong, but not for the reasons I thought I didn't."

I'm not quite sure what my feelings are. Fear, anger, and shame are mixed in there as I grab my purse and hop off the stool, ready to storm out of the bar, out of this town. After I finished up with Elmeer's shop because I promised Elmeer I'd do a job. I'll forge the map but no more MCs, no more heartsongs, and no more sex with Axe. I'll keep my head down and avoid all orc'i.

I ignore Raine calling out to me, my vision tunnels, blurring red with repressed rage, I don't notice the great, broad muscled chest belonging to enemy number one until I collide with it.

"Dammit," I snap. "I'm leaving. Just like you wanted."

"What? Where did you think you were going?" he growls. His focus snaps to Raine who is somewhere behind me and already denying he said anything to scare me off. "What did you fuckers say to her?"

I wait for a heartbeat that seems to take forever to hit. Maybe because we are glaring at each other. "Does it

Property of the Green Bastards

matter, Axe? I'm going. Just like you wanted from day one. I'm going. I'll do the map and then I'm going."

"That's not happening," he tells me and grabs my waist. I'm tossed over his shoulder like I weigh nothing.

"Put me down, you fucking asshole!" I squirm, refusing to fall for more of his hot-cold shit. He might want to fuck me, but Raine is right. War drums in the mar are more important than pussy.

He smacks my ass so hard I scream and try to reach back to protect it. Fuck him. He knows my ass is still sore from last night, but he doesn't seem to care and starts peppering it with smacks. Fucking asshole is tenderising me like a piece of meat he wants to eat.

Then, unexpectedly, he drops me onto shaky feet. "Princess, listen carefully. You aren't going anywhere until I damn well say you can. Now get upstairs like a good girl, and stay put."

I dodge around him, not expecting to escape through the open door. Axe is too big and too fast. But I'm not going quietly. I'm gonna fight and claw and bite and scratch. If he wants to fuck me, he will have to earn it. This bastard. I can finally admit to myself I'm mostly upset because I wanted him to be my heartsong. Instead, he is an orc with an amazing cock that gives me orgasms simply by looking at me.

Axe grabs my ponytail, causing me to screech and kick out. My foot connects with his knee, which buckles. The big, bad orc MC president, horde king doesn't care. He just flings me over his shoulder.

One of his big hands is back on my ass, groping it, reminding me exactly what we did last night. "You want me to make my point here in front of my brothers? I already told you, I don't mind someone watching me fuck you and I meant it. I'll spread you out on the bar. Eat your pussy until you pass out. Then I'll stuff you full of my cock for anyone to see you. You want that, Didi?"

His question is dangerous. My heart is hammering out of my chest and each shaky breath presses my tits into the hard muscles of his back, my sex throbs because this man makes me wet and wanton, no matter what.

"I can take whatever you think you gotta give," I declare. But in a softer whisper, meant just for him. "Not in front of them…please, Axe."

He grunts and squeezes my ass. Then louder for the room, he snarls, "I'm gonna fuck some sense into you."

Someone I can't see catcalls, and Dumbo bangs the bartop. As Axe pushes through the door, I catch Raine's eye. One corner of his mouth twitches up in a crooked, amused smirk. Two-faced traitor who tells me to go and then relishes when I'm getting hauled off to be fucked by the very orc he warned me about.

Axe practically runs down the hall I remember from my first night. We go past his office and up another flight of stairs. He is moving too fast, jostling me and making it harder to fight. But I know he'll put me down, so I bide my time. I gave in too easily, but like hell am I going to make this easy for him.

He opens another door, and after a couple of long strides, I'm being tossed through the air. When I land on a firm mattress, I literally bounce.

The room we are in is huge, almost set up like a studio apartment with an entire living section against the opposite wall with a little kitchenette under one of the windows. Everywhere is traditional orc textiles which are known for their complicated freeform designs. The beauty of everything steals what little part of my brain that isn't dominated by the orc towering over me.

"I told you that first night that if you were going to

Property of the Green Bastards

run, you needed to run then. You stayed. That was your choice. Now, I get to decide if you stay or leave. If you tell me not to fuck you, I won't. But you don't get to retreat from this."

There is something deeply possessive in how he says the words. He has me pinned beneath him. One of his hands holding both my wrists above my head. As he looks down at me, I am reminded of what this is.

For him, it is a game.

For me, it is every dream come to life.

Even when he sits up and reaches for something in the bedside table, I stay frozen with horror at how twisted this is. But I'm jolted into action when he takes advantage of my compliance and handcuffs me to the bed.

"What the fuck?" I buck against him, pulling at my restraints. He rolls off without saying anything about my curse, a devastatingly sexy smirk making me question my sanity.

He pulls his leather belt free and I thrash when he tries to tie my ankles together over my jeans, but he just growls.

"Be careful," he commands. "You aren't leaving until I'm done with you."

"You have no claim on my time. I need to go back to work."

He clenches his fists and mutters, "Tw'ti br'tas."

"I am not a twittering bird!" I snap back. "You aren't even going to fuck me, are you?"

He answers my question with one of his own. "Why did you want to leave?"

"Because you were right that first day. I don't belong here. I'll finish the map, keep my head down, and then leave just like you want!" I don't know why I am yelling but my heart is screaming that things can't get worse. But they do.

"Don't dictate to me, Dinah. I am the Ash'orde. If I tell you to stay here in my bed, that is what you will do."

"Fuck that." I'm hissing and spitting like a cornered cat.

"Your tone—"

"You aren't my heartsong. You aren't anything to me."

"No. I am not your heartsong. If I was, you wouldn't be fighting me all the time. Now. Stay here like a good girl."

He leaves, slamming the door so hard that the large battle axe bounces in its fitting.

I'm choking on my anger and the tears that start when I accept that he isn't coming back.

Chapter Eleven

AXE

I pause for a moment on the other side of the door, listening to her scream and curse me. I'm hard and angry because I've just lied to her.

She might be my heartsong. Her three genetic markers are enough for a heartsong and the thought of another orc claiming her makes me see red. But the thought of claiming a heartsong now? After I've uncovered a traitor and the plot to bring war to the Badlands? I'm not bringing her into that. If I took her, formally declaring she was my property in front of the MC and the people of my territory, she'd end up with a target on her back. And I could end up with a different orc claiming to be her heartsong. I punch the wall hard enough that the plaster crumbles, exposing the hard brick beneath it.

Fuck. She's mine or no one's.

"Why the fuck was I dealing with a screaming banshee?" I ask when I enter the common room to find Raine and Dumbo propping up the bar. "She was not contemplating cutting my balls off this morning."

"Why do you have your panties in a bunch? It isn't like she is your heartsong." Raine takes a long draw of his beer, eyes on me, daring me to react.

Finally, one of them said it. Dared me to claim her as my heartsong or reject her. My heart's pounding too hard for me to snap back at my enforcer. The silence is awkward. "Why was she screaming at me when I did jackshit to piss her off? Give me a beer."

Dumbo opens a beer and puts it next to the one she was drinking, just out of reach. I let that shit slide because I now have a good excuse to get in her space. And close enough to Raine to throat punch the rockfucker if he gets fresh.

"She grew up poor," my pretty enforcer tells me as he plays with that butterfly blade that seems to never leave his hand. "I think she thought well…fuck, I don't know. She got pissy when I told her she wasn't your heartsong."

The girl left scraps of the beer bottle label all over the bar top. What was she so nervous about? It bothers me that I am learning about her past from someone else. Particularly a brother whose tastes in women were pretty fucking close to mine. In fact, if I am being honest, and I'm in that kind of mood, the idea that they had been getting close behind my back is enough to make me want to claim her in front of the whole town. Then brand her as

Property of the Green Bastards

if she was my heartsong...just to remind handsome fucks like Raine from even thinking soft thoughts about what belonged to their prez.

"Don't see what being poor has to do with anything." Dumbo begins cleaning up the mess she made. I snag her half-drunk beer and drink it. "We grew up poor. Hell, we are poor."

"Yeah, but I think it is different." Raine takes a drink. I trust him...just not to fuck my itch. We didn't grow up together but when he prospected, he proved himself. His instincts, especially about people, are rarely wrong. "I don't know, but she was real pissed about it. Like, somehow, we lied. More pissed about thinking we were rich than the fact she isn't Prez's heartsong."

He's still daring me to come clean and tell them one way or another, my little princess with her fancy hair and dresses is my heartsong. Except, I don't have a firm answer to that question. All I know is that I can't get her out of my system, no matter how many times, places, or however I fuck her. I grunt. At the moment, she is locked in my room. Locked down tight because her wrists are handcuffed around the bedpost and her legs tied up with one of my belts. Just the thought of her being so helpless has me hard.

"She's not one of us—she didn't grow up in an MC or the Badlands. Even if she takes orc cock like she was born for it." I have to give them something. Some crude reason why I've not dropped her. Except that sweet little second clit confirms she has orc blood—a lot of it. And now I know she has the cutest green freckles. It won't be long before I strip her naked and see just how much of her body is covered in them. Who cares that I'm addicted to her body? Who wouldn't be? So I'm not going to try and hide how hard she makes me just thinking about those freckles and clits.

Flora Quincy

But Raine doesn't look too sure. "Have you seen her ears? She also speaks old orcish. She has two clits."

I grab him by the throat and slam him against the nearest table. "And how exactly do you know that?"

"Jaysus. She told us," Dumbo says. "Let him up, Prez. Raine wouldn't touch her. None of us would touch her." I'm gonna need to have a conversation with her and explain she shouldn't be talking like that. And until I say otherwise, her two clits are mine and she doesn't go around talking about them. In fact, I'm about to let my brothers know they don't think about her either when my mom walks in and looks around.

"Where is the girl?" The silence is broken with a snort from Raine. So when I meet her eyes, there is a little smirk on her face. "Elmeer is ready to leave. So, why don't you bring her down?"

"Fucking hell." I'd planned on fucking Dinah until my point was made, never in a million years did I think my own mother would cockblock me.

"She has a job, Axe."

"Fine, I'll go get her."

The hellcat is twisted on her side when I come in, giving me a perfect view of her ass in those black jeans that leave nothing to the imagination. Her t-shirt has ridden up too, exposing a sliver of skin. My heart skips a fucking beat at the sight of a couple of freckles dusting her lower back like a tramp stamp. I wonder what she'd do if I made her my property and had her get the Green Bastards' colours inked above her ass. Yeah, the idea of my brand on her body and the club's colours on her skin has my cock growing hard again. Only, I can't take care of that when I know my mom is downstairs with the others and even though I can smell the lemon-scented soap she used to clean up, my scent is still all over her.

"Are you here to fuck me?" she asks. It's then I realise I've just been standing at the door watching her.

"Nah, gotta let you go. Seems like you gotta go to work."

"Told you." She sounds smug.

I grin. She really is a brat. I wonder if she is provoking me on purpose. She must want me to take her over my knee again. Even if we never fuck again, she needs discipline in her life. Someone watching out for her. "I wouldn't mind reminding you about manners before I send you downstairs—"

She rolls over to glare at me, which is when I see that her eyes and nose are red.

"Asshole." Except there is no bite in her words.

"Were you crying?" Frey. She shouldn't be crying. I don't like those tears or the idea I caused them. Moreover, I know she doesn't want me to see her like this. I wouldn't want her to see me like this.

"What do you care?" She sniffs which is worse than if she was actually crying. "You aren't a gentleman."

"I'm not like your gentleman callers. You take me as I am. An orc. A child of blood and bone."

"None of you get it. I am not crying about just some guy who gives me orgasms but isn't my heartsong."

"Low blow, Princess." I sit on the edge of the bed. "Okay, tell me. Raine said you were upset about being poor?"

"Can't keep his mouth shut," she hisses. "Angry. And I'm crying because I'm angry at myself for thinking I could ever fit in here either. Humans don't want me. Orcs don't want me." She is working herself up and I let her because it is good seeing her with fight rather than defeated. "If I'm lucky, I might meet a nice werewolf who wants to bite and breed me. Or maybe I'll go to the mountains and find a dragon shifter with two dicks."

She isn't taunting me, but I growl. A werewolf? What can one of those knotted fuckers do for her? Who prefers a knot to an orc cock? To my cock. Not Dinah. Somehow, I know she needs to get this shit off her chest and my job is to listen. Then I can remind her that wolves and double dicks can't compare. She talks herself out and lies on her side, looking calmer now. Even her heartbeat has levelled out with her breathing.

Shit. I can feel her heartbeat. It has to be hers because mine is now racing.

Pah'pah, pah'pah, pah'pah…

Another heartbeat. Her heartbeat. Hers. I can tell the difference between hers and mine. But one look at Dinah tells me she hasn't figured it out yet.

Pah'pah, pah'pah, pah'pah…

It clicks into place. We aren't meant to sync. We just hear, feel, whatever our soulmate's heartbeat. So that is why it is called heartsong.

I grin. Oh, fuck yes. It ruins everything but she can't leave now. Impossible. She is my soulmate. It should scare the living shit out of me. Or make me angry. Nope. All I feel is light and easy, the tension in my body unwinding.

"Yeah. I don't think that will be possible, Didi. You see you got that pretty little double clit and those ears and freckles. You gotta heartsong out there."

"What about you?" She sounds nervous. "It clearly isn't me."

"I'm thirty-three. I should have met my heartsong. Makes me heartless," I say. Biggest lie I've ever told, but this is not the time to break the news to her. "Need to let you go now. Promise you won't castrate me?"

Property of the Green Bastards

She rolls her eyes. "Deh. Sh'war nee Ash'orde's ban'di so'hah."

I'm laughing as I release her ankles first, massaging them a little. When I go for her wrists, I growl another warning not to fight me until she is sitting up. There is some chafing which pisses me off. "You shouldn't have been struggling so much. You've marked your wrists up."

She opens her mouth—probably to point out that I'm the one who cuffed her—but thinks better of it.

Now that she is free, my itch doesn't move. Looks at me, sure. And she's as wary as a rabbit in front of a warg. But she doesn't move.

"Baby." I pinch her nose. "Do you think I'm a monster?"

She glares.

"Use your words, Didi."

"I want to go to work. I want to absorb all the knowledge that map has to offer. I want to…"

"You're going to ignore my question," I say, understanding. Whenever we are together, it is a lot for her.

Her chin goes up.

"Fine. If that's how you want to play it. Git." I jerk my head to the door. "Now…before—"

She scoots off the bed and stomps to the door. What was the word Swot uses? Dudgeon? Yeah, that's it. She is in a dudgeon.

"That's some attitude you—"

Her pace picks up, and I jump off the bed to follow. I'd make some smart-ass comment about her ass. But, while I like that fire, she seems brittle, fragile almost. I don't want to touch her and see her crumble like sand.

We enter the common room seconds apart. I stay by the door, hiding my clenched fists by crossing my arms. Meanwhile, my heartsong—yeah, I'm down with that—

snarls something at Raine before sweeping past everyone else, head up high. Fuck, she even ignores my mom when she says goodbye. But that rigid posture and frosty silence doesn't stop my mother from handing her a large casserole dish or giving her a friendly pat on her cheek. Whatever they say to each other makes Dinah's shoulders relax. She looks over her shoulders, allowing our eyes to meet, and the brat taunts me by sticking her tongue out. My heart skips a beat. She isn't leaving in tears.

Soon. Soon, I'm going to sit her down and explain how things are going to be from now on.

Just not today.

I need to deal with the shit that puts her at risk. Once I've eliminated that threat, there is enough time to fuck the knowledge that we are heartsongs into her.

I watch the door close then look at my brothers. Time to take care of business.

"Let's go." I signal them to follow me. What happens next is going to be ugly. I already wasted time with Dinah this morning. Not her fault. No one's fault but fuck, my thoughts keep spiralling back to her when I need to focus.

Traitor, or traitors because Kid didn't do this on his own. There are orc'i across the Badlands terrorising my people—even those I don't have a connection with are mine. I won't ignore the way the other MC presidents answered my call, agreeing to the Meet because they're scared shitless and need a real leader.

In the courtyard, in front of the Compound, the large potholes are like mini lakes after last night's storm. We'll need to patch them before the weather turns and they get worse over the winter. The club has the money but I'm pretty sure the mayor is gonna want help taking care of the mar's roads as well. Preparing for the winter which the wise ones are warning will be bad.

Property of the Green Bastards

I get on my bike and head to my next meeting with the fucking sheriff for a second time and the mayor. This morning's meeting was a disaster with the prick wanting to discuss what I did to the kvar fucker who beat war drums in my mar. Saying he probably met with an unfortunate end wasn't good enough for the shiny star carrying shithead.

Now it is about discussing the Meet.

Mayor Greta is Mom's age and that is where the similarities end. Mom keeps to the old ways and Greta wants us to move into the twenty-first century, which is reflected in how she decorates her office. Greys and chrome like she lives in the capital rather than the oldest mar in the Badlands.

"Axe." She nods when I walk in, but you could have hit me over with a feather when she brushed her fingers over her heart in a shine of respect to the Ash'orde. I smirk at her but I don't trust her. I never will.

"Greta." I stay standing even when she offers me a seat.

"The sheriff will be here in ten minutes. I wanted to say I take the drums seriously. You have my support."

"Well isn't that gracious of you. Accommodating even considering you wrote up five infractions against club businesses…while taking our money to repair the roads last year. I suppose you want more money now?" I scratch my chin in exaggerated consideration. The bitch can barely contain her snarl. Yeah, all that goodwill has a price tag.

"You know none of those violations would ever stick. You had the last sheriff on your payroll."

I shrug. "He was a good man."

"I don't think the new sheriff will be as…open to your methods. I heard he wasn't too happy to learn one of your prospects got lost in the scrubland. What did that boy do?

Not make your bike shine pretty?" Sometimes when she opens her mouth, she betrays those country roots.

"You care about someone who drove a cage through the town a couple of nights ago making a racket? And scaring your little girl?"

Her face blanks. She is spared having to answer the question because the knock on the door has her straightening and calling, "Enter."

Okay, maybe she has the arrogance Boonie has but at least my mom earned it.

The sheriff walks in looking as tense as this morning, but he gets straight to the point. "This Meet. How many people are you expecting?"

"Most of the clubs will come in full force. The Bastards will take care of security."

"That is a big ask. It isn't a secret that the clubs hold to the old ways and the old rivalries."

"Fine. I…" I emphasise the word. "I will be responsible. They'll camp on club land."

Which is shorthand for they'll surround the town because my family, by extension the club, own most of the land and property in this territory.

"I called the Meet as the Ash'orde. So expect more than clubs," I say. "This isn't about the clubs. This is about all of us. All the mars and the whole of the Badlands."

I cut a glance at the sheriff. "You too, sheriff. Little private citizen in this world."

"You have all my help." He takes a deep breath. "I'll keep an eye out. But–"

"But? Humans, always obsessed with asses." I smirk at Greta who looks like she has been sucking on lemons. Weird, but I think that if it was Dinah making that expression, I'd find it cute, but on this woman, it just pisses me off. "Aw, come on, Greta. Don't you think–"

Property of the Green Bastards

"Vulgar," she hisses. "This is meant to be a serious meeting. Hundreds, maybe thousands are invading my town."

I slam my hand on the desk and get right up in her face. "My town," I snarl. The feeling of or'gre builds at her ignorance. "All of this. The air you fucking breathe, the shit as soon as it leaves your wrinkled little asshole, it belongs to me. I am the horde king, the Ash'orde. She'sra meh weh 'are goki se' or ent sol. Dwen'mar, meh'mar. The Badlands, meh'cre on Grsil. Got me, Lady Mayor?"

I hear a barely suppressed snort to my left where I know the sheriff is standing.

I stare at her long and hard, letting or'gre cool. "The clubs are here for a Meet. They won't start anything. I hope you'll do the same."

I leave her gaping like a fish.

"Did you kill the prospect?" The sheriff asks as he catches me up on the stairs.

"You gonna keep asking questions like that, I'm gonna think you're as dumb as you look." I swing around. This fucker seems to think it doesn't matter he is just a human and not worth a minute of my time. He keeps pushing in, and I wonder how he'd squeal if I pressed Cuddles to his throat, and asked what the fuck he really wants with my town. Asshole doesn't know she'll only cut him if he is a liar.

"I'm not your enemy. And I'm looking out for her," he says. I don't have to ask who. You know what. I don't even have to be nice.

Yeah, fuck nice. I have him against the wall with my forearm pressed against his windpipe, putting enough weight into it that he is turning purple. "Keep her out of your head. Got me?"

I realise too late that I've made a mistake. Revealed my

hand that Dinah means something. And now I want to find her, fuck her, and get her face out of my head for long enough to prepare for the fucking circus that is coming to my mar in a couple of weeks.

He garbles, gasping for breath. I let up and he sucks in oxygen. "You need–"

"I don't need jack shit from you. Stay out of my way. Plot with the mayor but know she is more scared of the war drums than me. And she needs my help. She doesn't need yours. Back. Off."

"I just want to prevent war." He gasps. "The drums mean war. I've been keeping it from the authorities, but I don't know about the other sheriffs."

I drop him and walk away. If I stay longer, I'll ask what he means because war isn't going to happen. I'll make sure of it.

I get out onto the street, and Dumbo pushes off the wall and jogs up to me. "Prez. You have a call, it's Ryder."

If my day could get worse, it will be because this fucker is calling.

I get back and Grim signals me to his office, where the phone is just sitting there.

I pick up the receiver and put it to my ear. "Yeah?"

"It's Ryder."

"What do you want?"

"I got our guy...girl, actually."

"Yeah? I don't care if it is a she, he, or they. Stupidity and bad blood doesn't give a shit about your pronouns."

"Fuck, Axe. This is serious. Went on and on about a prophet and the Disavowed."

"So?" I'm losing patience. He's got nothing new for me and is wasting my day.

"You know that already? Why didn't you tell us? We all

spoke this morning on that fucking call and you said nothing."

"Neither did you," I point out but don't deny his accusation.

"We just caught her. Thing is, she has no connection to the Disavowed. Nothing. Yours?"

I consider whether to tell him, but in the end, sometimes you have to share information to get it. "Yeah, he did. And the Steel Prophets."

"We need to do a Meet before. Just presidents. At the Allteng."

"Then set it up."

"When?"

I squeeze my eyes closed. I need to think. I need this shit taken care of and for some reason, all this is my responsibility. Nah, I was born for this. It is in my or, my blood. The universe didn't conspire against me. My ancestors just continued to fuck and breed until I came screaming into this world.

"Axe?"

"Tonight. It needs to happen tonight."

THE ALLTENG IS HUGE, rising out of nothing. I've got Raine and Grim with me because they are big fuckers. An added bonus is Raine was born Old Horde, and before she passed, Grim's heartsong came to us from Demon's Disciples, the biggest of the clubs. These fuckers need to remember our creator, Frey, was smart. We find our heartsongs outside of our territories. It doesn't stop all the feuds, but it stops an all-out war—until the war drums are sounded. Then blood gives way to bone and your hearth becomes your only home.

Because the Silver Amazons are the protectors of the

Allteng, they are historically neutral, which is why we are walking five miles from where we leave our bikes with Hawk's dad's homestead.

Heddy, the Amazon's prez, meets us on the slope about a hundred feet from the entrance to the grand hall where we are meeting. She is young for a prez of the Amazons who tend to hold the title until they die, but the last prez died of cancer and they were forced to elect a new one.

"Greetings, Ash'or'ash-den, Ash'orde, President of the Green Bastards." She touches her heart and bows.

I grunt at her formalities. This is a fucking nightmare if they start treating me like the horde king. The fucking title is symbolic but already, I've been treated like–dammit I can't even pretend that I haven't acted like their king in the last week when I called a Meet, signing the paper with my full name and titles. "None of that, Heddy."

"Whatever you say, Axe, but get used to it." She looks me up and down like a hunk of meat. My heartless status is well known and she isn't the first woman who wanted me in her bed as a chance to be the mother to the next generation of Ashi. The Amazons in particular would love to get another one of theirs to be mother to the Ash'or'Ash.

If she is half as possessive as I am, Dinah is going to claw this woman's eyes out when they meet.

"Keep your eyes to yourself." Raine smirks. "Our prez is jer'se he'dsar fin rea Didi."

I bark a laugh. Yeah, that is a pretty good way to explain my relationship with Dinah. Balls deep in a sweetheart's cunt. Crude and true. Heddy flushes red, shuts up, and walks away. Her back is ramrod straight and there is no sway in her skinny hips.

Grim mutters something under his breath at Raine, but I ignore them. My people still believe we aren't heartsongs. To them, she is just some fun while she

Property of the Green Bastards

forges the map or until I get bored of her. Even if that was the case, if she left and found a heartsong, I'd let her go, no regrets because I was there first. I fucked her, sucked on those clits, had my hands on every freckle she has first. And on her deathbed, she'd remember that.

Lucky for her, I'm not ever going to be only a memory. I'm her now and her future.

I grin. Yeah, I'm that fucker. And I don't mind the itch this time or the way my heart tugs in the direction of Dwen'mar. I know where she is, safe and watched over by Tool and Hawk who is also on babysitting duty.

I roll my shoulders, now ready for the meeting that will lay out our plan to deal with this threat. This close to the mountain, you have to really crane your neck to see the snow-capped peak. About fifty feet above us is the natural cave where the horde leaders used to meet and discuss the future of our people. We enter shoulder to shoulder and I see we are the last to arrive.

"Where are the Steel Prophets?" Heddy asks. I fold my arms and shrug. I see Ryder shift in his chair.

"Ryder, you wanna explain?" I smile. "You were the one who called this little gathering."

"I didn't invite them," he says at last.

"Good," Heddy says, surprising me and probably every other orc in here. "The kvari cowards who beat the drums on the sides of the Allteng were first-generation Steel Prophets. I hunted them down. They claim the Disavowed have returned. That their princess is back to take back her crown."

Pivot, the gnarled Demons president, laughs. "What crown?"

"I don't know. That is what they said. That their prophet says the princess has returned."

"What bullshit. We call club daughters 'princesses.' That is—"

My mind blanks as I remember that I call Dinah Princess. Dinah whose background I don't know. I signal Grim close. "Look into it."

"Look into what?" he asks.

"This bullshit about a crown for the Disavowed Princess."

"Anyone else learn about this princess?" Heddy asks.

"Yes." Ryder stands and pulls out a gun. Causing a couple of people to reach for their own weapons. "Relax, you assholes. I got this off the bitch who sounded drums in my mar. It is Disavowed property. Spelled though. Only someone with the blood of the Disavowed can pull the trigger."

"Fuck. We had something similar."

I listen to the stories. Seems everyone has found their traitor. They are all prospects or young. Whatever, we are fucked. The fear is spreading as people hear about the drums and once all the reports are given, they look to me.

"So, we agree that this bullshit needs to be stamped out? Find this prophet and end him?"

"Or her," Heddy says. "I think—"

"Yeah, let's not jump to conclusions." I wave her off. "Him is, uh, general? 'Kay? You keep your ears open. Bring your people to the Meet. Weapons left on the All'whia ridge. I've got someone to protect them." I smirk thinking of the mayor learning how I plan to use her and the sheriff.

"Not giving up our weapons while you have yours." The Demons prez shakes his grey head of hair. "Not that I don't trust you, but people are going to be on edge. The last Ash'orde who called a Meet and demanded we leave

Property of the Green Bastards

our weapons on the All'whia was your grandfather. Heads rolled that day and children died."

"Bring a truth rod and I will promise to only cut off the heads of those who mean harm to the Badlands and the territories." My words hang heavy in the air because I'm not promising to not execute any threat. "Well?"

"We lost family that day. Heartsongs, who knew nothing about—"

"Do you deny or?" A new voice breaks in. We all turn to see an ancient Amazon–not a heartsong. She wears the white robes of a wise one but there is a brand on her forehead that belongs to the Disavowed. Vesta. The sister of the Disavowed president. She was heartless and devoted herself to the Allteng. She was the one who alerted the clubs to the thefts, and she spoke against her brother and the rest of the Disavowed. Her testimony swayed the judges and jury. Determined that her kin would be executed and to ensure none forgot, she branded herself. "Do you deny or?"

"No, wise one," is the united response.

"You should. The superstition of var'or has held our people hostage for a millennium. If you had any balls," she sneers at me, "you would declare the or of all goki sa or'sol clean. Purify it. Find my great-niece. Make her yours, Heartless King. Break the cycle."

Her words send a chill up my spine, but seem to burn a fire under everyone else's ass. Heddy calls for her to be taken away. All I want is to get the fuck out of here. The only thing we've accomplished is learning there is some Disavowed bitch who is going to overthrow the status quo according to a prophet. Oh, and it will all be just okay so long as I claim this person that we don't have any proof exists. Fuck that.

I have a heartsong. She exists. I'm not sticking my cock into any princess but Dinah.

The rest of the meeting is a waste of everyone's time. The only thing agreed is no guns. So Raine, Grim and I have another long ride back to the Compound. I get back too late to hunt down my heartsong, which is like being kicked in the balls because the minute I lie down, Dinah's scent assaults my senses. I consider stealing her from the barracks and bringing her here. I can fuck her until I pass out from exhaustion.

I roll on to my back, then get to my feet and strip, heading for the shower where I turn it to scalding. I grab my half hard cock and stroke myself root to tip and imagine Dinah on her knees in front of me. Her mouth open, pink tongue held out so that I can come and just see my cum filling her mouth before she swallows it down. I groan as the desire deepens and I start to fuck my hand even while I stroke myself harder. If I screw my eyes closed I can almost see her like that. I come hard, but even then, my balls feel full–I'll only get a real release when I bury my cock deep into her tight cunt.

Hers and no one else's.

Chapter Twelve

DINAH

I show up at the shop early on Monday. The dark clouds on the horizon threaten rain, and I don't have an umbrella. Like always, Tool grumbles about the fact I'm walking. Then walks back fast when I ask if he'll give me a ride. Frey, help me because supposedly it wouldn't be appropriate to give me a lift. Fat drops of rain dapple the sidewalk when I see Elmeer squatting out front. His hands covering his mouth and tears leaking out of his ancient eyes.

"Elmeer?"

"Don't go inside," he whispers, the words are full of raw emotion. That is when I notice that the door isn't open but has been ripped off its hinges. I swallow back the questions, ignore his warning, and step inside. Nothing. Literally nothing has been touched but there is an uneasiness in the koltop that makes all the hair on my body stand on end. I edge further in, waiting for the carnage I know must be there.

"No." The map. My map is destroyed. Ripped along the seams to remove the two hides outlining the territories belonging to the Steel Prophets and the Disavowed. But why? Why would anyone steal only two hides; it makes no sense?

And the hidden map I was told about? Nothing. I rush to the side and run my fingers along the edge. There was never an inner layer of hide like I'd been expecting. No lining at all, just the backing hide and that is bare. I sink to the ground and press my palms to my eye, trying to keep the tears at bay. How could I have been so stupid? Only the original would have had a hidden map. A forger wouldn't bother with one, might not have even known it was there in the first place.

"I'm sorry," Elmeer says. "I know–"

"I am the one who should be sorry. Why are you apologising to me? Your store! Your space."

"He didn't take anything but the sections of the map. I came in when Eel was ripping them off. I don't know–"

"We have to tell Axe," Tool says. I forgot he was there.

"I called Boonie," Elmeer tells us. "She told me to stay outside. I should have stopped you going in. They are bringing in a warg."

"Oh. Right...we should leave then."

I wrap my arms around the ancient pilgrim. His pain is devastating, but my own worries blow away. Perhaps my

Property of the Green Bastards

father was wrong and there never was a map that would reveal my connection to the Disavowed.

Outside, the rain hasn't started yet, perhaps aware of what has happened and waiting for the wargs to pick up the thief's scent.

Boonie stands with her hand on a warg's shoulder like it is some normal-sized dog. Hawk is there as well but on his bike. His eyes are sharp when our eyes meet, and he gives me a sharp nod. The wargs scare the living shit out of me.

She scowls at us. "I told you not to go in."

"We didn't touch anything," Elmeer assures her. "And we know who it was. Eel. I saw him."

"Fuck. Rher gre'iss," she orders the warg.

Watching the giant, wild animal slither into the shop reminds me of a raccoon I once saw stick its head out of a drainpipe. It comes back out and trots off down the road. Boonie mounts another warg and is off after the tracker.

"We'll get the fucker," Hawk assures us before revving his bike and following the wargs.

Just as I turn back to talk to Elmeer, the sound of a car door slamming is the only warning we get for the sheriff running up to us, his face pinched and angry.

"Why are a pair of hunting wargs running through–" He sees the door busted open and curses under his breath. "What happened?"

"Sheriff, I need to report a theft," Elmeer says. "But, if you can take the girl. She can give you more information."

I want to protest. I'm not the best person to answer the questions. He saw Eel and can give the information. But he must have a reason, so I slide into the sheriff's car for the short and silent ride to his office.

. . .

"Why didn't you call me? Why did you call them first?" Logan asks, a latent fury in his features as he parks the car. "I could have helped."

"I got there minutes before you. How am I meant to call you?" I square up to the bigger man. "Anyway, the MC protects this town."

"Security footage. I have access to that—"

"It could take ages and a warg tracker is faster."

"Why won't you trust me?"

The question hangs heavy in the air. For a moment, the only sound is the chugging AC that probably uses more energy than what the Compound uses in a week.

"You aren't one of us," I say and hold the back of my hand to his face which has a smattering of green freckles I haven't bothered to cover with makeup. "Or maybe, I am not like you. You could ruin me and my family. Why should I trust you not to report me to the human authorities?"

I get out of the car and walk in the direction of the Compound. He scrambles after me, getting in front of me.

"Jaysus. You think I care if you are half-orc? Or whatever percentage? I don't. Okay? Maybe I was curious at first, but it isn't my business. I've got Axe hating my guts because I'm human and a lawman. You hate me for pretty much the same reasons. I just want to do my job and make sure the peace holds."

"Great for you, I'Jat." I smile when he flinches. "But you are human. And you know that I am not."

"Fine. But my advice? Get out of here. Leave this town. Leave the Badlands because war is coming. Or have you forgotten a coordinated sounding of war drums in every town with an MC? Or that the people responsible are claiming that the Disavowed have an heir?"

My blood freezes in my veins. "Bullshit. I've never heard about an heir."

"Yeah? You asked your precious MC prez? Or are you just fucking him?"

I throw the best punch of my life, connecting with his nose in a way that leaves me shaking out my hand while I watch him cup his nose like the squealing pig he is.

"If you aren't holding me for anything…"

"You can be so naive. I'm going…fuck!" he howls in frustration. "I should lock you up for assault and battery of a police officer."

"But you won't."

I spin around to see Eel stalking towards us. Where the hell did he come from? This is the asshole who stole the map and his eyes are full of a wild haze that has me stepping back. Logan pushes me behind him, but Eel moves faster than his age should allow and he slams his fist into the sheriff's face which knocks him out.

"Come, girl." Eel grabs my upper arm. "I'll walk you back to the Barracks. Then you pack a bag and we get out of town."

"What? No. Fuck—"

"For your own safety, Di'or'nah-Fi."

Bile rises in my throat at the sound of the orc name my father gave me. I don't have a right to the "or" because my mother was human but he had insisted on it. Claimed that as an MC princess, I should have a proper orc name. "How—"

"You are the Driftas princess. My near-kin. My mother was of your line. But we must save you so that the kvari Green Bastards don't destroy our last hope."

"No." I back away. "I don't want anything to do with the Disavowed or any of it."

"You must be protected. It has hurt—"

"How did you know?"

"I was told how it would be. I have the letter your grandfather sent to honour your birth. The photograph with your father on your naming day is in my personal safe. I have the map."

This time, when the acid rises in my throat, I can't stop it and I throw up. "Please, leave me alone."

"Princess—"

"Don't you ever call me that…" I jerk away from him, shaking my head and not believing what was happening. He was saying there is proof. More damning proof than an old map that might not exist? I must surprise him because I manage to break free. "Get the fuck away from me."

I don't wait. The sheriff's car is there, and I dive into the driver's seat, more grateful than I can say that the key is in the ignition. Eel bangs his fist against the hood of the car, and you know what, I do not care if I run him over and he dies. I hit the ignition and drive straight for him, knocking him over.

As I speed away, I see Tool. He sees me too, shock clear on his face. I can't wait. Getting out of this place is my only option because if I stay, I know I'll die.

I ONLY MAKE it two hours out of Dwen'mar when the car stutters to a stop. I bang my hands against the steering wheel and twist the key, trying to turn the car on and off but the motor gives a pathetic grumble and then shuts off completely. "No. Please…" I plead with the hunk of metal. "I need to go. Please…"

But no one is going to hear my cries because I don't even know if I'm on the right road, and the storm that had been threatening this morning caught up with me. Tears leak from my eyes, and I give into hopelessness. I can't get

Property of the Green Bastards

out of the car and find better shelter. I can't call for help because there is no cell phone, no police radio, nothing to get a message out. Even if I could, I wouldn't. Tool will have told them I fled the scene. It looks bad for me; an innocent person would stay, but I was so scared. Stupid. I was so stupid. What's worse is my heart is screaming at me. It's wild and irregular like one heartbeat keeps time with my fear and an anger so fierce, it scares me even more.

Amidst all of this, a moment of clarity has me climbing into the back. Logan has left a jacket back there, which I wrap around myself to ward off the cold that has begun to seep into my bones.

At some point, I must have drifted off because I jerk awake and scream when I hear the door of my car being ripped off. Instinct tells me it isn't the storm, which seems to have ended. It is pitch black outside. The only light is the weak one that snapped on when the door was pulled off.

I recognise the monster in front of me.

Axe.

He never looked more threatening than he does now. Or'gre. Battle blood. I don't say the word out loud because I don't want him to think I am scared of how fucking terrifying he is. All of his muscles exploded in an inhuman way, like he has been on steroids. His jaw is somehow squarer, and his tusks have grown as well. But it is the black talons, which must be six inches long, that protrude where his fingers used to be. They could shred me to pieces. And I'm scared. I'm relieved he has found me. Whatever the outcome, he is the one who found me.

"Dinah..." My name doesn't sound normal on his tongue because his voice has dropped at least an octave. "Why?"

"Eel has the map," I cry. He hasn't killed me yet.

Maybe he doesn't know…but it will only be a matter of time.

"No. Why leave?" Shit. Even his words are more… what? Primal? Like some kind of Frankenstein's monster.

"Because that is why I was hired. The map is destroyed." I'm full of shit, and he knows it.

"No," he snarls, reaching into the car and grabbing my ankle so hard I know it will bruise.

"Axe, you are hurting me," I whimper.

His eyes grow round and he notices how his talons cut into my calf. He shakes his head, trying to clear the magic that still has him in its grip.

The magic wears off slowly. I watch his tusks recede, his muscles relax, and those deadly talons shrink until only his hands remain.

"It's me, Didi…" he says softly. I should be more scared that he has his rational mind back but a little sob escapes. I launch myself into his arms, burying my face in his neck. I know, I know that I won't be able to stay, but maybe for a moment, I can be near the person who came after me.

"My car broke down," I tell him. As if that is the only reason I'm a shaking mess.

"No. It ran out of gas. Get out." He doesn't wait for me to obey, just reaches in and pulls me out. We stand there for a minute, his hands on my waist, my heart hammering in my chest. Those hands that could have killed me moments before, gently glide up my body until he cups my face. His eyes grow dark, and his voice is harsh with anger. "You don't leave without my permission, Princess. We talked about this yesterday."

"I can't."

"You don't have a choice."

I'm an idiot. The biggest, stupidest, most naive idiot to ever draw breath because I throw away the impulse to run

Property of the Green Bastards

away and give in to the instinct that tells me to hold onto him for dear life and never let go.

He gets onto his bike, and I gracelessly follow him. "Wrap your arms nice and tight," he warns. Irrationally, I feel a bubble of nervous laughter build inside of me. As if I would do anything but cling to him. "Forgot a helmet for you and the roads are wet, so we'll go slow."

THE RAIN IS a faint drizzle when we ride into the courtyard in front of the Compound. I'm soaked through, and even with the heat radiating off Axe, I shiver–though it could be from the shocks my psyche has suffered in the last twelve hours.

When we enter the Compound's common room, the conversations stop. Forty pairs of eyes latch onto us. I recognise a couple of the brothers, including Raine and Hawk who sit at the bar where Dumbo and Tool are pulling beers. The others are patched members of the MC I haven't met, but there isn't any distrust in their eyes.

I will change that soon enough because with Axe at my back and his people watching our every combined breath, I know I need to tell him the truth. No matter what the consequences are, I can no longer keep the secret of my heritage from him. If someone is going to tell him who I am, it has to be me.

Boonie jumps up first. She runs over and gathers me into a warm embrace. I stiffen at first, uncertain how to respond to her murmuring promises that I am home and safe. No, you aren't, the devil whispers to me. Once they know the truth, you'll be dead or you'll have to leave. You'll be on the run for the rest of your life.

"Oh, sweetness. Thank, Frey. We were so worried. Get

her upstairs and warm," she tells Axe, who hasn't said a word; he just stays pressed against my back, a hand resting on the back of my neck, a heavy weight that feels like a blanket.

Her words prompt him into action, and he herds me through the crowd and up to his room in silence. The door clicks shut. With his chest against my back, he walks me to the giant bed.

Abruptly, my brain catches up with where we are. He isn't questioning me. Instead, we are in his bedroom.

"Why are we here?" I dare to ask. "What are you going to do with me?"

"Get on the bed," he snarls and once again, he manages to cuff me to his bed. "And you will listen, you will behave, and you will keep still for one fucking second so that you don't pinch a nerve. I need to buy some restraints if you keep trying to run off. Maybe a tracking collar."

I freeze. "That is a lot of information to take in."

"Don't care. I got shit to do. You aren't going anywhere–"

"What if I have to pee?" I tug at my wrists but he grabs them, easily controlling me with one hand.

"Stop fighting it."

"I'm not–"

"You are my heartsong," he says, holding my eyes. If I was standing, my legs would give out. But trapped on his bed, I freeze and blink at him, unsure what I'm meant to say.

"So. That means you are my heartsong," I say softly. I want to argue because I am a little scared by how fierce and possessive he sounds. We haven't seen each other since the last time he had me in this position. I want to ask him

Property of the Green Bastards

what is going on but the berserker scent—similar to ozone—clings to him.

"Good."

"Good?" I'm confused.

"Good." His eyes are hungry now, roaming over my face like he is seeing my freckles for the first time. Our eyes meet again and something flashes through his that I miss. He stands, rubs his hands down his long, strong thighs. "Good."

"Good?" I ask in disbelief. Is he going to leave me here? Somehow, the question doesn't form because my eyes are now caught on the growing bulge in his pants. He shrugs out of his cut and folds it over the back of a chair. My heart catches at the sight of his back flexing before he turns back around and stalks to the edge of the bed.

"Good." He crawls over me. A knee splits my legs and one thick thigh presses against my sex. Instinct demands I arch into him, trying to increase the pressure. I shouldn't be so turned on given every fear swirling inside of me, but everything about this orc has my mind reform around one overwhelming drive to spread my legs for him, and let him fill me with his seed.

"Good." My heart is hammering. I don't know what else to say. Heartsong. He said it, not me. I shift on the bed, uncomfortable with the way my arms are tied above my head. Axe undoes the cuffs and massages my wrists.

"Good?"

"Good." I swallow back a moan.

"Good," he growls. Rearing back, he grips the top of my jeans and pulls, ripping the zip apart, before dragging them down my legs, taking my flats with them. I'm naked from the waist down. "Good?"

"Good," I pant. I want to ask for more. But Frey cast

some kind of spell over us and if I say something, perhaps the spell will break.

His face is level with my cunt and he licks up my sex, his tongue swirling around my bottom clit, up the centre to give the top clit the same attention. The broad sweep of his licks is coupled with the way he rubs along my folds. The gold caps increase the sensation and I spread my legs as wide as possible, hoping to tempt him to turn their pressure to my clits instead, repeating the delicious torture from the night before.

"Good?"

"Good," I moan.

He kisses up my stomach, pushing my shirt up until it bunches under my breasts. His hands come up and cup my breasts over my t-shirt, tweaking my nipples through the thin material.

"Is that good, Princess?" he asks, the tip of his cock teasing my entrance, brushing against my clits.

"Good," I moan when his cock pushes in. "So good."

"Good."

His thrusts start even, but I'm squeezing around him so hard that his groans are matching mine as our fucking becomes desperate. His cock swells impossibly bigger, harder and then he is coming inside of me. When he withdraws, he rolls me onto my back, tilts my pelvis back, and cups my sex, preventing any of his cum from leaving. The action feels familiar.

I search his face, trying to understand what he is thinking but he hasn't lost the fierce, lust-filled heat. It burns into me, stirring my own needs. "Axe…"

"Ash'or'ash'den. Say it. Say your heartsong's name," he orders.

Heartsong. After days of saying it was nothing but sex, he is claiming to be my heartsong. My heartbeat tumbles

Property of the Green Bastards

through different rhythms. Suddenly, I realise there are two. His heart beats hard and sure. Mine skitters about. This is what I've been feeling since we met. Two hearts. I suck in a breath. "Pah'pah...Ash'or'ash'den is my heartsong."

"Who do you belong to, Princess?"

"I belong to you." I can't believe it, but I do.

"And what am I?"

"My heartsong."

He collapses against me, pinning me beneath him. "Good, now sleep."

I'm too exhausted to argue, and I want this moment to last. Tomorrow, I tell myself, tomorrow I will tell him everything.

I DON'T KNOW when he wakes up. Fuck, I wouldn't have woken up except that he rolls off me, removing the comforting weight and warmth. I watch him disappear into what I assume is a bathroom. He returns with a wet cloth and cleans us up. This is the first time he has ever removed any of his cum from my body, but I don't say anything. My thoughts have escalated from bleary sleep to high alert.

My heartsong deserves the truth. And if I don't reveal it now, he'll never trust me again.

I make a half-hearted attempt to prop myself up. I don't want to tell him I'm Disavowed while I'm naked. "I need my clothes—"

"I'll get you something to wear." He reaches over me and plucks his shirt from off the floor. "Put this on."

"I need to tell you something," I say once his t-shirt has settled around my body.

"Not tonight…unless it can't wait? I'm really fucking tired, Didi."

"I…" I can't stop the hesitation. We are tired. I can see it in his eyes. I feel it in my bones.

"Then it can wait until tomorrow."

I open my mouth to protest because it can't wait. Only my cowardice makes me pause, terrified of what he will say–what he will do–once he learns.

"Sleep, heartsong…my Pah'pah." The orcish term sends my heart soaring along with his, but my stomach plummets. I've never felt two emotions so strongly simultaneously. All we have is this one perfect night. I am a coward, but I refuse to turn my back on my one chance at happiness, however short-lived.

"Pah'pah," I whisper before melting into him, kissing him, sucking on his bottom lip. "Always."

Chapter Thirteen

AXE

I don't do some girly shit and roll on my side to watch my heartsong sleep. I turn my head to the side like a fucking king. She's face down on a pillow. I could get on top of her, fuck her like my cock wants.

Then, because she is a girl, she rolls on her side and gives me the sexiest morning smile I've ever seen. "Heartsong." Her voice is pure sex. "I can't believe it."

"I never should have let you leave this bed." She frowns. So I decide to admit the truth. "I knew we were heartsongs yesterday."

"Axe—"

"None of that, Didi. I was wrong to let you out of my sight. When I heard Eel attacked you, and that you drove off. I was ready to kill all of them."

"I had to," she whispers.

"You should have come straight to the Compound."

She hides her face in the pillow and huffs. "I need to tell you something really important. It is about my orc family."

This is what she wanted to talk about last night. "Yeah, sure."

"It starts with my grandmother." She pushes herself into a seated position and makes sure my t-shirt is tucked down so it covers her body. "I never met her but she was a missionary in a POW camp for orc'i fleeing the conflict."

"Fuck." We both know the only orc'i in the POW camps were Disavowed or connected to the Disavowed. Our eyes meet. We both know where this is going.

"Do you want me to keep going?"

"Yes." The word is clipped, and she flinches. I grab her hand. "Finish your story."

"Thanks." But she doesn't relax. "That is where my grandfather was born and he met her when she was just a teenager. I never learnt anything about their relationship. She raised my dad there. The only thing I know about my orc grandfather is he committed suicide. My dad could pass as human and that was what mattered. He could open a human bank account and everything, but it meant they could have a place, get a job. My parents met in the Capital. My mom…I don't even know what she was told because she died giving birth to a quarter orc."

"That wasn't your fault."

"Yup." She makes the "p" pop like you do when you want to make a point. I just don't know what her point is.

Property of the Green Bastards

Then she glares at me...she glares through me at someone else. "But her family blamed me. Everyone but my human grandfather." My head kinda flops back against the headboard.

"This is a lot, Didi. You wanna take a break?"

"No, this is the first time I've told this story and if I stop, I don't know if I can start again."

"Fair enough, but come here." I don't wait. I pull her into my lap and hold her head against my heart. She smells good.

"I didn't pass when I was a baby. My mom's mom was a midwife, which was good because it meant I survived. My Uncle Frank forged my birth certificate. That was all they did until my dad died. Alcoholism. Then I was an extra mouth to feed."

Part of her story is missing. She knows too much about our culture. She never flinched when she saw me as a monster. She was my fucking heartsong and knew what that meant. But she acted like she was all human. The woman had two clits, the cutest fucking points on her ears, and those freckles, which she'd stopped hiding with makeup, were even cuter. I'd cut an arm off before admitting that to anyone. Orc women, even only those with part of a bloodline, were not cute. Fierce, beautiful, vibrant if you were feeling sentimental but not cute. Di is cute enough that I might believe her even if she wasn't my heartsong.

"Fuck," I mutter.

"What?" Her brows draw together in a frown.

"Nothing, Princess. You know which horde? Or MC? Did your dad say?"

She bites her lip and shakes her head. "It wouldn't matter to you, would it?"

I want to say that her family doesn't matter. But that is

a straight-up lie. If she is Disavowed, her life is forfeit. That was the agreement and the treaty. All the Disavowed are gone. Killed by my grandfather. I grit my teeth thinking about the bloodshed. Babies. The mothers had been allowed to choose how they died. Given more kind options than beheading. But some escaped south…

She's also my heartsong.

"Nah, Princess. It wouldn't matter."

"You are thinking about the Disavowed. Aren't you?"

"Yeah. I'm sorry, Princess. It is hard not to."

"Axe—"

"Call me Ash'den," I tell her. "My heartsong should call me by my name."

"Don't make this harder than it already is." Her voice is full of anguish. "I have to finish…finish my story. I… when my father died, he left nothing valuable. The only thing in the apartment worth keeping was a folder with some paperwork and photographs of his parents. Him, his mom, and me as a baby. Another one on my name day…I didn't know anything about orc'i then. It wasn't until I was seventeen that I even looked at the folder properly. I spent most of my teen years avoiding even thinking about orcish things. I spoke the language because it was all my dad spoke to me as a kid, but customs? No."

I brush her hair off her forehead to look at the cluster of freckles that are so close together they are almost a solid green patch. "You had to hide these that whole time."

"Makeup. I started wearing it when I moved in with my human family. So, like, eleven. Anyway, I couldn't bring myself to look at the file that made it clear I was different. Then one day, I caved and opened the file. I saw the pictures; my grandfather was clearly an orc. And I'd learnt a bit about the camps…I went to the public library and Googled his name."

Property of the Green Bastards

"What was it?"

She shakes her head as if trying to deny the knowledge. When her eyes meet mine, they are pleading and scared. I physically feel her heart breaking inside my chest and know the answer. Not his name but at least what it will start with. "Ash'den...he was the son of the Disavowed. Their president's son. I didn't know what to—"

"Don't say it."

She continues, the story spilling out of her. "He...I don't know why he got with my grandmother...you know that part of the story. I came here because the only other information in the file was a picture of a map. On the back, my dad had written 'proof of who I am.' Elmeer put the map up for auction. Then he advertised the job."

She sucks her lips between her teeth like she is waiting for me to yell at her. "I have to tell you all of it. But I was so conflicted that day. My dream job. Working for Elmeer? At the best place for orcish artefacts. And I had the chance to destroy the one thing my father thought could prove I was Disavowed. To somehow destroy my past because living among humans was always a risk to my family. You see, the week before, a law passed punishing hiding magical blood with prison time."

I put her aside, and start to pace. That law. It doesn't affect us. And she's here too. Far away from those racist assholes.

"I knew I had to leave. And the only place I wanted to come was the Badlands. I could continue to lie about my heritage like I had my whole life. I was going to fake papers or even do it legally. My Uncle Frank was going to forge a death certificate for Dinah Smith. I'd disappear from the human records. Create a new identity. It was the only thing I could think of."

"It makes sense," I say because she needs something

from me. But I turn away from her. Everything I've known about her is a lie or a kind of lie, because what did I know about her? Nothing. I just…she drew me to her like true north because some fucking magic decided she was my soulmate. My heartsong carries the blood of traitors. She is the great-granddaughter of the orc who coordinated and planned the theft of sol from the Allteng. "Go on. Tell me the rest."

"Eel found me and said he had proof of who I was." She's crying those quiet tears that are worse than if she was screaming. "He had pictures of me as a baby with my grandfather. I swear, by all that is holy, I didn't even know it existed. I didn't know that he was even alive when I was born. You have to believe me. And I know nothing about the drums. I swear on my life. I know nothing about the drums or what has been happening. I only came to start a new life."

When she stops talking, my body is shaking with or'gre. There isn't space for everything I'm thinking and feeling.

"I should execute you." The words are out there between us. "You…you lied."

"Yes."

Somehow, the fact she admits it makes me trust her. Or, at least, believe her enough not to explode with the righteous anger I feel. This woman, my heartsong, is the greatest threat to my family, my club, my territory, the Badlands. She doesn't know a prophet is out there claiming she'll be the one to bring us all down. Or that her great-great-aunt told me I could fix all of this by claiming her.

But even if I do, the people who hate what happened in the past will rally around her and make her their mascot, symbol. And my connection to her? Fuck. She had a target on her back before I knew the truth.

"I should execute you, Dinah. You–"

Property of the Green Bastards

"I know."

Our hearts are breaking. Two hearts that came together perfectly torn apart.

"What am I supposed to do?" I ask, but there is no answer. I cross back to the bed and drag her to me. I invade her space until our noses are touching. "What am I supposed to do?"

"You have to—" She swallows. "You need to do what is right."

"I can't execute my own heartsong," I snarl at her blindness to the fact she is the centre of my universe. Has held me hostage from the first day that I saw her and thought she was nothing but an itch I needed to scratch for it to go away. She is an itch that will irritate me for the rest of my days because I refuse to stop scratching it, so she will always be there. Like she should be.

"But I have to tell them," she says. "We have to tell your people. They must be told. What if they learn from your enemies?"

"Fuck." I roll off the bed and pour us each a large whiskey. She sips hers slowly, but I throw mine back and pour another. I turn back to the bar when I see my jeans in a pile on the floor and lying next to them, Cuddles. An idea forms and once it is lodged there, I can't let it go. It will work. I grab my jeans and Cuddles, then grab Dinah's wrist and pull her from the room. I know she is only wearing my shirt and scent but I don't need the club or anyone thinking there is anything staged about this. That she is trying to impress them. She needs to be exactly what she is: my heartsong and innocent of trying to hurt the club or any of the people in my territory.

Innocent until Cuddles pierces her skin and her blood flows out and she—

I cut the thought off. This will work. I know my people.

217

Flora Quincy

They are more than family. We chose this life. We chose this club. I know where their hearts should lie. It is just time to find out whose side I'm on.

She protests and asks what I'm doing, but I keep my mouth shut. At the stairs, she digs her heels in. "What is going on, Axe?"

"Weh'frisa," I tell her. "Your trial…Pah'pa neh gra sheuh dwea meh weh so on orsol. Don't be afraid, Princess. If you are telling me the truth, if you tell them the truth, you have nothing to be afraid of."

"At least, let me put clothes on."

"No. And no, I'm not telling you. You have to trust me as your heartsong, right?" I stare at her hard. "I'm putting everything on the line for you. If you are my heartsong, that reflects on me. I'll explain it to them in a way they'll understand. Me weh neh var. K'var pewt'a neh orsol."

A tear slips free, then another, but she nods. Brave girl. Of course, she is. My heartsong would be brave.

It is still too early for many people to be in the common room. Kendle is behind the bar cleaning glasses and she squawks out a sound of surprise when she sees us.

"Go get mom. Round everyone up. I want them here in an hour," I say in my hardest voice, letting her know this isn't some fucking game.

"What the fuck is going on?" she asks. "Why is she crying?"

"Jump, Ken. Get them all here."

Kendle gets a move on, frowning when she passes me. I feel Dinah's heart skitter all over the place, but when I look at her, her face is a mask, hiding any fear she might feel. I push her onto one of the sofas and cross to the bar where I make her a Jack and coke. Not strong but I need her to mellow out a little because there is too much coming through the bond. I never believed my dad when he said he knew everything my mother was feeling. Now, I'm just learning to deal with the thundering, pattering of her heart and how my own emotions work to align with them. "Drink....slowly."

She cups the glass in her hands and takes a sip. "Thanks. What are you going to do?"

"Not telling." I begin pacing, waiting for people to arrive. Mom is the first with Sandra. They take one look at us and settle on the sofa across from Dinah. Normally, Sandra wouldn't be permitted to be here but I can't find the strength to kick her out. Mom might need her support because this could turn ugly fast.

People begin to trickle in and every fucking one looks at Dinah first. A growl builds in my chest. I hate them looking at my heartsong when she only has my t-shirt on, but their eyes aren't lecherous, just curious. Some even wink at me, grinning. Raine is the worst, catching Dinah's eye and giving her a thumbs-up and a smile. Hawk rolls his eyes but even he looks pleased when he passes me and gives me a pat on the back.

"Good work, brother."

Dinah twitches on the sofa and I turn a quelling–another nice big word from Swot–look on my cousin who throws his hands up in mock surrender before stretching out on a nearby sofa. Raine drapes himself over his heartsong...Exactly how I want to have Dinah all over me right now.

"That is all who is around. Including the old ladies and heartsongs," Grim lets me know. The big orc seems to be the only one who picks up on my tension, and after scanning the room, he steps in front of me blocking everything out. "Well? Ash'orde, Shay t'weh don?"

"I'll need a judge," I say in the common tongue. Asking explicitly for a or'gre'l-weh'ki turns my stomach. I don't want Dinah to hear me ask for a battle judge.

This is club business first. The bylaws, not me, will choose her fate, but she gets a fair hearing in front of the whole family first. Then the patched members will vote. Then if she is deemed safe, I take my heartsong to the people. I have more sway, more absolute power, outside of the clubhouse. I rub my tongue against the caps, reminding myself of the heavy burden I carry. One I always wanted until today. I might be sentencing my heartsong to death.

And if that is the case, I'm grabbing Dinah and my bike and getting the fuck out of dodge fast. We can go south. We can go anywhere; I don't give a fuck. No one is taking her from me. I'm ready to leave them all behind for her.

But first, I need to give them a chance to prove they are decent folk.

"Brothers and sisters. Your heartsongs." I look at Dinah and smirk because this is one fucked up situation. I am about to hurt her badly–she'll end up with multiple scars on her body by the end–but it is the only way I can think of to protect her. "You know I enjoy fucking this human. I have a fucking great time doing it and she enjoys it too."

Her face is hard and her heart is hammering like a jackrabbit. I take a deep breath, calming my own racing heart. She blinks, looks at me, and I see when she realises I'm asking her to trust me.

"Well, I learnt something this morning that makes me wonder why she came here in the first place. What brought her to our mar the morning after war drums were sounded? What made me want to have her choke on my cock?"

Property of the Green Bastards

My mom makes an outraged protest as do a few of the other heartsongs. I ignore it. Inside, I'm relieved. She has their sympathy. And she looks fucking pathetic right now. Messed up hair, no makeup, tears drying on her cheeks, and my black t-shirt pulled over her knees. She looks small and fragile.

"Turns out, she's my heartsong."

They cheer. A roomful of orc'i cheer. I meet Dinah's eyes and re-centre myself. The jubilation won't last.

"Shut up, you fuckers. Yeah, well she fessed up something a couple of hours ago. It doesn't concern just me but all of us. All of us in the club, the town, the territory. The whole fucking Badlands. And now she is going to tell you."

From joy to still silence in a breath.

"Axe, no. Please..." Her eyes are begging. "You said you'd explain it."

I lean in close and whisper in her ear. "They need to hear you say it. Prove the truth to them. Demand the law."

"Sha'dweh," she says softly. I smirk. This fucking woman. She speaks our language, she knows our laws, and she is going to prove to everyone in this room she is no danger to the club.

"Sha'dweh," she says, a little louder. Then again, almost a shout, "Sha'dweh."

Everyone and their ancestors start talking. Kendle glares at me, then Dinah and back to me. Others just frown or whisper to those nearest them. Whatever they are doing, none of them expects her to submit to being forced to speak the truth.

"Who will stand in? She wants to speak the truth..."

There are lots of ways, lots of magic or herbs that can be used as truth drugs but I pull out Cuddles and ram her point first into the nearest table. "Hold this to her throat. Ask her whatever questions you want..."

"What the fuck? What is this about?" Queenie, one of my road captains who has been away on a run, asks.

"The war drums," Dinah replies. She straightens her shoulders and goes to Cuddles, pulling the blade free before offering it to Queenie, handle first. "I don't know you. Be my first truth-judge."

Queenie takes the handle and puts it to Dinah's throat. My heartsong holds my eyes the whole time.

"For the record," she begins. "My name on my government papers is Dinah Smith. The name my parents and orc grandfather gave me is Di'or'nah-Ni."

The sharp point doesn't cut her. Queenie nods, lifts the blade away and places it on Dinah's forearm. "A lie."

"I am a man." The blade cuts in sharp and deep at the obvious lie. Dinah curses and I let it go—I have to or I'd be ripping the hand off my road captain for marring my heartsong's skin. Queenie pulls it back, cursing, but sets it at her throat again.

"Why did you ask for Sha'dewh?"

"Because I want everyone to know that even though my grandfather was Disavowed, I would never join their ranks. I would never intentionally hurt Axe, this club, its people, or any orc."

Shouts erupt from across the common room. Some are damning, but the majority are pointing out that Cuddles hasn't cut her.

The questioning begins. It is long. I refuse to sit because I won't show weakness in front of my people. I also won't let my heartsong stand alone. Hours pass. More detailed questions are asked by different members of the club and their heartsongs, each gets to hold the knife. There are two faint pinpricks of blood on her throat from when she told small lies—it seems she prefers fake strawberry to real strawberry—and five further cuts on her arm when she was asked to lie for proof that Cuddles works.

And she looks fucking stunning. Her chin is high, her voice grows surer with each ridiculously tricky question.

At last, my mom takes up Cuddles. She's been silent the whole time. Just watching, listening.

"Do you love my son?"

The only sound in the room is my growl. "Boonie," I bark. "Ask something people actually give a fuck about."

"I think they want to know." My mom smiles like she was the one who asked about strawberries.

"I haven't known him very long."

"Answer the question, girl," Boonie says, digging the knife into her throat.

"No." Dinah's cheeks are red and she won't meet my eye. Which I'm fucking grateful for because I don't love her either. We are soulmates but that isn't instant love. Our pull makes me want to fuck her and brand her, but I'm not stupid enough to confuse that with love. And it seems neither is she.

"You got a hearthstone handed down to you?" my mom asks. I freeze. How the fuck could I forget about hearthstones and the test?

"No."

"I'll get you one." She leans in close and says something to Dinah. Whose eyes get big for half a second. Boonie then hands my heartsong Cuddles and turns to face the gathering. For the first time, my attention shifts from my heartsong to the orc and orc-kin in the common room. They are drinking and chattering amongst themselves. "Listen up. I know the club will need to take a vote. And I want to thank Axe for letting us heartsongs and family be here to take part in the questioning."

Murmurs of agreement filter in from all corners.

"But! Regardless of the vote, we know from yesterday there are people–our people–who are traitors. Who sought to use this girl to harm us and our kin. That is no cause for celebration. I invoke Eve-tide as it is my right as the senior 'ajda and as the senior ole lady. It ends on the Eve of the Meet which is in two weeks. During that time, Ash'or'ash-Den and Di'or'nah-Ni will compete in the Dwen-weh'sen. You stay close. You watch over these two. Lay your bets, take sides, follow our old customs. But we are not to celebrate this mating until the kvari scum are taken and shown justice by our Ash'orde. We do this to protect the future of our or and our sol. May the safest hearth find you. Nam'dwen on lak're."

"Fuck, I'm bleeding and now I have to play games with a fucking king," Dinah mutters but people nearby hear her and laugh at her annoyance.

"Take your heartsong–"

"Hey, I never said he was my heartsong!" she shouts. Still as a tomb. This little brat! She meets my eyes and I finally, for the first time today, see some life in her. She waves Cuddles at me and grins. "We both have to acknowledge we are heartsongs, and I never said it...Ouch."

The blade has nicked the finger that was resting above the hilt.

"Fuck."

I snatch the dagger from her and spin her until she is pressed against my front, my hand on her ass, pressing her against where my dick strains against jeans. I rest Cuddle's point above her jugular.

"What did I say about swearing, Princess? Now, say nice and loud for the class. Who are you?"

"Your heartsong."

While the crowd voices their approval, I bring my face close to hers. "Do you want to play a game? Do you want

Property of the Green Bastards

to pretend you can outwit me? That you can escape? When we both know I'll catch you, fuck you, make you beg for my cock without any effort. What do you want, Princess? Do you think you can beat me?"

Her eyes dart around the crowded room before she dashes through the crowd. It howls and blocks her before parting to let her slip through.

I do some exaggerated stretches for the crowd. Cracking my neck and stretching, causing my brothers and sisters to catcall. Already, I can hear people making bets.

I'm fucking proud of my heartsong because the odds aren't so bad. Some people think she can win.

I watch her slip through the back door, probably knowing I'll guess where she's gone. There is no fun if I'm wasting my time tracking her down.

"Gre'dwen!" I shout to my people. Time to bring the battlefield to the hearth.

———

I CATCH her scent too easily which tells me she was waiting for me on the stairs. "Come on, little rabbit, you can do better than that."

"Oh yeah?" Her voice comes from the shadows.

"Yeah, Princess–" The word has us both stopping, the spell disappearing. We haven't really discussed the fact she's an MC Princess. "Dinah–"

"You don't have to do this…" she says softly, stepping into the dimly lit corridor. "If it is too difficult, I can leave."

I see red. Clearly, she doesn't feel the same. Clearly when she told my mother she didn't love me, that was it. Not all heartsongs love each other. "After all that–"

"Axe." She presses up against me. I soak in her scent,

the warmth of her body. "I want you more than anything in the world. Your mom let me save face when I said I didn't love you. I shouldn't. We don't know each other… but I couldn't live without you. You are my world. I realise who I am makes your position difficult. You aren't just the president of this club; you are the king. And people look to you, Ash'den…" She reaches up and runs her finger over the gold caps, symbols of my place in orc society. "You have to keep your people safe. I'll stand by that decision, even if it means leaving."

I know then I am going to make her my property. Honour her with every mark of respect my people, my club can give her. She understands our values without growing up with them. Or'dwea'ki runs through her.

"You aren't going anywhere. We'll figure it out. The club…the brothers and sisters, their heartsongs and families are gonna stand by us. You told the truth. They put a knife to your throat when you answered their questions and you didn't flinch. You revealed every secret you have, and I've never been more prouder."

Chapter Fourteen

DINAH

All my secrets. Not just to Axe but to the entire club. I should feel vulnerable, exposed. Instead, it feels like my burden has been spread out. The flood gates opened to create a lake. It fucks up everyone's life for a bit, but with time, the water will settle, some absorbed by the land, some moving on. But no longer mine to carry on my own.

All thanks to the monster before me. My monster.

"Mine. You are mine," I tell him. "Kiss me."

I tilt my face

"What a needy girl…but, yeah, I like that." His lips

come down on mine. A hard press because no one really tells you how hard it is to kiss with tusks. The moment I feel him step closer, grinding his cock against my body, I pull away just enough to slip under his arm and dash away. We have a game to play. It is ancient and primal, and I won't make it easy on him. My monster needs to prove himself to me.

"Catch me if you can, fucker!" I shout over my shoulder.

I know the Compound now just well enough to pick the exits which will take me to the back and towards the scrubland. He'll catch me, throw me to the ground, and fuck me like a beast. Then drag me back, caveman style, to his room and we'll fuck some more.

I hear his roar of frustration and it brings a fleeting grin to my face. He thought he had me caught already, but I'm going to prove to the most powerful orc in the Badlands, the monster who will protect us all, that he isn't going to have it easy. I'm not meek or sweet or any of the things he thought when he first saw me. I'm a fighter and that runs deep in my human DNA. Generations of hard-working people who never got a break. Yeah, those are the ancestors I call upon. Not the kvari cowards who sold our ancestors' bones for a quick profit.

Turns out, though, I don't know the Compound well enough. I skid around a corner expecting to find an ally to hide in. Instead, I'm face to face with the warg kennels. These beasts are scarier than Axe in berserker form. I freeze and begin to back up, hoping that Axe's scent covering me will make them think I am a friend and not a threat.

However, all hope of that flees when the largest jumps—without a run-up—over the gate, landing on silent paws in front of me.

Property of the Green Bastards

"Fuck." I hear a shout from Axe and then the pound of his heavy boots on the cement. The warg paces forward. "Down, Shadow," he barks. "Don't move, Dinah. Stay still."

I couldn't move if I wanted to. Then my heartsong presses against my back and the warg just watches us from where he lies down in front of me. I've never met a sphinx. Don't want to either because I value my sanity, but staring in the warg's eyes tells me what it might be like to gaze at the world's only creature without a shred of empathy. They say even a psychopath has more humanity than one of the great sphinx.

"His mate just had pups," Axe pants behind me, his arms wrapping around me. "They are feral in their desire to protect their pups…"

I can hear them now, the little yips as they search for their mother's teat.

"I didn't know."

"Of course not, Pah'pah. Let's leave them."

He backs us away, never turning his back on the warg he raised from a pup. That is how much he respects this predator and its urge to protect its young.

We edge out into the courtyard. When we're safe, his hands roam over my body, cupping my breasts over his t-shirt, gliding down to cup my unprotected sex.

"So wet for me. I should mount you here. Rut you like a warg on a bitch in heat. Everyone will come and watch me take you, see what a needy, seed-starved pussy you have."

"Meh Ash'orde…" I'm almost shaking with desire. Just as desperate for his cum as he claims. "Please. If you aren't inside–"

He cuts me off by biting hard where my shoulder curves into my neck. I feel the loss of his heat as he steps back. "I'm feeling generous, Didi. Run...go on...I know you want to."

I bite my lip uncertain if I want to pick up where we left off or if I just want him to hold me. Then the decision is made for me. The emergency exit opens and two people tumble out, their bodies pressed hard against each other and the sound of their masculine groans bouncing off the hard concrete. There is no direct way to get back into the Compound.

I begin walking, slinking through the shadows as much as possible–painfully aware that Axe is watching me, letting me get a head start so he can hunt me down like prey.

I skip past the line of bikes and wish I knew how to ride one because that might be a nice surprise for him. Instead, I'm left with my feet and wits, and he knows this place so much better than me. And there are so many people. My hesitation seals my fate.

Axe is on me, picking me up and depositing me on the back of a bike with a grunt. "Changed my mind, Princess. I like the idea of your naked, hot cunt on my bike. I want you to stain the leather with your slick. Come, be my good girl. You've ruined me, now ruin the leather of my bike."

He gets on and I scoot forward until I'm clinging to him, my arms around his waist. I rest my cheek on his cut inhaling the heady combination of leather and our scents.

"Ready for the best ride of your life, Princess?" The growl in his tone has my already needy body perk up.

The moment the engine revs to life, I feel my pussy pulse with a small, begging orgasm. The fucker is edging me.

"Go on, rub one out if you want." I retaliate by palming his erection. "Yeah, just like that. Fuck, Dinah. I never thought I'd have a heartsong, and I never thought she'd be as fucking kinky as you."

Property of the Green Bastards

We ride for an hour along roads I've never been on until we are cresting the north ridge which points in the direction of the Allteng. I know from the maps that there are caves dotting the cliff face, and my body tingles with a primal awareness. This is what I have been craving. We pull to a stop at the top of the ridge.

"Be careful when you go down the stairs. There is a rail but I don't know the last time it was checked. I'll give you five minutes…but after that, anything goes. Do you understand what this means, Dinah?"

"Yes," I breathe. "You are going to fuck me in one of these caves like the Teng did centuries ago. When we were spread across the Badlands and we were not yet civilised."

My breath catches in my throat. It is the first time I have referred to myself in any way as an orc. But tonight, my humanity seems to have slipped away, even if it is just until tomorrow. "The sun is setting…Better get going before you can't see."

I scramble off the bike and look at my orc. He was handsome the first time I saw him, he had looked so unconcerned and dominant. It is the same tonight, except now I am aware of the way his heart crashes against his ribs. We are in tune, not in sync. And my own heart fights to meet the raging need the rhythm of his pulse demands.

Five minutes isn't long, so I dash for the steps. The railing is actually chicken wire hanging from a pipe. I hug the walls, fingers brushing along the stone which is still warm from the sun. I pass the first cave and scent it, but there are lots of scents, so I move on. My long-buried orcish need for a cave that is safe and mine hums in my ears, and I begin to be less careful with my steps which seem even and natural as I run down them. At each cave, I inhale to see if it is right.

I stay too long at one when I hear the slap of Axe's

boots on the stone. I know he is letting me know he is coming for me. If he wanted, he could be as quiet as deep water. I hit a ledge and a fresh breeze touches my face, I look to my right and there it is. A crack in the rock. Big enough for Axe to get through if he army crawls where the gap is split wider at the bottom and a small stream trickles out along a channel.

"I can see you…"

"Fuck."

"What did I say about swearing?"

My heart is jack-hammering in my chest, and I drop to my stomach and crawl in. A strong hand grabs my ankle and begins to drag me out. I claw at the stone and kick with my other foot at him because if he wants me, he needs to fight me for it. He needs to prove himself. A particularly vicious kick loosens his grip and he lets go just enough for me to pull myself loose and crawl into the cave. My t-shirt is soaked because of the stream but I'm in.

I get to my knees and look around. The light from behind me isn't the only light source. There is a hole higher up and a shaft of evening light catches the veins of milky quartz that cut through the stone. The crack opens into a wide chamber that has clearly been worked on by others because there is a platform that could be used as a sleeping or eating area. And the freshwater means you could be here for days…if you brought supplies. It is perfect. I move back and wait for Axe to crawl through.

"You are going to get it, Princess. When I get to you. FUCK. Why? This is not what I had in mind."

I giggle and get down on my stomach to watch him wriggle through. It isn't so tight and I taunt him a little, relishing the way he growls and begins to drag himself forward.

"Looks like you couldn't just grab me." I smirk when

Property of the Green Bastards

his head first pokes into the cave. I watch with delight as he looks around.

Stupid, stupid, *Princess*, I berate myself. *You're now trapped with nowhere to hide from him.*

"Fuck."

I scramble away, looking for anywhere that might give me the higher ground, and all the while, I feel my nipples ache with need and the place between my legs swell with a need that fills my whole being. Suddenly, every fantasy comes rushing back. Getting stalked by some faceless monster, thrown against a cave's wall while he pounds into my pussy, filling me with cum. Now I have that, I'm scared of how turned on I am. It's so much more intense when I know it is my heartsong, and I see him standing to his full height. Or the way he shrugs out of his leather cut, folding it on the floor. The water from the stream drips down his chest and over the front of his jeans. There is no bulge there but I swallow my nerves when his hands go to unbutton his jeans and shove them down his thick thighs, just far enough that his cock hangs free.

"Take my boots off," he growls. I shake my head, knowing that if I get within touching distance, he will automatically gain the advantage. "Dwen'gri shej'd, Didi."

I flush. He wants me to perform a ritual of homecoming. "Shej wa'd? Then you'll let me go?"

He nods, and I take a hesitant step closer, then another. A feral animal being tempted with food…or in this case, a ritual where I welcome him into my home by taking off his shoes. Orcs don't wear shoes in their homes, a carryover from their nomadic past, and a host taking a guest's shoes off was a way of saying that they were equal. It's a way for the guest to submit too, showing the vulnerable soles of their feet, or putting their femoral artery in easy range of a hidden knife.

It is hard to ignore his cock, which is perfectly outlined in his jeans, so I focus on his boots, on carefully untucking the ends of the double bow then loosening the laces until I can ease first one foot and then the other out. I take his socks off, wrinkling my nose in anticipation of the smell but there's nothing rank. Of course not. The King of Orcs and my heartsong doesn't have smelly feet. I giggle.

"You like my feet?" A gruff voice says from above me.

"I like that your feet don't smell like ass," I say, sitting back on my heels and looking up at him, a smile tugging at my lips. His arms are crossed as he stares down at me. So in control…or that is how he wants to appear, but I see the way he is breathing through gritted teeth. Axe is holding back. "I didn't expect…"

"Yeah, well, that'll teach you to pick a cave I have to crawl into… Git, Princess. Unless you want me to feed my cock between those pretty plush lips of yours?"

Frey, I want that. But I also want our game. I straighten on my knees, my face now level with the monster he calls a cock. I marvel at how it hardens under my gaze. Thicker, longer, the texture becoming more defined, the veins bulging and the blood filling his shaft. I lean in, nuzzling at the crisp hair at the bottom, mouthing at the base and then trailing my tongue down to where his balls hang heavy and full of seed. I know I have milked him dry before but thank fuck nature will fill his balls again so that I can taste him, feel the warmth of his cum on my skin and in my cunt.

"Di'or'nah'fi…Princess…Didi…meh'pah'pah…if you—"

I suck one of his balls into my mouth, cutting off whatever he was trying to say. Primal instincts changed their mind the moment they were confronted by the most perfect cock and balls ever created. I'm compelled to taste him—all of him—so I release one ball and move to his twin,

Property of the Green Bastards

but I have hands as well as a mouth and I use one to cup the ball I had my mouth on. The other goes to his dick, my fingers don't touch but I give him a good hard squeeze at the base like he showed me. A groaned curse is my reward. Then a hand is in my hair, threading through the dark strands before gripping it in a ponytail. He pulls me back, and I reluctantly follow, my lips making a deliciously obscene sound as his ball leaves my mouth.

"What a tricksy little wench," he growls, using his hold on my hair to shake my head like you might shake a naughty puppy. "Sucking my balls like a little slut. What did you call me before? Daddy? You really are a good girl, my perfect little slut."

His words rush through me as potent if he was covering me with his cum. I have to take back some control, or I'll go mad with lust.

"Since when is having one lover a slut? Are you slut-shaming?" I ask, raising an eyebrow. He frowns, and I realise I wasn't teasing enough, that he thinks I'm being serious. "I don't think you are slut-shaming me. I'll be your slut, Daddy. If it makes you happy, I'll be your good little slut?"

I leave it as a question. This whole play is a totally new world for me where I am trusting him to teach me the rules. My own imagination is running wild but with no experience to back it up, I feel like I'm swimming blind.

"Give me patience, Frey. And turn your eyes elsewhere while I fuck this naughty, good, slut..." He tugs me up until I'm standing, then lets my hair go, smoothing it around my face. "Get naked. Kneel on the platform. Head down, ass as high as possible."

I narrow my eyes and step closer, my hands going to his cock. "I want to suck your cock."

"I want to fuck your ass, but we don't have any lube.

So, I guess neither of us is getting what we want right now."

"Fuck my ass?" I ask. That was not something I had ever thought much about. "Nothing has ever gone into my ass before, Axe…"

"You've got a lot to look forward to."

I reluctantly turn from him and head to the rock, pulling his t-shirt over my head as I go. Underneath, all I have are a pair of his boxers which I had to tie a knot in so that they wouldn't fall down. I kneel on the rock and then lower myself until the tips of my fingers to my elbows are lying flat on the cool stone. I wiggle my ass a little to settle my knees, and to get his attention which I discover I have in its entirety when one of his huge palms comes smacking down on the sensitive zone between my ass and thigh. I even feel the sting on the part of my pussy that is exposed.

His hands glide up the outside of my thighs, pressing my legs together instead of pushing them apart which has me confused. "Axe—"

"Trust me."

Then I feel it. His cock is pushing between my thighs and gliding between my folds, rubbing against my clits. I'm wet but not that wet, and there is a roughness to the way he pushes that creates a different kind of friction than what I've experienced before. When I try to shift he delivers a quick slap to my ass. "Just want to feel you like this. Imagine it… I've been chasing you. Your feet are sore because you're barefoot. Your knees, elbows, hands are cut up from when you fell earlier…"

His words spin out a fantasy where instead of stalking me through the Compound we are out in the Badlands. The way our ancestors claimed each other. I grind my palms against the stone trying to heighten the sensations. It isn't polished smooth so I feel the burn as I scrape up my palms. I do the same with my knees, gouging them into the rock. The fantasy becomes more real when he grabs one of my wrists and pulls it back.

"Bad, heartsong," he snarls, twisting my arm behind my back. He grabs the other and does the same. Transferring my wrists into one of his hands. "I told you to imagine. Not do. Bad." He pops my ass again. My sex gets wetter and I know he feels it because his cock is sliding between my thighs that are now clamped together. "You do not hurt yourself. Do you understand?"

"Yes."

"Yes, what?"

"Yes, I understand."

"You understand what?"

"Yes, I understand that I shouldn't hurt myself when you tell me to imagine something. Axe, it feels too good. Please...I need more."

"Who am I?"

I have to think. Does he want to be called Ash'den? Heartsong? What? But the only thing I can focus on is how he rules my body.

"My king," I cry out just as his cock notches at my entrance. I arch my back, hoping he will slide deeper, but he withdraws. "No. Please..."

"Call me that again," he growls, deep, low, and menacing.

"King. Please, my king." He thrusts forward, filling me, twisting my body so my shoulders protest. I just bend into it, hearing my back crack when I bare my neck to him. Orcs don't do mating bites but they like to mark up their heartsongs. I've seen Raine and Hawk covered in love bites, but their dark green skin disguises them. "I won't hurt myself–"

"Good." He holds me down by biting my neck, his

tusks are an ever-present reminder of how dangerous he is. I don't move because even the tiniest shift might cause them to bite through and cut into the sensitive skin.

Now that I'm pinned in place, he fucks me hard. A dangerous thrill takes over me. I'm no longer afraid of his tusks, instead, I thrust back against him, hoping to make him come without any consideration of my own pleasure. He is the centre of my world. When his cock swells and he comes with a shout, I feel him pulse within me and the warmth of his cum filling my womb, breeding me, marking me as his.

Chapter Fifteen

DINAH

Crawling out of the cave the next morning is less pleasant than crawling in. Big surprise there. Worse still, the smell of ozone is in the air, threatening another storm. I stick my cold hands under my arms hoping to chase away the chill that has nothing to do with the temperature.

I crawl through the crevasse and use the ruined t-shirt to dry off. Axe lies on his back snoring softly. His morning wood calls to me.

"I want to wake you up," I tell his sleeping form.

Biting my lip, I consider the best way forward. Do I take him into my mouth? Do I ride him? Do I just tease him with my tongue and hands until he wakes and turns me over to fuck me? And if he wakes up and tells me to stop? I'll do that. But for now he is mine to use.

"All three and in that order," I mutter. Crawling over him, settle over one thick thigh, rubbing my pussy against the bulging muscle. I make sure to take my time to fold in half and wrap my lips around the flared head. Sucking hard, I let the suction pull him further into my mouth. The deep groan from my heartsong has me repeating the action. With every suck I retreat just enough to create the kind of friction I think would drive me insane if our places were reversed. Hands, I remind myself. I grip the base of his cock and squeeze him in a pulsing, rolling motion like I imagine it feels to have my pussy milking him. With each new movement, I am vaguely aware of my hips grinding against his thigh. When he begins to push into my mouth instead of lying still, I slow. I have plans for him and they don't involve him coming in my mouth. There is something vulgarly erotic about how his cock bounces against his abs when I release him. A smear of wet left on the hard muscle.

Half afraid he'll wake up, I straddle him. Leaning forward until my breasts brush against his chest I rock back along his cock, smearing my slick over his length. "I'm going to fuck you," I moan into his ear. "I'm going to fuck you so hard, Daddy. Make you feel so good. You're going to wake up covered in my cum…"

I risk it and sink my teeth into his neck. Simultaneously I reach between my legs and hold his cock steady so that I can sink him into me.

"You make me feel so good, Axe," I tell him. All the dirty words and thoughts I've been holding close spill out. I praise this terrifying, sleeping orc for how he makes me feel. "You have so much cum. All for me. I bet you never had this much cum for anyone. You were saving your cum for me. Such a good heartsong, saving cum for your Didi."

I work my pussy up and down his cock. I clutch my breasts, rolling my nipples between my thumb and forefinger. I watch his face with heavy-lidded eyes. He's biting his bottom lip and the tendons in his neck stand out as he exposes his throat, making himself vulnerable in a way he would never be when he's awake.

"Meh Ash'orde dw'near he'dwe pah'pah. Give your heartsong your cum, Ash'ode," I growl as I grind down hard on him.

"Fuck," he groans as his hips unconsciously buck into me.

"That's it." I clench around.

"Fuck!" His eyes snap open. Now he is wide awake staring at me like he can't quite believe what he sees. "Dinah! Frey. Fuck. Yeah, that's it." He mirrors my words. "Shit. Not a dream."

"Do–"

"Harder, baby." He wraps his hands around my waist and urges me to move. "Best way to wake up."

I do what my heartsong wants and make each rise and fall more deliberate until his cock reaches deeper inside of me than ever before. I don't know which of us comes first. Does the pressure building because his cock is getting impossibly thicker tip me over the edge or is it the pulse of my pussy around his length that does him in? Regardless, we are coming together, making this raw fucking the most intimate moment between us.

I collapse on his chest, luxuriating in his racing heart which I simultaneously feel in my very being and hear where my ear is pressed to his pec.

"Morning," he says gruffly. He pats at my hair almost absently. "I think you blew my brains out."

"I promise I won't tell," I tease him.

"Brat." He punctuates the word by spanking my ass, before groping the abused flesh.

"Can you do me a favour?" he asks after a few quiet moments.

"Sure."

"Cuddle me?" He sounds so unsure. I make a sound of agreement and he eases me off him. I'm surprised as fuck when he rolls over so that I'm looking at his back. "Be big spoon, Didi."

I never thought I'd be big spoon with Axe but he seems to like the feeling of my breasts pressed into his back and one of my legs thrown over his hip while he holds my calf with one of his hands.

"I need to stop by the Barracks," I tell Axe once I'm settled behind him, nose buried into his neck. "To pack up and get clothes. Assuming you want me to move in?"

"What the fuck do you think?"

I roll my eyes, grateful he can't see me mouthing curses at him. This is all new. I know how things were done, not how things are done. "You didn't just shack up," I mutter. "Historically, you didn't move in together."

"Dinah?"

"Yes?"

"First, fuck history. I expect you in my bed whenever I want to fuck you there." The silence that follows makes me worried about what is coming with number two, so I try to turn him so I can see his face. "Two, when we get back, you are my heartsong. That means playing by my rules, the club rules. You aren't a citizen anymore. Do you understand?"

"Surprisingly, I don't know all the rules."

Property of the Green Bastards

"No sass." He pops me on the ass. "I'm not discussing club business with you. If I'm telling you to do shit, you don't ask questions. You can be friendly with patched members, but no more drinking with Raine—"

"We both have heartsongs," I point out. "Other than you, he is my mean friend. Well, him and Tool, who is my nice friend."

"Fine," he growls out. "Just don't do something inappropriate, like drinking in Kin'helm. If you want to drink, do it at the Compound. Tool is going to shadow you. It is still dangerous out there. You can get hurt. Until the Steel Prophets are dealt with, you and all the heartsongs are liabilities for the club."

I bristle and hate admitting to myself that right now, the biggest direct threat to Axe and the club is me. Axe wouldn't hesitate to take out a traitor or external threat. His words remind me that the club will always come first for him. I rest my head against his chest. Even with the truth out, I'm still a minor part of his life.

"The club might not trust you at first. Cuddles is fine, but it doesn't change the fact you have var'or in your veins and grew up with humans. You aren't one of them."

"Yet," I whisper. "I'll do anything to prove I belong here."

"I know, Princess. But it might take some time, and I can't be seen to take your side against the club. It doesn't work that way. If the club doesn't want you around, we'll go somewhere else. The club is important. It will always be the biggest thing in my life. But you are my universe, if you aren't there, how can I exist?"

I hold back tears and fall a little bit in love with him at that. I've never been this important to anyone. And there are no words to express what it means to me. All I can do is

243

clamber over him and kiss him. I can use my body to prove how precious his words are to me.

"Heartsong," he growls into the kiss. "I want to fuck you again. But you need food more. I need food. Then more fucking."

I would protest but the minute he mentions food I'm hungry. Ravenous. And, for once, not for cock.

Instead of going back to the Compound, Axe pulls into one of the motorcycle spots and drags me into the diner. Cherry is on duty and when she sees us, hand in hand, her eyes just about pop out of her head. The whole place is busy because it is lunch time and the silence is unnatural. Roughly fifty sets of eyes watch as Axe moves us to the same booth as before. He pushes me in first before draping his arm over the back of the banquet, fingers combing through my loose hair.

"I'll have a burger with everything," I tell my friend, who winks at me. She's full-on smirking at us as she backs away before Axe can order. When he looks up from the menu, she is gone. Suddenly, I remember how in a fit of indignant rage, I paid for his kids' meal the last time I was here. Fuck. This is going to be interesting.

AXE

There is a kids' breakfast plate in front of me, and Cherry is running away so fast, I don't have time to ask her why the fuck I'm eating this bullshit meal.

"I'll explain later," Dinah says as she slides my plate towards her and begins to cut up my food. In front of her

Property of the Green Bastards

is a burger that makes my mouth water, but she has pushed it far enough away that I can't reach it without making a big deal. Before I know what is happening, my "food" is in front of me, and my heartsong is telling me to, "Eat up." That is when it hits me. Offering food. Fuck. I take the bite fast before anyone sees what a complete simp I am for her. My reputation in tatters, I grab her meal and cut it up.

"Open up, Dinah." I hold a fork to her lips and she has to stretch her mouth wide open so that none of the burger sauce ends up on her lips.

While she is preoccupied chewing, I take a bite. Fuck, this is actually good. The maple syrup is covering the crisp bacon, and if you say there is a better combination of flavours in the world, find a new place to reside because Dwen'mar, fuck it, the whole Badlands, isn't for you. The combination is practically a national dish. I moan around a bite of the silver dollar pancakes as well.

"You sound positively sexual. I could watch you eat all day," my heartsong croons. "But I think you need more food. Want a burger?"

I grunt, and she signals to Cherry.

"Right. You wanna tell me about this?" I indicate the now empty plate in front of me.

"So…I was a little annoyed when you just left the day you brought me here." She looks at me through her thick eyelashes. My dick twitches because I've seen that look before she sucks my cock. "Anyway. You paid, so I paid for a kids' meal for you the next time you came in. I guess Cherry remembered."

I feel the corner of my mouth kick up in a smile, then there is a soft kiss printed right over it, followed by a quick lick.

"I like the taste of the maple syrup from here," she says quietly.

"Didi…" I growl in warning. "I'll fuck you right here if you push me."

Her breath catches and for a second, I consider doing it just to prove a point. You don't flash red at a bull, and I'm hung like one so yeah, the analogy is good. Swot would be so proud of me; I didn't call it a metaphor…Fuck. Maybe it is a metaphor. "What is a metaphor? You got book learning."

"Axe, I'm an artist. I don't know the difference between a metaphor and an allegory."

"Analogy," I correct her, feeling a little smug.

"I meant allegory." She counts them on her fingers. "Analogy, metaphor, simile, allegory."

"Why are there so many words for basically the same thing?"

"U'sea neh fret, Daddy." She pouts.

It isn't the first time she has called me that and I wonder if she is using it to get around saying pah'pah in public or if she wants me to go daddy-dom on her ass. "You need correction, little girl? You want a bedtime? Do you want me to cut up your food? And time outs when you're naughty?"

Her cheeks heat, and I'm not surprised that my cock swells. Yeah, I'd be her daddy if she wants that. Okay, fuck that, the idea of it really has my blood going. I feel her heart galloping the way it does when she is really turned on.

"Axe—"

"Burger!" Cherry announces loudly. I look up to see her two tables away. Dinah eases away and settles next to me. She looks all proper, except her hand is riding high on my thigh.

"You have something to say?" I ask the fiend when she puts my plate in front of me but doesn't leave right away.

Property of the Green Bastards

"Uh...Congratulations?" she says with one of those smiles only human-like mouths can make, lips pressed into a thin line and stretched wide across her face. She looks like a duck because the fillers in her lips still pout out.

"Thanks, Cherry. Girls' night soon?" Dinah leans forward, snagging one of my fries.

"Nice idea, Didi, but only if your friends are willing to come to the Compound," I warn her. Cherry's eyes get big and she nods, finally understanding that we aren't just fucking but that Dinah has moved in. That she is under the protection of the club.

"Sounds good," Dinah smiles. "I'll...Maybe you could stop by Elmeer's?"

Cherry just nods again. I watch her back away and then spin on a dime. Probably gone to gossip, spread the word. Which is exactly why we are at the diner instead of going straight home. The town needs to know the situation. Not just the bitches who want to bounce on my dick, but the mayor and the business owners too. And nothing spreads gossip faster than a waitress.

I WAIT outside the Barracks while Dinah packs, but Miss Krystal comes out for a chat disrupting the first moment of quiet I've had in a while. The brownie clearly has something on her mind, but I'm happy to wait her out.

"Axe, youse gots to be takin' care with that one," she says. Her accent is a strange mix of the highlands where she was born and Badlands. "Nows I's knowing a bit about what's goin' on up at the Compound. Your momma is a friend of mine. Buts I's gots to say youse takin' a risk bringing her to stay at the Compound. Lawman had his both eyes on her before."

"Don't give a fuck about that, brownie." I use her title

to ease the anger I know is seeping into my voice. "She is mine. I'm putting my claim on her."

"And if she gets the rocks in your pocket?"

Hearthstones. She's talking about the ritual that decides whose home new heartsongs will live in. There are rules but at the same time…

I mask all my feelings. That would cause problems. "She is the last of the Disavowed," I say at last. "I don't think the hearthstones will be an issue. 'Sides, I'm president of the Green Bastards."

The old creature, "Hmms," like I just said the sky was blue. And then rests her fingers on my arm. They are the colour of tobacco and the nails are stained yellow from age. "Then the territory is hers. You'd be uniting them. That land has been untended for too long."

"It is forbidden."

"And you know there are people on it."

I don't want to think about it. I don't have time to wonder what is going on there. I'm about as far from it as possible…until I remember that Kendle is going to be, or already is, heartsong to Ryder whose territory has the longest border with the old Disavowed lands. To protect her, I need the Badlands locked down.

DINAH

Back at the Barracks, I take a shower while Axe waits outside, then grab clothes, but I don't put on foundation or anything to hide my freckles. No, I throw that shit in the garbage. It is only while I'm brushing my teeth that I notice my bottom teeth are looking… more tusk-like? I lean in close to the mirror and run a finger along the

Property of the Green Bastards

straight, even edge of my front teeth until they bump into the tiny protrusions where my canines used to be. "Shit and cookies…"

This is information I want to keep to myself until someone else notices because I cringe at the possible embarrassment of someone looking at me oddly and saying they think I'm loopy.

Axe is ignoring the sheriff when I step out into the open. The younger man gestures about something in an undertone, and Axe just stares at his nails. I know the moment he senses me by the slight straightening of his body and the almost imperceptible way he turns in my direction. Our eyes meet and everything falls into place once again. This is the one person in all creation I was meant to find. There must be a logic to it because the necromancer who created the first horde was so skilled, she is worshipped as a goddess by three different magical species. Somehow, she decided fated mates was the way to go. If I could ever meet her, I'd want to buy her a drink.

"Nice work, Sheriff, finding Kid's body," Axe says when I walk up. I don't know whose benefit it is for, hell it could be both because my stomach drops at his next words. "I'll make sure he is dumped on the side of the Allteng."

The sheriff sucks in a breath. "Axe, this is bullshit. You know I have to report it. And the fact his jaw was broken. The coroner told me his eardrums were ruptured as well."

"Must have fallen down. You know how dangerous the scrub land is…"

"Axe," I interrupt because I'm not liking the way the sheriff is talking to him. I wonder if he is trying to scare me by revealing what Axe did to the prospect. What neither of them knows is that Raine already told me. "I'm hungry. And this conversation is boring."

His smile turns from taunting to lascivious in a heartbeat. "I know some meat I could feed you."

I can't stop the flush heating my cheeks or the way my body responds to his words. The bastard is playing two games. Getting me worked up and needling the sheriff whose nostrils flare when he turns to me.

"You can't be serious. You're idiots. Fucking idiots. You think this is going to make my job easier? I'm going to have to report this."

"What that Di'or'nah'Fi is Ash'or'ash'den's heartsong? Pretty boring gossip. Didn't know you were a fishwife as well as a lawman. Look, my heartsong is hungry. I'm hungry. So, fuck off."

Axe drags me to his bike. I glance once over my shoulder at the sheriff and notice for the first time this morning, he isn't in full uniform. Instead, he wears jeans and a button-down with the shiny star pinned to the breast pocket. My thoughts flash back to his comments, and once again, I find myself wondering who he really is, and what his motives are.

Chapter Sixteen

AXE

It is almost embarrassing how few boxes Dinah has. Three and a large suitcase.

"This all?" Tool asks, scratching his neck.

"Yeah." She tilts her chin up, daring him to say more. I see the insecurity there, underneath the forced word. I want to ask more; I will one day. She hasn't said she grew up hungry, but I am starting to think I owe her an apology for the way I talked to her in the beginning.

"Just pack it up," I tell the prospect, refusing to let

Dinah help as I dump her on the back of my bike and leave him in my dust.

"Your mom is going to be pissed we are only getting here now." Dinah puffs out her cheeks. Yeah, I'm gonna get a kick out of Boonie taking Dinah under her wing. I don't think she has ever been fussed over. Hell, Kendle will love her just because Didi will redirect mom's need to smother.

I'm not wrong. Kendle practically skips into the courtyard, a big grin on her face as she singsongs, "Mom is going to have your hide for not coming home first."

Boonie does look like a thunder cloud when she comes out, but that clears the second she sees Dinah. I'm completely ignored, which gives me a chance to talk to my sister.

"How's it going?"

"Good. Heph is coming to collect his bike. I'm…" She clears her throat, seeming nervous about whatever she's about to say. "I'm thinking of applying to the technical college down in Mayfair."

"What the fuck?"

"Well, you see…Boonie has a new project and I don't think I can learn much more here. If I was closer to the mountains, I could learn some of the dwarvish skills. I got sent a bunch of brochures–"

I growl. Only one person would dare try and tempt my sister like that. I'm going to castrate Ryder. "No."

"What? I thought you'd be happy. Besides, I haven't met my heartsong yet…"

"No."

"I–" Her face clears and you can practically see the lightbulb going off above her head. "You know who it is, don't you? Holy Frey. I should have figured it out ages ago.

Property of the Green Bastards

That's the reason you are so happy I'm working in the garage. Why you don't mind if I go partying with people outside the club…You know who it is!"

I look to where Boonie and Dinah still have their heads together but their mouths aren't moving so I'm pretty sure they are eavesdropping. Fuck. "Who your heartsong is, is none of my business."

"Bullshit, Axe. Bull-fucking-shit."

"Do not speak in that tone of voice to me," I bellow. Kendle stiffens and a single tear slides down her cheek. I look up at the sky and count to ten, but I can't get the sight of her crushed face out of my mind. When I look back down, the first thing I notice is the horns curling out of her head. They are small but they show off her fiendish blood.

"Shit," I mutter and reach out to her, pulling her into a hug. "I'm sorry, Ken. I'm sorry. I shouldn't have lost my temper."

"I just—"

"Yeah. Let's talk, but not right now. Okay? I mean it. Who your heartsong is isn't my business. I'm not telling you because it wouldn't be right."

"Fine." She sniffs. "But I deserve to know."

"Yeah…at the Meet. You'll probably see them then."

"Axe," Dinah says my name like she is talking to a wild animal. Fucking hell, I hate taking care of emotional women. Why are they always crying and bitching about shit that isn't their business or my business? "Your mom has something for you."

My sister steps away, wiping her face with the back of her hand which smears oil on her face. It is a kick in the gut. She'll be gone soon.

In her place is Dinah, her eyes reprimanding. Really? I want to say. You're going to take my sister's side? But she just raises an eyebrow. I shouldn't be able to read her expressions so easily. The magic of our bond, however, seems to act like an automatic translator. I know I'm not the only one because her face softens like she can read my thoughts too.

"Fine, what is it?"

Boonie reaches out her fist, palm up, and opens her hand. In the centre sits a stone, smooth but not polished. "Your father's hearthstone."

I pick it up, testing the weight of it in my hand. "You know what this means, Princess?"

"Check your pocket." She grins. I pat my pockets with my free hand and find something. When I pull it out, there is a rock with a thin vein of quartz running through it, the edges are a little rough which I recognise immediately. "From the cave."

I smirk, putting it back in my pocket and handing her my hearthstone. "Let the games begin."

Moving her in takes an hour, but by the end, we are sweating from carrying an extra wardrobe upstairs for her clothes.

I can finally slam the door on Boonie's back and turn to my heartsong. "I'm going to have to start with some rules."

"Now?" she asks. "I thought you've put them down already."

"Neh, didi. Weh'yu seh'she."

"Deh, Daddy." She smiles, coy and knowing. Smart prey. I close my eyes and beg for patience. "But you can't be with me at all times."

"No. I've got to settle for Tool."

"The map!" she says, clearly remembering for the first time since everything happened. She sounds so anguished.

Property of the Green Bastards

"I don't know what to do about it. I can recreate the drawing. Make a forgery to fool most people but...why? I still can't figure out why someone would want to steal it. The proof I am Disavowed isn't there, probably never existed."

"Does it matter?" I can talk about this later with her if she wants, but right now, I want to be buried balls deep in her tight cunt. Maps? We don't need old maps. "They probably took them for symbolic purposes."

"I thought about that...I'm missing something."

"Did I do it right, Ash'den?"

I run my tusks up and down her back until I can look right at the jewelled plug in her ass.

"I can't believe you own this," I mutter. I tug on the end, twisting and pressing it in.

"It was an impulse buy..." She wriggles her ass in my face.

"Dirty Didi." I bite the plump flesh in front of me. "One day, you'll take me here."

"Yes, Daddy," she whimpers as I spread her wide so that I have access to her hot, wet pussy. "Please, Ash'den... my king. I need you..."

"And what does my princess want?"

"I want you to...I want to ride your face," she says in a rush. "I want to come all over your face because you are... doing things to me."

I cover her back with my body, grinding my hard cock between her ass cheeks. I lean close so that I can whisper in her ear. "Are you sure you are ready for that?"

"Yes," she begs. "I want that."

I hold her hips hard enough that I know she'll have bruises tomorrow. My heartsong is still a little dainty thing.

I groan when she gives in and rests her pussy above my mouth. "When you said you were going to ride my face, I thought you meant you were going to ride, not hover. Good girls don't hover, pah'pah. Be a good girl for me and smother me with your perfect pussy."

She whines with need and embarrassment. Good. I like knowing I can affect her as much as she affects me.

"I love your taste. Like nectar from the Gods. Give it to me. I wanna stick my tongue–"

"Axe!" she snarls. Only fucking person who makes my government name sound like that. "Enough talking. If–"

I hook one of her knees over my shoulder, the other under my arm, and I now have perfect access to her two clits.

"I love when you…" she moans when I add my tongue. "I never knew it could be like this."

Her body shifts strangely and then I feel her warm breath on the tip of my cock.

"Fuck," I gasp as she takes me into the back of her throat in one smooth motion. I'm not losing my mind because of that though. And yeah, her mouth is perfect. Nope. Nope. Nope. There is another pressure on either side of my cock. The clamp-like sensation of getting a blow job from an orc. The way tusks can only add to getting head. I've never given it a second thought since I've been with her. Now though? The image of tusks on my girl has my balls tightening and ready to blow my load too soon. There is only one way to distract her.

I run my tongue from clit to clit before fucking her with it. Her mouth leaves my dick with a sloppy wet sound, giving me some relief from the heaven of her mouth.

"Axe, please."

"Give me one, Princess. Come for me."

"What about you?" she pants, her lips brushing against

Property of the Green Bastards

the base of my cock because she can't stop touching it even while she's moaning and gasping as she grinds her perfect pussy over my tusks.

"Go on," I tell her, running my hand up her back, wrapping my hand in her hair and holding her over my cock. "Open."

I thrust up into her mouth. Like this, I have complete control of her body. Taking and giving to her at the same time. Shit, this woman was born for me.

When she starts coming, I let go of her hair, letting her take over, so that I can focus on sucking on her clits, keeping her going, forcing orgasm after orgasm from her. She's protesting that it is too much before I let up. Allowing her to flop onto her back.

But I'm not done.

I move her into position before sliding my cock until I'm balls deep and rutting into her like a warg on his bitch. She's such a good bitch too, milking my cock and crying out my name, urging me to fill her with cum.

I'm a fucking softy for this freckled beauty that when she begs me again, this time in orcish, I let go. Coating her womb with my seed. I'll breed her tonight, tomorrow, the day after until her body swells in all the right places. "Fucking perfect, Didi."

She flashes me a tired smile, which reminds me of that fantom feeling of tusks on my dick.

"Can I have a glass of water?" she asks before I can look.

"Sure." I tuck a pillow under her hips before filling two glasses.

She's leveraged herself up on her elbows when I return, but smart cookie hasn't done anything to risk losing a drop of cum.

I wait for her to drink all the water before taking the

chance to see if she has tusks that I never noticed before. I've got her face in my hands, my thumbs pulling down her bottom lip. Tiny tusks like you might see on an adolescent have started to grow.

"When? How?"

"All that good orc seed," she says.

I kiss her, brutal in the way my tusks press against her mouth. I can taste my cum and it makes my blood hotter. My seed? Prompting her latent orc blood? I doubt the magic or the science of it. But fuck if the idea doesn't turn me on, make me ache to fill her with more of my cum.

"Hands and knees, Princess." I slap her ass. "Need to give you as much of my good orc seed as possible. Gotta keep you healthy, right?"

"Axe I'm tired."

Fine. I roll her over, slipping another pillow under her hips to give me a good angle. "Sleep, Princess," I tell her as I slip my cock into her prone, resting body. "Just let Daddy give you his cum."

"Will you mind if they don't get any bigger?" she asks while we are brushing our teeth the next morning. She's talking about the little tusks she showed me earlier. They are bigger than when we first met, and I'm happy if she is happy, but if they go back to their normal size, I won't mind either. There are more important things about her body I like.

"No. I'll be pissed if your freckles go away though."

"My freckles?" She wrinkles her nose, her mouth full of toothpaste. "Why the freckles?"

"Well, I figure you don't want to only have one clit. So I'll save my 'one thing I don't want Dinah to lose' to protect your freckles."

Property of the Green Bastards

Her cheeks balloon while her lips tighten around the toothbrush with repressed laughter. I pinch her nose, then she is choking and spitting into the sink. I stare at myself in the mirror. It hits me. This is the first time I've brushed my teeth with an adult. All the honeys I slept with never stayed over to get to this point.

Whatever happens, I'll keep her safe. I'm too much of a coward to say the words out loud yet. It isn't "I love you" so why make things awkward by saying something close to that?

I'm on my second cup of coffee when Hawk comes to tell me everyone's ready for church.

"It'll be fine. They voted Raine in, and he's a pain in the ass."

But before we can discuss Dinah's future in the club, we have to let the rest of the members know what we've learnt.

"First order of business: Eel. He's in the wind. The wargs couldn't track him down. So, stay on high alert."

We are sitting in the conference room and everyone looks like they've just seen their grandparents having sex.

"What the fuck?" Seems to be most people's response.

"Oh, there is more. He also stole part of the map Dinah was working on, which she thought had some information about her identity," Raine fills them in. "Don't make a big deal about it, but that is probably important."

"Eel?" Queenie asks. "Eel stole the map?"

"That is what Elmeer said, and the security camera from the gunshop picked it up," Swot confirms. "Don't get it…What good is a map?"

"Fuck knows. But why Eel? He's been a brother since before most of us were born."

"Are these maps the real reason you are having a Meet?" Vice asks. He was one of my dad's closest friends. Never wanted to be an officer—his heartsong is wary of the club—but he's a good brother and loyal to the club. "We need to know, Prez."

"No. That is for the war drums. We don't even know if they are connected."

"You know who sounded the drums?"

"Kid. And Eel is his kin. Orsol-kin." People shift in their seats. We haven't had time to have a proper meeting about it, and I'm pretty sure that there have been rumours, but the facts are always harder to swallow. "We don't know where Eel is or what he wants."

"Whatever he wants, it isn't good for the club," Grim says. "Look, he's a brother. But even good orc'i go bad. People do stupid shit. Get blinded by stuff. But I'll personally crack the spine of anyone who shares what we are talking about tonight with him. Got me?"

It is extreme, what Grim says. I expect the older ones to protest. They've known Eel longer. Instead, it's just stoney silence and a few people nodding.

"What do we do if he shows his face?" Hawk asks. Trust him to sneak in a question to get a hard rule that he and Raine can enforce.

"Same as we did with Kid," I say. "Truss him up for questioning." I meet every eye in the room. One after another. "We need information about what's happening. And if you hear anything. Keep it on lock down and bring it to the club. No selfless shit. We do this together. That is how a club survives."

I say all that unity shit but I worry, yeah, worry that if I get to Eel first there won't be anything left of him to question. He'd scared Dinah. Wanted to steal her from me.

"Does Dinah know?" Vice asks. The quiet is deadly.

Property of the Green Bastards

"That Kid and Eel are related? Because I know what we put her through, but none of us knew about Kid then. You kept that from us, Prez. I'm not sure how I feel about that."

"Vice, I get it." I put my arms on the table and lean in. "But I didn't want to bring speculation. I got the information about Kid a week ago. Had a meeting with the other clubs' presidents a couple of days ago. Then one of my brothers attacked my heartsong. Maybe there was time, but I'm not putting Cuddles to my heartsong's throat unless she asks for it."

Raine has the fucking nerve to laugh. "Yeah, don't think she's into knife play after the other night. No blood play either."

It breaks the tension. Everyone laughs. Smacking the table and smack talking.

"Right." Hawk stands. "Let's get onto something like debating whether we accept the fact our prez, the self-dubbed monster who rules the Badlands, can become a total bitch for Di'or'nah'Fi. I mean, we all know he's been fucking her every chance he gets. I can confirm he hasn't handed over his balls to her because he cut the colours off Kid. We also heard what she had to say–"

"Less talking!" Swot shouts. "Just vote. If you want Dinah to stay, raise your hand."

Everyone does. No hesitations or awkward glances to see how others are voting. Until I see those hands in the air, I didn't really get how much these fuckers mean to me.

"You realise she is Disavowed," I say, making eye contact with each one. "I'm going to draw a lot of heat for this."

"Prez, her or is weh. Stop stressing. We have your back," Queenie says. "Besides, bitches stick together."

"Fucking hell, you've all turned to mush. Anyone

261

saying no? Okay, dismissed. We can talk about what we do later."

Vice steps in front of me when I'm trying to leave the conference room. "I didn't mean to be rude about Dinah. Just thought, seeing as she is so smart, that she might know something."

I don't say anything and the old orc shifts on his feet.

"Seriously, Axe. Your girl? She was brave. We all saw it. Any say otherwise and the brothers would be on them, pounding their ass into the dirt while the sisters dig a grave."

Those are fighting words. Orc'i don't bury their dead. A grave is the biggest insult to any orc's dead body.

"Yeah, brother." I nod and pat him on the back. "He approached her. Scared the living shit out of her which is—"

"Freeda told me," he says, referring to his heartsong. "She saw how Eel went after her in front of the sheriff's office. Went and told Boonie."

I'm thrown back to that day. How my mom had come to find me in my office and yelled at me to find Dinah before the storm got too bad. I'd never asked how my mom knew Dinah had run but now I do. "Why didn't you tell me, Vice?"

"Shit was moving fast. You've been busy, man. You've been taking care of your heartsong. Figured it would come up. Just sorry I spoke out of turn like that."

"Nah, you're all good." I pat him on the back, and he lets me walk by.

"You're a good Ash'orde, Axe. Your dad would'a've been proud," he calls after me. My spine straightens, and my heart squeezes at the mention of my dad. He was some kind of mythical figure when I was a kid. As I got older, everything I wanted to be I saw in him. Fucking years of trying to live up to who he was. And now I have to be my own man. Face challenges he never had to. I'm starting to think, I don't know what kind of president, what kind of king he would have made in these times.

I raise my hand in a salute, letting him know I heard his words. "Thanks, brother."

Chapter Seventeen

DINAH

I curl up on the sofa in the common room with a shawl around my shoulders and an abandoned cup of coffee on a beat-up table in front of me.

Like a bolt of lightning, a long-buried memory throws me back years to waiting outside of the adult's bedroom while they discussed my fate. Could they keep me? Put me up for adoption? Returned to my dad's people? I suck in a breath and focus on soothing my heartbeat so Axe doesn't feel the change. The memory is hazy and unfamiliar like most of the ones from when my dad died, but the emotion

Property of the Green Bastards

remains sharp. What if they sent me to the Badlands? A child would be accepted. Only my grandfather had protested. Told everyone I would die if they didn't take me in. That long-forgotten conversation is when the fear started. And though I know in my sol—my bones—I am safe with these orc'i and my new family, my fight or flight instinct sparks to life. I sit up straight and look for Boonie who sits across from me.

"Boonie, what if they don't accept me?" My heart tugs in the direction of the conference room where Axe and the club are voting on if I can stay. It is almost a sure thing but…I'm Disavowed, and now everyone knows. A secret I'd wanted to take to the grave will probably be out in the mar by the end of the day. The only thing that had been decided on after we left for the cave was that no one would talk about my family until the club had voted. The only ones not in the room are the prospects. Tool is outside watching the bikes, and Dumbo is behind the bar cleaning glasses.

"Bitch!" Boonie howls with laughter from her place at a table where she works on making charms for the Meet. "You think those chrome dog riders are going to keep out a girl who was brave enough to let them stick a knife to her neck? You bet half of 'em woulda pissed themselves in your place. Ain't that right, Dumbo?"

"Yeah, whatever you say, Boonie," he says, but he winks at me. "Only reason they won't vote you in is if they want you to prospect."

"Axe would never," I say. Heartsongs can't prospect. "He'd never let me clean a toilet with a mascara brush."

Both of them nearly bust a gut laughing which makes me start laughing. This is nice. This is what it is like to feel accepted. And it scares the shit out of me. Before I came here, I had family, sure. But it was conditional, always a

265

quid pro quo arrangement. Since I got here, not one of them has called or written. I managed to look at my social media this morning–dial-up is a bitch–and nothing. Not an email or a silly meme, even though they've filled each other's feeds with messages and in jokes–ones I get but which I was never a part of. It hit harder than I want to admit. Even the "friends" I had hadn't asked how the new job was. They don't hate me; they just don't miss me.

And I don't miss them.

"Where did you go, sweetie?"

"Just happy," I say with a smile. "Axe said I could have some friends over…"

"Oh. What about two days before the Meet? Trial run before the chaos of the Meet?"

"If that is okay?"

"Come here." She flops down next to me and crosses her legs. Even at fifty-three, she is enviably flexible. Boonie grabs my hand to look at my palms. "Hmmm…this is good. Very strong lines and no breaks. You were always meant to be where you are. Your home is here. When the week is over and my son finds two stones in his pocket–"

"But–"

She puts her hand up. "Don't give up on the game even if you've already chosen to settle here. Pride, Di'or'-nah'Fi. Hear me, Fifi? For all the heartsongs coming into this family, we do not give up. No matter how crafty those orc'i are; we are smarter."

"Whatever you say." I think she is joking, but Boonie is steel and steel doesn't bend.

"As I was saying, once the week is over, you will be the most senior heartsong. You will be in charge of the parties. Of the Meet."

My heart drops. "I–"

"I will help."

Property of the Green Bastards

"But I'm not his property." I flush. We haven't talked about that other position. One that not all heartsongs have. "I know there is a difference."

"If he hasn't branded you by then, I'll make sure he does before the Meet is over. You will do it because you are by his side as his heartsong. The club will stand behind you the whole way so don't worry about that. Okay?"

I blow out a deep breath. "I wasn't exactly planning on all of this. There is a difference between the romance of heartsongs and the practical side."

"Ha! No shit. You look more scared of organising five hundred orc'i than you do of my son."

"Your son makes sense; I understand him."

"Then you'll be the first," she says with so much warmth in her voice that I crumble into her arms. The emotions of the last few days erupt and I'm crying huge gasping sobs into her shoulder, that have her pulling me close for a hug. She begins to sing a lullaby but instead of comforting me, it makes me cry harder. There is a vague far off memory of someone singing once, but I don't know if that is real or something my mind made up to comfort me.

> *"Sra'hwer dura hun'neh sura*
> *hua meh'lew'ka*
> *Sil'ra kwa'n say goki raem…"*

I feel her blessing. Magic. Not many orc'i have it. They were made from magic and therefore they have little ability to gather power of any kind. Boonie, however, is from the Silver Amazons, and I remember Axe telling me she could have been a Wise One, if she had decided to stay on the Allteng. As the blessing moves through my body, she rocks me back and forth like an infant. My sobs die and the heaviness of too many tears takes over, lulling me to sleep in her arms.

The next thing I know, Axe is picking me up, and carrying me back to our room.

He covers me with his heavy body and just lies on top of me, not saying anything. It is like the weighted blanket some people talk about. They seemed like such an extravagance, but I might beg for him to get me one now because I feel the stress melting away. "Axe."

"Yeah?"

"Are you going to get jealous if I try to steal all your mom's hugs?"

"Nope." He laughs and it reverberates through my body. "You are voted in. Now we have to play the game. I'll be branding you at the Meet. Symbolism and shit like that."

I roll my neck, releasing the tension there and in my shoulders. "That's good."

"You sound tired. I was going to fuck you, but I think this is better."

"What is?"

"Sleep."

Two weeks later, Axe enters the bathroom, eyeing me up like we didn't fuck a few minutes ago.

"Wait! No. No sex. I'm late already. I have a job, Axe. Fu…fudge. I'll get fired. Elmeer will fire me." It is easy to focus on getting dressed for work when you actually like your job. Besides, I just took a long shower and I don't have time to take another just to clean up.

"You don't have to work. You could just laze about."

"Absolutely not. I will continue to work. I'm not just going to lie on this bed, legs spread for you to fill me with

Property of the Green Bastards

your seed whenever you want! I am going to be more than a womb for your heirs."

He is on me in a flash, bending me over the sink. What I see in the mirror is hot. I can't deny it.

"Quick. Make your decision quick. I'm going to be working all day and I need to fuck you once more."

"Can you be quick?"

I want him to fill me with his cock. I should be too sore, too used, too something to enjoy the way he is using my body.

"Touch yourself. Make yourself come all over my cock," he orders as he fills me in one fluid movement. Practice makes perfect, and all that. But it doesn't wipe the smug smiles off both our faces as he begins to pound into me. "Didi, touch yourself."

I'm coming even before my fingers touch my clit. I know this will be quick, brutal. The hottest fuck we've had so far just for the way he is pounding into me, hand in my hair to keep me bent over at the waist.

Unable to form any coherent thoughts as that monster cock pumps into me. "I'm coming," I finally manage to gasp.

"Good." His hips smack into mine and I am arching back, wrapping my arms around his neck.

I go boneless so he catches me up in his arms. My back is to his chest, and he's spreading my legs over his forearms. It looks better than any porn the way I can see how his cock disappears into my slick sex. And like this his cock is putting more pressure on the second clit than normal. Almost too much. I close my eyes, trying to clear my mind, steady the fierce beating of my heart because otherwise I'm going to lose my mind to hedonistic pleasure. Which will make me useless for the rest of the day.

"Open those eyes," he orders. "Watch how I split you in half, little heartsong."

"Axe! Axe…Oh, Goddess."

"I'm going to breed you. Fill you full of orc seed. Put a baby in you. More than one. I want to fuck you while you are full of my child. The next generation…" His hand rests over my belly and he presses in as his cock begins to batter my g-spot. I feel my body begin to shake with the force of the orgasm that is coming up right by my cervix. "You feel so perfect. Milking me."

I can feel him coming, the way his cum floods my womb, and begins to leak out making a sound as it lands on the floor.

"Fuck, now I need to take another shower."

Second showers aren't so bad when your heartsong washes you, though.

My day off.

I'd forgotten about weekends since I started at Elmeer's. I've pretty much forgotten about the days of the week, but it has been about two weeks since I parked my car.

"Dinah? Are you coming with me or are you going to keep being gross with my brother?"

"Wait. You're hanging out with my sister now?"

"We are the same age. She is taking me to buy some new clothes."

"You need some money?" He catches my chin, tilting my face up, up, up until I have to meet his eyes. The emotion in them makes me blush, squirm…it's concern. "What? Why are you looking at me like that?"

"Looking at you like what?" I want him to tell me because I have no clue what my face is saying. I have zero idea how I feel. Weeks ago, I might have been angry, hurt, or have lashed out at his offer. When I took this job, I swore I'd never be a financial burden on anyone. Axe offering me money doesn't make me feel like a leech, but I still don't know why he'd want to do this.

"Like you swallowed a lemon but are excited to do it again?"

"I mean, no one has given me money before. Not without strings or guilt trips."

"People haven't bought you gifts?"

I remember solstices growing up. In bad years, there were donation boxes. Good years, we picked names out of a hat. One present each. They did try, I tell myself for the millionth time. "At Solstice, I got makeup to hide my freckles."

"That isn't a present," he growls. "A present is special. It should make you feel special."

He reaches into his pocket for a beat-up wallet. He pulls out some bills, not even bothering to count them. "Take these. Next time, I'll buy you stuff. I can't today, but I won't forget."

"You can't be serious."

"Didi, pah'pah she'es meh Ash'ni. Gha'ws hoo'er b'ine." His words translate into the sweetest thing anyone's ever said to me. Sweetheart, heartsong. My only queen. The one who shines brightly.

"I'm not a queen."

"You are my queen, Princess." His grin is crooked and so sexy, I want to stay here with him. "Get going. Buy pretty things. Something sexy that only I get to see."

"I knew you were giving me money for selfish reasons," I tease to break the tension. Kendle is still watching us and if I don't distract us both, I'll be begging him for his cock.

He leans in and raises an eyebrow at me. "Yeah, cause the only one orgasming will be me…"

"Oh…" I swallow. Axe derives an unhealthy pleasure from edging me.

"Shit, you'd like that, wouldn't you? How long do you think you'll last if I edge you? How long before I let my good girl come."

"I'm stubborn."

"Brat." He kisses my forehead, his arm wrapping around me, pulling me into his chest so that I can hear his heart and smell the leather of his vest. Two weeks and Axe gives me more affection than I ever got from my family. I soak it in until the sound of retching breaks the spell.

"Please get a room or can we get going to spend all that money?" Kendle whines.

Shopping with Kendle is akin to fighting for your life, especially with Dumbo restlessly pacing, waiting for us to finish up. He acts like we have five minutes before we need to run for our lives, while she acts like we have all the time in the world. After the pharmacy–where Kendle indiscreetly throws a couple of pregnancy tests into my basket– and a generic clothing shop for underwear, we end up in a shop in orc'helm that is full of leather and loose-fitting dresses and items you can layer. The clothes are nothing like what I've worn before, but she assures me I need to shop here and nowhere else. She drowns me in clothes, stacking them over my arms before ordering me into the changing room.

"Hey, Kendle?"

"Yeah?"

"You aren't into clothes…So, why all of this?"

"Just because I hate clothes doesn't mean I know nothing about them." I can practically hear her rolling her eyes. "You need to look the part."

Property of the Green Bastards

"Have you ever thought about looking the part?" I ask as I push the curtain back to show her the outfit of leather trousers that'd be perfect for riding on Axe's bike.

"I won't. I don't want to leave my family."

It hits me. "You're shy."

"No kidding. I hate people for the most part."

I deliberate it for a heartbeat. If I were her, I wouldn't want to be hit out of the blue with the truth. At the same time, it isn't my place to tell her because if there was ever someone who'd resist Ryder, I'm starting to think it is Kendle. Axe might not like it, but men stick together and I assume that Ryder is as much of a caveman as Axe.

"Just be prepared," I say softly. "You might have to leave—"

"You—"

"I'm only trying to say that finding a new place can be scary, but it is also a chance to explore new things."

She laughs. "I'm not sure if that is blunter than Axe or more subtle."

"Let's call it both."

"Fine, let's spend all of his money."

"Deal, but I'm not spending the rest of my life dressed properly. I need to find out where Cherry buys her clothes and blow the bank there."

I GET BACK FROM SHOPPING, carrying my bags and Kendle's. The minute we stepped back into the Compound, I'm immediately being dragged into the kitchen where Boonie has laid out all of her lists and notes from all the Meets she has ever organised.

"Boonie…I need to get these things put away."

"Yes, yes. Just give me a little bit of your time. I know it is your day off but there are going to be thousands of orc'i and other kin descending on the mar soon and there are details we need to go over."

She prattles on and begins showing me all the things she has learnt over the years. This is her life. From eighteen to whatever her age is, Boonie has been the senior heartsong, the most important woman in Dwen'mar. Fuck, her husband was king. She might as well be a queen. And I'm taking on that mantle from her. All of what I want–the art and the artefacts, hell even the forgery–will have to be put aside.

"Boonie, I need to find Axe about something," I say after a desperate minute of freaking out.

"Go, go, I'll be right here." She makes a shooing gesture. I dash to her side to give her a back hug.

"You're amazing," I whisper. Her hand comes up and pats my hair.

"You're a sweet girl. Now go find that boy of mine."

"Thanks." I kiss her cheek and run off.

Axe is in his office, squinting at the monitor and using one finger to type something out.

"Hey, do you want to dictate?" I ask when I get to his side. "Or is it club business?"

"You can type?" he asks, amazed. I roll my eyes.

"Better than you." I slide onto his lap then decide fuck it and straddle one of his thick thighs. "Begin."

"This is going to the other MCs for the Meet. Rules." He talks fast and while I can type, I'm not perfect and this operating system is so old that there are none of the red squiggly lines to let me know there is a spelling mistake.

We get to the end and I lie back with a sigh as his arms wrap around me. One of his hands cups my sex over my jeans while the other rests over my left breast.

"I want to keep working at Elmeer's," I say after a minute. "Boonie was showing me what she does and…I'm not good at that kind of thing. I want to be useful but the club needs someone to rely on."

"Did my mom say she was retiring?" he asks.

"No. Just that it was going to be my responsibility."

"Ha. Princess, you think Boonie is going to hand over the keys to her little kingdom? She turned fifty-two years ago. She might stop when you have a kid, but most likely, she'll just take on more babysitting duties."

"We haven't talked seriously about kids." I bite my lip. "I mean, we've talked about it during sex but that is kinda different."

"I want to see you round with my kid. I want to fuck you when you are complaining that you can't see your feet. I'm going to lick each stretch mark you get…"

"Axe, what if I'm pregnant?" The words come out in a rush.

"How? I mean, it hasn't been…" He frowns and I imagine he's counting. Maybe not the number of times we've fucked, because I've lost count, but definitely the days. "What twenty days? More? I was away… You weren't talking to me—"

"We fucked that day too," I point out. "I haven't been on birth control, and we haven't used condoms."

"When can you know?" His heart is hammering so hard I feel it in my chest more than normal.

"Now, I guess? I have a test."

"No point in wasting time," he growls.

"Yeah," I breathe.

He pulls me into the bathroom across the hall and orders me to pee on the stick.

"You don't need to watch," I protest. He just crosses his arms. It is the longest three minutes of my life because he paces back and forth.

"You had more chill when people had a knife to my

neck," I snap when he looks at the stick for the fifth time, causing him to storm back into the hall, and leaving me to watch the second line become visible. "Axe!" I shout. "You want to know–"

He must have been standing just outside of my line of sight because he is back, snatching the stick from me.

"Pregnant, good. Good." His voice is gruff. Instead of saying anything to me, he turns the shower on. While it warms up, he begins stripping my clothes, hands lingering on my curves, ghosting over my flat stomach, and dipping between my legs to rub my clits.

"My good, very good, heartsong. Fertile. Should have known," he mutters.

"Axe…"

"I'm going to fuck you," he continues to talk, mostly to himself. "But you need to get back to mom before she sends a search party, and I have church. While I want to walk in there smelling of you, I need to focus. So it will have to be shower sex. Can't be hard while I'm making decisions. When I'm done, you'll be riding my cock until you pass out and then I can fill you up more. I won't stop fucking you until the sun rises."

"Then you need to be naked too," I remind him.

"Get under the water," are the first words he says to me. He strips. T-shirt flying, jeans and boxers left in a pile on the floor. His dick is so hard it slaps his stomach when it springs free. When he steps under the stream, he crowds me against the wall, the cool tiles on my back. I know what he is going to do the second before he cups my ass with his hands and hauls me up his body. The head of his cock notches my opening, creating the most perfect friction against my second clit. But that is all he does. No moving, just teasing me with the flared tip.

"Please, you have to move," I beg.

"You have no idea how the first moment is. The first inch. How tight and wet you are against my cock…You just don't know," he groans. I squeeze around his tip, feeling empty and full at the same time. "Fuck, Didi. Do that again."

I clamp down again and when I'm at my tightest, he fills me with a single, brutal thrust. I feel every inch, every ridge creating delicious pressure along my inner walls.

"Oh, god. Oh, god. Oh, god. It's too much," I pant as I lose control and begin to uncontrollably pulse around the invasion.

"Yeah, you feel it, don't you? How I make you come just by sticking my cock inside of you. So fucking desperate for my cock," he growls against my throat before latching onto the muscle, biting into the flesh while he pounds into my cunt.

I'm a mess. My brain and body are dislocating from reality as he claims me. Already, I'm his. Already, I exist for his whims. But for the first time, I think he might exist for me as well.

"Mine," I gasp on the next brutal thrust. "You are mine."

He finishes with a shout. His cock swells, and the unmistakable sensation of my womb being flooded with his seed sends me over the edge in one last earth-shattering orgasm. He leans back just enough to look at me. "I belong to you? No shit. Fuck, yeah. I'm yours."

Chapter Eighteen

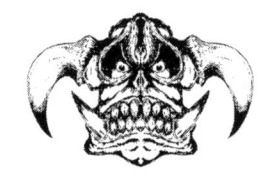

AXE

She is asleep, but I can't stop touching her. Resting my head on her stomach where she is growing our child. She peed on seven sticks last night. After the first one showed positive, there was something so satisfying about seeing the scientific confirmation. I went out and bought more while she kept drinking more water.

The pharmacist is a basilisk who wears blackout glasses which ensures the safety of clients but also the privacy of people like me who don't need the entire mar knowing they are buying pregnancy tests. Soon, though. I'm consid-

Property of the Green Bastards

ering taking her south where there is a hospital with human tests and scans that might make Dinah feel more relaxed.

Our child.

I'll be a father, something I'd accepted I'd never be. Even a conversation with Sandra reminds me I considered my heartless status and having no heir a good thing. There's a whole mystique around the horde kings and I wanted that to die with me. No future generations to bear the responsibility.

But now, there will be an heir.

NEAR DAWN, I'm jolted from a dreamless sleep by the sound of drums.

At first, I thought it was a mistake. But the second hit resounds in my head like the kvari bastards had brought the drums into my room.

I roll off the bed and drag on a pair of jeans, my cut, and my boots. Then I rip open the window and jump out, landing with a jarring crunch on the hard concrete. Fucking hurts to do that but I don't have time to waste. I take off for the gates and arrive at the same time as the rest of the members. Orcs are already mounting their chrome dogs and shouting to let the wargs loose.

Whoever these cowards are, the club is ready. We see them as we approach the empty plaza where the roads all meet, and the fuckers must either have mush for brains or balls of iron because they stand in plain sight. There are three of them; the biggest stands, shoulders thrown back, beating the drum like he has an army behind him. The other two are smaller, probably adolescents, too stupid to know they are throwing away their lives on a useless cause.

All around us, lights are being turned on, candles lit,

and people flicking their curtains back to look down. I get off my bike at the same time the sheriff arrives. He is flexing and fisting his hands, but when I catch his eye, daring him to take my prisoner, he just shakes his head, making it clear he won't be interfering.

I'm not surprised to find out the leader is Eel, but from the muttered curses around us and the sound of people spitting, it seems the others weren't ready to see one of their brothers leading the traitors. The boy is Kid's cousin, again, I'm not surprised. The last, I don't know. A girl, probably the same age as the boy. Maybe they are heart-songs? Who the fuck cares?

"Gris'e Driftas Nem w'esha! Jjit hwe'a Driftas OrSol weh orc'i!" the girl screams. It takes a minute to realise she is their leader. Eel bellows the words again, his deeper voice carrying them farther and over the snarling responses of the club brothers and sisters.

"Eel, give it up." I don't honour their defiance with orcish. I sure as hell don't acknowledge the girl. They want to cause a scene? They'll be treated like the outsiders they have proven themselves to be.

"Bring us the heir!" Eel says. He sounds bold, sure that whatever this bullshit is, he'll come out on top.

"Take 'em quiet," I say. Unnecessarily, apparently. The officers come forward, quietly menacing as the scent of ozone arises, signifying their shift to berserker. Each of them growing larger, more primitive.

Again, the girl is the one who shows the most backbone and the boy only protests when Queenie throws the girl to the ground, pressing a knee into her back while she cuffs the struggling varor'hew.

"Set the drums on fire," I toss the order out, not giving two shits who destroys them. I just want them gone in case another traitor or some idiot comes to get them. The

Property of the Green Bastards

burning drums has the prisoners shouting out curses again. "Fuck. Either shut them up or break their jaws. Don't want more witnesses."

"Where are you taking them?" The voice at my elbow has me twitching. I look down at the sheriff and my nose twitches as the feral scent comes off him. Fuck, he isn't human. Interesting, but for another day. At least I don't think he'll hurt Dinah now.

"Honest justice."

"Eoia'f le grah sews," he whispers in a language I don't recognise. "I'll come with you."

"No."

"I have my reasons, Ash'or'ash. I came to keep the peace…which means I am the person pulling the trigger."

"Well, fuck me." I chuckle.

"Thanks, but no. You aren't my type."

"Frey, when did you get a sense of humour?"

"When I realised she was going to be safe."

"You gonna tell me who you are?"

"Not today."

Guess I just gotta be happy with that because he moves away to talk to Dumbo. The prospect comes to me with a weird look on his face. "Prez, he said he was coming with us and wanted my bike."

"Put him on Tool's. You ride with us. Tool stays."

"He won't like that."

"He gets to protect the most precious—"

"Yeah, yeah. We know you think your heartsong shits roses but—"

I cuff him—not hard, but to knock some manners into him. "You wanna ride bitch with the sheriff or you wanna tell Tool he has to loan his bike to the sheriff?"

"Yeah, fine."

I go in search of Raine then. He's talking with Swot at the edge of the crowd. "What you got, Prez?"

"Call your little shit of a cousin."

"Which one?" He smirks.

"Ryder. Find out who else had drums."

"I'll take care of it," Swot offers. "Take Raine with you."

"No. I need you to gather intel on the girl. Take her picture or whatever you need to do. Then hunt down her people. Fuck it. Break into the mayor's office if you need better internet. You can send her flowers."

"I'm gonna fuck her daughter." He smirks.

"You sick—" I shake my head, remembering he catches more tail than anyone in the club. "Fuck. Just deal with it okay?"

THE SUN IS UP ENOUGH that we can go to the ridge to take them to the ledge. The patched members line up, spitting and cursing as the strangers walk past. But when it's Eel's turn, one by one, they spit at his feet and show him their backs. Eel growls at the first brother's rejection. About halfway down the line, he is level with Vice, who is maybe ten years younger.

"Shelly wouldn't be able to look at you. Her sol and yours will never be reunited. I'll make sure of it," Vice sneers before turning his back. Shelly was Eel's heartsong who died when I was a baby. Some kind of cancer.

Eel makes a start to wrestle free to get to Vice, but the ease in which he gets dragged away is pathetic, eventually, he gives up everything and stumbles off. He'll be useless in the questioning, too broken to be able to give a shit. Still, I'm going to get some answers out of him before his execution.

Property of the Green Bastards

We take them to the ledge where we questioned Kid, chaining them to the cliff. No one cleaned up the mess and dried blood stains the rock. The crazy girl continues to scream, so Queenie gags her with some rope.

"You know what you did," I tell Eel. "And on top of the drums, you scared the shit out of my heartsong."

That surprises him, his eyes blasting open and focusing on me for the first time.

"Driftas weh quirl jar'neh varor I'car Di'or'nah'fi." His voice takes on this pathetic longing when he claims that the Disavowed's honour is cleaned because Dinah's blood isn't spoiled. "Her or is human. She is pure. Frey blesses us."

Dumbo gets there first, his hand going around Eel's throat. "The Disavowed have nothing to do with seesee Dinah," he spits.

"I patched in before you were born, dickless cub," Eel snarls.

Dumbo roars, and if Hawk hadn't been there to pull him off, Eel's neck would have snapped like a twig.

"Varor. I don't want his words, prez," Queenie snarls. Never, I want to point out to Eel and his sidekicks, should you piss off Queenie. She's a Road Captain for a reason. Tougher than most dick swingers and vicious when she needs to be. Right now she looks ready to castrate Eel with a wet fish. "Give me his blood, Prez. Make the fucker bleed."

I rub my hands together. Make a big show of loosening my wrists. Shaking it all out. Fucking show, that's for sure. I need to plan. Nothing like a show of force but we need more intel.

"Eel? You gonna help out your brothers? Answer our questions? Get some weh back before you meet your ancestors?" I ask. "Come on, you slimy shitter. What do you want?"

His face goes hard.

"He's not going to speak." Grim scowls like he just doesn't understand. Fuck, I don't either. Turn your back on your club? The people you chose to live with as more than family?

He really isn't. Shit. I don't know if I'm surprised or not.

"We could make him talk," Raine muses. He's got that butterfly blade out, dancing between his fingers. Something about that end isn't right. I can't shake the need to… be better.

"You know what? I'll let you stand and fight."

His eyes bug out like he didn't expect it. Well fuck you, asshole, not all of us are without weh.

I pull Cuddles out of its sheath. "Cuddles can only hurt liars. You really believe the Disavowed are cleansed of their varor because Dinah is pure, Cuddles won't make a scratch. But I'm not a saint. You'll still earn a bullet between the eyes."

"You sure, Prez?" Vice asks. He wants to know if Eel deserves this honour. I nod. I'll give him this. He's a brother. This madness is new. Never knew him to be anything but loyal to the club…and, yeah, as much as he deserves to have his bones buried in the dirt, he was part of this club.

"He needs to lose those colours first," I say. "You want to do the honours?"

Vice nods and pulls out a lighter. It'll take time to burn off the tattoo on Eel's shoulder with that little flame. Fuck. He must be madder than me. But then he's known Eel for a long time. Queenie tosses Vice a flask, probably full of her favourite moonshine. He takes a swig and then pours the rest over Eel's shoulder. Neither of them looks at each other which creeps me out. Fuck, the only sound is the

Property of the Green Bastards

crazy bitch screaming behind her gag. Even the adolescent male is silent. Pissant actually pissed himself as well. Coward. Never stops to amaze me that people without honour are cowards. Like somehow, they can do their shitty little stunts in the dark but the minute you shine light on them, they scuttle away like cockroaches.

The first hiss of pain makes me look at Vice. He's got the lighter against Eel's shoulder. The skin begins to burn, and it's not pretty, but it's fucking satisfying to see him in pain. Can't even think how Dinah felt when he came at her, but it was bad enough that she ran.

He starts screaming when the skin chars black and the flesh underneath is revealed. He stamps his foot into the stone. I'm not sure if it's intentional or not but he looks like he's trying to beat those war drums again.

By the time it's done, I'm ready to move on. "Unchain him. Time to let him earn a bit of honour back."

Eel stumbles, fucked up by the pain. But follows like a freaking lamb when he's pushed into the circle of patched members.

We slowly dance around each other, crouching low. The only sound is our bare feet on the sandy stone. His hands are raised in fists. Against me and Cuddles, he has no chance.

With a shout, he charges straight at me. I catch him, feeling Cuddles go straight into his guts like butter. I'm almost surprised. He didn't believe it. He didn't believe whatever he was thinking about as he charged me. Fuck. I hold him close while I twist the knife so that I can whisper in his ear, "I'm wiping you and the other traitors off the face of this earth if it takes my whole life. Your bones will be buried in the dirt. No one will mourn you. No one will remember you."

"Meh Ash'orde y'or dwea ent dwen ent weh crill meh'-

varweh," he somehow manages to say through the blood bubbling out of his mouth. But I am in no fucking way using my responsibilities and honour to kill this honourless shit. "Tell the Ash'ni that I'm sorry."

"Criw," I snarl, never. I take Cuddles and spear him in the abdomen again, dragging the blade down, splitting him open. His guts spill on the floor, steaming and stinking. There is less blood than you might expect, but the floor is going to be slick with the stuff in a minute. You can survive being gutted like this. It's not enough; I need more. I need to see the fear in his eyes when he realises I am going to take my time. I'm not satisfied with disembowelling him, so I carve an X into his forehead, then bury Cuddles into his eye.

I step back and he falls to the ground, the life draining out of him. Somewhere above us, vultures scream. "We'll leave the body for the carrion birds. Then bury the bones," I tell them. "Well, boy, do you have anything to say for yourself?"

He shakes his head, tears pouring down his face mixed with snot. Real fucking classy.

"No," he croaks.

"Let me?" the sheriff asks. I look at the other members, and they nod or shrug. He isn't one of us, they don't care about him.

"We are going to have a nice long talk when we get back," I tell the human lawman. He raises his chin in acknowledgement.

"For disturbing the peace, you are going to miss dodging this bullet." He pulls out his pistol, twirls it like he is some kind of circus sharpshooter, and puts a bullet in between the eyes of the boy. I wait for him to do it to the girl who is foaming at the mouth with her meaningless, powerless curses.

Property of the Green Bastards

"You want to talk to the girl?" he asks. "Girl, you know you are lucky you are getting my justice instead of theirs?"

"This is not justice," she hisses in an oddly accented common tongue. "I demand–"

He pistol whips her. "You were hissing curses in the language of the Gods, you fucking piece of shit. Be grateful that they are not here to hear you."

Yeah, this fucking lawman is sitting down and telling me who the fuck he is when we get back.

"You–"

He raises his arm for the second time. Then thinks better of it. "Can you unchain her?"

I signal Dumbo to remove the manacles.

He waves the prospect away and walks up close to her. When he is within touching distance, he whispers, the wind carrying his words to the rest of us, "Fly, little bird."

Her face goes still and she nods, then like a zombie, walks to the edge of the cliff, spreads her arms out like wings, and falls into the canyon. At the last moment, he raises his gun and fires a single shot which catches her in the back of the head as she falls to what would have been a certain death.

"You can never be too careful," he says as he reholsters his gun.

"Shit, what are you? A god?" Queenie asks.

"No." He laughs like the idea is absurd. God or not, we are the orc'i and a necromancer–not a god—created our race.

WE GET BACK to the Compound, and there are a bunch of people standing around the gate wanting to know what is going on.

"I'll take care of it," the sheriff says.

"Thanks." I hold out my hand, and we shake on it. "Move out of the Barracks though."

"Yeah, whatever." But we both know he and Dinah shouldn't have been there from the beginning. Fuck, maybe that is part of it, maybe it's a bad luck trigger having non-humans in there. Except, for my heartsong, and as much as I don't want to admit it, the sheriff are not bad luck. Fucking blessings.

Blessings. Shit. I left without telling her where I was going. Not like I think she thinks I'm hurt…but, yeah. Not a great look when you abandon the mother of your kid and take most of your best people with you.

I slam through the Compound's main door, stopping abruptly in the common room where I see her going between tables and pouring out coffee for the other heartsongs, calm as fuck. She sees me, nods, and gets back to what she is doing. I'm pissed because I want to know why she isn't running into my arms, asking if I'm okay. Fuck, even if I am fine, she should be worried. What is wrong with her? Then I just can't help the smile curling at my lips. I think it is time for her to get taught a lesson.

Stalking my heartsong soothes my more primal side. She senses my presence and picks up her pace. I hear her tell someone she needs to go, and she places the coffee pot down. There is one nervous glance over her shoulder and then she really is moving through the gathered orc'i, not even bothering to acknowledge them.

I intercept her at the door that leads into the back. "Well, well, well…The little rabbit running away from the big, bad warg. And why is that, when you should be running towards me?"

"You look a little pissed off." She shifts so the door is at her back. I know her game and sling her into my arms before opening the door and carrying her into the still dark hall.

"You can put me down," she says even as she puts her arm around my neck and pulls herself up until she can press her lips to my neck.

I don't bother going to our room. The office is closer, and my cock likes the idea of showing her a bit of discipline in an official kind of place.

"Does my heartsong not worry about me when I take down three murderous traitors?" I ask, pitching my voice low and dangerous.

"I don't think it is possible to worry about you." Her voice is breathy, needy. "I know you are strong, powerful, relentless, without peer. Nothing in this world is a match for you, Ash'den."

Fuck, does she know what she does to me when she calls me that? How reverential she sounds?

I put her down, ready to bend her over my desk like that first night.

She drops to her knees, hands on my belt before I can stop her. I'll let her have what she wants, for now, then I'm taking what I want. I'm already hard when she pulls me out, but, yeah, my cock gets harder than steel when she puts her mouth on the tip and sucks. Her cheeks hollow out while her tongue runs up the slit, putting pressure on the sensitive underside. She'd never had a cock in her mouth before mine, but she works me over like we've been doing this forever.

Means I'm also on the brink of an orgasm far too quick. I want to make this last, to torture her in a way that makes her realise I'm the one who owns her.

"Princess." I fist her hair and pull her off with a wet sound, a trail of spit from the tip to her lips. "I need to make something clear."

"Yes?" Her mouth is slack, her pink tongue reaching out and running along her plump bottom lip.

I pull in a breath. Frey, I want to paint her face with my cum, but I need to tell her a truth I hate admitting. "I'm not invincible. Something could have happened…We never know."

"Ash'den." She runs her hands up my thighs. "Don't. For me, you will always be invincible. That doesn't make you immortal, eternal, all-powerful. You were born for this time and you cannot be defeated. Should something… unspeakable happen to you. You will live on."

Her hands drop to her still flat stomach.

I want to fall to my knees, but she needs my strength.

"And this morning, the heartsongs of your club brothers and sisters needed strength as well. Boonie made it clear that times like this, we need to show all our faith in you. We put our fear to the side until we are with our heartsongs again. Then we can be weak. But screaming and carrying on? What does that do?"

I pull her up by her hair, not hard, just guiding her movements. On her feet, she is still so much smaller than me.

"Fuck. Fine. Next time I come back to you though, fall to your knees like you just did and suck my cock," I growl. I need to keep control here. Not let the emotions blurring my vision take over. My brave pah'pah. Mine. "Mine. Tell me."

She stands on her toes and kisses my cheek. "Yup, gotcha. And don't–"

I turn my head, capturing her mouth in a kiss. "Say it, Didi. None of this bratty bullshit."

"Yours," she whispers with one hand fisting my cock.

I need to be inside of her. I'll lose my mind if I'm not inside of her. She must have the same idea because she is reaching behind her, struggling to tug down the zip of her dress fast enough.

"Leave it," I say as I grab her hips and spin her around, bending her over my desk and pushing the skirt of her dress to her waist, exposing the round globes of her ass which I squeeze until she is squirming in my hands, rocking into my grip. Just like that first night.

"Please…"

"What? Use your words."

"Fill me up with your seed. Breed me. Make me messy so that everyone knows I am yours. Brand me. Please, Axe."

I smack her ass. "Please, who?"

"My king. Please fuck me, my king. My only. My pah'-pah. My heartsong–"

I slide one hand between her legs, spreading them. Her panties are soaked. I hook my fingers into the gusset and pull the lace down her thighs. With my other hand, I fist my cock. "So wet for me, Princess. You want this pretty little cunt blasted open by my thick orc cock? You want me to ruin that tight hole?"

"Fuck," she moans. "Fuck. Axe, FUCK."

I suppress a chuckle. She can't see my grin, and I have to force a stern tone so that she doesn't figure out how cute she is when she curses. "Bad girl." I pull out until just the tip teases her opening and spank her ass, first right then left. "Bad girls don't get fucked. Remember? Bad girls get un-fun punishments."

"I'll be good. I'll be good," she rambles, bucking back into me. "I'm a saint. I'll be so good…Just fuck me already." She stamps her foot.

I pause. We both pause.

"Daddy," she growls. "Don't be mean and fuck me."

"What a temper." I cover her back and clamp down on

the back of her neck like an animal locking their unruly mate in place.

We came here both knowing I was going to turn her ass red and then we got sidetracked. But Dinah was being such a good girl and putting us back on the right course.

"What did I say about swearing, Princess?" I keep my dick buried in her quivering cunt.

"That you don't like it when I say words like fuck, cunt, shit." She's panting but not fighting. How could she? I've got my whole weight on her.

"That's right. And what did I say I would do…"

"You'd spank me."

"That's right. But you were bad. Very bad. You tempted me with this perfect pussy."

"Yes," she moans. I reach around and find her clit. I strum the sensitive bundle of nerves with my thumb. Like this, I don't need to move. I can have her milking my cock with some dirty talk and playing with her pretty little clit. "Please."

"You wanna come, Didi?"

"Yes. Meh Ash'orde shwa'en dw'ni…"

"You want your king to stretch you good?"

She's just whimpering at this point.

"Words, Didi."

"I want the king of the orc hordes. The monster of the Badlands to fuck my cunt." She shouts out the words because she's coming hard. Harder than I could expect when we're connected like this. I fuck her through the rest of her orgasm which seems to return again and again like waves on the shore.

I feel my balls draw up as a particular strong convulsion of her pussy makes my eyes cross and I'm coming inside my heartsong. Jaysus.

Property of the Green Bastards

My legs are shaky but I get us to the sofa and collapse with her in my arms.

"I don't think I can handle getting spanked right now," she giggles. "Hells, I feel like I'm coming down from a high."

"Maybe I should wash your mouth out with soap instead?" I tease. I'd never do that. Sandra did it to me once, and no way am I putting Dinah through that. Of course, she doesn't know that.

"No." She struggles to get upright and look at me. Her eyes wide. "I promise to never swear again. Please, anything but that."

I frown at the sharp way she pleads. This isn't part of our play. "Did someone do that to you?"

"Once. Please…"

Irrational anger fills me that anyone would do something to upset her so much. I pull her to the sofa where I drape her over my lap and lay a quick pair of smacks on her ass. Each word I speak next is punctuated by another. "You. Should. Have. Told. Me. That. Was. A. Hard. Limit. For. You."

On the last one, I rest my hand on her hot skin, soothing the sting away.

"I'm sorry," she hiccups. "I'm sorry. I never–"

"Hush…" I run fingers through her hair, massaging her scalp. "We know now. Another time, we'll go into more detail. I should have asked. Made sure I knew everything."

Her hand reaches back, searching for mine. I link our fingers, tethering us together. "I'm sorry."

"Not something you should be apologising for, Princess. You are being so good for me…always. From the beginning when you bent over my desk, this ass was in the air while you begged for my cock. What a brave, good girl you are. And good girls get rewards."

Flora Quincy

She makes a whimpering laugh. "I would like that, Daddy."

"I bet you would. Come on, stand up." She is a little shaky on her feet. I steady her with hands on her hips, then kiss her stomach, still flat but I can imagine how it will swell. Then down to her sex, slick seeping from her sex, her clits swollen and ready for when I suck the first one into my mouth. "What a pretty pussy you have for me."

"Axe—"

"I want you to tell me who this pretty pussy belongs to."

"You—"

A knock on the door interrupts us.

"Fucking assholes," she hisses. I smack her ass once because she shouldn't be swearing but I'm not telling her off for it.

"Yeah?"

"It's important. Swot's back."

"Princess, I gotta go. Take a shower, go to bed. I'll be back soon."

Swot is bouncing when I get to the conference room, a worried frown on his face.

"Any problems?"

"Mayor walked in while I was working but didn't make a fuss."

"Then why do you look like you got caught with your pants down?"

"Yeah, well, ignore that. Look. We got a problem, Prez."

Like we don't have enough shit on our plate, he wants to add more?

"That girl? Well, I got her picture from some CCTV.

She is in the database. Some crazy bitch claiming to have visions in Frey'mar. They locked her up but had to let her go–nothing to hold her on. She is the prophet…Please, tell me you killed her."

"Sheriff did. Bullet in the back of her head."

"Thank Frey. It is more than that. She has a record. Was in the Deep."

I freeze. The Deep is where the worst criminals are sent. Even humans send the worst of their kind up to Dragon mountains.

"Shit…" I want to kick something. The idea that someone as young as her was in the Deep. And then it hits me. About twenty years back, there was a crazy motherfucking serial killer, she'd been sent to the Deep and had her kid in there. "The Strangler's daughter?"

"Yeah."

"Shit. So?"

"Man, I don't know, Prez. Just freaked me out, okay? Like…that shit ain't right. Imagine being born there? Special kind of crazy having a psychopath mom…"

"Fuck. Okay. Just add it to the long list of problems."

Chapter Nineteen

DINAH

We've fallen into an easy routine with Axe taking me to work and picking me up. Tool still stays with me during the day, but he has proven to be useful in the shop. I spend most of my time prepping the hides for the forgery. And why work on a forgery of a forgery that has been ripped at the seams? Elmeer listed the piece in a high-end auction two days before Eel broke in. The interest is so great that I'm fielding calls from galleries and prospective buyers wanting condition reports, authentication documents. I haven't told Axe because

Property of the Green Bastards

even though I think the timings are connected, does it really matter at this point? Especially since we still don't know why they wanted to steal the map, let alone two panels.

And since shitstorms come in threes, tourists have been in and out of Elmeer's wanting their little piece of orc history in the dozens. So when Elmeer shuts for the day, I drag Tool upstairs to the attic room because the place needs cleaning. A lot of it.

"Why? We aren't even done with prepping the hides."

"Because, and if you breathe a word, I'll make you useless to your heartsong, a collector called yesterday and she wants to come up and see the map for herself. And I'd say no to anyone else but if she goes back and says it is genuine, the reserve will go up."

"Don't know what the fuck any of that means, but what you say goes."

"Yeah, I'm thinking we can stage a theft…Or maybe I tell her that I've taken apart the other two pieces for restoration? I'll figure it out." I spin around and jab a finger into his chest. "I am figuring this out. My shit to deal with. Don't tell Axe or Elmeer…Besides, I am not even sure I can make a good forgery without the other two hides. We still have so much to do."

"Dinah, seesee, you have this. You are good at your job. You are definitely more like your ancestors–"

I grit my teeth. He mcans the Disavowed. "You…"

"Come on, you need a thicker skin. People are going to say a lot worse."

"If I was like them, I'd have faked the bones, not stolen the real ones."

"Deh. Meh'seesee weh fro on Allteng shwear."

"My honour is heavier than the Allteng?"

"It is one big mountain."

Flora Quincy

I press my lips together. "Come on. I need to change the lightbulbs."

Why we don't have a real ladder up here is beyond me. But I'm able to con Tool into letting me stand on his shoulders. He cups my foot and launches me up there.

"If you die, Axe is going to kill me."

"Then hold tight," I snap. Looking down, I feel the blood rush out of me. "Fuck."

The word comes out long and low as I look down from where I'm perched on Tool's shoulders. The map. I'm seeing it from a bird's eye view for the first time. The two missing hides are like a gaping wound, the edges raw, but I'm only just noticing the pattern scraped into the hides themselves. It is disrupted by the missing pieces but is clear as day.

"Tool. Is there a ladder? A camera?" I'm trying to lean over to get a better look at the map and internally kicking myself for not doing a bird's eye look earlier. "We—"

"Dinah, I'm putting you down. Otherwise, you are going to fall and then I'm dead. Just—"

"Get me closer to the table. I'll stand on that."

He grunts something but does as I ask and bends his knees enough that I can carefully step onto the edge of the table not covered by the map. It isn't as good as being up high, but I'm not an idiot.

"So…Dinah? What is it?"

"There is something scraped into the hides and then they drew over it. We have to confirm who forged this map. And find the other hides, of course. I think there must be a connection between the timing of when the drums were sounded and now. There are gaps, do you understand? In the logic."

"It is probably a coincidence. But I'll find you a ladder." He walks off when he realises I'm not getting

Property of the Green Bastards

down so I have to shout after him to not forget the camera. His two-fingered salute is all the confirmation he gives me, but I know he'll bring me what I asked for.

When I hear the door close, I jump down and do a happy dance. Throwing my hands in the air and ululating.

This. This is everything.

Maps. Orcish maps.

Orcish artefacts are my jam; my whole research. Years of working in a department and then an industry that looked down on primitive art and objects, and now, finally, I have something that we have real proof of.

What I didn't tell Tool is that the scrapings prove the hides are original ninth century. The map itself is a forgery. Hell, the way the hides were cured is a forgery.

Okay. I sit on the floor for a minute and gather my thoughts because I'm going to need to explain this to everyone.

First, the map is a forgery. They prepared the hides to look like ninth-century map hides. Second, the forgery was made in the nineteenth century. Third, the hides themselves were original ninth century, but the reverse because makers signed the back. Fourth, the underside of this map would be, I hoped, an original ninth century.

And fifth, I have zero idea why this happened.

I blow out a breath and stretch out on the floor. My heart is racing. Whatever is hidden on the underside is what I came here to destroy. Now I need, or want, to see what would have been my death sentence.

I shoot up to hunt down some of the hides we were going to use to recreate the maps and slide them underneath. Then grab a sharpie, inkstone, and all the other tools I will need to very quickly recreate the map. I need to see the whole thing and then maybe I can put all the pieces together. Right now, they feel like a one-thousand-piece jigsaw puzzle.

When Tool returns with the ladder, he brings Raine who complains that "the prospect would be murdered if I fell and hurt myself." He also brings a digital camera.

"I could kiss you," I say without thinking. They both make a strangled noise. "Sorry. He wouldn't hurt you…If anything, I would be the one who couldn't sit for a week."

"Did not need to know that," Tool whines.

"So, what is this all about?" Raine asks as I climb up and begin taking pictures. "The idiot here made some garbled explanation that you discovered something about the map."

"Can I start from the beginning? Explain everything?" I ask. They both agree. "A map like this is made of hides from each horde. It is symbolic unity. Traditionally, the hordes would give their hide to the horde to the left from a bird's eye view. Another demonstration of respect. This, however, is a forgery. I don't have the ability to test if the artist made them from horde specific hides or if that means anything. However, when I stood on Tool's shoulders, I noticed that the hides were prepared so that each one had a scraping pattern. It is a play of the light. We were struggling to determine which technique but…but what if the hides are original and the map is the forgery. Again, I'm not sure if it was meant to be a secret or if it is in the original. But, I am convinced and my instinct says that the reason the two hides were removed is because of this pattern. Since I didn't see it before, I can't recreate it. I'm hoping that I can make some educated guesses based on the others. Hence the ladder and the camera."

"I have no idea what you are talking about, but it sounds intelligent so, sure," Raine says with so much sarcasm I want to ask if he has an ulcer.

"Thanks for the moral support, Raine." I put on my phone voice, upbeat and shiny, making them laugh. My heart twinges. The reflex to flinch away from any kind of sarcasm is gone. I no longer feel like it is a thinly veiled attack. These two assholes are my friends. Cherry and Erika are my friends. For the first time, I have friends who let me prattle and don't make fun of my intense interests. "This fucking sucks. How am I going to pull this off?"

"Wait, I thought you had one of those photographic memories?" Tool says as he moves the ladder so that I can get the next hide.

"No. I have an eidetic memory, but this is for the record so that other people can see and compare my working. I need to document it for you mere mortals."

"I'da what?" Raine cocks his head.

"Eidetic memory. She sees something and has perfect recall."

"Since when did you swallow an encyclopaedia?"

"We talk a lot when we work." Tool sounds smug. "Dinah seesee tells me shit."

"Hush boys. We need to focus on determining if the sub dermis was scraped before or after the design was applied."

"You keep saying you aren't fancy and then you talk about this kinda stuff. Sounding all official and shit."

"Are you teasing me?" I ask, pretending to be suspicious of their bullshit. I love it though.

"Isn't that what brothers are supposed to do?"

I grit my teeth together and roll my eyes. Not, mind you, in exasperation but because I don't want tears to start leaking from them.

"Seesee?"

"I have dust in my eyes."

. . .

Hours, literal hours, later, I slouch against the chair, my back killing me after hunching over the pictures and trying to determine what the rest of the pattern might be. Half-formed ideas are sketched on scrap paper.

"Well?" Axe asks. When I didn't make it home for dinner, he stormed in furious that we hadn't let him know where I was. Hawk came as well, giving Raine a sharp word before they settled on the trunk. I can't look at them, remembering exactly what Axe did to me there. Tool lies on the floor, his back as bad as mine.

"I think," I begin. "Going back to the beginning, my dad said this map would expose me as Disavowed. When I saw it, I thought the interlay would have a list of names. There isn't an interlay though."

"But, what does that have to do with the map?"

"The map we are looking at is a forgery." I wave that consideration away. "It was kept by someone and the real treasure is the map with the family tree—"

"OrSol Map," Axe interrupts. "It belonged to the Disavowed until my grandfather took it."

"Deh, meh'Ash." I smile. "My working theory is that the OrSol map is the real one. The forgery was made to hide the OrSol map. I thought it was separate—the interlay, that is. Now I suspect it is on the reverse of the hide. Now, there are only three confirmed existing examples of ninth-century horde maps all in human lands. I've seen them all, they almost always have the names of the horde leader and the orc who was the heartsong of another horde. Initially, it was suspected—"

"Didi, less rambling. Is any of this important?"

"Yes, Daddy." I wave him away. "I think the original map will show cross-horde heartsongs for this generation. So Disavowed with Green Bastards, Green Bastards with Old Horde—"

Property of the Green Bastards

"Why do you say that?"

"Because they are one over from the Disavowed." I sketch what I mean onto his hand. "You end up with the symbol of the Allteng and the Hre'dah, the dark place where souls go, where the fiends come from. Whatever the traitors or my dad were talking about, this is much older."

"From the time of Intentions," Axe says. I feel his heart stutter. The time of intentions is ancient, back at the founding of the hordes.

"We take it to the Meet." Raine steps in. "We argue it would go against the Intentions if Axe and Dinah are separated. Their names are on the hide…"

"Not my name. 'The princess who passes' is there, but there was no other name. The Disavowed will not have another leader in this generation."

"So, we need to find the bit with her name, or whatever?" Tool speaks for the first time since Axe arrived.

"No," Axe says the single word in such a final way that I flinch.

"You can't protect me if–"

"I want to see the other hides first. The ones we have here."

"It will take a long time. We'll need to take each hide apart."

"Why aren't you going around the edge?" Hawk asks.

"It would be too difficult to do it all at once, and we don't know the state of the interlay."

"Those kvari destroyed it," he presses. "Doesn't seem like it matters."

"Hey," Axe snaps. "If she says we do it this way, we do it this way."

I shoot him a grateful look. So much of my time here, of everything here is linked with this map. Already, taking the map apart feels wrong. Like dissecting something holy.

Flora Quincy

But what else can we do? They watch as I stand and pick up some needle-nose tweezers. Whoever stole the other hides ripped the seams; I'll not desecrate it like that. My hand hovers over the boundary between the Old Horde and Steel Demons.

"Pah'pa, meh'didi, du'weh shea'ts," Axe whispers in my ear and I feel him slip both hearthstones into my pocket. Two more days. I don't want to win but we've agreed I must. If we want to claim the territory and then name a regent, I need to win. But we are playing the game nonetheless. In this moment, the weight of the hearthstones soothes my fears. I'll always have a home at his hearth. "Frey sha'ki qui Allteng orsol Dwen'mar. Or'dwea'ki."

"Okay." I suck in a deep breath, trying to control the emotions swirling inside of me after his promise to keep me safe, that the protection of the Allteng's shadow would always follow me. I pluck at the first thread, then use a scalpel to make the tiniest cut. The work is painstakingly slow. But it is as if time stands still because the others say nothing. Only Axe stays near, his comforting mass keeps me sane as I finish with the first seam.

"Right then..." Tool sighs, pushing to his feet as he joins me at the table. He hands me a pair of gloves.

"Nope. We won't wear gloves for this."

"What? I've been waiting to use gloves this whole fucking time!" he complains, breaking the tension as Axe, Raine, and Hawk laugh.

"Awww... poor baby," I croon before getting serious and directing him to take the other corners so that we can lift the hide up. When it becomes clear I'm not tall enough to turn it over, Axe takes my place. My heart is caught in my throat as they lower it and I can see the Orsol map.

"Steel Demons hide but Old Horde map," Raine says.

Property of the Green Bastards

"Bet they pulled the wrong one and had to take the other as well."

"But why take both?"

"Does it fucking matter?" Axe growls. "What do you see?"

"The pattern is traditional for its type, a single mountain point. But instead of the founding member, it is someone alive. Someone from our generation."

"Ryder," Axe says without even looking at the inscription.

"Not Raine?" I reach into my pocket and palm the stones.

"I'm not 'the one who sings'," he laughs. "Can't carry a tune to save my life."

We free the Old Horde's hide next. "Do you know who the 'one with eyes of fire' is?" I ask.

"Drake? The second son of the current prez. He was blinded in a fire. Ugly stuff."

We know who will be on the next hide. Two peaks. I look close, half expecting to see Hawk's name because I still don't believe it isn't Hawk and Raine. Only the epithets couldn't be more clearer.

"The King. The Horned Princess."

"Shit. You mean Ryder and Kendle?" I can't imagine what she'll think about that. Everything about her screams that she wants to stay here. Perhaps even prospect for the club after going to mechanic school. I put my hands on Axe's hips, smoothing my hands down so that he won't notice when I slip the stones into his pocket. "Does she know?"

"Nope." Raine laughs. "My kin will be in for a surprise."

"Unless she gets both her stones in his pocket," I point out. All the men laugh as I wink at Axe.

He pats his pockets. "Very clever, Princess. I think we can all agree there isn't anything more to learn here. Fuck off, boys. I'll see you at the Compound."

"Jaysus. Are you ever going to let us watch?" Raine genuinely sounds aggrieved.

"Dinah?" Axe asks me and I can feel the race of his heart. There is a part of him that wants this, needs this. To show his people what we are. I bite the inside of my cheek. I'm not ready. And there is something not quite right about having sex in front of people I have to see every day…At least, not in such an intimate space.

"At the Meet," I say. "At the Meet, we will fuck to show everyone our union."

Axe doesn't take his eyes off of me. But tells the others, "You heard her. Get out."

We are in the attic room, lying on rugs, resting from more orgasms than I can count.

"How is this going to work?" I ask. "At the Meet—"

"We will do it on a dais. No one will be close, unless you want that."

"I meant telling people."

He fists my hair, angling my face towards him. "You are going to stand in front of our people, Cuddles at your neck, and tell them what you told the club."

"That won't get rid of the traitors."

"It will consolidate—"

"Axe! A four-syllable word! Have you been reading the dictionary?"

He slaps my ass so hard that I yelp. "Bad girl. None of your backtalk."

"Sorry."

"Sleep, Didi. Stop thinking for the night. There is a lot

Property of the Green Bastards

to get through but they begin arriving tomorrow. We need to rest while we can."

I grumble into his chest. Disapproving that we can't work things out while everything is fresh in my mind. At the same time, the moment he tells me to sleep, my eyes begin to droop and the deep breath that always precedes sleep fills my lungs. I snuggle into his warmth and wrap an arm around his waist.

"Dinah?"

"Axe?"

"If it doesn't go our way, I've made plans. We have passage into the mountains. Or we go north."

"Don't say things like that."

"I just want you to know."

Tears prick my eyes. I hate that he makes all the plans for the worst possible outcomes, even if it is just in case.

"Once this is over, no more disaster planning," I tell him.

"Nah, Didi. I'll always plan. I think about how my day will go before I open my eyes."

I know, or maybe I've learnt that about him. "I'll wake you up with my mouth on your cock."

"Baby, you wake me up like that and I'll be the happiest orc in the Badlands."

I choke on my laugh. My heartsong is a corny, horny motherfucker.

"Sleep deep, Ash'den."

"Sleep deep, Princess."

Chapter Twenty

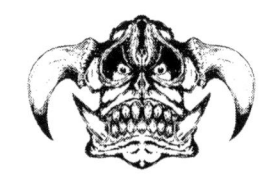

AXE

Three days before the Meet, Dinah bursts into my office, a smile on her face. Victory. I relax. For the last hour, her heartbeat has been erratic but no one has come to tell me something is wrong, and by now, the mar knows to be on the lookout for any threat to her. I even almost trust the shit ball of a sheriff who sits across from me.

"Sorry," she pants. "I didn't know you were in a meeting. It can wait."

Property of the Green Bastards

"You ran all the way here to tell me your news can wait?"

She rotates her shoulders, and I watch the way her breasts sorta arch out with the movement. So does the sheriff.

"Keep your eyes on your shoes," I snarl. The fucker blushes. You can't blame someone for appreciating a beautiful body…unless the body they are appreciating is my heartsong. Under those circumstances, I'll happily put them on disability after removing their eyes from their head. But I also can't miss the way she grimaces with the movement. "You hurt yourself?"

"Just stiff."

"Come here." I pat my thigh. This time Dinah blushes and the sheriff looks fucking scared. "You can leave, Sheriff."

"Actually," she draws out the word. "He might want to be here."

"Oh?" I now wonder why she was willing to wait.

"I'm starting to wonder if maybe we want more support…" she trails off, frowning, which I now know means she is thinking, trying to translate a human thing into an orc thing. Fucking adorable. "My first night here, someone tagged the Barracks telling Logan to leave. I'm worried that whoever took the pieces of the map might try and do the same thing. It is like a gang war, right? The drums were like a drive-by shooting, the snitches—"

"How do you know about this?"

"I grew up in the Stews. There was gang activity," she says like it is nothing. More pieces of the puzzle fall into place. The reason she is vigilant but not scared of everything going on. She has lived with it before. "We already agreed that they are going to use the map to create tension between the clubs, but I'm starting to think it will create tension between the clubs and citizens. I just came from the Diner and was talking with Erika and Cherry. Seems like everyone is blaming the club for the drums, the Meet, all of it."

"Way to bury the lede, Princess." I pinch her nose. "You heard about this, lawman?"

"No. But the town likes me about as much as the rest of you."

"Yeah, humans aren't exactly loved–"

"Exactly." She bounces up and begins to pace, which in my office isn't exactly easy. Her heartbeat, though, is calmer now. "What if someone is behind the prophets and the drums? Humans encouraged the thefts from the Allteng. Only your grandfather delivered a justice that the majority of the orc'i supported, so the civil war, or whatever you want to call it, was stopped."

"You think humans want to start a war?"

"It would give them a good excuse to send troops," she points out. "Come on, Logan. You know that."

The silence is awkward.

"Don't you?" She sounds less sure, maybe picking up on my own curiosity.

"I don't know anything about human politics," he says, his posture stiff. Then his features begin to blur and reform. His nose gets longer, hair lighter, and his body loses some of its bulk until a leaner figure with sharp features sits before us. His clothes haven't changed, so they look baggy. Somehow, he manages to look more regal in this new shape. I try to move, to protect Dinah and the life within her but I can't. Magic I cannot see or feel binds us. "Uh, apologies for the binding. You look rather murderous." He smiles, rueful and mischievous. "I did not plan on showing you this form yet. Perhaps if Dinah had not been fated to be with you, I'd have confessed to her... You may speak, if you wish."

"Who are you?"

"You can call me Logan."

"That doesn't answer his question," Dinah snarls. "Who are you?"

"I am, uh, an emissary. I did not choose the face I wore or the personality because we had to mimic the real Logan. He is rather...uncouth. My apologies, but we needed someone we could control. The humans had chosen a rather gun-friendly individual. Though completely committed to peace."

"Are you a god?"

"Heavens, me? No. Merely a neighbour to the north. We appreciate the buffer you create between us and the humans."

"So, you knew? You knew about their plans?"

"We knew there was meddling. But I was honest when I said I know nothing of human politics. As their technology does not work this far north, so our magic does not work that far south. There's been rumours and reports but only in the recent months."

"And you didn't think to tell us?"

"I didn't think you would need to know," he snaps. "We did not expect the drums. There are forces working here..." he trails off with a frown marring his perfect features. "I did not expect Dinah. Or the drums..."

"You—"

"I am here to help. Perhaps not in the way you would like. But I will be, uh, better at looking into the human side. I share the mind of Logan. Absorbing another soul is exhausting, keeping it locked away puts a toll on me."

"You killed him?"

"His body is in stasis. When it is time, I shall return his

soul. He will remember everything that happens, though, perhaps not immediately."

"And now what?"

"I will help you find the people who are a threat to the peace and end them."

"How?"

"By going into the lands of the Disavowed."

"Come on." I laugh. "Shouldn't you be here? Where will the Meet be?"

"You doubt your abilities? I can go where others cannot. Give me a trusted ally, and I can bring back the information you need."

I watch Sandra and the shapeshifter ride off before dawn. Sandra complained but Boonie said something, so I guess it worked out in the end.

"Do you trust him?" Dinah asks as she tucks herself more securely against me. Not even three weeks ago, I was pushing her away and now having her in my arms is natural.

"Sandra will keep him in line."

"He could steal her soul–"

"Neh, Didi. Dwe'r koll'she."

"You think he is good?"

"I think he doesn't want war."

"Now what?"

"Now, you work with Boonie or with the map."

"This is where heartsongs and club members are different?"

"Yeah."

"It isn't even sexism because Queenie is an officer," she snarls. "But that doesn't make it right."

Property of the Green Bastards

"If there wasn't a separation then we wouldn't have anyone to take care of saying the blessings."

"Bad argument. Raine—"

"Raine didn't know he was going to be Hawk's heartsong and was voted in before they met."

"One day, I want that story."

"Nope." We turn and see Raine swaggering towards us. He looks more relaxed but a quick look at his knuckles tells me that it isn't because of fucking but because he found a punching bag. "You're too sweet for that."

"Offended!" She laughs. "Nothing you say could surprise me. You forget, I read romance novels."

"Aren't they boring? You know what is going to happen."

"You clearly don't know anything about reading one-handed."

It takes me a beat to know what her smirk means and then fucking hell…I was not ready for that image because my dick is now very uncomfortable in my jeans. I have to see her. Legs spread, fingers rubbing her clits while she reads one of her dirty books. "Raine, you got something important to say?"

"Eh, it can wait while you take care of that wood."

"Great." I throw Dinah over my shoulder and stroll through the common room. The brat squirms and tells me that the safety of the club is more important than my other club. "Raine said it could wait, Princess. What kinda prez would I be if I didn't trust my enforcer?"

"But!" I slap her ass good and sharp, making her yelp. "You fu—"

"Do you want a red ass?" I ask. "It's been a while since you needed a reminder."

She shuts up quick, but those hips don't lie as she tries to get some pressure on her sex. Fuck, yeah.

Flora Quincy

I make it to our room and dump her onto the bed.

"Read out loud." I pull my shirt over my head and toss it to her. Then perch on the bed. "Put that on, too. I want to see your breasts. Keep it nice and high."

She breathes in my scent like a drug addict but puts it on. "Is me reading really going to turn you on?"

"You getting turned on by smut turns me on. Read. The. Fucking. Book. Out. Loud."

It is a human shifter romance. I don't know how far along in the book she is, but the sex scene starts pretty quick. Lots of dirty talk which is what gets my heartsong going. Not just the way her nipples pebble under her shirt, but she sits up, opening her legs for better access to her naked pussy. She looks so fucking sexy with her fingers spreading her folds, letting me see her clits. Damn, she is already wet. Has she ever gotten this hot and bothered so fast with me? It should dent my ego considering it, instead, I'm getting rid of that e-reader and making sure she only has paperbacks from now on. I want to know when she is reading smut so I can take advantage of it.

I reach for my belt and get it loose. She is so caught up in reading, she doesn't look up when I stand to push my jeans down and get my dick out. I've never wanted to jack off more but there is so much in my balls I won't try it.

"Baby girl…"

"Yeah?" She looks up, her eyes not even making it to my face. The horny little princess stares straight at my dick and licks her lips.

"Did you know that orc'i have more cum when they meet their heartsongs?" I ask. "Should have known that first time. I completely coated you. Made that whole office smell of sex for days. Had me hard every time I was meant to work."

Property of the Green Bastards

"Ash'den…" she moans. "I'll do whatever you want, but I need you to touch me."

"Of course, you will." I fist my cock, squeezing the base hard because I'm not coming until she does–lots. "You're addicted, aren't you?"

She whimpers, spreading her legs wider. "Put your cum in me…"

"Topping from the bottom? That isn't what good girls do."

Her eyes snap open and she glares at me, but her nipples are sharp. I'm gonna start with them, I decide. Haven't given them the attention they deserve.

I lean down, bracketing her with my arms, and begin by kissing her eyebrow. I haven't told her yet, but she is getting a piercing there. Trailing my lips along her face, I make it to her mouth, all so I can tongue the tusks. Fuck, when they get big enough, she's getting gold caps. First, though, I'm fucking her until she can't see straight, can't walk straight, and can't move without cum leaking out of her.

Shit. No. First, her breasts. She protests when I abandon our kiss to suck on her breasts. Dinah gets with the program fast. Moaning and arching her back as I take first one and then the other into my mouth. She's sweet as sugar, and soon they're going to be big and full of milk for our young. I'm mauling her, sucking and biting hard enough she'll be covered with my marks.

"Stop teasing me, Daddy. I want your cum…"

"You are going to get my cum. These beauties need attention too, though." I jiggle the one in my hand like they bounce when she rides me. "Plus, I'm trying to decide how I want you. Riding me? But I need to see that ass bounce. I like your tits too…"

"Axe," she snaps.

"Oh, baby, this isn't for me, Didi. This is for you." I nip the swell of her left breast. I'll never tell her this is my favourite spot because her freckles are so close together it is like a green patch. I don't want her feeling self-conscious ever, or think I want her to have green skin. Fuck that. I want her because of her. If that even makes sense. I can't define how I feel. "I fucking worship you, Princess. And if I can't sex up every inch of your skin when I have my cock inside of you…I'm doing my job wrong."

Her mouth opens to process. "I am not doing my job. You're thinking, which means I'm not doing my job."

Her little growl makes my cock jump. Dammit. I'm getting distracted.

I move down her body faster than I want because I need her taste on my tongue. Up close and personal with two clits and her hot sex is my favourite pastime.

"That reading material really got you worked up, didn't it?"

"Imagining you fucking me got me worked up," she moans at the first sweep of my tongue from clit to clit.

"Sinking into heaven, Princess. Every time I get inside of you, it is sinking into heaven."

STRANGERS CROWD THE MAR, clogging the streets and emptying the shelves of food. I send the word out that any farmers will be paid top price for their produce. At night, the campfires make midnight seem like noon. When Boonie asks Dinah how she sleeps so well, my heartsong claims that cities are brighter and noisier.

The Compound isn't immune. Members who live in the rest of the mar moved within our walls, filling the guest rooms and even the rec room where the kids had been set up in a crazy mess.

Property of the Green Bastards

"What happens if someone sounds drums?" Kendle asks. She's on edge, her childhood habit of bouncing her knee speaks louder than any words. Then the only thing that would soothe her was our dad's singing. Fucking Ryder being named the one who sings or whatever pisses me off even more because as her brother, I should want her calm and taken care of. But the idea of my kid sister growing up? Yeah, it pisses me off.

"No fucking clue," I admit. With her, I can be honest. She lied for me enough as a kid. Especially after she took "snitches get stitches" literally when she caught me and Hawk drinking moonshine when we were fifteen. She told our dad she couldn't tell why we'd been throwing up because "like Ash'ee, needles make me scared." Honestly, I couldn't ask for a better sib. "You gonna be alright staying here?"

"Fuck, like I want to run into some dick swinger or muff muncher who is my heartsong. I'm a Green Bastard." She glares at me.

"You've been talking to Dinah, haven't you?"

"And if I have?" She springs up and takes a step towards me.

"What did she say?" I can't help the menace in my voice. Shit and fucking shit balls. I should have known they'd become close. Same age, both of them independent and smart. "Well?"

"Just that I need to think about what might happen if my heartsong was in a different territory."

"Fuck. Can't keep her trap shut." I regret the words immediately because I don't mean it like it sounds. "Don't you dare tell Dinah I said that."

"Don't you dare talk about her that way. She cares. She knows something. She isn't telling me but she isn't keeping me in the dark like the rest of you fuckwads. I have guesses and if that means I have to sew my pockets shut and hide in the walls of the Compound, then that is what I'm doing."

"Ken…"

She slumps against the wall. "Axe, I don't want to go."

"Yeah, I get that. Can we talk about it later? After the Meet?"

"Axe?"

"Yeah?"

"You're a good brother…But since Dinah's showed up, you've gotten better."

"Thanks, seesee. You couldn't ever get better. Born perfect." I hate that it feels like a goodbye.

"You are such a goof. Oh, Mom wants you to know if you have an idea of which heartsongs will be coming. I'm going to bully Dumbo into helping me lift the tires for Heph's bike." Her smile, though, is like a kick in the heart. Somehow, I know this is the last conversation we'll have like this. And she knows it too.

Strange how you can say goodbye without words even to someone who isn't leaving.

"THE TREATY IS BULLSHIT," Dinah hisses that night. "It was written to hamstring the orc'i. All the hordes and MCs."

"What do you mean?" It was my turn to frown.

"Please." She laughs, bitterness and anger made it into an ugly sound. "They assumed the horde king would kill everyone with Disavowed blood. They wanted people who'd been born into the Disavowed bloodline killed… even if they lived in other hordes. It would have created chaos."

"It did create chaos. People hate the bastards because

Property of the Green Bastards

we are responsible for the death of orc'i born into other hordes."

"And if you'd killed those who—"

"I see what you mean." I grab her chin, surprised she is crying. "You don't have anything to cry about, Princess."

"Yes, I do. I can cry about the fact that people died simply because they were related or married to a couple of bad people. I can cry because there is a generation of orc'i who don't have a heartsong because of that bloodshed."

"Do you hate me?" I'd never considered that she might hate me.

"No. Unlike them," she spits the words. "I don't think the sins of the parents should rest on the child's shoulders. Shweers."

"None of that," I warn her. "What did I tell you about swearing?"

"You are such a hypocrite."

"The benefits of being King." I nip at her shoulder, right on top of where I bit her last night. Where I plan on branding her. I wonder where she will brand me. Wherever she wants, but I hope it is visible—I am proud to be her heartsong and won't be ashamed to let people know I belong to her as much as she belongs to me. Yeah, I am going to mark her up good now that I've laid my claim. She'll go to the women's baths and all those bitches will go back to their mates, families, and everyone else to gossip about how Dinah is mine.

What our conversation tells us is we need to make sure that the old superstitions, the ones that meant innocent children and heartsongs were killed, are left in the past.

Or should not be what determines the weh of an orc. Fuck, or shouldn't be what we judge anyone on.

Chapter Twenty-One

DINAH

Axe has me on his lap while we sit in the conference room with the rest of the club. I didn't resist when he insisted I join them. Our conversation last night stuck with him so much that he woke up asking me more questions than I had answers to.

"Didi, what are you up for?" Axe asks. Under normal circumstances, I'd think he is asking about sex. Right now, he wants to know if I'm down for another round of Cuddles at my throat.

Property of the Green Bastards

"Cuddles and I are best friends now," I say, and the others chuckle. "But we need more than Cuddles. I think…and this is just as an outsider, so tell me to can it if I make a mistake."

I wait for them to agree because I know my place isn't here. "I think that we need to unite the clubs. Everyone knows they are the Hordes. And Axe called the Meet as the Ash'orde. Why don't we use that to our advantage? I, uh, made a pretty bold claim that I was the Ashni'orde."

Axe's laugh reverberates through my body. "That is a pretty big leap, Princess. I haven't branded you yet. Or made you my property."

In retaliation, I grind my ass against the bulge in his jeans.

"That was very naughty, Ash'ni'," he whispers. "Don't think I'll forget you are trying to distract me during a meeting."

"Are you taking her as your property?" Grim demands. He was one of the few who never took his heartsong as property and I never learnt why.

"Dinah, you are my property. Now get out of here so we can vote on it."

"What about the plan? I have one," I ask. I'm not going to fight him right now about staying for the vote on the plan. I just want to know what the option is.

"We'll make sure everyone knows who rules the Badlands," Axe growls. "The Green Bastards are the King's Horde. Now and forever."

The members bang the table. I stand and put my hand over my heart in the traditional pledge to the horde king. Then lower myself to my knees, looking up at Ash'or'ash'-den, the Ash'orde. "Meh'i'sh for meh Ash'orde. Gre ent jwar meh'orsol for meh Ash'orde."

Flora Quincy

The others follow. Pledging their breath for the king in war and peace, their blood and bone for their king.

I don't know what Axe will do. I can guess my heartsong's actions more often than not but when it comes to his role as the Ash'orde, to be polite, he is fucking unpredictable. Right now, his heart is beating like it did the night he tracked me during the storm and claimed me as his heartsong.

"Ch'tur Ash'orde, meh'weh, meh'or ent me'sol, she'h tu weh ent orsol."

He pulls me up as the room erupts in shouts. I expect him to kiss me, instead, he presses his forehead to mine. "Princess, you are dangerous. This vote will be quick. If I get upstairs and you aren't spread naked on our bed, you won't be sitting comfortable until the next full moon."

I know he means it. Emotions are running high, and he needs to let his excess energy out either by killing something or fucking me. I'm an avid fan of the latter option, so I run out of the room.

Boonie, Kendle, and some of the other heartsongs are hanging around outside. They straighten when I come out, but I forestall all their questions.

"All good," I say. "I think they'll be out in a minute, so be prepared. We are going to make a splash at the Meet."

AXE COMES IN QUIETLY, like he has been stalking me instead of knowing exactly where and how he'll find me: naked, on my back, arms over my head with the wrists together, and my legs spread just wide enough for him to see everything. I was never shy with my body before but the weight of his gaze makes me feel like this is our first time all over again.

"What a good, good heartsong," he croons. "I think

Property of the Green Bastards

you deserve a reward…Tell your Ash'orde what you would like."

My chest rises and falls with a mixture of lust and emotional need. "I want it like the first time. I want you to fuck me like you didn't know I was a virgin. I want to be ravished in our cave…"

"Oh, you wicked girl." He grabs my ankle and pulls me until my ass is at the edge of the bed and he can lean over me. "You ask for the one thing I want more than you. And the one thing I cannot give you today. The next time I fuck you in that cave, I am going to take my time. I'm going to tie you up and use you exactly how you want…because you are mine and you will beg me to do whatever I want. So pick something else before I put all our plans aside and do what we both want."

I whine in disappointment, but I didn't think about the fact we have to be at the great Amphitheatre in an hour.

"Fuck me hard and fast," I say. "However you want. But hard and fast. I want to feel you in between my thighs when I walk in front of everyone, your cum dripping from me, and bruises—"

He straightens, looming over me, reminding me just how much bigger he is. How easy it would be for him to do all those things I just begged for.

He kneels between my thighs and puts his mouth over my sex, lapping at the slick that has gathered. As ever, I can feel the ridges of his tusks against me, the way the gold caps run along my folds.

"Hold on, Princess," he growls before burying his tongue into my cunt. I make a desperate sound and cup his head, holding him in place as I grind my clits against his face. He makes a satisfied sound that only makes me want more. He draws my legs over his shoulders, gliding his hands up my back until they wrap around my shoulders, pulling me closer and holding me in place. Suddenly, he rears back and stands so that I am riding his face, only supported by his strength.

"Axe! Oh, Goddess, Axe. It is too much." I hold his head to keep my balance.

In response, he tilts his head so that each rock of my hips puts pressure on my clits.

I'm boneless when he relents and allows me to slide down his body. My release coats his face.

"My turn." He releases me so that I drop onto his cock. The sudden stretch causes me to cry out, but he forces me further until I'm split in two, my legs stretched wide over his thick arms.

My eyes roll into the back of my head, and my mouth opens in a soundless scream as I come again on his cock.

"Your cunt is so needy," he snarls in the same tone he used that first night. "Look at me when I fuck you."

I force my eyes open. He knows how weak I am for him. How I'd do anything for him. That his cock is only part of what I love about him but I can't form words when he fills me. Just helpless moans.

He walks us toward the bed and tosses me onto the soft mattress.

"Axe, no. Please, I need you."

"You are such a good girl for me, Didi."

"Yes…You said I could have a reward."

"You will." He holds my thighs apart and slides in, slowly dragging his length along my too sensitive walls.

"Please, I need you to fuck me. Make me scream…"

"And what will you scream, Princess?" he asks, pulling out so just the tip teases my entrance.

"Ash'den, King who rules the Badlands."

"And you?"

"You own me. You rule me. I am yours to command."

Property of the Green Bastards

It is so easy to say the words. To acknowledge what we both know makes him happy. And what makes him happy makes me happy.

"What a good girl." His thrusts stutter and I feel that familiar pressure as he swells inside of me before filling me with his cum. He doesn't allow all of his cum to be released inside me, but pulls out and covers my naked body with the rest of his release. "Fuck, the best thing in the world is seeing you covered in my cum."

He says the words almost absently as he rubs his seed into my body, scoops up what is left and smears it over my face, encouraging me to suck on his fingers until they are clean.

"Now, Ash'ni'orde. You aren't a princess anymore. But a queen. Give me the stones. I want to walk out in front of the orc'i with your hearthstones in my pocket."

I'M FINISHING up the hides for the forgery when I feel a hand on my elbow. I lash out like Axe taught me, catching my attacker in the diaphragm and knocking him to the ground. When I spin around, I see Elmeer on the floor.

"Elmeer! You scared me." I reach out to help the old man to his feet. "I am so sorry."

"No, don't be. I should have shouted when you didn't respond to your name."

"It is the map." I indicate my work. "I don't know how accurate the pictures you sent were…"

He shakes his head and pats my hand. That same grimace as the first day when he looked almost regretful when he showed me the map for the first time. "What is it?"

"This is all my fault, Dinah," he sighs. "I only wanted to help my old friend."

"My uncle?"

"Your great-grandmother was a Steel Prophet until she went to the Disavowed. She told me about the map, how it presented a time when in one generation, all the hordes would be united through heartsongs, making it impossible for there to be war in the Badlands. She confessed it was a great relic of her family that had been hidden by painting a map of the Badlands. When Axe's grandfather took it from the Disavowed, I knew I needed to get my hands on it. I convinced Boonie to let me sell a forgery…" He drifts off looking around the koltop. "I thought I could keep the knowledge safe here."

I'm speechless. Elmeer had known? All along, he'd known about the map?

"Your grandfather passed what he knew down to your father. All I knew was that it would prove you were Disavowed. And when your uncle Frank mentioned you and that you were part orc. Dammit, but I knew I needed you here. To see and destroy the map. That the knowledge would continue even if the object did not. The knowledge—"

"You…tricked us."

"Do you want me to say it is in my nature?" he asked.

"No. We cannot help who our families are." But I'm sick to my stomach, knowing I'm here not because of my abilities, but events orchestrated by a man I thought was my friend. He doesn't even wince when I move away from him. There's an understanding and sadness in his face that I haven't seen since my grandfather hugged me after my dad died. My dad. My dad was part of this prophecy. Creating the child who would pass as human. They made the prophecy happen. Did my father know? Did my grandfather?

More importantly. Do I fucking care about the kvari

Property of the Green Bastards

scum who desecrated the sol of the teng, who are without weh or faith, whose shadows will never find a home under the mountain knew?

No, I fucking do not.

"Can you forgive me? Your skills are without question. A wonderful bonus."

"You didn't know me before you put my life in danger."

"I didn't know you. Doesn't make it right."

I look him dead in the eye. "Meh'or is human. Meh'sol is mine. Meh'goki are ash'or'ash."

"Say that when you face the Meet."

"Why?"

"Because you sound…" He looks up at the ceiling. "You sound powerful. Your father's father's people are stuck in lore and myths that are new, that feel fresh. I am more than two thousand years old. I don't remember my exact age."

"You are…" My mind spirals as it assimilates to beings so close to a god. More powerful than Frey who was a mortal necromancer, even if she could create an entire species from the blood and bones of the dead humans and monsters. A sudden fury overtakes me. "You are a god and you meddled with the affairs of mortals. That is illegal."

"Demi-god," he corrects but he doesn't contradict me. "I am still one of the Pilgrims. Just an ancient one."

"Still one of the eternals. And now, I bet you will say you cannot offer me your protection because that would be interfering with fate."

"That is the case."

"They could condemn me to death at the Meet. Axe would have to kill me. Either chopping off my head or offering me poison. Do you understand the lives you have ruined? People have died already because they believed in a prophecy—Kid, Eel, and others. My children, the children of countless others still carry this varor. The belief in tainted blood exists. It will continue to poison the minds of the orc'i. The Badlands will never survive a war between the clubs." I'm on the verge of screaming by the end. Fury fills me as if I was one of those women who calls lightning.

"If you are there, alongside their king—"

I spit on the floor between us.

"Proud Queen." He shakes his head, his eyes sparkling with excitement. "Proud, proud Queen. When you came to me, you didn't care about the orc'i or the Badlands. The world was a simple place for a little city rat who only knew how to survive. I've never seen such a skilled liar. But kindness? It cured you of lying. When was the last time you spoke a falsehood?"

"This is no longer your place," I tell him. "Leave it. I'll find—"

"You will take care of it. Remember that is the only thing I asked of you on that first day. For you to protect this place after I am gone. Farewell, Queen of the Orc'i. I look forward to watching you lead these—"

I leave the room before he finishes. It hurts too much to think about what he's done. Hurts more to think he is leaving.

I GO STRAIGHT to the Diner after I'm sure he's left. It has become a gathering place for the citizens who object to the Meet. Strangely, I'm considered acceptable. Maybe it's because I still look like an outsider, or Cherry and Erika have scared them straight.

That's where I am when they come for me.

Two hulking, unfamiliar orc'i whose patches are from

Property of the Green Bastards

the Screaming Demons. Drake with his red eyes and Vicious, an older orc with unusually curly hair.

"You're your father's second son," I say the minute I see the patch.

"Witch," he snarls.

"She is orc like you, boy." Vicious tuts.

"Only a witch could capture an orc as powerful as Axe. Look at her. Not even a real orc. You—"

"Sh'a me weh fri'sur," I cut him off, the same frustration with Elmeer flashing inside of me. I've had enough of these games. Ones I played for so long, even if the rules were different. Games that were never mine. That changes now. From now on, I make the rules. Everyone else? They must pay to play or they will be left behind. "Re's dwen kre'm shwea. Kvari driftas sol'ji. Ash'orde meh'pah'pah. Meh'sti Di'or'nah'fi, Ashni'orde."

The silence is almost comical.

"Do I need to say it in common tongue? My honour is protected by the King's Horde. I reject the Disavowed. I am the heartsong of the horde king. My name is Di'or'-nah'Fi, Horde Queen."

"I know what you said," Drake spits. "I know who you are. Disavowed. That is why we are taking you to jail."

When he drags me outside, there are orc'i from the other clubs. They all glare at me but other than the Demons, no one makes any move to touch me. Which tells me that while they are all in on it, they are being fucking cautious and nothing as I'm hauled by them.

And there is no way they can keep this quiet because the only jail is in the sheriff's office. And even that is a bit laughable since it is a bright, spacious cell. Sure, there are iron bars over the window and along an entire side, but the cot has a real mattress.

Now that I am playing by my own rules, when I'm

thrown in the cell, I do the one thing I know will piss everyone off: I sing. I have a terrible singing voice. Shockingly bad. A screeching banshee sounds like a choir of angels compared to me as I sing my favourite pop songs. I consider dancing, but I don't know how long I'll be here.

At first, Drake is growling at the cell, telling me to shut up, threatening me, shouting, and being an asshole. Vicious drags him away during an excellent rendition of "Into the Night, I'll Stay By Your Side." It is a ballad sung by someone with an eight-octave range. Not pretty.

The other good thing about singing is it helps you track time. Most songs are around three minutes, and I can't imagine it will take more than five for Axe to come storming in. But when I get to the tenth song, I begin to worry. At the twelfth, I promise to stop singing if I can have a glass of water and a trip to the bathroom.

"This sucks." I sigh when I lie back.

"Don't worry," Vicious tells me. He's taken out a book and is reading.

I scoot so that I'm sitting. "So, do you really think Axe and the Green Bastards will turn their backs on me?"

"Me?" He closes his book and stretches his legs out in front of him. "I think you have a lot of powerful friends, but you also are Disavowed. You speak orc'ish, but that doesn't change your heritage which carries a death sentence."

"I bet the last time they sounded drums was when you all suddenly learnt about me?"

"Yes."

"Axe will kill all of you."

"Axe is smart. Not as smart as you, it seems, but smart."

I lean forward. I met this orc forty-ish minutes ago. "When did you come to that conclusion?"

Property of the Green Bastards

"Axe wouldn't piss us off by singing. And he wouldn't go full-on royalty. That scared the shit out of all the orc'i."

I laugh. "I'm a brazen little bitch."

"You are smart. You know how to get people to see what you want them to see."

"And you saw right through that?" I narrow my eyes.

"No?" He frowns at the sound of a question in his voice. "Just...I know Drake. Drake is very hard to rile up. But you got under his skin very quickly."

I snort and lie back, arms crossed under my head.

I'm on my way back from the bathroom when I hear Axe shouting. An or'gre's roar...If I didn't know it was my heartsong, I'd piss myself in fright.

"Shit." I take off with my guard on my heels because if I don't stop him, Axe might just be the one to start a war by killing everyone who stands between us.

"You took my heartsong. Put her at risk." Axe pulls the hearthstones from his pocket. "You want proof? Our stones. Or would you prefer Cuddles? Stick it in my heart and ask whatever questions—"

"Ash'orde, me weh neh 'sdet. Gri'j ow'der. Or'dwea'ki. Shreh." I push between two of them and dash to his side. "Back off, demons. You want him to claw your throats out?"

But before I can reach him, both sides reach for guns. My heart stops. Guns misfire north of the border. "Put them back," I plead. "Guns cannot be trusted."

"Says the human..."

"Watch your tongue, demon," Axe snarls, his gun levelled at the other orc's head.

"You are the fire eyes," a familiar voice breaks through the deepening growls. I look around Axe and see Raine and Hawk striding to us. He has that same swaggering walk as always, but it is hurried like he would rather run. "Drake, right? Well, you sorry sight of a rockfucker, got a reason why we shouldn't put you in the ground for taking our prez's heartsong? 'Cause that breaks a lot of rules, no matter whose rules you play by. And right now, you are in Bastards' territory, so you play by our rules."

"Or'saw. Blood denier."

"Yeah, I like a bit of Bastard, but a bit of Bastard likes me as well. And he is a mean motherfucker who likes a bit of blood when he plays hide the snake. Meanwhile, you've got your hand and a hard-on for Vicious who is a proven heartless." Raine looks like he is having the time of his life, which is not de-escalating the situation. "What will your heartsong say when she finds you balls deep–"

"Enough, Raine!" I cry out. "All of you, enough. Hyped up on or'gre. You say you want a trial. We will have your trial. Take us before your judges. Before our people. I'll stay."

"No!" Axe shouts.

"If it means things go smoothly, smoother, then I should stay. I'll be a reluctant guest."

The Meet takes place in a natural amphitheatre north of the mar.

When we step into it my bravery melts like ice in boiling water. The rows of seats carved into the cliff ledge are crammed, not just with orc'i but the citizens of the mar. Cherry catches my eye right away since her outfit matches her hair and horns, but I'm more anxious to find Boonie and Kendle. As I search the crowd, the faces blur until I cannot distinguish except for the colour of skin and clothes like blobs of colour in a pointillism. I remember my cousin saying that your brain shuts down in stressful situations making you temporarily deaf and blind.

But I see Axe. My heartsong smirks from where he lounges on a stone chair—I won't call it a throne—carved straight into the rock. I will him to come over and tell me what's going on because since I agreed to stay in jail, no one has spoken to me about the Meet.

"Get moving." Drake gives me a push. Not hard but enough that I enter the stage stumbling. I straighten slowly.

The sound of the crowd explodes in slow motion. The soft cacophony of whispers amplified and bounced around until sounds blended into an identifiable buzz.

"Ho! da Frey! Goki sa Orsolki gre on Gresil." The Silver Amazon President says, the natural curve of the landscape carrying her words to everyone in the space. She wears a wise one's robe rather than her leather cut which rests on the stone reserved for her. "Ours are the first made people. We are the children of blood and bone! We are the ones fated to live on the ancient battlefield. The Badlands are ours!"

Her words should have people cheering and stamping, instead, there is silence. Even the children know to shut up.

"This is a Meet but we have—"

"Who is 'we'? The orc'i are no longer led by the hordes! You are nothing but criminals continuing systemic injustices in our communities. You own the lands—"

Two Amazons cut off Erika's rant by pulling her on stage.

"You dare to interrupt your wise one?"

"I want to know why you dragged a woman to prison and left her there without food or water or a simple blanket!" Her words ring clear. She's pushing it a bit. I had a bed, blanket, and food. But it paints the right picture. I look like I've been dragged from one of the lesser hells. I need a shower and to brush my teeth.

"Take the intruder away," the Amazon says. Erika protests and they manage to just about get her off the stage. I guess they didn't want to risk her going crazy on them, and the way she was arguing definitely makes her look crazy.

"Give your name, prisoner."

"Di'or'nah'Fi, Ashni'orde," I say clearly like Axe and I had agreed. That starts the crowd off buzzing. Ashni'orde haven't been acknowledged in the Badlands for five hundred years. Cat. Pigeons. Chaos. The result exceeds my expectations. "I am the last Driftas Princess."

My heart races…I focus, hoping to calm myself, only to realise it is Axe I feel. Our eyes meet, and it hits me. I have not told him that I love him. Somehow, the words never needed to be said until this moment. Terrible timing, if you think about it.

"She is Disavowed. Her blood is var. Do you think that the great-granddaughter of the worst orc ever to breathe deserves any place in our society? She was brought into the world through subterfuge. Her whole existence is devoid of weh." The shouted words come from everywhere but are so loud they blend into a single, visceral attack against my very existence. Instead of many voices, it sounds like one violent declaration of hatred.

Every Green Bastard is on their feet protesting.

"Do you ignore the laws of our people? Will the Ash'orde break the law because she is his heartsong? Does he have the right to be Ash'orde?" The Silver Amazon's president asks Axe.

"Ignore the laws? Pretty much. But those laws should change," Axe says. There are hisses throughout the crowd. The orc'i are turning against him. "As for the right to be

Property of the Green Bastards

the Ash'orde? Yeah. I kinda do…if you believe she is varor, you have to accept my or is weh. Only logical really."

I stand on the other side of the stage from Axe, my heart beating an uneasy cacophony, everyone stares at him like he is the one whose blood is kvari. Like his or carries the taint. And I'm too afraid to do what I want, which is to scream that it is my fault, that I have tainted their king. And then lecture them on how humans had manipulated the situation. Anything to turn their condemnation away from him.

"So, you won't do this because she is your heartsong?"

"Correct."

"And you have come to the end of the mating trial?"

"We have," he says, looking even more smug.

"Who has the hearthstones?"

I freeze. I know. I know he has the stones. Axe has both stones. There is no way for him to have given them to me because we haven't been close. He hasn't touched me. If he has the stones, he is meant to move to my hearth. The gathering won't care that I picked up a rock from our cave. They see me as Disavowed. He'll be mating into the varor rather than the other way around. Fuck.

"Who will see who has the stones?"

"I will," says Ryder, Kendle's heartsong, although that's unknown to most.

He is on our side, I tell myself. But it doesn't feel like it when he pats me down. Axe is growling, clearly furious with how thorough a rival MC prez is being with me.

"Here!" He pulls out two stones. Flashing them first at the crowd, he then asks me to confirm they are ours. I nod.

A sleight of hand. He went into my pocket first…I look at Axe whose eyes twinkle. They planned this? I look at the President of the Silver Amazon who nods, she doesn't seem surprised at all. Did they plan this and not tell me? I could–actually, I will–strangle Axe when I'm next with him.

"So Dinah's or is not var because she will stay at the Green Bastards hearth?" One of the other club presidents asks. Oh yeah, they planned this. Fuckers.

"But she is Disavowed! She is varor!" a voice cries out from the audience. It is so on the nose that I wonder if they've planted a convenient dissenter in the crowd.

"Yes, Axe. We must address this," Ryder says. He is still standing close, obviously antagonising Axe but I'll give him credit. If they really did plan this, he is the best actor so far.

"We believe or carries the weh of the teng. But have we ever determined the truth of it?" Axe takes his question to the audience. "But I vow to you meh'kin orc'i weh af'ar meh'weh ni cor. Orsol c'rum dwea. I will spill her blood if she is varor."

He told me to trust him the first time Cuddles judged me, so I focus on his heartbeat. It is faster than normal but steady. His blood exhilarates in the anticipation of the next move.

"How about Cuddles?" he asks pulling the dagger from her sheath. "I have put it to her jugular twice already. Asked all the questions, but if you want…my blade is yours, Wise One."

The Amazon sniffs dismissively but she takes it from him. She tucks Cuddles to my throat and asks her first question.

"Is your blood var?"

The point pushes in. This bitch wants to shank me, splatter my blood all over her pristine robe. Her eyes flash with hatred. I've never met her before. Oh, shit. She must be one of the female orc'i, even ones with heartsongs, who wanted to give Axe children. I smirk. This bitch is out of

Property of the Green Bastards

luck. All that orc seed has already planted a babe is my fertile womb. Fuck you, bitch. But it is my body that smells of him, my thighs that are covered in his cum.

"Cuddles can only hurt liars," I tell the gathered crowd. "Meh'or shr'ew neh Var. Meh'or ent meh'sol ent meh'weh ta'k dwel."

Cuddles can't pierce my skin and after a moment, she relents and hands the knife to Ryder. The orc is larger than Axe, but one look at him tells me he will be putty in Kendle's hands.

"Tell me a lie," he commands.

"I have green skin." Cuddles slices the skin of my forearm, adding another line to my skin. Axe has already told me they will scar.

"You called yourself 'Queen', will you accept the crown of the Ash'ni?"

"I–"

"Do you know the crown of the Ash'ni?"

"Yes."

"Tell it to us."

"The Ash'ni'orde is the horde queen. There hasn't been one since the Horde Wars one thousand years ago. The crown was lost."

"Describe the crown."

I blink at him, confused. But Cuddles tickles my jugular. I could lie and it wouldn't nick me.

"What are you doing?" I ask. "How…"

"How do the records describe it?"

"It was made of stone. Carved from the Allteng and engraved with promises to unite the hordes."

He nods, and Axe relaxes, cracking his neck like he does before getting ready to start in on some bullshit. Oh, nope. He knew. He knew this was coming and didn't warn me. We had time. Even a "Hey, Didi, you are going to be asked about the Ash'ni's crown." He knows he is going to get it as well because he won't meet my eye.

"In your expert opinion, is this the Ash'ni's crown?"

Another orc steps forward carrying a large wooden tray on which there is a stone crown.

I lean over to pick it up, the weight is right but it is so clean and too fancy to be the original.

Chapter Twenty-Two

AXE

Dinah glares at me, and my balls do the smart thing and retreat–metaphorically–inside of me.

Sure, we could have given her a heads up. Sure, she is a good liar. Sure, she could probably pull all this off without our shenanigans. But the fewer people who knew the pla,n the better. Just me, Ryder, and Heddy.

Crown us, shatter the crowns, restore the integrity of the Badlands by rejecting the past. That is the outline, the rest we are making up as we go along…because, you know, democracy.

"Well? Is it real?" Heddy presses Dinah.

"Yes." Just that one word. Then she opens her mouth again. "This is an Ash'ni's crown."

Truth. Fucking hell. She found a way to speak the truth with Cuddles still gracing her skin. I scratch my nose to hide my smile. She's ripping me a new one the next time we talk. Then I'm fucking her hard. After that, who cares?

"And as the heartsong of uri Ash'orde, does that not make you the Ashni'orde?" Ryder asks all casual like he wants to know if I think he is a rockfucker.

Twenty-three years of playing a part means my girl was fucking made for this moment. She looks me right in the eye and then turns to the crowd.

"Earlier, the Green Bastards took a vote. They claimed him as their king. They claimed him…and so should you. We—"

She pauses, daring the gathering to correct her. Her heart's racing though. She's flying by the seat of her pants and doing an amazing job.

"We are the made people," she continues. "We are not ruled by anything but the or and sol, which knows no king. But symbols have meaning. Ash'or'ash'den is a symbol. A monster ruling the Badlands, the one person between the humans and you and the rest of the world. For, should they come for us, they will want a leader, a symbol to destroy. Very well. Make him your symbol. Make me your symbol. We will die for you. Tell me, orc'i and kin, is that enough for you?"

Queenie stands, her hands raised above her head as she ululates. Her heartsong, Stevie, does the same, adding her voice to the cry. More orc'i stand and some kin as well. The sound echoes, growing and growing until the only other shouts I can hear is the pounding blood in my ears.

The or'gre and my need to touch the fucking radiant

Property of the Green Bastards

heartsong I am a pussy-whipped bastard for are competing for who wants to take over. The or'gre is strong and my body shifts to accommodate the battle urges. My strides eat up the distance between us.

"Bad, Axe," she admonishes. "That was not cool."

"Whatever," I scoff. "You weren't there to help plan so we came up with one on our own. Once we've said those vows, I want you to take the crown off and shatter it. We need to make a symbolic gesture that the crowning isn't going to be something that goes forward."

"What?" she hisses, looking around the amphitheatre. "That is not what I just promised them."

"We should make it clear our kids won't wear crowns or be kings or queens. Say something like you accept the crown but we will be the last ones to wear them because orc'i have no royalty or some shit like that."

"You and the rest of your little group of MC presidents got together and made me authenticate a freaking crown." She sucks in a breath before continuing her tirade. "That was fake, might I add. I had to work around the fact that if I lied and said it was the ninth century lost Ash'ni'orde's crown, Cuddles might have gotten enthusiastic and gone for my jugular. What the fuck were you thinking? Our plan was good. Uniting everyone under one leader. Fucking hell, Axe."

"Don't swear," I say and then have to roll my shoulders to control the tension building in them because the or'gre has nowhere to go.

"If there is ever a time to swear, it is now. You want to destroy the symbol of unity? Do not think I've forgotten that we decided you would fuck me in front of everyone. We need—"

"What do you want more? To crown me a king or for me to fuck you in front of hundreds of people?" Okay.

Fuck, yes. I love this woman. And so does the or'gre. My cock is also on board because of the adorable yet angry pout she is shooting in my direction. "Is that right, Princess? You want me to split you open? Let them see how much cum you can take in that tight pussy of yours? Are you going to be my good girl and beg for Daddy's cock?"

"You're smart. You figure it out."

I don't have a chance to say anything because Heddy has started to drone on and on about all the king stuff I never paid attention to. We aren't like other races. We have no formal robes. If we have any ornamentation, it is the caps on my tusks and like fuck am I giving those up. My kids will have them too…Just, no crowns. The crowns are stupid. This whole crowning thing is stupid but this was our plan. Create a symbol and destroy it.

But claiming Dinah in front of the largest gathering of orc'i in a century? That means something. Not just to us, to the Green Bastards, but to everyone in this arena.

"Are you ready?" I ask her even though I'm looking at the crowd.

I look down at Dinah and she licks her lips, then reaches up and moves her thumb over her lips like she's smearing red lipstick. The sight sets my blood on fire and my cock gets hard so fast that I feel lightheaded.

I run my fingers through her hair, wrapping it tight, and guiding her to her knees.

"The first day we met, I told you I put good girls on their knees. You said you weren't a good girl. But what if I want you to be my good girl."

"No matter what, you are meh Ash'orde. Meh Ash'-Den, ash pah'pah. King of my heart. For you, I'll be whatever you want."

Her words hit me in the gut, hit me in the solar-fuck-

Property of the Green Bastards

ing-plexus. This itch of mine is leaving me speechless in front of thousands.

"Take me out," I tell her.

Her hands go to my belt. She bats the ends aside so that she can open my jeans just enough for her to reach in and pull my cock out.

I'm vaguely aware that everyone has gone quiet. Their eyes focused on my heartsong as she leans in to run her tongue along my cock, pausing to suck on the ridged length. I'm keeping a grip on her because I know that clever tongue and mouth, and I know fucking well she wants to drive me out of my mind with lust so that I fuck her hard and fast.

"Princess, no topping from the bottom. Be a good girl for me and take this slow. I want you to show off for all these people how you take my cock. So no tricks. Just open that pretty mouth, open for me while I fuck your face."

She protests but relents as I pull her back and she opens her mouth, her pink tongue out, looking like a wet dream. I fist the base of my cock and tap the flared head against her cheeks. Don't know why it is so hot, just love how I can put my cock in or on her, wherever I want and she'll stay wet and needy for me.

"Axe…"

"I know." I rub the tip on her tongue. Then ease, nice and slow, into her mouth. There is nothing like making her gag on my cock. Watching her adjust, relax her throat, and let me fill it until I can see how her throat bulges. "Perfect, perfect, Didi. You know how pretty you are like this, don't you? How jealous every person is that I am the one who gets to fuck you like this. They want to be me. They want to be the one fucking your mouth, dominating you. But I'm the only one who touches you."

I pull out so that just the head rests on her lips, letting

her breathe as much as she wants before I slide my cock right back down her throat. In and out, long, slow movements, each time I wait and wait for her to catch her breath.

It's hot, but I nearly lose my control the next time I fuck into her throat. My sneaky, sexy heartsong wraps a hand around her own neck and rubs my length through the column of her throat.

"Bad girl," I growl. "Trying to make me come before I'm ready…"

I drag her off my cock with a pop and tug her to her feet. Instinct drives me to bend down and kiss her. Yeah, everyone here probably knows I'm a total pussy when it comes to my heartsong. But give me half a chance and I'll remind them just how much of a monster I can be.

First, though, I gotta fuck my girl.

She's wearing one of her black work dresses.

"Didn't say how pretty you look in this. You weren't wearing it yesterday."

She rolls her eyes, but her hand is on my cock, stroking the length so I let her sass go. "They let me change."

"Lucky me. That material is begging to be ripped." I grab the collar and use the or'gre to do just that. Right down the front. "Frey. Princess, your breasts look so perfect and heavy." I pause to grope them. Her little whimper of pain tells me I'm being exactly the right kind of rough. "You ready? You want Daddy to fuck you in front of all these people?"

"Yeah. Sure. Fuck me." So cute when she pretends she isn't dripping for me. Bet if I put my pinky in her tight little hole she'd come without me touching her clits.

Which is why I'm not wasting her time with playing with her clits. They need to see my cock splitting her in two.

Property of the Green Bastards

Her dress drops to the ground leaving her in some pretty little lace thingy. Not having that on her, so I rip that off as well. Then I turn her so that she is facing the crowd.

"Meh Ash'ni'orde seh lon'i Didi. Meh'Pah'pah ist go'wn. The greatest fucking treasure in the Badlands. They are going to watch your Ash'orde fuck perfection." I say against the shell of her ear. My hands are back on her breasts.

"Yes." I'd ask for more words but a simple yes is still the sweetest sound when it comes to her.

"You're wet. Is it because you know they are all looking at how well you take my cock?" I ask, grinding my hips against her soft ass. She bucks into me, begging for more, even though the only sounds coming out of her are fucking animalistic.

Primal mating. Exactly what all these people need to see.

"Hands and knees, Didi. Stick that ass up for me."

She gets in position. Fisting my cock, I observe the curve of her spine and the way her hair falls to one side so I can see her face. Then I get to my knees. I spread her wide. Her pussy and asshole on display. At some point, I'm taking her there but for today, I let myself thumb the tight hole. She shudders. Perfect.

When I fuck Dinah, I have to take my time with that first inch. Nothing better than the moment her body stretches to accommodate the thick flared head of my dick. She feels it too, contracting around the intrusion. I pull back, using the tip to tease her clits. Okay. I might have said her clits don't matter, but what can I say? I have a sentimental attachment to them.

"Stop teasing," she begs. "Fuck me."

I land a stinging, snappy thwack to her ass for swearing. Then, because she's a good girl I give her the fucking she deserves. Hard. Fast. My balls slap against her pussy with each brutal thrust.

"Axe." She pants. "Axe. Give. Me. Your. Cum." I enter her so hard she falls to her forearms, head resting on the stage. "Oh, please. Please. Please."

She's a quivering mess, pulsing around me each time I am buried balls deep inside of her. We could have the whole world watching and everyone would know she's mine. Her moans. Her breasts. Her freckled skin. Her black hair. Even the way she shakes her head–because one more orgasm will make her pass out–is mine.

"That's it, Didi. Your needy little pussy desperately milking my cock. Desperate. You've been desperate for orc seed since I put you over my desk and fucked away your virginity."

A memory of her blood on my cock, a flash of satisfaction that I was her first, rips away my control and I rut into her. She'll make it over the edge, but I can't think straight because I'm coming. My balls draw up and fill her with cum.

I shout my release. Making a show of it but, fuck, if it isn't one of the most powerful orgasms of my life.

Our audience slowly comes back into focus. Dinah tenses beneath me, remembering exactly where we are. I run a hand down her sweaty spine, soothing her nerves. "Don't mind them," I tell her. "Focus on me. You look so pretty though. So, if they look…take it as a compliment."

"Axe, they are going to be looking at your giant dick," she mutters. "But it's mine. Don't forget it."

"That's right, Didi. All yours. You up for the next part."

"Sure." Then she's giggling. "None of this was on my bucket list."

"Axe?" I look over my shoulder to where Queenie waits

Property of the Green Bastards

at a respectful distance.

"You two ready?"

"Yup." Dinah pops the 'p' letting me know she is psyching herself up for it. Hells, I wouldn't be able to tell she's nervous from her heartbeat. It is hammering away but that could be from sex or nerves. Fuck. I hate not being able to tell.

My road captain steps forward, carrying the heated brand in one hand and a flask in the other.

Dinah eases back to her knees and I get the satisfaction of seeing my cum leak out of her. Queenie hands her the flask, which she takes a deep swig from. She coughs as the liquid fire burns down her throat.

"Right. Where?" she asks me with a bit more confidence.

I'd love to brand her face. That shit hurts though and she's pretty image-conscious. "Neck?"

She thinks for a minute and nods. I'm not sure that is the enthusiasm I wanted but if she's letting me go a bit over the top with the branding, I'll take it.

Everything changes when she gets into position. And I catch sight of a patch of skin, about the size of one of those silver dollar pancakes, bare of freckles. It's right over her heart.

"Changed my mind," I say and then press the red-hot metal into the skin above her heart. "Sorry, Princess. Breathe through the pain."

She does, hissing and puffing out her cheeks like she's been running a marathon.

I pull the brand off.

"Here." Queenie hands Dinah the brand.

"I can't." She shakes her head vehemently. "I can't."

She doesn't mean brand me. She means with this brand. The symbol of the Driftas.

"No, it's good," I assure her even though I am not pleased I'm going to be carrying–stop that thought. The Driftas are gone. Dinah. My heartsong is a new thing entirely. This brand is hers. "It's good."

I finish off the flask and toss it to Queenie who catches it with a twinkle in her eyes.

"Same as I did it, Princess. Straight on, no angle so that the mark is even."

She goes for it. I mean, does. Not. Hold. Back. Presses the brand into my skin like I just got kicked out of the doghouse for being such a shit. The crowd is cheering. Thousands of orc and kin cries drown out my bark of pain.

"Did I do it right?" She drops the brand on the floor and gets in close, examining her handy work.

"Yeah, and I just confirmed I'm not a masochist," I tell her. "Gotta finish this off and then we can party. Okay?"

"Can I have some clothes?" she asks, a pretty flush spreading from her cheeks down her chest.

I clear my throat realising I still have most of my clothes while she's naked. I give her my shirt which covers her up good enough…I'm starting to not love the way people are looking at her. When she's dressed, I put myself back together and stand to face the crowd.

"Meh she'or'oth! Meh'orsol." My voice carries in the amphitheatre without the need of a megaphone but I kinda wish I had one. Might scare them if I could get it to do some feedback. But my ancestors didn't need them, so why the fuck should I?

"You have heard my heartsong's words! She had the dagger of truth at her neck. She answered the questions put to her by the hordes…"

Some parts of the crowd shut up; others start shouting.

"You don't like the word horde? You know why we

Property of the Green Bastards

don't have them anymore? Humans were afraid of the hordes. Of our power, of our unity. We fought, sure. But when it mattered, we were united against our enemies. So they wanted to make us weak. And they did that by manipulating the Disavowed. They stole from the Allteng. They desecrated the sol of the Teng. They gave away their weh for pennies. But where were the hordes then? We did not see our brothers and sisters suffering. Orc'i! Hear me. We did not hold true to or'dwea'ki."

"They broke faith!" someone shouts.

"We allowed their children to starve. How would you have felt if your family was in that position?" My words sink in and the people who were shouting are now back, sitting on their asses and listening for once. "That famine hurt the smallest hordes. Even today, we know that to be true. Prophets have been struggling. Only they didn't ask for help, did they? And you want to know why? Because they didn't trust us."

"Who are you to tell us what to do?"

"I'm the motherfucker who will do whatever it takes. I am the horde king. The Ash'orde. Meh'weh 'sh Ent OrSol. Meh'weh har'na. If that means killing every single one of you to protect the future for my children–" I want them to realise that while they might hate Dinah, she is pregnant. "I will do what is needed. Will you?"

"And what is needed?" Erika demands from the sidelines.

"A vote." I shrug like it is obvious. "Do you want the hordes–"

I let the words hang in the air. We are territorial, so this next part will hit home. "Are the hordes going to maintain the old territories or are we going to make the Badlands one? I'm not talking about giving up what you have. Just erasing the boundaries. Maps without horde-hides."

"That will take days."

"So?"

The crowd's murmurs fill the air.

Finally, Heddy steps forward. "The Amazons are willing to host a vote. To be taken in two full moons' time. Return to your homes, discuss with those who were not here and then the Badlands votes. I declare this Meet over."

Just like that, it all ends. Kind of a let-down but better than an all-out rebellion, or having to grab Dinah and getting the fuck out of dodge. We are standing around chatting when I hear my name being shouted.

My mom storms towards us, her face twisted with an emotion I can't place. Kendle holds onto her sleeve like she's been trying to slow her progress but when Mom has a bee in her bonnet, it isn't going away until she's had her say.

"We did not talk about this. Since when did orc'i decide to be a democracy?" Boonie shouts, giving no fucks about who might hear her. "We have traditions for a reason."

I wince. Her whole life was about being my dad's heartsong and his property. His pillar of strength. We ripped up the script she's read off her whole life and it sucks to see her like this, but it can't be helped.

"Boonie." Dinah sneaks between us like she knows I was about to tell my mom it isn't her business anymore. "Think about it. Isn't this better?"

"No." One word and my mom turns her back on us and walks away.

"She'll come around," Dinah says. "It is just a big shock for her. Come on. She's organised a big party. Let's go. Have some fun… Make her feel appreciated."

We ride back to Dwen'mar on my bike. Grim's at the

gate glaring at everyone trying to enter but when he sees me his ugly mug breaks out into a smile.

"Welcome back Ash'orde, Ash'ni'orde."

"Hey, Grim." Dinah waves.

I give him a salute then pull up in front of the Compound, parking my bike right out front. No matter how many fuckers are here, no one will touch my bike or any bike belonging to a Green Bastard. Especially with Tool watching.

He's a lot cooler than Grim and just gives his friend, my heartsong, a chin nod. She responds in kind.

"Okay, what now, Axe?" she asks after we get off, and I've given her a good, hard kiss.

I want a moment with my heartsong before we have to spend time with everyone but that isn't happening. Erika and the sheriff are standing outside the Compound. As far as I know, they've never been inside the gates yet they look relaxed like they belong there.

"Fuck."

Erika straightens, her arms crossed. "I approve," she says like I give a fuck about her opinion. "I really approve and that pisses me off."

"Am I meant to give you a gold star?"

"No. I had you wrong, and I don't like being wrong."

"So..."

"You are a good leader. I just hope you stop with the illegal businesses and run for mayor."

"Who says I'm doing anything illegal?" We all know I'm not giving up the "work" the MC does. Why should we? It doesn't hurt anyone except bleed the pockets of travellers and pay us for protecting the mar. The sheriff says nothing.

Dammit, I hate that I've stopped hating him.

Erika lets out some kind of exaggerated breath. The

kind people do when they are calming themselves. "You're such a–"

"Don't finish that thought," Dinah interrupts her friend.

"Whatever. But if you don't run for mayor, my mom will keep getting elected."

"Why don't you run?" Dinah asks.

She shrugs, looking away. "That isn't for me."

"Will I see you at the party?"

"No. I'm not really feeling it. Look, I'll see you two around?"

I watch the girl who played a weird role in what happened today melt into the crowd gathering for tonight's party. Her actions make zero sense. Fuck, women make zero sense ninety percent of the time. The rest of the time, I'm just glad they speak the same language, even if the words mean different things.

"Right, do you want to know what Sandra and I found out?" Logan goes next. I wonder if they planned who spoke first.

"Is it important?" Dinah asks. I like her passive hostility towards him. It's kinda cool watching her push back. She might as well have been born in the club; she's taken on the role so naturally.

"Yes. The Prophets and their allies are using the old port to take in shipments from human boats. I'd guess arms and drugs."

"And?" I urge him on.

"And what?" Logan smirks. "Are we allies now?"

"If you want to be allies, you'll tell us everything."

"You could ask Sandra."

"I want you to say it," I tell him.

His sigh, unlike Erika's, sounds tired and frustrated. "I don't know. Why would humans take allies like the

Property of the Green Bastards

Prophets? Are they trying to undercut your clients to the north? Or are they just pawns?"

"Trolls." The word comes out too fast but other than humans, trolls are our natural enemy. They wanted the Badlands after the Great War. But our teng were given them according to Frey's wishes.

"Don't jump to conclusions." Dinah pokes me in the side. She glances around checking to see if there are any troll'kin who've come to the party.

"Fuck."

"Unless you want me hanging around…" the sheriff trails off.

"I don't."

"Hey." Dinah steps forward, stopping the asswipe from leaving. "Run for mayor. Fuck, the humans. They can send another sheriff. You should run for mayor."

His face drains of all colour. "No. No. No," he says not exactly sounding like himself. "No."

"That's the real Logan talking. You're losing control, aren't you?" Dinah smirks. He frowns and backs away. Damn. My girl is good. She cups her hands around her mouth and shouts after him. "See you around, Sheriff."

"Fuck, Didi, you're hot when you go all heartsong of an MC prez."

"Did I do good, Daddy?" She grins. "We have about an hour. Come fuck me, Ash'or'ash'den, meh Ash'orde et pahpah…"

She's off before I give her ass a love tap for saying fuck.

"Good girl, Princess," I say to no one. Then stalk through the crowd, ignoring the well-wishers, the club and its kin, and the strangers here for a good time. I've got a duty to perform. *Fun*nishment for my good girl. And everyone knows I take my responsibilities really fucking seriously.

353

Chapter Twenty-Three

DINAH

The party to celebrate my branding and the end of the Meet is wild, spilling out into the courtyard and even into the square just outside of the gates. The music is loud and the crowd is a mix of familiar faces; citizens and members of other clubs who have dared to come into Dwen'mar. Outside of the mar, there are more parties as the other clubs relax and socialise with each other.

The only person who declined my invitation was Erika. Cherry said not to take it personally because she has always avoided the club. And given Erika's attitude to the

Property of the Green Bastards

club when it's brought up, I'm starting to think maybe her heartsong is a member. I scan the crowd looking at the Green Bastards, wondering which one is the most likely. Most of the guys have a honey with them. Swot has two, clinging on either side. The women all have heartsongs, so there is no chance of Erika being with them.

I don't have much longer to contemplate it and barely manage a goodbye to Cherry when Axe steals me away early to carry me to our room. Not long after, we are in bed, his dick inside of me and coming hard while he stares at his brand. I don't blame him; I can't stop looking at the fresh wound just above his collarbone. It must have hurt but I wanted every ambitious idiot in the Badlands to know he was taken. Everyone probably has heard by now, still, the idea of my mark on him is satisfying.

"My property." I grin when we are resting afterwards. "Mine."

"It's so cute when you get possessive," he says. I open my mouth to ask if that makes him cute but he gets there first. "Don't say I'm cute. I'm scary. Have to keep all those horny assholes away from you."

"Ha." The idea of anyone taking me away from Axe is hilarious. "You know da-fudging well no one would touch me."

"No shit. Doesn't stop you from being the hottest piece of ass in the Badlands. It would be insulting if they didn't look."

A repressed giggle turns into whoops of laughter. "You are such a raging misogynist."

"Hey, it isn't misogynistic if Hawk calls Raine a hot piece of ass."

"I did not need that visual, Axe."

It devolves into a bickering "discussion" but I can't

keep the grin off my face. My cheeks are going to hurt from smiling so much.

That fortune cookie said I was destined for great things. It really should have said I was destined to smile even when my heartsong behaved like an arrogant asshole about treating women like, well, pieces of ass. I'll never tell him his best look is when he turns into a hulking caveman. Because whatever his words, he treats the women in his life like queens.

"Is Erika's heartsong a member of the club?" I ask Axe the next morning while we are lounging in bed. I've got one of his t-shirts on. Dumbo has painted "Property of Axe" on it in red. We were talking about the party last night and how we should have more events that invite members of the town. Or rather I'm advocating for integration and Axe is refusing to get mixed up with a bunch of self-righteous bigots.

"Not your business, Didi." He is so final that I feel he is trying to put me off. I tweak his exposed nipple. "Look, I have my suspicions but if they don't want to do anything about it…"

"Axe…Ash'den."

"Can't say no when you call me that, Didi." Ooooh… he sounds so sexy when he grumbles. Although, he's a total pouty baby before coffee.

"Who?" I press because now I really want to know.

"My guess? The biggest manwhore in the club."

"Shit, fuck balls." I don't get the reference but does it matter? Fucking around when you know who your heartsong is…never a good look. Also, none of my business.

"Oh, Princess, I have been hoping you would make a mistake like that…"

"Wait…" I back away. "Since… Come on, Axe. You cannot drop–"

"You agreed to the rules, and you've been so good for me. So good, I'm so proud of you."

I swallow because I have been good, and he has been good to his good girl. "I am your good girl, Axe. You don't need to…It was a slip-up."

"Oh, Didi–"

I dash for the door and get through it before he reaches me. Fuck, he is fast because I hear the door bang on its hinges before I've made it ten steps. I shove the hall table in his way and run down the stairs. At the bottom, I nearly crash into Boonie who catches me, her eyes sparkling with laughter.

"You are a wild child."

"Hide me."

"Why?" She looks up the stairs.

"Because I want to be able to sit like a normal person tomorrow."

"I said, 'Shit balls.'" I hiss under my breath. This is mortifying. Not only has she seen her son have sex with me, but now she is about to learn I am not allowed to swear in front of Axe.

"You swear all the time," she reminds me.

"Yeah, but not in front of your son. He doesn't like it."

"Axe! You didn't tell us she wasn't allowed to swear," she says as he joins us at the bottom of the stairs.

"Has she been swearing?"

"Oh, all the fucking time." Boonie crosses her arms.

"Didi…" The growl in his voice will always be my undoing. So sexy. So animalistic. "Good girls take their punishments and don't look for loopholes."

"Meh Ash'orde. Frey'ja or'ney. Remember I am carrying your child…"

"I am sure you can handle it," Boonie says as she pries my fingers from her arm.

"I'll be careful, if that is what you are worried about."

I'm not. I did my research on the computer in Grim's office, and then cleared the browser's history. But this early on and if he is only using his hand, we are a-okay for a bit of spank and tickle.

"I…"

"Come here." He holds out his hands and, on instinct, I take it.

"Axe, we are revisiting the rules. I have–"

"Sure thing." He capitulates so quickly; I don't trust him but that is a fight for another day. "But right now the existing rules are in place."

He explains as he would to a child as he leads me back upstairs.

The slam of the door is so final that I twitch.

"Now…now. Why don't you tell Daddy what his little princess did wrong…"

Summer ends overnight.

It is almost poetic the way I wake up in our cave and crawl out to see frost on the ground.

People don't think that you can have frost on rocks. But you can. Beautiful, delicate, lace-like frost that crunches when you step on it.

Or frost catching in the fissures of the rock like veins of quartz. Huge boulders can shatter because of it and you can see it all over the Badlands.

This morning, though, the frost is the delicate kind, but my breath still clouds the air.

I left the city a month ago. A month and everything has changed. Right now, though, all I can think about is the different landscape.

Property of the Green Bastards

The openness. The way the light is almost blue. The smell. The taste of the water–never again will I drink city tap water. Only fresh, clear Badlands' well water. Shit, if humans tasted it, they would pay whatever we wanted to charge.

I laugh.

"What's so funny?" Axe's voice is thick with sleep. "Why the fuck are you out there?"

I crawl back inside. "I was thinking we could make a fortune bottling and selling Badlands' well water."

"Capitalist." He snorts

"Says the king." I slip under the blankets and stick my hands and feet against his warm body.

"If you don't want to freeze my balls off, keep your hands to yourself."

"What about my mouth?"

"That warm?"

"And wet."

"Let me see." He pulls me onto his chest, urging me close enough for a kiss. "Yeah, I think my balls would be happy to have your mouth near them."

I laugh into our kiss. He makes me happy. I push myself up so that I can look him in the eye. "I love you, Axe."

He blinks. If I didn't have his heart beating in time with mine, I might have worried when he doesn't say the words back right away. I don't need them right now, though, not really.

"Pah'pa, Pah'pa, Pah'pa, the song of my heart. Meh'weh te'dwa shurl. Didi–"

"Your honour is the cloak keeping me warm," I repeat the words. Allowing them to hang between us. "Meh'muth te'dwa cock."

"Frey. I try to be romantic. And you switch it up…

Flora Quincy

Fucking hell. Jaysus. Really?" But he is laughing. "You are something else."

"Just yours. You know, I think I'm perfect for you because I make you laugh."

"Yeah? And what do I do for you?"

"You take care of me."

"That's right. And Daddy will always take care of his princess. So don't ever worry. You get a sun burn? I'm pulling the sun out of the sky for a chat."

"You'd do that for me?" You do not call orc'i like Axe romantic. But if your orc isn't threatening the sun after UV damage to your skin, is he really even your heartsong?

"Yeah...you going to suck me off or am I gonna have to take care of myself?"

I look down at the thick monster he calls a cock.

A drop of precum has pearled at the tip, making me thirsty for his cum. I lick it away and my vicious orc is groaning, his hips arching. With my mouth open the tip slips in. I suck down his length, using my tongue as much as possible to get him good and slick for me. When I pull back up, I meet his eyes and wrap my hands around him. Even one on top of the other, there is still another handful. And I'm going to take all of him in, choke on him, and finally drink his cum.

Our eyes hold steady as he wraps his hand in my hair, guiding my motions, up and down. Holding me down longer sometimes when I swallow around the thick intrusion.

I love this. The way I choke around him, knowing he loves every second of it. But taking him into my mouth makes my pussy ache with how empty it is.

"How's your pussy?" he asks like he can read my mind. "Bet it wants to be stuffed full of orc cock, huh?"

I cup his balls and give them a little tug in response.

Property of the Green Bastards

"Dammit, Didi," he groans. "Do that again."

This time when I play with them, I use my middle finger to reach up and rub against his taint. Slowly, I extend my finger until it ghosts over his tight hole. His hips thrust deep into my throat before dragging me off him. "That was good. Another time, maybe? But your little pussy…I just can't stop thinking about how neglected it must feel."

"Axe. I was supposed to—"

"Yeah. But what if you showed me your other talent? You know the one. Where I completely blast you open? Climb up on that cock and ride me."

I lean in for a kiss. "Whatever my king wants."

I sit up and grip the base, holding it steady while I force him into me. Force because it is tight and the stretch is sharp and delicious. I'm wet and ready. Hells, I'm so turned on I'll be coming the minute I have him inside of me. "Axe…"

"Fuck," he mutters. "Just look at you. Taking my cock so well…If you weren't already pregnant, I'd make sure you got pregnant today. Right fucking now."

His hands wrap around my waist and hold me steady while he thrusts into me. Fuck, I think he likes being in control even when I'm on top. I feel the way his cock swells and then the flood of warmth as his cum fills me.

"Frey!" I shout out our creator's name. A prayer to the fact she made it possible for someone like me—a quarter orc, unwanted orphan and burden to her family—to find a freaking soulmate and a cave in the Badlands to be ravished in whenever we want. That's like buttering both sides of your bread.

I slump forward, letting him roll us over so that he is pressing me into the blankets we've brought here.

"Let's just stay here for a bit longer," I plead. "Shadow's fine. They don't need us either."

The fucker is already snoring. I giggle. This is my life and I don't half mind it.

"Good shake," I tell Shadow when he shakes when we get off in front of the Compound that night.

"You can't say that to a warg!" Dumbo complains. "He could bite you in half. You are a snack to him."

"But he did a good shake."

"Axe, come on, Prez. You can't let her talk like that. Shadows' balls are gonna shrivel and crawl back up inside him."

"You so insecure in your masculinity, you gotta project onto my warg? She could put a big pink bow on him and he'd still have bigger balls than you." But in an undertone, he warns me that if he sees any pink near Shadow, he'll make sure I wear nothing but coveralls for a month. "Check your pockets."

I know the stones are in my pocket already, felt him put them in there while we were riding back from the cave. Suddenly, an old bone I have to pick with Axe comes right to the front of my consciousness.

"We never talked about that prank you played at the Meet," I snarl. "When Ryder pulled the stones out of my pocket."

"It worked didn't it?" He smirks. "Come on. I want a shower."

He swaggers off. Asshole. I love a fucking high-handed asshole who would tear the world apart for me.

But damn, I can forgive all the over protective and other bullshit because he looks damn fine in a pair of tight jeans. I'm a simple woman. Hells, who wouldn't be?

Property of the Green Bastards

. . .

WHAT WE DISCOVER the next morning is that there are a pair of Silver Amazons with the instructions that I need to perform the Rite of Weh'ni'teng before the vote is finalised in a moon's time. It is the rite adolescents undertake before they are accepted as adults. It sounds a lot more intense than it is. I hope. I'll be stripped naked and left in the heart of the Allteng. I've twenty-four hours to find my way out.

"I don't like you going away." Axe glares over my shoulder at the two Silver Amazons who will over see the ceremony.

"Twenty-four hours, Axe." I squeeze his hand. "And I'll meet my great-great-aunt. The last of my family."

"Yeah, but it could wait."

"It can't."

"You're branded."

"I should do this. Stop coming up with excuses. In two days, I'll be home and we can go to the Diner."

Genius. I'm a genius because he licks his lips when I mention the Diner. I'm not an idiot. He's been ordering the kid's breakfast every time we've gone. And first of all, we haven't been in a little over a week. Secondly, he would never go on his own.

"You are such a temptress." He slaps my ass. "Get going, Didi. Have fun."

He doesn't mean it. This new casual, gives-no-shits attitude is just him trying to play it cool. I give it to him. He worried. It's nice. No. It is the best feeling in the world, knowing he worries about me.

"Axe, don't forget. You are my heartsong. You'll feel, you'll know if something has gone wrong."

Flora Quincy

THE AMAZONS ARE NICE. A one-eighty from my experience with their president. We have the car's radio turned on and are singing along to some decades-old pop song that seems to be the most popular music in the Badlands. Then it happens.

"Fuck, tyre is blown," the one driving says. "It shouldn't take long."

She has her hand on the door handle when a head-splitting bang goes off. A gunshot a couple of blocks away might sound like a car backfiring, but when it is right next to you, that shit hits differently, especially when the gun isn't a normal handgun. A sawed-off shotgun has blown a hole through the centre of the windshield. Glass is flying into the car, hitting the Amazons first.

My ears are ringing, and I press my hands over my ears like that will protect me from the psychos with the guns.

One blessing is we are all screaming. At least that tells me the other two are still alive.

Two orc'i wearing motorcycle club cuts that have their patches ripped off drag me out of the car by my hair. I look back and see that another three have their old flint-lock antique pistols pointed at the Amazons in the front seats. They might look like props in some historical movies, but they are still more reliable than a semi-automatic.

"Let them go!" I shout. But the dread is there telling me they are dead even before all three guns go off. The one with the sawed-off shotgun moves in closer and fires once more.

Eerily married with my screams is the sound of the radio which hasn't cut off yet. Something about finding that right man for the solstice.

"No!" I scream again. "What are you doing? Axe will—"

Property of the Green Bastards

"Shut her up," one of them growls. There is a dull pain at the back of my neck and then...nothing.

"Rumour is our king is hiding his little human heartsong...and that she is Disavowed. Hasn't killed you yet? Doesn't look good for you, bitch."

I scoot back until my spine is pressed against the wall of the cave prison. I've woken up in a cliff prison, sometimes called a pit prison because they are literally holes carved into the cliff edge. The one way out or in is a hole about six feet above my head. An orc could jump out if they were pumped up on or'gre except they'd then have to push off an iron grill that is locked over the entrance.

"You're Steel Prophets," I accuse them. "You rode wardrums–"

"We must start again. Do you think we want our or to be tainted? Green Bastards, Old Horde, even those uptight virginal Amazons. They all think they are better than us. Well, they guessed wrong."

I don't know how much time has passed but my throat is dry from asking questions. "Why?" I ask for what feels like the millionth time.

"We need a war," the orc says. "And we thought the war drums would be enough...but it turns out all we needed to do was grab you."

I don't say anything, knowing my gaoler will keep talking. I know what I'm meant to do right now. Survive. That doesn't necessarily mean escaping. But delaying whatever bullshit is happening right now is right up my alley. So, I ask another question.

"Since it looks like I'm not going anywhere, can you tell me why you want a war?"

"Come on, you went to university," he says in a mocking, singsong way. I'm a little worried that he knows that detail. "But, you are also female and so not that bright. Look, it is simple really. The humans pay us in contraband they take from the other clubs. We then sell it at a premium."

"They'll kill you." I'm, to use a word Swot loves, aghast. "The humans don't care–"

"They want war too. They–"

"They want resources. Yeah, I might be a woman, but I'm not feh'oo or some rockfucker."

"They need someone to rule. The Steel Prophets will be crowned. And I will be their king."

I bite my tongue until it bleeds. How can they be so stupid? "You are being lured in by the same lies as my kvari forefathers."

"You think I'm an idiot? You are nothing but Disavowed scum."

"You aren't any better. Your brothers killed Amazons. They killed wise ones."

"I'm not Disavowed. I am a Prophet! My blood is pure."

Oh, shit. He's crazy.

Jaysus. Why didn't Axe's grandfather do some kind of inkblot test and get rid of all the crazy in the Badlands? My train of thought borders on hysterical but staying alive is my top priority. Dissociating from the genuine terror I should be feeling is natural. Normal, I tell myself. You are being normal by having weird intrusive thoughts.

"Rot, bitch." He spits down at me but misses because of the dark. I listen to his footsteps retreat.

The worst part is I don't know how much time has passed. Five days? Two hours? I wish I had a watch or something but my mind races and stands still at the same time. I try to regulate my heart rate to send Axe a message

Property of the Green Bastards

using morse code. I know he knows it because Kendle said they used to use it to pass messages back and forth in case one of them got into trouble.

Frey, however, did not think ahead enough to allow us to use our connection to send messages. I think of the dragons who have a psychic link with their mates, or the elves who read auras even from hundreds of miles away.

"AXE!" I scream his name, taking comfort in how it reverberates and echoes off the walls of my prison.

Chapter Twenty-Four

AXE

If my heartsong isn't here, I might as well get drunk. Drunk and stupid. I'm lying on my stomach while Tool of all people is doing the outline for a tattoo of the Green Bastard's colours.

"Damn, Prez." Hawk sits at my head, sipping his beer with a smirk that the minute I stand up, I'll wipe off his face. "Never thought you'd have the balls to let someone needle your skin."

"Ignore him," Tool says. The buzzing stops.

"Thank fuck that is over," I groan.

"Nah, we got another hour, maybe two to finish the outline."

"The fuck?"

"Yeah. You wanted it big. And you got a big back."

"And then?" I know I sound like a pussy but fucking needles. Who puts needles into their skin on purpose? "Tell me how much longer it is going to be."

"More hours."

"Just let me pass out."

"That would be unethical."

The door bounces on its hinges when someone slams it open. "There you are!"

Boonie crashes into the room looking terrified.

"They took Dinah. The Amazons just called saying she didn't arrive and wondered if they haven't left yet."

I instantly feel sick. I thought the rapid beating was excitement or nerves. Fuck, it could have been my nerves because of the needles. But not fear. Never fear. 'Cause I swear to Frey, the only thing she ever feared was being alone and the minute I claimed her, my family and club embraced her. There was never any doubt. She would never be alone again.

I sit up and feel faint.

"Head between your legs." A big hand forces my head down. "Deep breaths."

I rear back, throwing Tool off me. "No. We go. Gather everyone. We ride."

"Prez…"

"I know where she is." Fuck knows how I know, but everything tells me that she's been taken to Disavowed lands. "And someone get the sheriff."

. . .

Flora Quincy

A SHITTY STRING of barbed wire stretches post to post along the boundary between us and the territory the Disavowed used to live on. Sure, we know there are people who live here, criminals and those who reject our ways, but we usually leave it to itself.

Logan and Sandra meet us in the piedmont, having scouted ahead on wargs. Sandra leans forward, her legs resting on the pommel of her saddle. "We saw you coming along the highway. No more chrome dogs. Wargs only unless you want to spook the bad guys."

"Don't have time for that shit, and we didn't bring any."

"Lucky for you, Someone called around. Old Horde brought back-up. We're camped over that ridge."

"The fuck?" Raine growls. "We do not need them. Dinah's our Ash'ni'orde."

"Well, they're here." Sandra sounds none too pleased. Shit, she probably knows about Kendle and Ryder.

The camp is small, efficient, and full of fucking Old Horde shitheads.

"Thanks, Ryder." The words taste bitter in my mouth. Not like I'm ungrateful, but because he saved my ass, he probably thinks he can ride to the Compound and take my sister with him.

"Weh kres'aw eh'whe, Ash'orde. We should get you and the Ashni back to Dwen'mar." He's pulling this friendly stuff off better than I am.

"Jaysus. Stop with the king stuff?"

"Nah, I like the idea of being the brother-in-law to the King of the Orc'i," he jokes.

"You're getting us back just so you can take my sister? You think it is going to be that easy?" I ask, ready to pound this fucker into the earth if he steals her.

"I'll ask," he mutters.

Property of the Green Bastards

. . .

WE'VE BEEN WATCHING for an hour or more before there is any movement. A metal shipping container begins to appear just over the cliff's edge, moving slowly on some kind of rig.

"See that?" Logan points at a dark shape on the horizon. "If you get close enough, you'll see it is a lift for the shipping containers. They are smuggling things in and out of the territory. Guns and drugs. They've got humans with them."

"Have you done anything useful?" Hawk snarls at Ryder.

"Yes, I've made sure that none of this gets back to the other clubs."

"So?" Dumbo takes up an aggressive stance.

"If the other clubs know about this it could get ugly. We have that whole vote coming up? You really think they want to hear about shit like smuggling and whatever justice we are about to hand out?"

"Fuck."

"You are supposed to be a wart on the tip of a dick," Queenie says behind us, causing everyone to laugh. But it is brief, everyone too nervous to take the edge off.

OUR CAMP SITS in the shadow of the Allteng three hours before dawn. None of us like hiding out, but this operation needs to be handled as Boonie put it "delicately". Under the cover of darkness, we mount wargs and stalk towards the collection of shipping containers that back onto one of the prison caves that run along the cliff face.

Sticking to the shadows, we creep along the edge of their operation, carefully taking out the guards. Sloppy fuckers only have five and they are easily disposed of by our superior strength. Yeah, okay so we brought a bazooka to a fistfight, but I'm not complaining about the extra strength.

"Take what prisoners you can," I hiss at Ryder before we split up and circle around the edges to deal with the orc'i working on the dock. He gives me a thumbs-up then melts into the shadows with the rest of the Old Horde. It is the signal for the Green Bastards to split up, as well. I'm skirting one of the shipping containers when I hear the sound of a gun going off. I'm moving fast, no longer crouching low but full out running towards the prisons. I'm not getting involved in guns. Not in the Badlands. But seems like there are more folk than we expected. Because bullets are flying everywhere, one whizzing past me, sticking in the metal siding.

Fuck.

The bullets are flying around like gnats unable to land a target. When the humans realise they aren't hitting us, they start shouting and then running when they see the wargs. They were instructed to stay on the outskirts but clearly don't want to miss out on the fun. They've rushed in, riderless, like the fucking cavalry. I watch, impressed and reasonably scared, as one of them leaps over my head and charges down one of the humans, who backs away pulling the trigger of a gun that has no more bullets. The giant warg grabs the human by his head and in one smooth movement shakes his head, breaking the asshole's neck.

"This way!"

I turn in the direction of Queenie's voice. Signalling to the others, I high tail it in her direction.

"The caves are this way," she tells me.

I fucking recognise the orc standing at the entrance to

Property of the Green Bastards

the prison caves. Grass, the Steel Prophets president. Don't know how stupid this shit is, but not running from us and the only weapons he has are a short sword and dirk.

"You touch my heartsong?" I ask because that has been tucked into a little black box in my mind. Now my anger, the or'gre roars forward.

"She is very pretty." His words are weirdly slurred, and his grin reveals that he is missing front teeth and the others are bloody.

"Did. You. Touch. My. Heart. Song?"

"Does it matter?" He has to spit out a mouthful of blood before he can talk again. "She's gone. Dead."

Now, I know this isn't true. I feel her heartbeat inside of me. And that alone allows me to keep a grip on reality instead of ripping him in half.

"Don't bother yourself with this rockfucker, Prez," Dumbo snarls. "Let one of us take the trash out."

"Hold your horses, prospect. Let a real orc do the job." Queenie cracks her neck and I can imagine her flexing her fingers with their brass knuckles. A lot of men underestimate her, but if I let her, she'd destroy Grass in a second.

"Grass, Grass, Grass." I shake my head. He's even more stupid than I first thought. "The newest Green Bastards prospect could take you apart. But...you know, your human friends have been cowards and have run away–don't worry, they're being hunted down. And your varor friends have been dealt with on the sharp end of a blade. They'll leave their body where they are. That's a lot of honour to give a bunch of traitors. Me, though? I haven't gotten to kill anyone, and my ole lady is gonna be pissed if she finds out I didn't defeat anyone to rescue her. Kinda embarrassing."

"Ya!" he screams. "Stop. Talking. All she did was talk. She wanted to talk. Talk. Talk. Talk. And then, when

I went in to tell her to shut up, she hit me with a fucking rock."

"Score one for Dinah." Queenie laughs. "Come on, Prez. His face is already messed up. Let me rearrange it a bit more?"

"You have no shame, letting others do your dirty work."

That. That right there is going to be the last full sentence he ever speaks.

"Stand tall and fall," I tell him. Now, I'd happily kill this kvar scum in the least honourable way possible, but doing it formally works just as well. Besides, I'm going to enjoy using my axe. I reach over my shoulder to pull it free. The relic of my ancestors feels right in my hand, the weight, the edge ready to bite into his flesh. "Or are you a coward and unwilling to fight me?"

He makes some unholy noise and his eyes blank with fear when he recognises his life is going to be over in a few minutes.

A small shift in his weight is the warning I get before he rushes me. Long hours of practice all contribute to the easy movement of the war axe rising up over my head, exposing my entire body to attack. The idiot takes it, putting all his energy into his reckless attack. As he comes close, I step back and allow the swing of the axe to come down, slicing through his spine and separating his head from his body which tumbles forward a few steps before crashing into the floor.

The death is too quick, but there is a certain poetry to executing him.

"Throw him in a hole."

"I'll start digging," Queenie says.

"No. I want you with me." I don't want to admit Dinah might need a female.

Property of the Green Bastards

"These caves are deep. I don't know how long it—"

Then I hear it. Fuck, we all hear it.

My heartsong is screaming bloody murder. Smart girl.

I run down the unlit corridor, not checking my steps even when I trip over a crack in the stone floor. The or'gre rises inside of me, enhancing my vision and hearing. Her screams. I'll never forget how shrill they sound.

"I'm here!"

She's at the bottom of the last prison hole, banging her hands against the walls. "Axe! Axe, get me out of here!"

Queenie helps me lift the iron grid off the top. "I'll go down, lift her up to you," she says. I grunt but don't object. "That way you…yeah. Dinah? I'm coming down, move to a far wall."

She drops into the depth quietly.

"Are you injured?"

I freeze. I don't want to hear the answer unless she says she's fine.

"No. Some bruises and cuts but nothing major. I am thirsty and hungry and I need—"

"Okay, babe. But let's get you up to Axe."

I can see my road captain crouch and help Dinah onto her shoulder. I get down on my stomach and grab her wrists, pulling her up until she is lying on the floor next to me.

"Didi, come on, I'm taking you home." My voice isn't completely normal. My body is still too heavily muscled to look normal, but she jumps into my arms, burying her face into my neck. I hold her against my chest, grateful she is alive. Fucking grateful she isn't running away from me when I look like a monster. Not that she has before. But still. I don't ever want her afraid of me.

"Jesus fucking Christ, I hate that place," she whispers. I

Flora Quincy

know she isn't going to be able to go into small, dark places again. Not anytime soon, anyway. "It smells."

"You okay down there?" I ask Queenie. She jumps and catches the edge before hauling herself out of the prison.

"All good."

Scooping Dinah up in my arms, I make sure to cup her head into my neck when we pass by Grass' body and head. She doesn't need to see that. We get out into the fresh air, and her body relaxes. Shit.

"Didi? You okay?"

"Just hold me a bit."

"Okay. The others can take care of clear up."

Her body tenses again. "There are still people out there? Can you check?" she asks. It fucking breaks my heart and makes me feel like a god at the same time.

"Sure, Princess. Dumbo! You and Queenie wait with Dinah so I can do the final sweep."

Ryder and his people have done an annoyingly good job and it takes maybe an hour of us working together to cover the whole place and secure the guns. We'll split the contraband between the two clubs, but Old Horde will be the ones to patrol this area. The map is changing and so is the game.

When I get back, Queenie is helping Dinah put on some fresh clothes. Fuck, I run a hand over my face. I hadn't even thought about that. Just came straight out here as fast as I could.

WE GET BACK to Dwen'mar tired at hell. Not going to lie, all I want is to fall asleep. Help my girl process—get her heartbeat back to normal—what the fuck happened to her? Killing the rest of the kvari scum can wait a couple of days because there are others who want to get their hands

Property of the Green Bastards

on them just as bad as me. Let them take some responsibility for once.

I wait for her to get off the bike, and like the queen she is, she waits, shoulders back, holding her shit together even while I feel her heartbeat skittering about.

Huh, just like that first day. Bet she was just as scared when I crowded her against that beat-up tin can, but she held it together then too.

Swinging a leg over, I stand up and pull her to my front, holding her against me.

"Welcome home, Princess."

"Axe." She turns in my arms. "Make me yours?"

"You don't want to sleep first?" I check in 'cause I don't want her doing anything she doesn't want. Not today, not never.

"Make me yours. Remind—"

I wrap my hand in her hair, tugging it back so that I can kiss her. Because it's all I've wanted to do since I had her in my arms again. "Never letting you go. Understand me?" I ask, yanking just a bit so that I can make my point.

"Harder," she whispers in an undertone like she doesn't want the others to hear. Like she wants the show we are putting on to be good for them.

"Whatever my little heartsong wants." Louder, I order her onto her knees. "Show all these people how good you look choking on my cock."

For someone who was so uncomfortable with the idea of public sex a couple of days ago, she overflows with confidence as she drops to her knees, her hands going to my belt. "Keep your eyes on me," I order. "You don't need to look anywhere but me."

I'm not hard yet but that mouth and those hands of hers have me like steel in seconds. I could come like this. Any other day, I would but as I watch her watching me, the urge to take her to our room, bathe her. Clean her up and just hold onto her grows stronger until I'm almost blind with the need for something more than a public blow job.

I ease her off and watch her kneel at my feet while I tuck myself back in. "You mind if we take this somewhere private?"

She stands, dusting off her knees. Her smile is soft, just for me. And I'm such a sap that I miss the moment she makes the decision to run.

"Fuck." I run a hand over my face. "Always. She loves to run."

"You gotta go after her, Prez," Queenie says.

"No shit, Queenie." I stalk in the direction of my heartsong.

Pushing into the common room, I see Boonie holding Dinah in her arms, tears glistening on her cheeks. Kendle stands close, holding one of my heartsong's hands in hers.

How any of us thought she didn't belong here is beyond me. Seems like years ago, even though it was only weeks.

"Come on, Didi."

She disengages from my mom and sister and dashes for the door like she wasn't just getting hugged and cooed over.

"Go get her, Ash'ee." From Kendle this time.

"What is with all of you?" I ask as I push past them. She's just on the other side of the door, waiting for me. "You gonna run?" I ask. "Or are you going to let me—"

"Carry me," she says. "I don't think I can…"

"So all that was a show?"

"Yeah." She sucks her lips between her teeth. "I wanted them to think I was strong."

My heart breaks a little. "Jaysus. They'll never think

Property of the Green Bastards

you are weak. Fuck. Even if you came in crying, they'd still think you're strong."

"I don't feel strong. I'm shaking like a leaf."

I pinch her chin and tilt it up. "You know how I know you are strong? That heartbeat of yours. Remember? I can feel that. Anyone who can feel you the way I do would never think you're weak. That's what I love about you."

"You love me?" she asks.

One good thing about being green is she can't see my blush cause feelings aren't really something I talk about. "Yeah."

"Okay."

"Wait. You gonna just…you just let me say that and all you gotta say is 'okay?'"

"Axe, I love you. But I don't want you to be uncomfortable. I don't like words anyway. I like actions."

"Yeah, I can get down with that." I bend over to throw her over my shoulder, and the cheeky thing jumps to make it easier for me. I pop her ass because that kinda behaviour? Cute as fuck. Too cute not to tell her how fucking cute she is.

She wiggles her ass. "No shit."

"You are a brat too though." And I have to give her a good smack on her sit spot, causing her to yelp. "And adorable."

I take her straight to the shower and turn it on, letting her strip while I begin filling the bath.

She doesn't wait for the water to get warm, just goes straight in, letting the water wash away the dirt on her face. I clamp down tight on the anger that rises in my chest at the sight of her so vulnerable.

The water is just warming up when I get in there with her. I've got a comb and I start at the end of her long black hair. Carefully teasing out the tangles until it falls like a cape around her.

This tub we have now is perfect for what I have in mind. A shelf-like seat going around half of it so I can sit and have my heartsong straddle me at the same time. The air is heavy with steam, but the water is crystal clear, meaning I can see every freckled inch of her skin as she mounts me.

I line her dripping cunt over my cock, teasing us both, but I want to see the way I split her open. See every fucking millimetre disappear.

"Put your hands on my thighs," I order. She arches her back to get into position, forcing her breasts out, presenting them to me. I could lean forward—I will lean forward—and give them the attention they deserve.

"I wish cell phones worked up here." She gasps as I urge her to lower onto my length. "I want you to film this. So that if you ever spend the night away, we have something to watch…to relive this."

"What a dirty little slut," I growl.

"Your dirty little slut," she moans. "Only yours. Please, I need more, Daddy."

This woman is perfect. How the fuck did–but then, we were fated for each other. Of course, my heartsong would come ready and willing to indulge every single fantasy I have, ones I didn't even think about.

"I wanted you to ravish me," she whimpers. "That first night…I wanted you to catch me and ruin me in front of everyone."

I pull her further onto my cock. "Tell me, what did I do to you, Princess?"

"You stalked me like I was prey. The king popped my cherry while I was bent over a desk. You didn't know my name and you took what you wanted. Please, I need my king's cum."

"Soon, Didi." I thrust in, my tongue running over my bottom lip because there isn't anything more erotic than her body, trembling with need as I slowly use her to cover my cock. Fuck, she feels like a vice. "Don't come yet, Dinah," I snap when she begins to buck, trying to take more of me. "You don't get to come until your clits are grinding against me."

"Oh." Her mouth drops open with a gasp. "Oh."

"Yeah, like that." I encourage her to rock in my lap. "Don't work at it. Just…"

"Hmm…" She leans in, hugging me close while she kisses my throat. "I could fall asleep like this." She sighs.

"Is my princess tired?" I ask her. It's hard to be all serious with the way she's moving. I want to fuck her hard when she squeezes down on me like this. At the same time? If she falls asleep, that's a good thing right? She's been through a lot. "Dinah?"

She hums something, nuzzling against my chest.

"I'm going to take us to bed?" I ask.

"Okay."

I stand, and we make sure she's got her legs wrapped tight around my waist before I step out of the bath. And, of course, my cock is still buried in her hot quim. It isn't easy to roll us onto the bed because Dinah is completely passed out by the time we make it to the bed.

I get us sorted and, in the process, lose my boner. Not romantic or sexy but for a minute, a whole fucking sixty seconds, I couldn't hear her breathing. I had to focus, a hand on her heart, another under her nose, just to make sure she was alive. I knew she was. But the fear gripped my heart hard.

"Not again, Di'or'nah'Fi. Ash'ni'orde until you smash

your crown. I'm not letting you out without one of my most trusted brothers with you. I'll take you to work. I'll pick you up. All that shit, I'll take care of it. Just don't ever scare me like that. Okay?"

She murmurs in her sleep.

"That's a promise then," I say.

Next morning at dawn, I take her to the ridge, carrying her down the narrow stairs until we are in front of our cave.

"You think you can go in there?"

"Yes," she answers, turning into my chest. "I just don't want to be in a prison cell again. Screaming and singing kept my mood up."

"You can be not okay too. Didi…"

"Ash'den, meh Ash'orde. You are everything to me. I'll be strong and weak at the same time for you, for us. Now, right now, I want to crawl into our cave and have the most wild, kinky-out-of-this-world sex."

This. This is how we are going to spend the rest of our lives. Fucking in this cave. Sure, there will be adjustments when she gives birth but I want more than one kid. I'll keep her breeding until I've got enough kids to start a football team. Okay. Maybe five…kids or football teams, I'll let Dinah decide.

Epilogue

AXE

My brothers and I leave just after the witching hour. As soon as I've got Dinah asleep in our bedroom after our day-long fuck sesh in the cave, we are out. I need to make some things clear to Ryder before he steps into the Compound.

He and his veep with a couple of other Old Horde members are waiting on the side of the road. Rather, the veep and the others are waiting; Ryder looks like a worried heartsong. Pussy. I don't say the word out loud. I'm not a fucking hypocrite. I can even admire him for being so patient and waiting until I told him it was a good time. It isn't, but better now than him storming in unannounced.

"You want something that you are still on my land?" I ask as we roll up next to them. He surprises the shit out of me when he gets on one knee. The guys behind him don't even blink.

"Ash'orde, I offer Dw'or weh. Our clubs are to be tied together by the bond of or." He stands, brushing the dust off his jeans.

"Yeah. Your kids will carry the blood of my ancestors."

I see the moment he realises that reminding me Dinah has Disavowed blood would be a serious mistake.

"I thought you wanted to make this easy?" he asks.

"Oh, I *am* making this easy. Kendle is going to have you eating her shit."

"Not my kink, but if she likes—"

"Nah, man. That is gross. No one needs to be thinking about my kid sister like that." I feel physically sick at the thought.

"Yeah." He looks down. The big orc is embarrassed. "Sorry. Fuck. Look, neither of us like this. I've been patient. But that ends now. I'm not having my heartsong in some other territory. She belongs under my protection."

I keep my mouth shut. As her brother, I want to argue I can protect her just fine. As an orc with a heartsong, the idea of Didi anywhere but safe in my bed has me reaching for that or'gre and preparing for battle.

"I won't stand in your way. But I can't make Kendle go with you."

There is a beat where I think he might argue but he doesn't. I really need this fucker out of here before I offer him a beer and some advice on how to handle my sister. Nope. Not gonna get friendly with him.

Property of the Green Bastards

"Let's go." Grim revs his bike and backs it onto the quiet road and waits for me and Ryder to go first.

We don't waste time. Probably breaking the speed limit but who cares? Logan? That asshole is probably in bed at this hour. Don't like that fucker either because he might actually not be all bad.

"You look like you ate shit, Prez," Tool says as we pull in front of the Compound.

"Nah, just thinking life used to be simpler. Fuck it. Come on, Ryder, let's see if my sister is willing to go with you."

Dinah sprints across the common room and leaps into my arms, her arms and legs wrapping around me. I get a handful of ass and a good whiff of her clean smell. "I need coffee, Didi."

"Yeah." She buries her nose into my throat inhaling deeply. "Thanks for coming back in one piece, Ash'den. Is this where I get on my knees, and you fuck my face in front of everyone again?"

"Not right now. You aren't going to like what is about to happen," I whisper into her hair. "Sorry, Princess."

"What?" She pulls back. When she sees Ryder, her body stiffens and her face goes hard. "No."

"He saved our asses when we rescued you. Proper cavalry shit."

"Shit. Now isn't a good time, Daddy."

I pop her on the ass because you can't let the little things slide, but I kiss her forehead to make it better.

I set her back on the ground, but keep her close. If we are in the same room, she is either on my dick or in my arms. I only got her back yesterday. I didn't realise how empty I'd felt until I pulled her out of that hole in the ground. The magic tied to the heartsongs is way more powerful than anything I could have imagined. Shit, maybe that is why I'm so understanding of Ryder looking like a complete psycho standing just inside the door, staring at my sister like she is his last meal.

And Kendle? She just looks him up and down with as much interest as staring at a fence post. This moment might just take the number one spot of pride for my sister. Heph's bike was a big deal, but looking at your heartsong like he means nothing? That stuff is solid gold.

Boonie rushes in and declares that since Ryder is a visiting prez, we need to have a feast like she's planned the whole thing. We all settle in and my mom keeps Ryder and Kendle at opposite ends of the common room all day.

"Thank Frey for your mother." Dinah sighs. She crawled into my lap after the first course and has curled up like a little kitten. "But I want this over and done with. I need a nap and I need to wake up to your cum—"

A hand slams onto the table causing every conversation to stop dead. I growl. The most perfect piece of ass was about to propose kinky sex and now I have to listen to the drama of Ryder being a bitch about asking my sister to be his heartsong.

The asshole stands and stalks down the table until he stands across from her. The girl just sits there, cleaning her nails with a long wicked-looking knife.

"You're coming with me." Those are literally the first words Ryder says to my sister. All afternoon, we've been eating and drinking. They've been avoiding each other like the plague and then he comes out with those four words.

"Yeah, fuck no," Kendle says, crossing her arms and giving Ryder a dirty look. "No offence. I don't know you or anything but I am not going to spend the rest of my life just a heartsong to a club president."

"Jaysus, it isn't that bad," Boonie mutters behind her.

Property of the Green Bastards

"Don't fucking care what you want, you are coming with me. Peh'or'Ash'ki, I claim—"

"I cry Weh Jraw'dwen. Honour of Shared Hearth." She shoots up, knocking her chair over. "Raine prospected here. And I will prospect with the Old Horde in exchange. That is the tradition…And you za'orde love your traditions."

"What?"

"No!"

The words ricochet around the room. I can't tell which club is more pissed off. But I'm not. That sneaky, sneaky kid. Ryder can't say no to that.

"You're a girl."

Dead fucking silence. I search out the sexist shit among the patched brothers in the MC that is taking my kid sister from me.

"Your bylaws prevent women from joining? Is there actual language that says women can't join?" Dinah asks from my lap. "Because I've got the bylaws memorised."

"Shit…You plan this, Dinah?" Raine looks impressed, but I'm thinking he knew and helped them because that smirk didn't come out of nowhere. Old Horde was Raine's birth club.

"I am a font of wisdom. In fact—"

"No," Ryder cuts her off.

"How dare you interrupt your Ash'ni?" Kendle sneers.

"There is nothing in the bylaws saying you can't prospect," he confirms. "You want to prospect? You can prospect. But we aren't soft in the north. All the ass-kissing you are used to? That's gone. Hard floor for a bed. Cold showers. And for once in your life, you'll have to follow the rules. Understand?"

"Jaysus, help orc'i with shit for brains," Boonie prays.

But Sandra, looking like one badass motherfucker,

leaps over the table until she is standing in front of the huge orc. "She is my blood. You are taking my girl. So if I hear anything, I'm coming for you and your club. Got me, little boy?"

I'll give Ryder credit, he doesn't flinch when Sandra bares her pointed teeth and flashes her tail with its razor-sharp tips.

Everything happens way too fast after that. Mom, Sandra, and Dinah surround Kendle. The Old Horde members move so they are near the door. I stand in the middle, the last barrier between my kid sister and the orc who could be my friend in another life.

I can hear the women talking.

"You're going to be fine. And call Fren'as when the babies are due. I want you here for that," Dinah says. "I'm sorry we didn't get to do all the fun things we talked about."

"We will. I'll prospect and then come home. I can patch over and they won't want to keep me as a…I'll make them patch me. This won't be goodbye. Just a really shitty vacation."

We all know that is a lie. The pull of a heartsong means she won't be able to leave once it is formalised. And it will be.

"You'll always be a Green Bastard," Mom says. Her voice is strong like when my dad died. Nothing to let us know she is hurting to see someone she loves taken away from her.

"She's Old Horde. There will be rubies in her tusks." Ryder just can't keep his mouth shut.

Ken struts over to me next, her hand sneaks into mine, squeezing it in morse code…SOS. She'll never say it out loud. I pull her into a hug. "Don't back down," I remind her. "And no matter what anyone says, you can always kick him in the balls."

Goodbyes are quick because Kendle makes none. Just hitches her bag over her shoulder and walks towards her fate.

Dumbo surprises me when he comes forward and drags Kendle into a hug. They stand, arms wrapped around each other for a lot longer than makes Ryder happy. The Old Horde prez rips her away, growling something I can't make out.

"Get your filthy hands off her!" Dumbo snarls. "You don't deserve to eat the dust she walks on."

Dinah grabs my arm, preventing me from interfering.

"Jeal, no." Kendle doesn't struggle against Ryder but she isn't relaxed either. She twists and glares at her heartsong. "I have to go. Honour. Meh'weh shail den orc'i kr'awl."

Her honour is the fire that will bring orc'i to their knees?

Shit. My sister seems to be pulling out all the old traditions today. Does she really think she can take over the Old Horde? But with Ryder staring at her like she just confessed her undying adoration, maybe she can.

Bonus Epilogue

DINAH

20 years later

"Don't do it," I whisper under my breath as I stand outside Elmeer's, no my, art and antiques shop. It's a perfect midsummer day but I have my arms crossed because my nipples are pebbled and visible through my thin silk blouse. I cross my arms tighter like it will hold the words inside me. "Really, do not do it."

I repeat the phrase as a mantra while I watch Axe swing his leg over the motorcycle with an audible groan of discomfort. He refuses to drive the truck, insisting it is beneath him and he won't be caged just because his joints ache before a storm.

Twenty years since we first met and at fifty-three he is getting stiff and crotchety. The great president of the Green Bastards isn't what he was. Even so, he makes my heart race. Hells, he's the reason I've got my breasts covered. According to our kids it's not dignified for me to be panting after my heartsong. Gods, help us if we remind them that's the reason are alive.

Kids are a chore.

Watching the orc who made me his? That is a pleasure I'm not giving up.

Axe's put on weight, his face has some lines that he blames on our daughter, but he's still the orc who fucked me in his office the first day we met.

I glance at my watch. He's late. Now that I can bitch about. A client is coming in an hour and Axe needs to be out of here at least twenty minutes before the elvish couple arrives.

"You're late," I say with a little more snap than I wanted.

"Shut your mouth, woman," he snarls. "Your son thought it would be funny to paint the wargs pink."

I try. Truly, I try to hold in a whoop of laughter. "Which son?" I ask with as much decorum as possible.

"Mason." He rolls his right shoulder which has been giving him problems, though we aren't sure why.

"He always took after me." I love this. Fighting over which child took after who is probably our favourite contest. Raine keeps tally and announces which of our progeny belongs to which of us at the end of every week. Hilarious. Even the kids love it, trying to provoke responses in one of us to that we take credit or disown them.

"Which is why he's your son." Axe is now close enough for my blood to heat. He feels the same. Desire dances in his eyes as he watches me slowly back towards the open door.

"Come on, then." I pivot away from him and take off into the shop. My assistant gives me a weak smile as I dash past her. Poor thing is probably scarred from watching us get it on like teenagers most days of the week.

He moves slower which is how I make it to our attic room with enough time to duck behind a huge stretched canvas that is ready for Dumbo paint. His being an artist is still a surprise but when it gives me a choice hiding spot…

"Didi…come out, come out from wherever you are."

After so long together, he can probably trace my heartbeat and pinpoint my exact location. I can certainly follow him around the room, our heartbeats acting like echo location.

Which is how I know to brace when the entire canvas is lifted and tossed aside. Wisely, I don't remark that if it rips we are in for a world of hurt. Hells, I'm not even thinking when I see him. In the few minutes he's had, he's stripped.

Naked. Hard. Mine.

"You need this to be quick," he growls, fisting his cock from root to tip. "But you've been wet from…"

"Since I knew it was time for you to arrive." I lick my lips. "Can I have a taste? Just the tip?"

"Just the tip," he concedes. "Come here and give Daddy a special kiss, Princess."

I rise to my knees so that I can shuffle towards him. He wraps his hand in my hair and holds me still. He knows I'll try for more than the tip if I have my way.

Slowly he paints my lips with his precum before pulling away. His hot gaze grows darker, more feral as he watches me lick my lips. "Hands and knees, Princess," he orders with a rough growl that goes straight to my sex and makes my breasts heavy with need. "Present. Show me what belongs to me."

His cave man act doesn't change the fact he is the one asking. He needs my submission but, even as he gets my consent to every filthy act, we both know I have as much control as him. Our twenty years have only grounded every moment in a layered push and pull that inevitably ends with us bound tighter and tighter together.

Knowing this, I turn, I lean forward until my back arches, presenting my ass.

"Pull your skirt up." His voice takes on the same breathy, uncontrolled quality as my pants. I have to lower my cheek to the soft rug so that I can reach behind me and gather the full skirt and lift it around my hips. I go to push myself back up but his hand falls heavy on my back, holding me in place. "Not wearing panties, Didi?" He huffs as his hand ghosts over my ass and cups my sex. "What a dirty girl."

"Axe," I'm pleading. Needy and pissed off, when it isn't my fault I'm bare underneath my dress. "You put them in your pocket after fucking me this morning."

"Had to make sure I had easy access to this pussy. Brought them with me because I'm a gentleman and don't want my cum running down your legs. You wanna tell me where my cum belongs?"

"Inside," I whisper or I'll be moaning at the way his thick finger splits my wet folds to play with my clits. Circling first one and then the other. He's an asshole. Arrogant. Edging-his-heartsong bastard.

"Inside where, pahpah?"

Frey, he's going to make me say it. "My womb. My fertile womb."

He doesn't use words; I know what he'd say if he did.

"That's the fucking truth." But, no. We are past the great President of the Green Bastards using words. Instead, he fucks his cock into me with a single, sure thrust that forces me to take his entire length.

"Not gonna be long." He grunts. "Just the thought of filling you, breeding you. Making you big with our fifth."

He's groaning, fucking into me with the same self-centred focus that got me off so many times on our first night.

"Touch yourself," he commands. "Go on, rub one out while you are getting fucked by your heartsong."

I reach between my legs and press hard against my clit "rubbing" just like he ordered me. Even if I could, I wouldn't try to play with the other because with each vicious thrust he's dragging the ridges of his cock against my second clit. Any more stimulation would be too much, especially as his cock's reaching places only he's been.

We're moving in tandem. In and out. Fighting for that final toppling flight off the cliff. Our bodies know each other. Some magical connection that recognises before we do that the other will be coming. So by the time I'm begging for his come. By the time he is shouting his release, I'm there with him exploding like a star with the strength of my orgasm.

Afterwards we can only pant. His hand running up and down my back.

"You aren't half bad at this. Took me twenty years to train you, though," I tell him with a huffing laugh.

"Jaysus. You… You do remember you were the virgin when I popped your cherry?" He asks like I'd forgotten. Still, I can hear the smug smile in his voice.

"Yeah, yeah." I start to shake with laughter. "You popped my cherry. Big whoop-di-do. Virginity is a social construction."

"Shut up, woman. Let me have my moment."

I hum in agreement and pleasure as he pulls out and cups my sex so that his cum doesn't run down my legs. There is a moment and then a cool wet flannel cleans the mess he's made of me. I roll over onto my back and watch as he carefully fits my panties over my hips.

"You're pregnant," he says with so much conviction that I'm inclined to believe him. "We'll do this until we're sure but I'm calling it. I impregnated you today."

He's so serious I don't tease him but then it strikes me.

"Would you care to explain why you are so determined to have five kids?" I ask him as he sits behind me and begins to brush my hair. I can't remember when he started the ritual after we have sex. I love it. L.O.V.E. Love it.

"No."

"There is something…" I narrow my eyes even though I know he can't see my expression. "Tell me Ash'den."

"No."

"Are you embarrassed?" I turn around to get a good look at his face.

He clears his throat. I open my mouth to press the issue then close it with a snap as the reason comes to me. "Boonie had a dream," I say softly. We lost her four years ago. Heart attack. She was too young, especially for one of the orc'i. "You could have told me."

"Princess, that isn't why. But if Mom heard you she'd probably say that is exactly why. Only she'd claim ten."

"Wait. If not Boonie, is there a bet? Did you and the members make a bet?" I should be angry but after twenty years nothing surprises me.

"Football team," he mutters. "I want enough kids for a football team."

"What? Are you insane? Do you…of course, you do. No. That is way too many."

"Yeah, but if there are five, they can play five-a-side against some of the other goki."

"There is going to be a twenty year age gap."

"So. The youngest can start when they are five."

"Out." I point to the stairs. He's lost it. Absolutely fucking lost it. I keep inside. I'm still not allowed to swear and…I also have no clean words for what he's jus revealed. "Get out. I'll count to ten."

He gets up and pulls on his jeans. That selfsatisfied smirk on his face. Oh, boy. He's in for a world of hurt. See if I let him fuck me ever again. "Don't give me that look. We're fucking when you get home. I know you're pregnant but just to make sure you're fertile for a couple more days."

"Axe, you fuck me like I'm fertile every day of the week."

"Didi. No. Swearing."

The bell signaling someone has entered the shop saves me a sore ass. "Clients are here," I say as I rush downstairs.

Even though I'm expecting them, the immortal couple are intimidating to the say the least. The king of the elves and his changeling wife are strolling down the aisle the preternatural grace and lethal ease that only their kind possess.

"Good afternoon, Your Highnesses." I smile.

"May the dappled light show you the way," she replies. Very formal. Shit.

"Fallan," the high king tuts. "There is no need to be so…ceremonial. The orc'i no longer have royalty."

"Phæn," Axe strolls up to his…counterpart? We did give up the titles but Axe is Ash'or'ash until he dies and orc'i still call him Ash'orde.

"Axe," he replies with a small bow but it is impossible to miss how he slurs the name so it sounds like "ash", king. "I've come here looking for an item my family lost."

Fallan rolls her eyes at me. "He's so dramatic."

"Aren't they all?" I sigh dramatically.

"You owe me a fifth." Axe pops me on the ass. "She'll find the horn for you. My heartsong convinced the orc'i to give up their obsession with passing the sins of the parent to the child. She's the best thing to happen to the Badlands. It was her destiny."

My cheeks heat at his praise. Suddenly, I'm reminded about the fortune cookie's message. The prediction for great things. Maybe not destined for great things but I certainly have a lot of great things in my life. Including the orc who's swaggering out of my shop.

Fallan clears her throat and brings my attention back to my clients.

"Right, let's see what I have in the archives," I say with a bright smile.

The End

Thank you so much for picking up
Property of the Green Bastards.

Reviews are one of the ways indie writers reach new readers, and it would be wonderful if you could take the time to share your thoughts on review sites like Amazon and Goodreads.

The Green Bastards MC Hierarchy

<u>President / Prez</u>
Axe

<u>Vice president / Veep</u>
Grim

<u>Sargent at Arms</u>
Payne

<u>Road Captains</u>
Queenie
Jax

<u>Enforcers</u>
Hawk
Raine

<u>Secretary</u>
Cam

The Green Bastards MC Hierarchy

<u>Treasurer</u>
Jessa

<u>Members</u>
Rift
Swot
Vice
Eel

<u>Prospects</u>
Dumbo
Tool
Kid

Glossary

Property of the Green Bastards
Glossary

Orcish is a relatively simple language where concepts/words are combined to make a sentence.

Mostly people speak common but will use orcish for specific contexts. It is rare for non-orc'i to use orc'ish.

———

Or - Blood; represents the connection between all orcs and especially their ancestors

Sol - Bone; represents an individual. They are only exposed in death and form the centre of ancestor worship

Orc - Blood person

Orc'i - plural of orc

'K or 'c - makes a concept into a noun (eg: Orc = blood people; kin = near people)

Teng - Ancestor

All - Mountain

Glossary

Weh - Honour

Meh - Makes something possessive (eg meh'didi, my sweetheart)

Ash - King

Kot - Knowledge

Kol - Place

Sil - Field (eg Sil'kot is a map. Orsol sil'kot is a family tree)

'gre - Battle (eg or'gre blood battle, a berserker state when an orc's strength and senses are heightened)

War - Beast (eg war'gre / warg is a battle creature similar to a giant wolf and the traditional mount for orc'i warriors)

Mar - Town/city

Dwen - Hearth

K'in - People (these are people who are close to the orc'i but are not orc'i)

Var - To make a thing or concept negative

Helm - Dwelling (eg or'helm blood dwelling, where orc'i live in the mar)

Dw - Prefix to make a thing or concept positive

Doubling a sound makes it a diminutive / familiar (eg: Didi di = sweet Didi = sweety / sweetheart)

Naming conventions:

Family name / blood / personal name / chosen name (eg: Di'or'nah'Fi)

Axe's name is different because he is the horde king. Ash'or'ash King'blood'king is a gender-neutral title. His chosen name is Den.

Also by Flora Quincy

The Badlands Orc MCs

Property of the Green Bastards
He is the monster who rules the Badlands.
Her humanity makes her fragile, her past tells another story.

The Hartwell Sisters Saga

Omega's Gambit
It is a knotty problem, and it will take some slick moves to mate these two together.

Omega's Virtue Part One
The heat rages when two possessive alphas and a fiery omega mate up.

Omega's Virtue Part Two
It Is out of the heat and into the fire for these protective alphas and their feisty omega.

Omega's Dream
These deadly alphas will tie one proud omega up in knots rather than let her get away.

About the Author

Flora Quincy is British-American author currently living in Glasgow with her Scottish Terrier, collection of stationery, and a daily pot of coffee. She fell in love with books at a young age. Reading romance, fantasy, and science fiction to escape into worlds far more exciting than real life.

With an overactive imagination, she had dozens of stories begun and discarded, before she decided to take writing seriously. Now those characters and worlds are finding their way to the page.

When she isn't reading or writing, she has a *healthy* relationship with the characters inside her head. So far she hasn't been alarmed too many people while conversing with imaginary men and women as she takes the dog for a walk.

Follow Flora for extra epilogues, teasers, and frolicking fun.

Email
   floraquincyauthor@gmail.com

Acknowledgments

The Solstice Society have been a huge inspiration. Their dedication to the craft and work ethic is inspiring.
For help with the cover and cheering me on, a massive thank you to Lizzy Bequin.
To the wonderful ARC team who caught the little things I missed.
To Kirsty of Let's Get Proofed. You whipped me and PotGB into shape and wondered why I used "freaking" instead of "fucking" in that one instance. Thank you.

Full Content and Trigger Warnings

This book is meant for mature audiences.
There are graphic depictions of sex and violence.
Consent rules.

Content and Trigger Warnings:
Explicit depictions of torture
Death of children (historical, not detailed)

Kinks included:
Primal play
Somnophilia (negotiated)
Daddy Dom
Domestic Discipline
Breeding